Dragon Tooth Gold

Volume 2 – Pioneers

By

Kent J. McGrew

Acknowledgments & Thanks

Without a doubt, everyone who creates has to wonder if their work is worthwhile. I have a lot of encouragement with this issue provided by the overwhelming response and acceptance of Volume One – Immigrants.

Thanks to the many, their warmth and well wishes are appreciated deeply, and in truth, keep me going.

Special thanks to those who stand out every day.

For my wife Sally – Morals, and Ethics Editor
For my daughter Tahtim – Creative Writer/Editor
For my Sister-in-Law Terry – Fun and Enthusiasm Director and Reader/Editor
Cousin Loretta – Punctuation Director and Reader
Brianna and Jay Barksdale – Readers, Illustrators, and great fun to work with

* * *

Table of Contents

PROLOGUE

West, the mantra of mid-Nineteenth Century America. From the congested slums, from the muddy streets, from the crushing poverty, from every beleaguered backwoods area of the country, young and old alike turned their backs on the Atlantic Ocean and put one foot in front of the other to embrace the vast unknown. Different from the throngs who blazed the trails west during the gold rush, the westward migration in the 1860s had only a few who dreamed of sudden wealth. Most looked to the west for a better life, one with land to farm, virgin forests to timber, one without the oppressive aura of civil war that clouded the soul of the young nation.

Pioneers of that time held only one thing in common; that was the hope for opportunity, the hope for a better life, the escape of the hopelessness of from where they came. The Government and the newspapers alike pressed the masses to emigrate west. The "waste people": the commoners, the landless, the unemployed; all were encouraged to move on to a better life.

It wasn't like that for the second generation Callahans. They had wealth. They had the privilege of their parent's hard work. They also had the crushing weight of the tornado's devastation. They had the oppressive dominance of a war-paranoid grandmother. They had the strength and optimism of youth. Regardless of their motivations, like any pioneer, they had to put one foot in front of the other to realize whatever would come next. Like their immigrant parents, the four young Callahans turned West for a life of their own making, a life free of the expectations of others, a life free of their family's past. A life for which they had control. Like river water finding its way to the sea, the pathways west lead to unknown, but infinite possibilities.

OLATHE

The brothers reached Fort Leavenworth in the late afternoon. They put their horses up in the livery and checked in with the Quartermaster. He had three huge, heavy wagons, each loaded with eight tons of rifles, munitions, and powder, each pulled by twelve mules, three teams each, four abreast. Eli and his brothers would take the wagons down to Olathe and await a large supply train entering the trail from Westport. They would leave early the next morning and spend two days getting to Olathe. There was an extra day in the schedule to allow for delays of the larger supply train. Suzette knew all this. She had good intelligence from military children at the school who pretty much knew all the business of the Fort week to week. The Quartermaster's son had a crush on her, and he was her most reliable source of information. She had anticipated that Denise would send riders after her.

She was impressed as she watched from the bluff above Raytown as six men riding hard stopped at William Ray's blacksmith shop. Suzette spent the night with Aunt Sophie, Hannah's close friend and confidant. Sophie told her to hide out in the woods, and if riders showed up the next day, let them pass and make your way down to Olathe on the back-roads rather than on the main trail. Sophie tied a medical bag onto the back of the saddle and told Sophie to make sure she and her brothers took the quinine pills to protect against malaria and yellow fever. There were enough pills to see the four of them to Santa Fe and beyond. Sophie patted Patches on the neck, and Suzette turned the stout mare west, saddlebags packed full of jerky, dried fruit, and several day's worths of oats. Playing hide and seek with Denise's posse was going to be a challenge. The only consequence of getting caught would be losing precious time as Eli headed his wagon train further west or getting abducted back to Independence against her will. That outcome would mean an unwanted trip around the horn with her grandparents. With one last look down at the settlement, Suzette saw William Ray hand several bottles of whiskey up to the riders. Eluding these riders was going to be easier than she thought.

By nightfall of the next day, Eli was more than halfway to Olathe. The heavy wagons were clumsier than he thought, and twelve mules were harder to handle than eight. He wished he had some time to train the mules better before they set out, but schedules were of princely importance in the Quartermaster's kingdom.

Suzette didn't follow the back roads. She followed the posse riding southwest on the trail at a gallop, resting and watering the mare at every opportunity. There was a camp by a blue water stream about ten miles from Olathe. It was a good bet that the posse would hold up there for the night. It was also a good bet that the bottles of whiskey would be empty by the time she reached them. She was enjoying reversing her position from hunted teenager to the huntress as she approached the camp around midnight; Denise's posse was there as she anticipated. She rode to the south of the camp and tied Patches to a tree. She took off her boots and put on a pair of moccasins Aunt Sophie gave her as her last parting gift.

The fire was just a bed of coals, and the snores of the drunken riders were a ridiculous uncoordinated serenade as she made her way to the corrals. She didn't stampede the horses; she just fashioned a hackamore over the snout of each one and led them quietly away from the camp and back to where she tethered Patches. There was just enough moonlight to ride for the rest of the night. About every two miles, she would leave the trail and turn one of the horses loose, one on the north side, then one on the south. By dawn, she rode into Olathe, tired but pleased with her stealthy attack on the posse. The hungover men would only find the moccasin tracks and assume Indians had stolen the horses. She gained at least a day on them, that is if they even found their horses or purchased new mounts.

Arriving in Olathe, Suzette remembered a trip here in the spring when the grasslands bloomed with verbena. The pink flowers with lavender stems were a vivid memory of the first spring she went out with her brothers on the supply runs from The Meadows. She put Patches in the small barn behind the Mahaffie farmhouse and asked the farmhand to keep her presence on the farm a secret. The young man was more than willing to conspire with the good-looking young woman. She had been to the farm with her brothers several times on their short supply runs and was sure that they would wait here for the supply train to arrive from Westport. The farmhouse was just a little way north of the trail, and from the hayloft, she would be able to see anyone passing. She needed a few things before they arrived, but first on her list was a hearty breakfast. J.B. and Lucinda Mahaffie owned the farm. Lucinda was glad to see Suzette and welcomed her with a warm hug. Lucinda asked Suzette where her brothers were.   Suzette just answered, "They'll be along shortly."

Eli and the twins pulled up to the farmhouse in the late afternoon. They put the mules in a corral next to the barn and went up to the farmhouse to beg a home-cooked meal from Lucinda. Lucinda already knew they were coming and had a large pot of stew simmering on the stove waiting for them. The young men ate, and when they got to dessert, Eli noticed a piece of paper under his plate of apple pie. He pulled it out and read it. Written in Suzette's hand, it said, "I'm in the hayloft, don't leave me behind." Eli wasn't puzzled by the cryptic note a bit. He saw the farmhand grooming Patches in the gloomy shadows at the rear of the barn as they were tending to the mules. He decided to keep Suzette under wraps for the time being. He knew Denise would have men out looking for her; that was why she was hiding.

Eli and the twins spent the next day waiting for the supply train and sorting the mules into the dominant and passive animals. The position of each mule was constantly shifted, moving the leaders to the front and the followers to the rear.

One by one, they would lunge the teams in a round pen next to the corral until they were satisfied with the performance of all three teams. The supply train reached Olathe early in the evening. They pulled up to the pond above the farmhouse and set up camp for the night. The drivers and hands still had a lot of work to do to feed and settle the teams. There wasn't any more room in the corral, so most of the teams were just left hitched to the wagons, fed, and watered in place. Eli could see that there would be a lot of problems on the trail. The animals always had to come first; teams left to stand in their harnesses would be extra unruly in the morning, and some would develop sores under the harness straps through the warm night.

Eli was watching the camp and saw two men he recognized from the constable's office in Independence. He walked back into the barn and paid the farmhand a dollar to ride Patches out to the east and stay away until dark. He would give the boy another dollar if he would saddle the mare and meet him on the trail a couple of miles west of Olathe the next morning. As he was walking out of the barn, a clump of straw fell from the loft and landed on his hat brim. He took off his hat and brushed it off but didn't look up. He was pleased Suzette would have heard the plan for the next morning. His sister was smart and cunning. Growing up with three older brothers, she was also tough.

Eli and his brothers strung their hammocks between the wagons and settled down for the night. Eli told Jacques and Roland that Suzette was in the hayloft, and some men from Independence were looking for her. They all started to laugh even though they didn't know exactly how she would choose to join up with them. They were just happy that they wouldn't be separated for months or years, depending on the future of their troubled nation. They all slept soundly and were up before dawn, feeding their animals and assembling the teams. If all worked out well, the mules would always have the same position on their team. Routine was important in managing the mules to optimize their pulling ability. They had the wagons hitched up and were ready to pull out when the wagon master of the supply train walked up and introduced himself. Brandon Armstrong was a man in his middle fifties, grizzled and hardened from years on the trails; most everyone called him Brady. Eli knew him by reputation, and not all of what he knew was good.

Eli wanted to leave, but the rest of the train wasn't ready to go. He convinced Armstrong that the heavy wagons would likely be slower, and it would be a good idea for him to leave early. They were in a safe place along the trail; there usually wasn't any trouble with Indians or renegades until farther west of Council Grove. The older man agreed, and before Eli left town, he and the twins each inspected their wagons. There was a large potato sack on top of the ammo boxes on Eli's wagon; it wasn't there when they pulled in two days before. Eli put a leather pouch of jerky and a canteen next to the potato sack and said, "Just in case the potatoes get thirsty."

He climbed into his driver's seat, released the brake, and led his brothers west on the trail. The young man from the barn was waiting for him as planned, and Eli flipped him a double eagle for his trouble. The young man looked down with awe at the coin in his hand and asked, "Can I come with you, mister?"

"Maybe just as far as Council Grove," was Eli's reply; he didn't want to steal one of J.B.'s farmhands, but an extra driver would be useful, and the young man already proved he was reliable. The young man's name was Horatio, and he didn't care if J.B. fired him. He had more money in his pocket than he could save working all year on the farm. He tied the mare to the back of the wagon and climbed up into the driver's seat with Eli. He was reluctant at first to take the reins, but the trail here was wide, and the ruts deep. Not much could happen, but Eli had him puzzled when he told Horatio that from time to time, he would have to ride the mare out of sight for an hour or so when *Inspectors* passed through searching the wagons. Horatio assumed that the *Inspectors* were hunting runaway slaves and left it at that. Towards noon, Eli looked back and saw the dust of two riders coming on hard. He told Horatio it was time for him to disappear with the horse, and the young man rode Patches over a rise to the north. The riders caught up with the heavy wagons. Eli made it easy for them and pulled over for a make-believe inspection of his gear.

"We're looking for your sister," one of the men said. The brothers just shrugged their shoulders and said she wasn't here. The two men were not the Constable's brightest men. They looked through the wagons and asked if Eli would share some potatoes. Eli declined, and the men rode back to the east, confident that the girl was still behind them.

As they ate a lunch of jerky and apples, Eli told Roland they had a lot of apples and to put some up by the potato sack. Roland did so and patted the potato sack as he put down the apples. "Humm!" He intoned. "These potatoes are already getting soft." Suzette stifled a giggle, but the bag twitched, and Roland said, "Stay hidden, there may be more riders."

That afternoon Eli stopped early under a grove of cottonwoods just west of Gardner where the California and Oregon trails branched off to the north. The supply train was still not in sight. "Green handlers and unruly mules," Jacques commented. They hoped this wouldn't become a pattern. They couldn't go more than three days without the oats and food from the supply train. It was almost dark when Armstrong rode up to their cook fire. When Horatio was out with the mare, he shot a deer and was cooking it on a spit. The wagon master was concerned. His men were going to chow down on hardtack and salt pork, the smell of roasting venison was going to drive them crazy. He rode back to the column and had them set up camp a quarter of a mile away from the three wagons. If there were a stream or a spring, he wouldn't have done that, but for tonight they would water the mules from the barrels; each supply wagon had two lashed securely to each side between the wheels. Eli carried eight on each cargo wagon, three between the wheels and two on the tailgate. He could go for several days without clean water even though he had more animals in each team. He watered his mules in their feed bags, not a drop of the precious liquid was wasted.

As the sun started to set and the secrecy of darkness descended on the prairie, Roland got Suzette down from his wagon. She hugged him and started crying into his strong shoulder. "There, there now. It's time to be happy. We're all together, and we're not going to send you back." Roland cut a slice of tenderloin off the deer and handed her a plate with baked potatoes and carrots. She ate like she hadn't eaten for days. She drank her fill of apple cider and then wandered off in the dark with a lantern to relieve herself. Eli explained the whole situation to Horatio. The young man swelled with pride that he was an important part of Suzette's escape.

Suzette was curious about the shipment, so when she returned, she opened Eli's message pouch and got out the manifest from the Quartermaster. The wagons carried mostly Harper Ferry Model .54 caliber muzzleloaders, lead shot, and kegs of powder, percussion caps, and accessories. There was only one exception; somewhere in Roland's wagon, there was a crate of Henry .44 caliber repeating rifles manufactured by the New Haven Arms Company in New Haven, Connecticut, and twelve crates of ammunition for the innovative weapons. Suzette remembered reading about the development of repeating rifles and how the Army generals were against them because they thought the soldiers would waste ammunition. Eli said that the Henry crate would be at the bottom of the wagon towards the front since the manifest indicated the rifles were for delivery to Epperson Hardware & Supply in Santa Fe, the last items to offload.

It was too late to unload Roland's wagon, so they agreed to do that somewhere along the trail when an opportunity availed itself. They hung hammocks between two of the wagons. It didn't matter that they only had three. One of the four men would always be awake on watch through the night. Suzette's bed was on top of the ammo boxes in Roland's wagon, and when she returned with her lantern from her walk away from the camp, she read Eli's manifest in detail. The new weapons were destined for forts and military outposts along the trail. They would be on the northern route to Santa Fe, and deliveries were slated to six forts along the way with the bulk of the load going to Fort Union in the New Mexico Territory. As the pioneers in Independence, Suzette was looking forward to the trip; she was already further west on the trail than ever before.   The next day she would ride tucked in front of the water barrels on the tailgate of the rear wagon watching the trail to the rear, gunny sack close by just in case she had to disappear again. She fell asleep thinking about owning a Henry rifle before entering the more dangerous New Mexico Territory.

As the day before, the supply train was slow to break camp. Eli was disgusted with Armstrong, and it was only the morning of the third day of what was supposed to be a two-month journey to Santa Fe. Traveling at Armstrong's pace was going to take more patience than he thought he could muster. Finally, about three hours after the first light, the supply train got on the trail. There were forty or more wagons, at least Eli would always be in the lead and not have to eat their dust. That was little consolation; they were going to be slow on this crossing, and while he didn't have any plans after reaching California, the wasted time rankled his efficient nature. It was going to be a long trip, and they didn't even encounter any troubles as of yet.

Eli wanted to get close to Palmyra by nightfall, where there were good wells and a camp where pioneers stopped to rest and repair wagons. There was a Post Office at the settlement, and he would mail his letters from there. At their slow pace, it would be another week or more to Council Grove, and then things would get tougher.   One of the worries was how Armstrong would respond to having a young woman along for the ride. They would handle that when the time came. Suzette had three strong, heavily-armed men that would die protecting their sister from harm, and she was a tough young woman in her own right. They would make it. They would survive the trail, but none of them were looking forward to their grandmother's wrath when they reached the other end. That thought was as dark as thunderclouds rolling over the prairie. Eli was thinking of how he would break the news to his grandmother that Suzette was with him. Denise was a worry that Eli could do nothing about; he had to keep his attention on the problems at hand. It was going to be a long, arduous journey to California.

FIRST TROUBLES

Predawn of the third day on the trail was kind with cool air and a gentle breeze from the southwest. In what would become her routine every morning before first light, Suzette walked away from the camp to find some privacy. She carried a lantern to light her way, and it kept her safe from stepping on a rattlesnake or other hazards. Upon returning, she heard wagons approaching, and Roland, who was on watch, had three rifles and two revolvers close at hand. He handed Suzette a revolver, she had her own on her hip, but extra firepower was always a wise precaution. In the gloom of first light, they saw three wagons approaching. Suzette stirred up the fire, and by the time the wagons arrived, she had coffee on and waited with Roland, weapons close at hand.

Two supply wagons and a chuck wagon pulled up, and six men got down and walked into the light of the fire. They greeted the camp in German, and Suzette answered the hale. The men were surprised that it was the voice of a woman, but they were relieved that language wasn't going to be a problem. Roland invited the men to sit on the logs around the fire until the coffee was warm, and he went to wake Eli and Jacques. One German, who introduced himself as Hans-Werner Schultz, was the spokesman for the group and told Suzette that they wanted to travel with them. They were more disgusted with Armstrong than Eli. The wagon master was drunk every night, and the wagon train was disorganized, and the morning schedule for breaking camp was non-existent. They didn't mind the slow pace so much as missing the two or three hours of travel in the cool air after first light.

Eli and Jacques joined the group, and Suzette translated all that was said to her brothers. The German went on, "If you let us travel with you, Niclaus will have breakfast ready every morning at first light. Our wagons carry grain and corn for the mules. I don't know if it is enough to get us to Santa Fe, but we can't just leave the supply train for good anyway; like yours, our contract says we stay with the train."

Suzette paused him so she could translate. It would be up to Eli, but he wouldn't approve unless all five of them chimed in with their approval. Horatio was the last to join the conversation, but he was the first to approve. Jacques was still thinking it over, and Roland brought up a concern that no one had yet thought of, "This is going to anger Armstrong. He is going to see that his wagon train is falling apart and sees this as a challenge to his leadership. Eli, he already doesn't like you; do we want to alienate him even more? More wagons from the supply train may want to join us. Armstrong could grow into a real problem."

Eli responded, "A bigger camp will be safer west of Council Grove. Armstrong is going to have trouble, no matter what we do. I am in favor, and having a cook ready with breakfast at first light every morning will be a luxury. We wouldn't have to stop for lunch, which we will eat on the go. Let's go over some ground rules with them, so we get off on the right foot. Suzette, I'll go slow but raise your hand if I get too far ahead of you."

With that, Eli laid out how they would work together. First, all of the newcomers would stand a watch except for the cook. The cook will turn in early, and all of us will rotate through cleaning up the chuck wagon after dinner, so it is ready for the cook in the morning. Eli went on, "No booze on the trail; if you have any, get rid of it now." Suzette raised her hand. The Germans all were nodding their heads yes, and when Suzette got to the news about the booze, all laughed – they didn't have money to waste on liquor.

Eli continued. "Clean drinking water is sacred. The two green barrels on each of his wagons are only for drinking and cooking. The barrels have spigots, so only draw water from the spigots, no dipping in the top for a quick drink and no sharing cups, each man has to have his own. We fill the green barrels when we have either a clean spring or clear blue running water.

There can't be any exceptions to this rule unless we are caught dying of thirst." Again, Suzette raised her hand. There was concern among the Germans, not all of them had a cup of their own. Suzette told them that they would fix that when they reached the next supply station or Council Grove.

Eli asked, "I need to know about your teams and your training?" The Germans talked among themselves then related a tale of woe. One of them was left behind in St. Lewis with a broken leg when a mule kicked him as they were hitching up at Fort Wiki the first time. We lost another of our team in Independence when a mule bit him in the neck and tore open a large wound. We left him at the hospital where a black woman stitched him up. There was already an infection, and she said if he continued before he was over it, he would surely die. We picked up another German just off the riverboat to replace him. The Army didn't care that they had no experience. They had learned a lot, but the mules were still their worst nightmare.

Eli said, "We will help you with the mules. One last thing, each of you will learn several words of English a day. Here are your first three words – *My name is* – Eli Callahan. Willkommen."

When Suzette got to the last sentence, Schultz jumped up and shook Eli's hand, holding it in both of his and babbling on in German to his mates. Then he said, struggling with the words, "My name is Hans-Werner Schultz, "please call me Hans, *Danke*." Each of the other men introduced themselves, and Niclaus brought over a Dutch oven and a frying pan of already cooked bacon and set it on the grate in the fire pit to warm. Roland and Jacques looked at each other and smiled, Horatio just stared at the food waiting to eat.

Suzette asked Eli why he didn't have any rules concerning her. Eli responded, "These are immigrants and more than likely men of character. If there is a problem, they will learn to treat you with respect quick enough." With that, all the brothers presented a doubled-up fist and punched the air assuring their sister that she would be well guarded. Horatio got the hint and repeated the gesture. The pact sealed firm with a good breakfast and strong coffee, and they set out in the early morning light. Eli's wagon train just doubled in size; he hoped for the better.

At 10:00 AM, with the cool morning already giving way to the hot of the day, Armstrong was riding up hard from the rear. Eli was on the first of the supply wagons watching the mules. He already switched the positions of the mules two times along the trail and was satisfied with this team. Hans had the reins and was doing well, talking to the mules in German. Eli didn't think the mules knew German, so Eli gave him his next three words in English: *whoa, gitty-up and walk*. Armstrong pulled up in front of the team when he saw Eli on the German wagon. He dismounted and started yelling obscenities demanding that the German turn around and get back in line with the supply train. Eli got down and kept Armstrong's attention on himself as Suzette walked up behind Armstrong, who focused on Eli, still raving and swearing like a lunatic.

Suzette took advantage when the angry man had to draw in a breath and said, "Mr. Armstrong, you can't yell at these men as if they were mules. "

Armstrong spun around, surprised at a woman's voice. He stank of sweat and whiskey, and his nose was spider-webbed with bright red blood vessels as he grabbed Suzette by her bandana and opened his mouth to speak. Armstrong cut short as Suzette drew her knife and pricked his neck in front of his jugular vein. The drunk stepped back and went to draw his gun, but lightning-fast, Suzette drew hers and shot Armstrong's hat off his head before he even cleared leather. Armstrong stumbled and fell backward into the dust of the trail. Suzette leveled the gun at his face and said with a strong voice of command, "Leave."

Armstrong got up; Eli led his horse over and stood with his arms crossed. As Armstrong mounted, he saw three rifles trained on him, and Eli said, "You or any of your men touch my sister again, and it will be me that kills you." He slapped the gelding on the rear, and the wagon master rode out fast. His wagons were visible in the distance. Armstrong wasn't a ship's captain that could have the Germans hung for mutiny; he didn't know how he would handle this, but he was resolved not to let it lie.

Eli got on the second of the German's wagons and yelled up to Horatio to head'um out. Like Armstrong, he knew this wasn't over. The next stop was Rocky Creek, a blue water stream with deep pools, one of their favorite stops. They would make camp there for the night, replenish their water supply and bathe. The afternoon was hot, and the flies were swarming, a black cloud over mules and humans alike, looking for a taste of sweat or a drop of moisture at the corner of an eye. Mosquitoes were starting to be ever-present but far stronger in numbers in the early evening. Among the medical supplies that Suzette got from Aunt Sophie were bottles of her garlic repellent. Suzette told everyone It was boiled garlic in a mixture of eucalyptus oil and lemon juice. Sophie filtered out the garlic when the tincture cooled, and bottled the liquid. Suzette had two-pint bottles of it and used it sparingly. That night she would make sure everyone had a small portion to ward off the annoying bugs, and she was going to make sure Niclaus had an ample supply of garlic before they left Council Grove.

About two miles from Rocky Creek, Eli sent Horatio out to hunt; there were always deer in the grove above the camp. The young man rode forward on Patches, and it didn't take long that a rifle shot echoed over the prairie as Eli turned off the trail up to the campsite. When they pulled into the camp a half-mile north of the trail, Horatio had a large buck hanging on a branch of a cottonwood tree and was gathering wood to start up the cook fire. Suzette started replenishing the water barrels from a large pool upstream that eddied around a large rock. She could see fish in the water, and the memory of the last day with her parents hit her like an unwelcome blast of cold Arctic air. She focused on the task at hand, and by the time the water barrels were full, the deer was cooking on the spit with Horatio sitting on a rock at the side of the fire, turning the handle. Niclaus had the sideboard of the chuck wagon down and was preparing the rest of the evening meal. They still had four hours of daylight. *What a waste,* Eli thought as he watered the teams one by one in the creek below the camp. The Germans followed his lead, watered their teams, and then released them on a grassy patch after hobbling them for the night. Eli had halters for each of their mules and tied them to steel stakes that the twins drove into the rich soil of the meadow, giving each mule a twenty-foot circle of private turf.

As usual, it was almost dark when the wagon train made camp down on the trail on both sides of the creek. Armstrong walked up to Eli's camp unarmed with his palms raised in supplication. "We need to talk," was all he said when he approached the camp. Eli sat him down by the fire ring, and Niclaus fed him a plate of venison, potatoes, and carrots. Armstrong was sober, and he ate heartedly. Eli hoped the sober would last for a while. In between bites, the hungry man said, "I lost a man today, and another is sick, I think it is cholera. They were fine at breakfast, and the one was dead shortly after lunch. I wasn't expecting this kind of trouble till after Council Grove, but it has hit early."

Suzette asked him if they had picked up their allotment of Dr. John Sappington's anti-fever pills at the hospital in Independence. Armstrong bristled; he didn't enjoy questioning by a woman but settled and said only Eli's Germans and several other teams picked up the kits. Suzette wouldn't share any of their medical supplies. She told Armstrong to take the kits he had and divide the pills up among the rest of the men. There were ninety-five men when he left Independence, six came with Eli, and one died, leaving him with eighty-eight. Each kit had seventy-five pills, enough for one spending two and a half months on the trail, some other ointments, and an assortment of bandages. Doing the math in her head, she said,

"You can give each man two pills and have some left to dose anyone else that comes down with diarrhea heavily with about four pills a day. I'm pretty sure there will be an ample supply of Sappington's pills in Council Grove. I'll saddle up my horse and come down with you to dose the sick man. Remember, you or any of your men touch me, and you will die."

Eli looked at Armstrong and said, "Take it to heart; it is not a threat if you get her meaning. Roland, please go down with her, Jacques, and I have a mule to shoe." Roland got a double-barreled shotgun and an extra revolver and left with Armstrong and Suzette. Two of the Germans fell in with them; they only had one rifle between them, so the other man carried an ax.

When Suzette got to the sick man, he was stretched out by a campfire stripped naked. His fever was high, and he was badly dehydrated. He was delusional and going into shock. He looked up at Suzette and thought she was an angel arrived to take him to heaven. She took out four anti-fever pills and made him drink a whole canteen of water. She told the men standing around to carry him down to the creek and keep him in the water until the fever broke. She thought the man was too far gone to save, but this was his best chance. She rode down to the creek and told the men to make him drink at least a cup of clean water laced with sugar and salt every fifteen minutes. She told Armstrong to assemble his men. It was time for a lesson about hygiene on the trail.

Most of the men were already there, seeing if the cholera victim would live or die. There were quite a few fires next to the creek and some light from the waning moon. Suzette was appalled that the Army would hire any man willing to climb up on a wagon and turn them west without a shred of training concerning safety. She told them how to keep their water clean and to only replenish the water barrels from springs or clear blue running streams. There was a thunderstorm approaching from the west, and she told men they could drink all the rainwater they could catch, as long as they caught it on something clean. She asked the cooks to come forward to see if any had any mint in their supplies. One did, and she told him to brew up a batch and let it cool and then mix in six egg whites and to see if he could get it down the cholera victim. Almost all the men were in awe of her and appreciated the advice. Roland overheard a ragged looking group of three joking that they had a lot better use for a woman than a lecture on the water supply. Regrettably, he knew there would be trouble sooner or later. These three were probably criminals, more accustomed to the whores on the back streets of the eastern cities, whom they could abuse at their convenience. Many men took to the trails to escape prosecution back home. Roland hoped these were the only three among Armstrong's ragtag crew.

At sunrise, Armstrong was back. The sick man was stable, but now that wasn't his worst problem. More than twenty mules and his horse had disappeared during the dark of the night, enough mules to pull three wagons. He was going to transfer the goods from three wagons and abandon the wagons on the trail. Eli told him to strip the tongues, axles, and wheels and any iron parts they could get off and lash them under the remaining wagons. He showed Armstrong his rigs. Each had an axle, and two spare wheels lashed up under the beds of the wagons. "Trust me; you're going to need them." Eli just shook his head as the sorry excuse for a Wagon Master walked back down to his camp. Along with his letter to Denise, he would be writing to the Quartermaster about Armstrong. He was going to do everything in his power to see that this was Armstrong's last trip.

Eli was already glad he had a cook join his team. There were some meat pies made with venison, bacon, and onions cooking in Dutch ovens on the fire. The smell was more than several levels above and beyond jerky and apple cider for breakfast. Suzette saddled up and rode down to check on her cholera patient and found him lucid. His fever was down, and he hadn't thrown up since he had the mint tea laced with egg whites. He had to be helped to get dressed, but he was going to try to eat and get his strength back. So far that morning, he hadn't been hit with diarrhea, and he was thankful Suzette had saved his life.

A little way away, the three men that were looking Suzette over the night before were watching her again. "Look," one of them said, "she doesn't have her guards with her today."

Another intoned quietly, "Calm down, Whitey; our time will come. That little cunt will be spreading her legs for us soon enough whether she wants to or not." The three men left it at that as Suzette rode around to make sure that the quinine pills had been distributed and taken. All of the men were respectful and glad to have a nurse with them on the trail, all but the three ruffians who just gave her wicked instead of friendly smiles. One of them grabbed his crotch; this one Suzette figured would soon wind up dead if he weren't careful.

Suzette didn't smile back; she just said, "French Pox on the little guy, heh? I don't have any cure for that, but amputation." The expression on Whitey's face morphed from the invitation to anger as black as his soul. Suzette nudged Patches and rode right at the vulgar man. Whitey jumped to the side to avoid being ridden down and cursed when he stumbled and fell in the dust.

"I'm going to kill that bitch after I rape her," he told the other two men as he got up.

Armstrong saw the exchange and walked over to tell the three not to harass Suzette.   His life depended on it, and he told them how fast she was with a knife and how she shot his hat off his head the first time he met her. "Leave her alone, boys, and we will all stay alive." Despite his dire warning, Armstrong could see that the three men were not going to heed his advice.

Unloading and stripping the three wagons didn't take long, with many hands organized into the task. Suzette saw that Armstrong had his men better organized and hoped he would stay sober for the rest of the journey. Maybe he was just out of whiskey, and his troubles would start up again when they reached Council Grove. When she got back to her camp, she told Eli and her brothers about the incident with the lewd man and his cohorts. Eli told her he would talk to Armstrong about the incident and went to unhitch his lead mule to ride down to the other camp. Suzette dismounted and told him to take Patches.

When Eli rode up to Armstrong in the lead wagon, he was pleased to see that the wagon train was ready to pull out, and it was only two hours after sunrise. With luck, they would make more than fifteen miles today. On his own, he would average twenty a day, but fifteen was a good improvement, and he let Armstrong know he was pleased. He asked about the three men, and they talked about the situation for a while. He saw Horatio lead out with his wagon from the upper camp as Armstrong told Eli he talked to the men, but he didn't trust them to stay away from Suzette. He didn't know what to do; he didn't want to die if something happened that he couldn't control. Eli suggested that they send the three men back, but Armstrong didn't trust that they would go back. They would run off and sell the wagon. Armstrong went on for a while, "They are only carrying supplies. It wouldn't be much of a loss, but we would be short drivers."

Eli was thinking ahead and told Armstrong that when they got to the next camp, Armstrong should pull in closer this time where they both could watch for the trouble they expected. Eli assured the older man that he lifted the death threat, but he was also sure that one or all three of the ruffians were going to be dead soon. There would be some drivers along the trail or in Council Grove that fell behind or had to stop for some reason and got left in the dust. He often gave abandoned drivers rides back to Fort Leavenworth or Independence, depending on where he was going on the return leg of a supply run. Armstrong was relieved, Eli wasn't sure it was because he spared Armstrong the death threat or because he wouldn't have to give up any more wagons. The Army didn't keep a wagon master long if his losses were too high. Eli rode ahead to catch up with his wagons. He was also relieved that the confrontation with Armstrong also seemed to be mitigated for the moment. Like everyone involved, Eli hoped the new partnership would last.

Travel was at a quick pace through the morning. A thunderstorm swept in the afternoon, intense with a leading front of hail. The cool ice and then the cold rain were at first refreshing, but then the ugly mud of the trail slowed progress. It took longer than Eli wanted, but they made the fifteen miles to a particular grove of elm trees where he wanted to spend the night. The further west they got on the way to Council Grove, the thinner the trees. This mature grove was large, and the ground was bare from years of pioneer traffic. Eli chose the southwest edge of the grove for his camp. The elm grove was a dry camp, so it didn't matter where he lay up for the night, but the trees were sparser on the southwest edge of the grove. The open spacing of the trees suited the plan he put together in his mind to draw out the three men who threatened Suzette. The ground was still a soggy mass of mud from heavy rains. The wagon train was only an hour behind this time, a big improvement in their schedule. Armstrong pulled in close to Eli's camp and started directing his wagons here and there as they arrived. When Whitey's wagon entered the grove, he placed them a hundred yards to the northeast of Eli. He purposely kept the area between Whitey and Eli empty of wagons. None of the other drivers thought anything of this; seeing Eli's camp a way off from the main body of the wagon train was expected.

Like Eli, his brothers, and the other drivers were tending to the mules; they saw a man working his way down from the wagon train. It was obvious he was reconnoitering their camp as he worked his way closer, hiding as best he could from tree to tree. Suzette walked over to Eli with a cup of water and said, "That's him, the leader of the three."

Eli hardly glanced at the man but noted that he had turned back to the wagon train as soon as he saw Suzette. He was sure an attack would come that night, and he wanted it to unfold on his terms. As Eli and his crew sat around the campfire for their evening meal, Suzette translated the details of Eli's plan to the Germans. She had each of the Germans repeat their part of the scheme to confirm that each man understood his part. There were only twenty trees between them and the wagon train. The Germans would be on a line about halfway to the other camp, each man armed with an ax or a shovel would hide behind a tree. Roland and Jacques would be armed with rifles and conceal themselves closer to the other camp. Eli and Armstrong would accompany Suzette up to check on the cholera victim about an hour before dark, and Suzette was going to start walking back on her own after dark. Eli would tail her and be watching for signs of trouble. Suzette needed no instruction; she checked her revolver and sat quietly, sharpening her knife, wondering if she would ever see a peaceful night again.

When the three of them walked up to the supply wagon camp, Armstrong pointed out the three men who were making a conscious effort not to look their way. They heard the notes of a banjo a little further on, and Suzette was thrilled to see that the banjo player was none other than her cholera patient. He was playing some popular songs of the day, and all the men around his fire were clapping and singing along as best they could. When he saw Suzette, he made a transition from a polka he was playing to *Annie of the Veil,* a J. R. Thomas ballad about a young soldier pining away for his girl to come to him. She recognized the ballad, and when the banjo player sang her the full score in a rich, deep baritone voice, Suzette experienced an unexpected emotion of affection. When he finished, everyone clapped and cheered and called for more. When they quieted, Suzette said, "I see you are better. Where did you learn that ballad?"

"I studied in New York with John Thomas. My name is Paul Hayman. I'm on my way to Los Angeles and plan to sing for my dinner on my way west. I'm a driver's helper, but Mr.

Armstrong said he would pay me an extra fifty dollars when we reached Santa Fe if I entertained every night. I missed a couple of nights, and if it weren't for you, I would have missed them all. Are you going to deduct the lost nights from my pay, Mr. Armstrong?"

"No, son, you only have to stay alive and keep singing. You're damn good at that." With that, he turned to make his rounds of the rest of the camp. Eli and Suzette waited for total darkness and then left together to return. When they reached Whitey's camp, they saw the fire had burned down low, but there was enough light to see the camp was empty. They hadn't seen the three men up at Hayman's camp, so Eli knew they were in the woods waiting to catch Suzette alone. He held back and let her walk about fifty feet forward in the darkness. Stealth was impossible with a heavy round ball of mud stuck to each foot, but Eli walked as quietly as possible and followed his sister into the woods. Suzette had her pistol in her hand at her side and her knife in the other. She was humming a stanza from Hayman's ballad to let Eli know where she was in the darkness.

Suzette was halfway down to the line of hidden Germans when she heard the swish of a rope and felt a lasso fall over her as she raised her forearms to keep the rope from pinning her hands. Whitey stepped forward and said, "I got you now, bitch." As Suzette spun around in the pull of the rope, Suzette could see Whitey clear as day, backlit with the glow of many fires among the wagon train. Suzette raised her revolver and shot Whitey in the heart. Another man charged her but fell as an ax cleaved his sternum, expertly thrown by a German from twenty feet away. The third man broke from the cover of a tree trunk and ran towards his camp but skidded to a stop falling on his ass in the mud with Roland's rifle inches from his forehead. Roland said, "You get to live for the moment because you were smart enough to run away. Eli walked over with Suzette, and Armstrong arrived with at least fifty men with lanterns that lit up the woods and took charge of Roland's prisoner.

Suzette and her brothers walked back to their camp with the Germans carrying on about the incident. Suzette told her brothers that the Germans were commending their compatriot on the good throw of the ax. The German was modest and shrugged off the praise, but passed the bloody ax around the light of the fire pit with a look of pride at his handy work. He had grown up with axes and saws in the forests of Germany. Ax throwing was a favorite pastime among the German lumberjacks. Niclaus took a Dutch oven off a grate on the edge of the fire and served up a berry cobbler for a victory celebration. Suzette wasn't in a celebratory mood. She had killed a man. That bothered her even though she was hardened towards rape, having read her grandmother's accounts of her rape aboard *The Blessed,* and the many books and articles Denise had written on sexual abuse of blacks throughout the South.

Roland sensed her mood and with a hand on her shoulder, assured her that she had killed the man only in self-defense. "There will probably be more killings before we reach Los Angeles. Don't let this one dwell on your spirit for very long. The man was a pig." With that, the party broke up, and everyone turned in to the crackle of dying embers and the howls of coyotes out on the prairie. Dawn would come soon enough, and once more, each day on the trail west would breathe its own breath.

The morning of the fifth day went smoothly. They were still ninety miles from Council Grove, but they could make that in six more days if Armstrong kept up the pace. Two miles from the last camp, Eli saw a group of Pawnee that included several men, seven women, and some children. There was a young brave standing in the trail holding Armstrong's horse. Eli pulled up as soon as he saw them and called back for Suzette. She and Horatio traded places, and Eli coached her on how they would handle this encounter. The boy in the trail with the horse was all of twelve and selected to show good faith. The horse would be for sale; the price was going to be haggled over. Suzette had command of at least one hundred words of Pawnee, and she would talk to the boy in some middle ground between broken English and the Indian language. Eli didn't want her to say that the Indians stole the horse. It was important for the Indians that they were allowed to maintain their pride even if it was a charade.

Eli pulled his mules up to the boy, and he and Suzette got down to negotiate the deal.

Suzette asked in her rendition of Pawnee, "Find horse?" The boy smiled and nodded his head yes with enthusiasm. Eli was looking the horse over. There was a lost shoe, probably from being ridden hard and sucked off by the mud of the prairie. The saddle was missing, but the bridle and bit were still in the horse's mouth. Eli lifted the shoeless hoof and shook his head in derision, looking back at the motley tribe. One of the older men just shrugged his shoulders as if to say, *not our fault.* Eli knew they had little use for money miles away from any settlement or trading post. He decided to offer food. He walked back to the chuck wagon and got out the open barrel of salt pork. It was more than half full. He carried it over and set it down in front of the Indian that had shrugged his shoulders, assuming he was the leader of the small band. The *chief* shook his head *no* and grunted, "Horse big. Barrel small."

Suzette walked over and asked in Pawnee, "What do you want?"

The Indian struck a resolute pose with his arms crossed and grunted a single word, "More."

Eli looked at the chief and then at the horse, shook his head *no* and picked up the barrel, and started to walk back to the wagon. The Indian women started to harangue the chief, and he finally gave in. The salt pork tasted a lot better than horse meat, and the band was hungry. The chief nodded at the boy, and he walked the horse over and handed Eli the reins. Armstrong pulled up and was amazed to see Eli with his horse. He jumped down from the driver's seat of his wagon and walked over to Eli to retrieve his mount. Eli crossed his arms and mimicked the serious expression of the Pawnee chief and grunted, "My horse." Even the Germans laughed. Armstrong rankled, but Eli smiled and told the Wagon Master, he could have his horse back later that night after he took care of the missing shoe.

Suzette waved at the Indian children as they scurried off after the adults. At least they would have a full stomach for a day or so. All of them looked like they could use many more than several good meals. With the horse-trading complete, the wagon train turned back to the tedium of the trail. The prairie was drying quickly in the morning sun, and that was good. It was still a long way to Council Grove, and dust was much more welcome than mud.

THE NARROWS

Armstrong announced that they would stop in Palmyra to replenish their water. If the trail stayed dry, Eli wanted to push up through a difficult stretch of trail to the west of Palmyra called The Narrows. The Narrows was a nine-mile stretch of trail that stayed on top of a low ridge that divided two drainages full of streams to ford and marshes impossible to cross. The nine miles were a challenge, even when it was dry. If it was wet with new rain, it was near impossible choked with deep mud. Wagons, especially his heavy wagons, would sink to their axles.

Eli pulled up to the well in Palmyra, and Eli rode Armstrong's horse over to the post office and trading post. He had written the letter to Denise the night before and mailed it. He held off on writing to the Quartermaster even though he felt the Wagon Master would slip back into his alcoholic ways as soon as more liquor was available. Thankfully, the trading post was stocked only with the barest essentials. The woman behind the counter did have about a dozen packs of the anti-fever pills, and Eli bought all of them along with tin cups for the Germans. By the time he got back to the wagons, the water barrels were topped off, and Armstrong was arriving with the rest of the train. Eli was ready to pull out, and he cautioned Armstrong not to waste any time at the well. The Narrows lay just west of the settlement, and if it was dry, they needed to make it through to the west end by nightfall. Armstrong didn't cotton to the young man acting like the Wagon Master. He had been through The Narrows many times and shrugged off Eli's advice.

Eli pulled out at a fast pace. Just west of Palmyra, the town of Baldwin City was growing rapidly. You could see the trail going up to the ridge where the infamous nine miles of The Narrows lay. The weather didn't look good out to the west, and with a sense of urgency, Eli drove up to the ridge at a gallop. From the higher ground, he could see a thunderstorm in the distance. The trail wasn't dry but not wet enough to sink the wagons. About halfway through it, he could see why many pioneers favored oxen for pulling in the mud. The mules were struggling, slipping back some for every step they took forward. The storm was advancing from the southwest. It would be a race to make it to the end of the nine miles before the storm hit. Eli and his brothers mounted their lead mules and were nudging them forward, trying to avoid the deeper ruts. Litter lined the sides of the trail, pioneer castoffs of every kind. From cookstoves and cabinets to a favorite piece of furniture; even a grandfather's clock lay weathering in the rain and sun. Suzette thought there was enough trash on the trail to outfit an entire village. She was riding Patches out ahead of the wagons, feeling her way through the driest parts of the trail and staying on what grass there was on the top edges of the deep swale.

They made it to within a half-mile of the end when the storm hit in earnest. The rain front was intense, and the swale was a natural collection basin. They went another quarter mile before Eli's wagon went down to the axles. He told everyone to stay undercover until the storm passed, and then they would unhitch the rear teams and use as many teams as needed to pull the wagons one at a time out of the swale to the end of The Narrows. This storm was a big one, and Eli was glad it didn't carry a tornado along with it. It took an hour to pass, and then came the arduous task to pull the wagons through the deep mud it created. They only had a quarter of a mile to go. Armstrong would be caught further back on the trail, or maybe he would just lay up waiting for the trail to dry. That would be the smart decision, and Eli hoped he would make the better choice. Getting six wagons out of the mud was going to take some major effort; forty more would be impossible.

Eli and the twins unhitched the tongue of the two back wagons and brought the teams around to the front. Each tongue was fitted on the front end with an iron ring the same as on the front of the wagons. The drawbars joined together, and twelve mules became twenty-four. They still couldn't move the first wagon. The Germans were going to jump in and push, but Eli waved them to the tailgate. He had told Suzette that many a broken leg occurred when a wagon moved, and the man pushing slipped in the mud and went under a wheel. They brought up the third team, and all hoped that would be enough because the tongues on the supply wagons were smaller and wouldn't be as easy to join up. With thirty-six mules and a lot of encouragement from the boys, the heavy wagon lurched up and moved forward. Once moving, they wouldn't stop until the wagon was safely out of the swale. Eli didn't like leaving Suzette alone to guard the wagon as they unhitched and told her to ride back at the first sign of trouble. They were near Military Junction that was a cutoff from the trail to Fort Leavenworth. Eli looked up to the trail to the north, but there wasn't a wagon in sight. Alone was good; his sister would be safe until they returned. He pulled his rifle out of his wagon and gave it to Suzette, more to reassure himself than his sister.

Eli turned the mules around. In a way, thirty-six mules working together was a thing of beauty. Riding back to the second wagon was easy. Getting all thirty-six mules to backup at once so they could hitch up the tongue, took more than an hour. It was going to be a long, long day. The second wagon was not as heavy as the first and not mired as badly; they pulled it out of the swale with no trouble. As they returned to get the third wagon, the Germans had two of their teams, sixteen mules, hitched to the chuck wagon, and were pulling it out of the line to go around the heavy wagon in front. The wagon leaned precariously on the edge of the swale and all the men, but the driver jumped on the uphill side to keep it from turning over. It would have been safer to wait their turn. Eli could see the making of the broken leg disaster and would talk to them about it later on. For now, they still had three more wagons to recover.

It was dark by the time they got the last wagon out. Suzette had to lead Eli out of the swale with a lantern. The night was black in the dark of the moon, and a light cloud cover obscured the stars. Everyone was dead tired, and they flopped on the grass around a small fire. Wood was scarce this close to the trail, and the cook, Niclaus, had worked most of the day with the rest of the men freeing the wagons. Suzette had a big pot of stew cooking at the side of the fire, and she fed her hungry men. She had made the coffee extra strong, but even with that, the men were nodding off one by one. Eli kept them awake. There was still work to finish. The mules had to be staked out for the night, and their hooves cleaned, or they would come down with infections in the frog of their hooves. There were a few acres of grassy sod about a hundred yards from the end of the swale. All the teams were moved up to the grass, and settling the teams down for the night took another two hours. The men finished the work by lantern light. The men were hoping they could get by with only one guard on watch through the night, but all moaned when Eli posted two, one at the mules and one at the wagons. Suzette took the first watch and saddled Armstrong's horse. She could stay awake longer in the saddle and on horseback, and it would be easier checking on the guard at the mules to make sure he stayed awake. The Indians in the area would know they were exhausted, and sleeping pioneers made easy prey. Suzette stayed on the watch for two rotations to spare Eli watch duty for the night. She woke Roland for his watch, and she climbed up to her bed in Roland's wagon. She slept soundly, and Eli didn't wake her until after first light.

Eli was up with Niclaus before dawn and was setting up the forge to cut down a mule shoe to fit it to Armstrong's horse. He would pick up a supply of horseshoes in Council Grove. He was turning the handle on the blower to build up the charcoal fire when Suzette climbed down from Roland's wagon, groggy from her short night's sleep. Eli told her she should have woken him for his watch, but Suzette just laughed, "You looked like you were dead." She walked to the top of the swale and looked back down the trail to the east. She could see about three miles, and there was no sign of Armstrong. She walked back and suggested to Eli that they ride back later and see if Armstrong was in the swale or if he had sense enough to stop and wait in Baldwin City for the trail to dry. The rest of the men were up and waiting for something to eat. Niclaus was admonishing them as they crowded around the fire. He had learned a new word yesterday, and he barked, "Back," when one of the men reached for a piece of bacon.

They all rushed in to eat when Niclaus finally rang his triangle. There were bacon and briskets and a pan of scrambled eggs. Eli and the men ate like they had missed a week of meals, but Suzette wasn't that hungry. She feasted on jerky through her long watch and figured that the men needed the food more than her. Eli took care of Armstrong's horse after breakfast, and they saddled Patches. Eli rode the gelding bareback. They headed down the swale, staying on the upper side on the grass to avoid the deep mud. They were near to the end when they found six wagons mired, sunk to their axles. Two of the wagons still had their teams hooked up, but there wasn't a driver in sight. Eli unhitched the teams and riding with a lead rope apiece; they took the hungry mules back down the trail to Baldwin City. They found Armstrong sitting with some of his men around a fire on the edge of town. The rest of the wagons were there, more than half still had the mules hitched up to their wagons. None had their hooves cleaned, and the rest of the men were disorganized, trying to figure out how to get the mired wagons out of the swale.

Armstrong found a bottle somewhere in Baldwin City because he was drunk and got belligerent when Eli started organizing the men and had them taking care of their mules. He was showing the green drivers how to hook the tongues together to pull the mired wagons out of the swale. Armstrong staggered up and accosted him, "Trying to take over again, I see." Eli didn't answer him; he just turned around and knocked the Wagon Master out cold with a hard-right cross to the jaw. Suzette led the gelding up, and Eli leaped upon his back. Together they rode down to the post office in Palmyra. Armstrong's grace period had come to an end. Eli wrote out his letter to the Quartermaster and told him he would take over the supply train if necessary. If things went on under Armstrong's leadership, a good deal of the wagon train would be left behind on the trail due to stupidity and drunken decisions. The mail courier was getting ready to leave, and he had the third man of Suzette's attackers mounted on an old mare. The prisoner's hands were tied at the wrists and tethered to the saddle horn. The mail courier would take the would-be rapist back to Independence. Suzette rode up to the man as they were leaving and leaning over in her saddle, whispered in her attacker's ear, "If I ever see you again, I will kill you."

As Eli rode back through Armstrong's camp, the men implored him to wait for them on the trail. It would take them a day to retrieve the wagons, and by then, The Narrows might be dry enough for them to clear it, given that there wasn't another storm brewing on the horizon. Eli told them that he would move west to a better camp and wait for them there. When they got to the swale, there were two teams hitched together, and the men were trying to get the mules to back up to the tongue of the rear wagon. Eli told Suzette he was going to stay and help and for her to go back to their camp and tell Jacques to move them five miles to the west. There is a blue water stream there; he assured her that they couldn't miss it. Neither of the twins had been west of Baldwin City before. His parting words, "Be sure to pull the camp in as close as possible tonight and keep the watch doubled. I'm going to stay with the supply train until I get them back on the trail."

Suzette was loath to leave Eli behind, but she was looking forward to some time to unpack a Henry rifle and make it her own.

A NEW PARADIGM

uzette watched Eli as he waded into the mud and took charge of the men struggling with the mules. She was gaining a new appreciation for her oldest brother and could see in him, the same strong, determined character of her father. She watched for a while as Eli finally got the mules to back up and hitched to the tongue. Eli pulled himself up out of the mud onto the back of what he thought was the dominant mule of the team, and with several men pushing from behind, he pulled the wagon out of the deep ruts of the track. He turned the team back down the trail and waved to his sister as she turned Patches to return to their camp. She would walk her horse the six miles to the camp. She didn't want to stress the mare. Patches would carry her nearly thirty miles that day before she was put up for the night. Halfway to her camp, Suzette came upon some Indians scavenging through discarded items, looking for anything useful they could use or sell; some looked her over but left her alone when they saw that she was armed.

Further up the trail, some children were looking over the grandfather clock. Suzette got down and greeted them in Pawnee and had the children help her stand the clock upright. She hoisted the weights and set the pendulum swinging. It was amazing that the clock still worked; the youngsters were mesmerized by the swing of the pendulum and the sweep of the second hand. Suzette was trying to get the clock to chime when one of the boys vaulted up over the back of Patches. The young brave turned to run the mare back to the band she passed on the trail. Suzette let him run a hundred yards and then put her index fingers to her mouth and let out an ear-piercing whistle. Patches turned so fast the young boy flew out of the saddle, and the mare returned to stand by Suzette's side. Suzette looked at the rest of the children and said, "My horse," in Pawnee. She rode back to the horse thief to see he wasn't seriously injured, then turned and rode back to her camp. She was no longer comfortable being alone on the trail.

By the time she reached the wagons, Patches was showing the first signs of going lame, favoring her right front hoof. Roland helped her unsaddle the mare and inspected the hoof. There was a rock pushed up into the sole of the hoof between the frog and the shoe on the toe. Roland went to get his hoof pick from his toolkit on his wagon while Suzette gentled the mare and drew some water to wash the hoof clean. She hoped the rock would fall out once free of mud, but it held solid between the frog and the outer hoof. Roland tried to use the hoof pick to remove the rock to no avail. Jacques looked over the hoof and told Suzette the shoe had to come off. He had her stir up the fire pit to warm up some water while he got a hoof jack and nippers out of the blacksmith tools. Roland set to pull the nails out of the shoe, and when he got it off, he started working on the rock with the hoof pick, Patches winced and nickered. He looked up at Suzette and said, "I'm sure she has a stone bruise, you're going to have to stay off of her for a couple of days. Roland pulled the left shoe so the mare could walk evenly, then set her hoof in the warm pail of water to soak.

Suzette told her brothers that Eli wanted them to move five miles west and to wait for him there. There was water, and they would be able to tether the mules in close. Jacques didn't want Patches to walk five miles and said it wouldn't hurt to stay where they were for another day. Suzette told him about the Indians on the trail. Jacques looked over the ground at the campsite, which was already drying out and said they would pull the wagons into a circle for the night, and increase the watch so that half the men were up at a time. Jacques summoned the Germans and had Suzette translate their plans for the night. When she finished, Jacques showed her how to wrap the sore hoof in burlap, with a leather pad under the hoof. He told her, "Tomorrow, you can walk her the five miles to the new camp, and when the pad falls off, we will stop and rewrap her. She should be fine by the time Eli gets the rest of the wagon train up the trail."

Late in the afternoon, the men started arranging the wagons. Here was a circumstance where more wagons would be better because to make a circle big enough to put all the mules inside left large gaps between the wagons. Jacques sent Roland and two of the Germans with one mule each to gather wood from a grove they could see in the distance. There would be fires outside the circle, so anyone sneaking in during in the dark would be backlit by the embers. They weren't expecting trouble, but preparedness was the rule on the trail. Those who chose to ignore it suffered the consequences.

Suzette told Jacques she wanted to uncover the Henry rifle crate. They set to shifting the ammo boxes in the front of Roland's wagon, and it seemed like they had half the wagon unloaded before they found the one crate they wanted. The crate was as heavy as the crates of muzzleloaders. Two of the Germans lifted it out and handed it down to Jacques and Suzette on the ground. They repacked the wagon so that the crates of .44 caliber ammunition and the Henry rifle crate would be on the top of the load within easy reach when they got back on the trail.

Jacques opened the crate with a bar and withdrew a rifle. Each rifle, wrapped in oiled paper, lay cradled in a slotted board; six rifles abreast stacked two tiers deep in the crate. There was a manual in the top of the crate, and Suzette paged through it. There was a warning inside the front cover; it read, "Do not dry fire the rifle." The men unwrapped a rifle and marveled at the beautiful brass receiver, the lever-action, and the hammer that cocked when you opened the breach. Jacques passed it around, and each worked the action and sighted down the barrel as they held it to their shoulders as men do with any gun they encounter and appraise as if it were their own. Suzette, ever the teacher like her mother, said, "Don't dry fire the rifle."

Suzette took the rifle and looked it over but was more interested in the ammunition. Like her 9mm Lefaucheux revolver that her father sent for after she complained about the mess of loading with black powder and lead balls, the Henry loaded with a single .44 caliber cartridge. The magazine tube under the barrel held fifteen rounds. Unlike her revolver that had used a pinfire cartridge, the Henry cartridge was rimfire, and the firing pin in the rifle struck the rim of the cartridge on both sides, improving the reliability. She wasn't quite as in awe of the rifle as the boys, but when Eli opened a crate of the .44 ammunition, she immediately saw the advantage of a self-contained cartridge for a rifle. She kept reading the training manual and soon had the rifle loaded. She levered a round into the chamber, raised the rifle to her shoulder and fired into the emptiness of the prairie south of the trail. When she levered the second round into the chamber and fired again in less than a couple of seconds, she knew that in her hands was a weapon that would rewrite the pages of modern warfare. She gave the rifle to Jacques, and he fired two rounds and then passed it to the first of the four Germans in the camp. Each fired the weapon two times and then passed it back to their instructor. There were still three rounds left; Suzette turned the rifle upside down and worked the lever three times, dropping the rounds into her hand.

"These rounds are bigger than my 9mm Lefaucheux, and the casing is a little longer." The Lefaucheux was deadly at close range, but it was not a long-distance weapon.

Jacques said, "You couldn't kill a deer with that at four hundred yards."

"True, but if we snuck up on a herd, I could shoot sixteen of them in the time it took you to reload."

Roland and the two Germans returned from the wood gathering, and Suzette demonstrated the new rifle to them.

Roland said, "Let's unpack one for each of us. Mr. Epperson won't mind if we borrow some of these until we reach Santa Fe."

Suzette just smiled. She had money of her own stashed in her gun belt. "I'm sure Mr. Epperson is a good businessman. I'm going to buy my rifle when we get there, along with a crate of ammunition." One of the drawbacks of the Lefaucheux was that she only had two hundred rounds for the revolver. If she ran out of ammunition or lost her saddlebags, the gun would be completely useless. Her father had bought the revolver for her twelfth birthday, and he had to send away to New York for the gun and the ammunition. The revolver was perfect for a lady and deadly enough for self-protection as it already proved, but a novelty that couldn't be supported any distance away from a post office.

As the evening was drawing to a close, Eli returned on Armstrong's horse and was more than a little upset that they hadn't moved the camp. Roland calmed him down and explained the situation to him and showed him their preparations for the night. Suzette put her two cents in and said, "We also have a secret weapon." She showed him her Henry rifle, and at first, he was even madder that they had broken into the shipment, but when Suzette put sixteen rounds into one of the outlying fire pits in less than twelve seconds, Eli just stood there with his mouth agape.

He finally said, "You know what, I'm going to quit worrying about you people." He would spend the night with them. If it didn't rain, he was going to move the supply train up through The Narrows the next day. Armstrong was worse than ever. Eli didn't know what the man was drinking, but whatever it was, rendered the Wagon Master completely worthless. If the drivers wouldn't follow him out of Baldwin City, he was going to leave them behind, and they would continue to Santa Fe on their own. He wanted Jacques to move their camp the five miles west at first light and to wait for him. With or without the rest of the supply train, he would be back by the early afternoon.

As evening approached with the sky radiant in the red of a prairie sunset, they hobbled the mules inside the makeshift perimeter. The mules weren't content being hobbled on the thin grass of the campsite but settled down in their feed bags. A bedtime snack of oats and water did wonder for their disposition. As total darkness fell, the outlying fire pits blazed away and lit up the night. Eli wondered about this. The light from the fires wrecked one's night vision. He could see pretty well just with the starlight on a clear night. Roland reminded him that they couldn't count on a clear night, and in a few hours, the fires would be burnt down to embers. He had them banked so that the glare of the flames would cast shadows toward the camp. Half of the men carried the new rifles. No one was going to get close to the camp. Eli told his brothers that when he joined up with the rest of the wagons, to keep the new rifles out of sight, everyone was going to want one, and he didn't want Armstrong's unruly crew plundering his wagons.

As she did before, Suzette took Eli's watch so he could get a full night's sleep. Two hours before dawn, she thought she heard something out in the darkness. She had put the last of the wood on her fire some time ago, and there was only the red light of embers casting their glow only a few feet around the pit. Three men appeared out of the darkness; they weren't Indians. Two had on cowboy hats with wide brims, and one was wearing a sombrero. All three had guns drawn expecting a fight. Suzette realized that they thought the fire pit was the camp instead of an outlying perimeter. It was obvious they were confused and advanced, putting the red glow to their backs. Suzette yelled out, "Hold it right there." She knew the men would be blind for another minute or so after staring at the fire. She heard the other guards stir at the sound of her voice. The three men froze.

The Mexican said, "Amigos, it's a *mujer*. Let's take her."

Suzette was lying down with the Henry rifle steadied on top of an ammo box. Backlit by the glow of the embers, she could see the gun in the Mexican's hand. It was an easy shot. She squeezed the trigger and shot the Mexican's gun out of his hand. The gun went off when it hit the ground; the round flew harmlessly into the night sky. The mules behind her were agitated and wanted to run. She hoped none would hurt themselves trying. The Mexican was roaring profanities in Spanish and holding his injured hand in his armpit. Suzette had a strange thought that an armpit on the prairie was probably not a very sanitary place.

One of the other men said, "Well, sweetie, it's going to take you some time to reload. How about I walk over and introduce myself." He started to walk in from the fire pit; he was betting that the woman didn't have a revolver and had wasted her only shot. Suzette fired two rounds over his head, and the man turned and ran back into the darkness. His partners were already gone. The whole camp was rousted and working desperately to settle the mules.

Eli walked up behind Suzette and asked, "Who were they?"

"Renegades! One of them left his gun behind. It probably isn't worth much. Sorry, I didn't want to wake you, but they were persistent. I'm glad I didn't have to kill one of them."

"Next time, kill all of them. There could have been a dozen more out there behind those three. You couldn't know, so play it safe. Think of it this way; they had a death wish when they walked in here. You would just be helping to make their wish come true."

Roland had some sage advice as usual, "Suzette, I heard the exchange. Men of that ilk will make you their camp whore for a while. But the white men or the Mexicans will kill you before they reach the next town to keep you from exposing them. If the Apache take you, your fate will be worse than that. You could live the rest of your life in slavery. Eli is right; kill them all."

The men lit lanterns and started hitching up the teams. Suzette walked out and found the Mexican's gun. It was a Colt cap and ball pistol but in very poor condition. She wouldn't trust to give it to any of the Germans. It was probably as dangerous to the man who shot it as to his target. She walked over to help Niclaus with the morning meal. She was anxious to move the camp now that the renegades knew where they were. They might still think they found a lone wagon instead of a heavily armed force and would return for another attempt.

They pulled out at first light. Eli was already gone an hour, and Suzette hoped the weather would hold, and the trail would be dry enough to get the supply train through to the west side of The Narrows. She was walking Patches with a lead rope, picking her way around the mud holes, and keeping the mare away from rocky areas. If she got a little way off the trail looking for good ground, Roland would walk out with a Henry rifle over his shoulder and walk with her. After a while, he just stayed with her on foot. Five miles wasn't that far. Some pioneers walked the entire journey to Santa Fe. Some didn't make it at all, whether they rode or walked. More graves lined the trail the further west they went; the crude crosses a grim reminder that there were many ways to die on the prairie.

She was glad Roland had stayed with her. They had to rewrap the hoof several times along the five-mile trek. However, Patches wasn't limping when they reached the grove by the stream. Suzette led her mare down to the water and let her drink her fill. She found a grassy spot, and Roland drove a stake and tied Patches off for the day. They would move her into the camp at nightfall. Suzette helped with the chores of setting up the camp, and then just sat watching the trail waiting for her brother to appear in the distance. It was late in the afternoon when the first wagon came into view. When it got closer, she could see that it was Armstrong's wagon, and Eli was at the reins. As he pulled up in the camp, Suzette climbed up on the driver's seat and hugged her brother. "Where's Armstrong?" she asked.

"Dead, he drank himself into oblivion." Eli reached into the bootbox and pulled out an earthen jug. "I think this is wood alcohol." He handed the jug to Suzette, and she pulled the cork plug and smelled the liquor. There was a faint odor of turpentine laced with the acrid smell of the moonshine.

"This isn't straight wood alcohol. It is contaminated corn whiskey. If it were pure wood alcohol, it would have killed him the first time he drank it. When he died, was his skin yellow? Wood alcohol kills the liver."

"Yes," Eli answered. He was impressed with how much Suzette knew about medicine. The booze he could understand, they grew up in the shadow of the brewery and remembered the care with which each batch of corn or grain was inspected before being added to the fermenting vats. Excluding wood chips or twigs was essential. "He was delirious and couldn't hold his eyes open in the sun. It was spooky; he died with his eyes open, and his pupils were the size of half dimes."

"That was wood alcohol for sure. I'll pour this out or start a fire with it. I don't think we have any other alcoholics on board, but let's get rid of this evil stuff just in case."

Roland was counting the wagons as they came in. There should have been thirty-seven, but two were missing. Eli said that they must have held back until he turned into The Narrows, then turned around and headed back east. They would probably sell the loads and then abandon the wagons. Not an uncommon happening among Army supply trains. He would hold a roll call that night. The Quartermaster needed to know who were the men in the missing crews. If the Army found them, the Army would prosecute them. More likely, once they disposed of the wagons, they would never be seen again. He was now officially the Wagon Master by a unanimous vote held right after Armstrong died in the throes of his last violent convulsion.

That night they had more than enough wagons to make a large circle with all the mules hobbled or staked out in the middle. There would be a man on watch on every third wagon. Eli let the men know this would be the way they camped every night until they reached the end of their journey.

Suzette walked her mare up from the creek. Patches wasn't limping, and that was a good sign. Eli unwrapped the hoof and was pleased. The frog was hard. They would set up the forge, and he would shoe both front hooves with a heavy layer of leather between the shoe and the hoof. Hopefully, the pad would protect the hoof for the next leg on the trail. Suzette said she would walk her mare as far as they went the next day. Many pioneer women walked to Santa Fe, some even with children. She could do it too. Eli didn't disagree. The horse was important, not just because Suzette loved it. An extra horse allowed them to hunt and scout and ride up and down the wagon train keeping everyone moving. He couldn't stop to rest the mare, but he would do everything possible not to lose her.

It was dark by the time they finished. Eli said, "No watch for you tonight, little sister. If you're going to walk fifteen miles tomorrow, you better get a full night's sleep."

RENEGADES

The next morning came early for the tired drivers and their hands, but with Eli and the twins waking the last of the reluctant drivers, they were hitched up and made ready to pull out at first light. The night had passed without incident, and Eli wanted to make it to Overbrook that day, a little more than fifteen miles. Eli was riding Armstrong's horse bareback. It was his horse now, and while somewhat unremarkable, the big gelding deserved a name, and Eli deserved a saddle. Roland was good at naming stuff; he would have him think up a name for his new acquisition. Suzette was on foot, leading her mare and watching for the first sign of trouble with the injured hoof. She didn't know what she would do if they had to leave her behind. Maybe she would stay with her and then catch up with the train after Patches was completely healed up. Eli told her there was a settlement named Marion a couple of miles below the trail a little way further on. If Patches went lame, she could stay there.

Before they reached the road down to Marion, a soldier was riding hard from the west. Eli rode out to meet him. It was a young lieutenant from Fort Leavenworth, and he was wounded, his left arm wrapped in a bloody sling. Eli knew the soldier; his name was John Sanders, First Lieutenant John Sanders. He was attached to the Headquarters Company at the fort. Sanders was the bearer of some unwanted news. There was a large band of renegades operating east of Overbrook. There were over forty men in the outlaw troop. They ambushed a small pioneer wagon train and killed all the men, women, and children, plundered and burned the wagons. The carnage they left at the site of the attack was not a pretty sight. The attackers had set fire to the prairie to scatter the wagons and then swept down to take the wagons one at a time. A dangerous but effective tactic, they could have been caught in the fire they set to scatter the wagons.

Sanders had encountered the outlaws riding out of Overbrook. The renegades killed the two men he had with him, and he took a bullet in his left arm; it broke his humerus above the elbow, and blood still oozed from the sling. He was lucky to have outrun them. Sanders advised Eli to hold up until he returned with the Army. Eli considered that suggestion, the Army would take more than a week to arrive, and the renegades were not that far away; the renegades could attack in the meantime. Eli made his first of many critical command decisions.

"I'm going to make camp at the Junction to Marion. We have more than 24 tons of rifles and ammunition. Most of my drivers and their hands are green pioneers, but I'm going to arm all of them and teach them how to load and shoot. We can't wait a week to head west, but we will be ready when we get back on the trail. You need to let my sister set that arm and dress the wound. You won't make it to Leavenworth with that wound bleeding. I could use your help in training these men."

"I'll stay and get patched up. It's only two miles to the junction. Is that your sister?" Suzette and the mare weren't lagging behind the wagon train. She was even with the lead wagon, and Eli waved her over.

"We are going to hold up at Marion Junction, there's trouble on the trail, and Lieutenant Sanders here needs your help." Suzette was relieved. Patches was doing fine, but favoring a lame hoof, she was tiring fast, holding pace with the mules.

She looked up at Sanders and said, "Let's stay with the fourth wagon. My medical kit is there. Did the bullet go clear through?"

"No, it was almost spent when it hit me. It is still in there, and I'm no coward to pain, but it hurts like hell."

They reached the junction, and Eli guided the supply train into one large circle with the Marion Junction in the center. Eli was pleased that his drivers were unhitched and tended to their animals without being told. He soon had the Germans unpacking rifle crates, barrels of powder, and shot. There were crates of accessories among the loads, and each contained a military belt with pockets for a powder horn, percussion cap dispensers, a bullet starter, shot, wads, and barrel grease. They laid out rifles and belts for eighty-eight men who would be armed and trained. Suzette was working on Sanders. She had the bullet out and was closing the wound. She would set the arm and splint it straight down through the elbow. Doctors in Fort Leavenworth could put on a plaster cast when he got there. For now, she did the best she could.

Eli assembled the men, and standing on an ammo crate addressed them. "We've stopped for some important training. I am issuing each of you a rifle, and for those of you who haven't shot one before, there is going to be training. There is a large band of renegades marauding west of here. They may leave us alone because of our numbers, but they have already murdered a small wagon train. When Lieutenant Sanders is ready, he is going to teach you how to load and shoot. Be careful; he has already been shot once, and he is a good friend of mine. I don't want to lose him." With that, Eli went over the range rules they had learned at Leavenworth. Suzette finished up with Sanders, and he walked up to take over the training.

Sanders was methodical. He had each man take a rifle and a belt and then asked which of the men were familiar with muzzleloaders. There were twenty or so that raised their hands. "You men that know how to shoot will each take several men and help them with the training." If any of the men bristled at Sanders' military way of speaking with orders, they didn't show it. Suzette said she would keep the Germans with her and anyone else having trouble with language. She was already translating every word Sanders said to the six non-English speakers.

Sanders went through the names of all the parts of the rifles and the items in the belts. Then he had Suzette take a rifle and had her perform each step of the loading process as he explained more about the weapons. "Your powder horn is designed to deliver 120 grains of powder. You hold it upside down and put your finger over the end of the tube. You push the lever, and powder fills the tube. You close the tube and line it up with the end of the barrel. When you tip the powder horn up vertical, the powder falls down the barrel." Suzette deftly demonstrated the move with one hand and loaded the charge.

Step by step, they finished the process: wad, a dab of barrel grease, ball, ball starter, and ramrod, and last, the primer cap. Sanders wasn't expecting it when Suzette raised the rifle to her shoulder, aimed high in the air, and shot the ball out over the heads of the pupils. Many of them flinched at the noise. Suzette wasn't going to let on, but the kick was much greater than the Henry, and it hurt her shoulder. Sanders said, "Make sure you pull the gun into your shoulder tight, or it will hit you with enough force to bruise you badly. Suzette shot the Mississippi rifle before, but now she was sure her father and brothers humored her with a lighter charge. Lt. Sanders continued, "The .54 caliber weapon can load with a charge up to 176 grains of powder. Maybe a sniper would do that, but for the average soldier, 120 grains is sufficient for combat.

Sanders spent about an hour in the training session and then got the men lined up on the top of the swale east of the camp. The men wanted to use empty barrels for targets, but Eli nixed that idea. Empty bottles, cans, and broken barrel tops were set out at about fifty yards, and the teams started banging away at the targets. At first, none of the green hands could hit them, and some of the men who never shot before were more than a little wary of the heavy guns. However, by the time they ended the shoot in the late afternoon, no bottle, or a scrap of a barrel top remained safe out on the range. Most of the settlers from Marion came up on foot, horseback or buckboards to watch the noisy attraction.

Sanders had the men replenish their ammo belts and told the men that the rifle they carried was now theirs. Roland asked him about the forts out west that were expecting the guns, and Sanders said, "Screw'em. We need firepower right here, right now. You may find some of those forts out west burned to the ground or abandoned. The Apaches are raising hell out there." With that, the cooks set to feed the men, and the drivers and their workmen drew lots for the first watch. Eli and his brothers walked the circumference of the circle and saw the men piling barrels and crates for barricades at the guard posts. The defense was straightforward common sense. He didn't sign-on to lead men into battle. He wondered what tomorrow would bring. He didn't want to lose any more men, and the safety of his family weighed heavily on his mind. He would spend the rest of the evening talking to Sanders about tactics.

As they walked back to their wagons, they heard Paul Hayman's banjo. They looked at each other as they saw him at their fire, serenading Suzette as she worked to change the dressing on Sanders' arm. Roland hoped this would be just one of many broken hearts Suzette would leave along the trail. This young man seemed more resilient than the rest of Suzette's admirers. Maybe he was going to be in his sister's future for more than the trip west.

Sanders had a good plan for dealing with the renegades. They were going to unload the three heavy munitions wagons. These were essentially bulletproof with high sides of thick wood backed by a steel plate. The armor protected barrels of gunpowder during transport, but now the heavy wagons would be manned by the best shooters selected from the previous day's training exercise. Only half the wagons would leave in the morning. Same as the cargo wagons, those were going to be empty so that they could react faster to the ambush. The remaining wagons and men would remain behind, circled, and barricaded to protect the cargo. With the planning complete, Eli walked over to his wagon and drew his Henry rifle from its hiding place. In the light of the fire, he handed the rifle to Sanders. "Careful, there is a round in the chamber. Cock the hammer, and it will fire. It shoots a 0.44 caliber bullet from a self-contained cartridge. Reloads with the lever, and the magazine holds fifteen rounds."

Sanders took the weapon and studied it with a look of reverence and awe. "I've heard about these. How many do you have?"

"There was a crate of twelve consigned to a hardware store in Santa Fe. Eleven are in the hands of my crew. There is one extra; if you had two good hands, I would give it to you." Sanders was deep in thought. There were going to be some modifications to his battle plan.

Eli had the camp up two hours before dawn. The men were unloading the three heavy wagons into a stockpile, along with fifteen of the supply wagons. The teams were hitched up to the empty wagons and lined up to the west on the trail. The remaining wagons were pushed by hand or moved by teams into a tighter circle. It was a monumental task, but a Chinese cook commented, "Many hands make light work."

By the time dawn broke, the men had finished eating breakfast and drew straws for determining who would man the "prairie gunships" and who would stay behind. Eli could see the men were eager to be on the armed wagons. No one wanted to stay behind. His simple observation turned to a deeper concern when he saw Suzette with an ammo belt over her shoulder. She had scavenged six bullet pouches off of extra belts and had them fashioned into a bandoleer, loaded with the .44 cartridges for the Henry she cradled in her arms. When Eli walked up to Suzette, she turned to him and said, "Put my medical kit in your wagon. I'm staying with you."

It was obvious that Sanders was going to be on her side of this argument, and he spoke some good logic. "The forward wagons will be the heaviest armed. We aren't going to lose this fight, but there are going to be casualties. Also, you tell me that your sister is the best shot among us. Why wouldn't you want her guarding your back."

"Because I don't want her to get hurt," was Eli's reply.

"Eli, you have to trust me on this. She will be safer with you. If the renegades are smart, they will attack this camp after we pull out of sight on the trail. They will be ready for a fight, but things could get ugly here before we finish this. These renegades had three days now to reorganize and gather more men. If I were leading them, I would have scouts watching our every move. I don't want to buck your leadership of the supply train, but I want your sister's rifle and medical kit forward with the attack wagons."

Burdened with the responsibility for his sister's safety, Eli turned to Suzette, "You're with me. You get hurt, and your grandmother will kill me. Keep that in mind."

It was time to load'um up and head'um out. Eli helped Sanders up onto his horse. He unstrapped his Colt and looped it over the saddle horn. "Just a little more firepower for you, I don't want you to run out of bullets; with only one hand, reloading is not an option." Sanders patted the handle of his saber in its scabbard but nodded his thanks. Eli shouldered the medical kit and walked with Suzette to the lead wagon. He noticed that the men walking with them all had bayonets either on their rifles or in scabbards hanging on their ammo belts. He hoped this fight wouldn't come down to hand-to-hand combat, but he was encouraged that the men were spirited and ready to take on the hardened criminals out on the trail. He gave Horatio an encouraging hug as he left him to guard the camp. He was relieved that the young farmhand had drawn one of the short straws.

Eli put Suzette up in the back of the wagon. The water barrels were off, and the tailgate was up. She would have a clear field of fire to the rear. He climbed up and climbed over the driver's seat and looked over his men. There were four of them, and each had two loaded rifles, one in hand and one on the floor. There were three barrels of lead shot behind the driver's seat where he could shelter when things got hot. He got into the driver's seat and released the brake. He clicked his tongue, and the wagon lurched forward, throwing him back into the seat. The mules expected the heavy wagon, and they were as surprised as Eli as they pulled without the heavy load behind them. Eli wondered how fast they could run without the burden of eight tons of munitions.

The morning was clear and warm, with a gentle but steady breeze from the southwest. The prairie was still damp, but it was dry enough to burn if the renegades used the same fire trap they used on the pioneers. Only three miles down the trail, Eli smelled smoke. Perfect, the first band of renegades was no doubt hidden behind the slight rise to the south where smoke wafted over the top. A little farther down the trail, he saw the second fire and then a third. The fires were spaced about a quarter of a mile apart; he could see at least twenty riders behind the first fire. The renegades spread the flames from their fires to the prairie grass. Eli smiled; criminals weren't smart; they should have had bundles of tinder ready to ignite and drag behind the horses to start the fire in a long line. Eli and the twins turned their wagons toward the fires and with whips cracking, drove at the gaps between the fires. Sanders charged the remaining wagons west and then turned them to flank the fire from the upwind side.

Now the smoke from the fires worked against the outlaws. They couldn't see the maneuver through the smoke but smiled when the first wagon emerged from the smoke and was running right at them, no driver visible, just a runaway team trying to escape the fire.

Eli was glad Roland had the foresight to lash the shot barrels to the front of the wagons. The ride was wilder than expected, and several bumps threw everyone aboard a foot up off the floor. He couldn't believe how fast the mules could run. Usually, a mule could run almost as fast as a horse for about a half-mile. Eli's teams were tough, well-fed, and well trained and terrified of the fire. They didn't break pace and covered the mile to the head end of the first fire in less than two minutes. The fires were now long wedges, spreading wider and moving northeast in the wind. He hoped Sanders made it around the last fire to the west. He had the longest way to go. No time to think of that, Eli was engaging the outlaws on his right. The band was mounting their horses to ride down the runaway wagon when Eli pulled the team to the left and stopped fifty yards away from the confused outlaws. The men threw the heavy canvas cover over the top of the ribs and in less than a second, fired six rounds, taking six horses down from under their riders. Eli and Suzette didn't go for the horses. Two men dropped to the ground. The second volley took four more horses and two more men. The remaining riders were going to charge them but hesitated when shots rang out from the west.

Sanders was at the lead of his wagons and was still out of range but firing his Colt at the remaining riders to get their attention and cause confusion. Two more riders hit the ground. There were about eight left, more than Eli expected. Suzette was dropping them with deadly accuracy. Shots rang out to their right. Roland was firing on the second group. The last of the riders were down, and the men on the ground dropped their guns and put up their hands to surrender. Suzette and Eli didn't want to kill unarmed men, but Sanders charged by with his wagons and his shooters killed the rest of the renegades and the wounded, with the same lack of mercy that the criminals showed the pioneers.

Eli released the brake and charged west to help his brothers. It was all over in less than five minutes. Renegade Indians, whites, and Mexicans lay dead on the prairie. The fires working slowly upwind engulfed the dead bodies, and they could hear the sound of guns discharging, cooking off rounds in the heat of the fire. Eli found a track to the east that ran back to Marion. He pulled up; it was time to open the field hospital. Sanders paused his column to offload his wounded. The casualties were surprisingly light, considering the number of dead men laying out on the prairie — not a single man killed in the gun battle. There were only seven injured, and all of those were trivial but one. That man was bleeding from a wound in his chest. Suzette would try to save him, but even if she could get the bullet out of his lung without killing him, he would probably succumb to infection within a few days.

Jacques and Roland joined Sanders' column, and they returned to the trail on the east side of the fire. With any luck, the fire would stop at the wide bare dirt track of the trail, and they could make a sweep of any of the renegades stationed north of the trail. Their luck held, and they caught two of three small outposts on the north side of the trail by surprise. The scrimmages were short, and Sanders took no casualties. The four men in the last band were riding west as fast as they could; one of them had a wide sombrero. Sanders would have ridden them down if he was able, but he was content with his morning's work and thought a few survivors to spread the news of the ambush, and the carnage that took place, would only serve to make the trail safer. He wanted an accurate body count. He sent Jacques and Roland back along the trail to count the bodies along with the rest of the wagons. He rode up on the east side of the fire line to make sure there were no survivors out on foot and to count the rest of the bodies. He needed to organize the men at the field hospital to police up all the weapons and ammunition from the dead. Leaving so many guns behind for the Indians to scavenge was not an option. Everyone would meet up later in the day back at the camp above Marion.

By the time Sanders returned to the makeshift field hospital, Suzette had the bullet out of the man's chest and was threading her curved stitching needle to close the wound. The man was lucky for the moment. The bullet was a small caliber ball, and it had hit a rib and came to rest outside of the lung. Suzette had her patient sedated with the last of the laudanum in her supplies. She was covered in blood up to her elbows but still working with total attention on the wound. The rest of the wounded men stood around, hoping for the best and waiting their turn to be doctored. Some even took care of themselves and bandaged their own or each other's injuries.

They would leave the seriously injured man with the people at the Marion settlement. Suzette hoped that one of the women there could be a competent nurse. Even if there weren't a nurse, the man's chances would be better there than jostling around every day in the back of a wagon. Sanders assured her that he would send a medical wagon to pick up her patient after he returned to Fort Leavenworth. He would ride out and take the military road north as soon as he had his body count tallied so he could make an accurate report to his commanding officer. Suzette finished closing the wound, and they loaded her patient into a supply wagon and headed into Marion.

Later in the day, they were back at the camp above Marion. Sanders gave the men an encouraging speech before he departed. From horseback, he was a commanding figure. "You men did well today. I know we have a serious casualty, and that is always regrettable. But consider how many of you would have been dead if you hadn't taken the initiative against those bastards. You killed sixty-seven of them today, only four got away. You are going to be remembered for a long time in the annals of the trail. No Army unit could have done better." Sanders raised his good arm and saluted the men. "I am proud to have served with you." He turned and rode off. Horatio made his mind up on the spot that he would join the Army as soon as they would take him. He was going to be just like Lieutenant Sanders when he grew up.

The rest of the day was spent reloading the cargo and putting the wagon train back in order. Several mules had taken some bullets in their rumps. Eli thought these must have been wild shots from the outlaws because none of them had a chance to stop one of the gun wagons by bringing down the leading animals. One-by-one, he had the men hobble a wounded animal and then dump it over on its side. Eli extracted the bullets and stitched up the wounds. Only one had to be cauterized to stop the bleeding.

When darkness fell, the men huddled around one large campfire, retelling the stories of their glorious day. One man was showing off his blood-stained bayonet. He was the only one in their party who had cause to use it when an Indian made it to the back of their wagon and tried to leap inside. The bloody bayonet didn't hold the center stage for long. The men talked about the repeating rifles until they retired for the night. Eli reduced the guard to only one man per six wagons. A sigh of relief floated through the cool night air as the men made their way back to the wagons. To a man, every one of them wanted a Henry rifle and couldn't wait to own one.

DELAY and BURIAL

Already six days on the trail and not yet halfway to Council Grove, Eli awoke with what was becoming an ever-present thought; they were moving too slow. He couldn't just shrug it off that there were events that he couldn't control, and there were no illusions about his responsibility to the Army as Wagon Master. He and his brothers had signed on as a way to get to California. To do that, he now had to get the whole wagon train at least as far as Santa Fe and then continue from there.

As he walked around the camp before first light, he greeted each of the guards; the night had passed quietly without incident. The cooks were up, and the smell of wood smoke and coffee wafted through the camp. Eli stopped at the Chinese cook wagon and was offered a cup of green tea with a few vegetables floating in it. It wasn't a substantial breakfast, but it was a good way to wake up. The cook's name was Mr. Sue, and he spoke in sentences only a bit longer than the Indians. He wore his hair pulled back in a ponytail, black clothes that looked like pajamas, and shoes that looked like slippers rather than boots fit for the prairie. Eli suspected that Mr. Sue could speak English as good as any other immigrant on the train. He sensed that Mr. Sue didn't have anything of significance to say. Eli wanted to get to know this man better, and he decided he would make the morning cup of tea a ritual. He also wondered if Suzette would be able to learn some Chinese by the time they reached Santa Fe.

As Eli started to walk away, Mr. Sue took him by the forearm gently and led him over to the back of his chuck wagon. There was a saddle there with a thick saddle blanket, and a bridle adorned with silver buttons. Mr. Sue gave the saddle and tack to Eli and said, "For your horse. Much better in an emergency than riding bareback." Eli was grateful for the gift, even though it was scavenged from the renegades and carried the saddle and bridle back to his camp. He cut Armstrong's horse out of the center of the wagon ring and saddled him. He was pleased that everything fit the big gelding perfectly. It was a shame that so many of the renegade's horses were killed in the attack. The fire ruined much of what lay on the ground.

The camp was starting to stir, and when he got back to his wagon, Suzette was returning from her privacy walk. "Suzette, do you think you could learn Chinese from Mr. Sue?"

She answered him in three languages, "*Non mon homme.*" No, my man. "*Nicht viel zeit, um zu studieren.*" Not much time to study. Then she struck the stubborn pose of the Indian with her arms crossed and grunted, "Too hard," in Pawnee.

Eli was glad to see that his sister could muster up some humor after the many men she had killed in yesterday's battle. "You should talk to Mr. Sue. He pretends to speak only a little English, but I overheard him explaining recipes and some Chinese remedies to the other cooks. He makes a really good cup of tea for breakfast; I wouldn't mind having him cook for us. You could learn six words a day." Eli looked at his sister with a tilt of his head and with his eyebrows raised, suggesting that it should be easy for her. Now they both laughed, and it felt good.

Roland walked over and asked what was so funny. Eli was quick to be the first to respond, "Suzette just promised me that she would learn Chinese by the time we got to Santa Fe." Suzette punched Eli on the arm in her sisterly way and walked off. The brothers watched her turn towards Mr. Sue's cook fire.

Roland joked, "I'll bet you my first gold nugget that she can do it."

"You're going to be a gold miner now?" The brothers laughed, none of them had to go prospecting to be wealthy, but every time the news of a new strike swept the nation, the family would talk about it. Their father always downplayed the rush to a new goldfield. Few got rich, most walked away poor. It was the merchants and the suppliers that made money in the long run. Trade was sustainable, that was always their father's last word on the subject. Roland always thought that their dad was molding them to stay at home and join the family business rather than join a gold rush, but he had a good point. Look at the money he made for everyone he touched, supplying food and materials to the trailheads, not to mention the whiskey. Another point, there wasn't a single nugget ever found on the Santa Fe Trail.

The brothers walked over to their chuck wagon. Now here was a real breakfast fit for the traveler. The cook had horse meat sausage, biscuits, and gravy. "That's what I smelled when I walked around the camp," Eli realized. The cooks had butchered the best parts of the renegades' horses, and everyone had feasted on fresh horsemeat the night before. It wasn't as tasty as beef, but it had made a good hearty meal.

Roland commented, "I wonder what mule sausage would taste like?" Jacques pointed out that they would probably find out by the time they finished their trek.

Dawn broke to another clear day. Hitching up went smoothly, and Eli led out onto the trail in less than an hour, riding Armstrong's horse high in the saddle. *All the men are working better*, he thought. *We could make more than fifteen miles today*. Three miles out, they were in the burned area from the day before. There were still fires burning south of the trail, but with no wind to carry it over, the fire had stopped at the natural fire break of the bare wide track of the swale. Eli looked south to the scene of the carnage and felt no remorse. Suzette was by his side, and she didn't even look over to the hundreds of turkey vultures circling and landing to ravish the carrion. Rarely did the vultures find such an easy meal.

Two miles on, though, held a far more gruesome sight. The remains of the wagon train slaughtered by the renegades lay scattered over the prairie. There were decaying bodies and smoldering remains of wagons everywhere. Four women were staked out naked near the trail, probably raped repeatedly and left to die. Eli was going to pass them by, but Suzette was leaning into him, holding on to his forearm with silent tears making wet-dusty tracks running down her face. Eli pulled up and set the brake and sat there, contemplating the horror. Suzette still clung to his arm and looked at him imploringly. The stench of death was everywhere, and the carrion eaters had been at the badly ravished bodies. There were ten or more vultures on every corpse. Suzette wanted Eli to stop the train and bury the bodies, especially the four women, but she wouldn't say a word. It was Eli's decision, and she would live with it whatever he decided. The horror of the scene, though, would play on her mind for the rest of her life.

Eli got down from the driver's seat and un-lashed a shovel from the side of the wagon. He walked over to the upwind side of the bodies and started digging. Before long, his brothers and the Germans joined him, and soon all the rest of the men in the wagon train were there, joined in one quiet effort to dig a mass grave. It took nearly four hours to gather all the remains and cover the grave. More than eighty men, women, and children would be buried and forgotten in this lonely spot. Suzette had saddled Patches and was riding her through the rushes on both sides of the trail, making sure they had recovered all the human remains. She was about a quarter-mile north of the trail and ready to return to the gravesite when she heard whimpering from the willows at the bottom of a rill. She dismounted and parted the willows. There was a girl about ten years old lying in the muddy bottom. The young girl had a broken leg, and her hands and her good knee were raw from crawling down from the trail. Suzette gathered her up and put her up on Patches and walked back to the trail.

The men were almost finished covering the grave, and when they first saw Suzette, they thought, *Oh no, another body.* But as Suzette neared, they saw that it was a young girl, and one by one, they started to clap and cheer when they realized the girl was alive. The men already had tremendous respect for their doctor, teacher, and heroine, but Suzette just earned another stripe on her sleeve or another ribbon for her heroine banner, if she desired either. She brought the girl up to Eli's wagon and started washing her up. The girl wasn't dehydrated because she had been drinking the feted water in the rill, and God only knew what else. As she washed the mud off the girl's face and out of her hair, it was apparent the girl was Mexican. Suzette finished cleaning her as best she could and dosed her with the malaria pills from her supply. She splinted the leg; it was a clean break in the middle of the femur. Mr. Sue gave the girl a tea laced with herbs and a trace of laudanum. When Suzette was satisfied with the splint, Mr. Sue gently picked the girl up and said, "I'll take care of her. You are too important to be a babysitter."

Suzette answered, "Xiè xiè, lǎo Sue," the respectful form of thank you to her elder. Eli and his brothers would never quit marveling at the seemingly endless limits of their sister's talents. Suzette was relieved that Mr. Sue took the girl. It would be all too easy to get attached. They already took on Horatio; if they kept taking orphans and strays, they could be up to fifty by the time they got to Los Angeles. She unsaddled Patches and gave the mare some water as the men gathered around the grave for a moment of silence. Roland said a few words that their deaths were vindicated, and with that, the men donned their hats and walked back to their wagons. It was time to head out. Suzette climbed up to the driver's seat and took her place next to Eli. She thanked him with a kiss on his cheek and then showed him what she found among the dead renegades. She had a rifle scabbard for her saddle. She would be riding with her companion, Henry, at her side from now on.

Eli clicked his tongue, and the mules pulled like all creation; they were tired of standing in the sun as the day warmed, and sharing the flies with the dead carcasses. Suzette took her Henry and slid it into the scabbard. She wasn't happy with the fit; the scabbard was too large. She was going to climb over the load to retrieve her stitching needle from her medical kit, but Eli nixed that, "You can't stitch while we are moving, you'll wind up stabbing yourself."

"Tonight then. Where will we camp?"

"It's already midafternoon; we'll stay on the west side of Overbrook, there is a good spring there. I'll have Roland and Horatio stay with you in town; you might even find a saddler there that can stitch that scabbard." Eli stopped the wagon and got down and mounted his horse. He would be riding back through the wagon train relating his plans for the night. Suzette took the reins, released the brake, and drove the remaining miles into Overbrook. The "town" wasn't anything more than a settlement, a few more buildings larger than Marion. She stopped and got off the wagon, and Roland pulled out of the line. Hans came running up to take Eli's wagon on to the spring, and Jacques waved to his sister as he passed. He was concerned for her safety but saw that she had her revolver, and rifle and Roland and Horatio would be well-armed as well.

It took fifteen minutes for the wagons to pass, and Suzette watched until they were gone. There were some small houses and one large building on what passed for Main Street in the tiny burg. The large building was well kept and served as a general store, bar, and barbershop. There wasn't a saddle shop, just a small building that served as a livery stable with a corral at its side. There were four saddled horses with heavy saddlebags and bedrolls tied behind the saddles. *More travelers for the trail*, Roland thought.

The three of them walked into the store side of the building and bought some candy and the entire stock of malaria pills. The girl behind the counter was just a couple of years younger than Suzette; she introduced herself as Sophie, the proprietor's daughter. Suzette saw a sign next to the entrance of the barbershop that listed the fees. At the bottom, she read **Hot Baths, 10 Cents**. Suzette couldn't believe that she could get a hot bath out on the prairie and needed one badly for feminine reasons. She tapped the sign and looked longingly at Roland. Roland said, "Let's make sure the bathtub isn't a horse trough out back."

The barber was the owner of the establishment and introduced himself as John Bassarear. There was a Mexican in the barber chair, and from the amount of black hair on his chest and the floor, it was easy to tell he was undergoing a major overhaul. Half his beard was shaved off, and he looked almost comic with the other half lathered awaiting the straight razor. The Mexican appeared to be asleep, but his eyes would open to slits from time to time to stay appraised of the newcomers. Suzette inquired about the bath, and Bassarear assured her it was a real bathhouse that he built for his wife. As he was yelling for his wife to come over from the bar, Suzette noticed that the Mexican had a bandage on his right hand. She nodded at Roland and then turned her head and looked at the hand, and Roland nodded that he understood. There was a large sombrero hanging on a hook on the wall behind the row of chairs.   Roland repeated the gesture and looked at the sombrero. Suzette wanted to leave, but Mrs. Bassarear, her name was Regina, already had Suzette in tow and was leading her out through the bar to her bathhouse. The Mexican opened one eye and watched her leave, a crooked half-smile spread on his lips as he closed his eye.

The bathhouse was an elegant little building with an elevated water tank fed by a windmill that squeaked a little as it turned and pumped.   There was smoke rising from a stovepipe, and Regina said that the bath was ready. Her daughter had started her monthly, and she was warming the bath for her. Inside, Suzette told Regina that she had the same problem and desperately needed to clean up. She regretted that all her spare underwear was in Eli's wagon, so it would have to wait for nightfall for her undergarments to get washed up. Regina said, "It's no problem, I'll fix up a bag of new stuff to take with you. There are always women passing through that left a little unprepared." With that, Regina left her to the bath, and when she closed the door behind her, heard Suzette bolt the door. Regina was startled when she turned around and saw Roland and Horatio standing guard with their strange-looking rifles aimed at the back door of the bar. "Just being cautious," Roland said as Regina turned and walked over to the back door of the General Store.

After a little while, Roland saw the Mexican leave the barbershop and walk to a small stable and corral down the street. He saddled up and rode toward the bathhouse with three other men. All four of the riders looked Roland and Horatio over as they rode by even with the bathhouse. Roland and Horatio kept their rifles leveled at the four men, ready to kill them at the first sign of trouble. "Not today, Amigo," the Mexican said as he passed. Roland knew they would see the four men again as they turned and rode to the west. He didn't know where and when the Mexican and his amigos would choose to die.

Regina returned after a while with a carpetbag. Roland assumed it contained clean clothes for his sister. She knocked on the door, and Suzette opened it wrapped in a towel. Horatio took a covert glance at his beautiful young friend and quickly looked away. Both women noticed, and when Regina closed the door, she looked Suzette knowingly in the eye and said, "Men." The simple one-word sentence conveyed all that had to be said. Suzette dressed; it was amazing how good it felt to be clean and in clothes that didn't smell like sweat, mules, and prairie dust. Regina combed out Suzette's hair and admired her striking good looks. They walked out together, and Regina noted that the rifles were leaning against the bathhouse as the four of them walked into the back door of the general store. Regina went behind the counter and retrieved a small bottle of lavender oil from her private stock. She handed it to Suzette and said, "Now, you can smell as good as you look."

Suzette opened a pouch on her belt and took out a double eagle and handed it to Regina, "Thank you, and God bless you."

Regina looked at the gold coin in her hand in disbelief. She came around the counter and hugged Suzette. "Thank you, and be careful out there. There are a lot of bad men on the prairie. Four of them were in here today, and I had my shotgun trained on the leader under the counter. I didn't like the way he was leering at Sophie."

"There are a lot fewer bad men out there today than yesterday," Suzette assured her as she turned and walked out the door with her two guards. Regina wondered what she meant.

Roland had the wagon parked next to the General Store. Horatio climbed up the back and sat on the water barrels. Suzette sat with Roland on the driver's seat, and they drove to the camp at the spring west of town. When they got to the camp, Horatio took care of the team, and they reported all that happened in town. Eli was concerned, but after wiping out over sixty renegades, he was sure they could deal with the Mexican and his three amigos.

Nonetheless, he wouldn't let Suzette out of his sight until this was over. Eli turned to his sister and told her, "Tell the Germans. I'll tell the rest of the men what happened in town tonight after dinner."

Eli did just that. In the evening, all the men were sitting around the campfire by his wagon, listening to Paul Hayman play and sing. Paul was paying special attention to Suzette, who looked great in fresh clothes and smelled good to boot. Eli waited for a pause in the music, then got everyone's attention and told them that the men who tried to sneak into their camp two nights ago were seen in Overbrook earlier that day. He had Suzette describe the man she shot in the hand, and any other details she could provide. She finished with the best she could remember, and Roland added that when they rode out of town, the Mexican was wearing his big sombrero and had a yellow bandana tied around his neck. Hans stood up and talked to Suzette. She translated, "Hans and his men are going to stand an extra watch around our wagon tonight. Eli knew the men were tired, and he figured that the extra guards around Suzette would be good enough without doubling the watch.

Suzette sat down at the campfire and started stitching the scabbard for her Henry. Mr. Sue had carried the girl with the broken leg to the campfire to listen to the music, and Suzette was sitting next to the girl waiting for the right time to talk to her. As the rest of the men started to drift back to their wagons for the night, Suzette started asking the girl some questions in Spanish. "Hola amiga! ¿Dónde está su casa?" The girl cowered against Mr. Sue and didn't answer. "¿Cómo te llamas?" Again, no answer. Suzette remembered the stories Rufus had told about Jackson and Goliath and how he had first called the St. Bernard *Sin Nombre*. The next sentence was a real challenge to her Spanish vocabulary. Suzette cocked her head and raised her eyebrows as if making a great discovery. "Supongo que sólo te llamamos -- sin nombre."

The girl looked incredulous and said quietly, "Mi nombre ne es sin nombre, es Maria. Maria Hernandez."

Suzette put her arm around the girl and pulled her into a hug with an arm around Maria's shoulder. "Bienvenida, Maria. Mi llama es Suzette, Suzette Callahan." Suzette looked up to meet Mr. Sue's gaze and said, "It will be a long day tomorrow. I think it is time for Maria to go to bed. Mr. Sue stood up, and before he picked up Maria, he clasped his hands together as if in prayer and gave Suzette the honor of a slight bow of thanks. Suzette walked over to her wagon and saw that Paul was still there. She could tell that he wanted to talk to her but probably didn't know what to say. She helped him out, "Paul, you played and sang beautifully tonight. I think it helped to break the ice with Maria."

Paul, who could play and sing hundreds of songs, was suddenly tongue-tied and finally managed to blurt out a sentence. "You look great tonight, and-and you did a good job with that girl."

"Why, thank you, Paul. Good night now, but come back around tomorrow and play for us some more."

Paul walked off on top of the world. An invitation to return tomorrow was about as good as a good night kiss in the young man's fanciful mind.

Suzette lit her lantern and retrieved her Henry rifle and started to walk away from the wagon ring into the dark. Two Germans started to follow her, but she turned and held up a palm to stop them. "Damentoilette," she said. She hoped that the four men would show themselves soon. This extra attention would drive her crazy long before they reached Santa Fe.

BURLINGAME

As the camp came to life for their eighth day on the trail, Eli was pleased as all the wagons were ready to pull out shortly after dawn. He could set a record for his daily mileage today, but he only wanted to go as far as Burlingame, where there were numerous blacksmiths to care for the shoes of more than fourteen-hundred hooves that supplied the motive power for their every move. Eli was on his horse, and Suzette accompanied him with the Henry riding comfortably, hanging from the front strap of her saddle with an extra strap over the saddle horn. The weather was clear, and the trail dry. Eli was looking back as the wagons were unwinding the camp ring and said, "Hopefully, there won't be any rainstorms or massacres to deal with today."

Suzette wanted to pick his spirit up a bit, "I'm not worried; we deal with thunderstorms and massacres routinely." Eli laughed, and his sister was glad to see that a little humor could still tickle the soul of her ever more serious brother. Eighteen years old and Wagon Master responsible for over eighty men and now two young women who he considered still girls. Suzette wondered how many bad guys she would have to kill to be considered a grown woman. It didn't matter; she knew who she was and didn't need the endorsement of anyone else.

Eli told her, "Stay close to Jacques with the lead wagon until I get back, and then we will ride ahead and take care of the toll for the bridge at 110 Mile Creek." He turned his horse around and rode back to inspect the rest of the train. Suzette wanted to go hunting, but she remembered the Mexican and his amigos and knew Eli would be angry if she ignored his order. She didn't want to break his trust in her, but she also didn't like the way he addressed her when he told her to stay with Jacques. She would let him know when the time was right that she didn't require commands; she just had to be asked.

Eli returned after an hour. There were over thirty mules that needed shoes. The Army should have included a blacksmith wagon instead of so many chuck wagons. Furriers were hard to hire, however. A blacksmith was rare enough, but one that was willing to shoe an ox or a mule could work anywhere.   Most that settled along the trail ran thriving businesses and didn't want to move on. When Eli returned, he looked at Suzette and said with a mischievous smile, "I'll race you to the bridge."

"No, I'll meet you there. I don't want to run Patches yet."

Eli rode ahead at a gallop. The bridge on 110 Mile Creek was still a couple of miles ahead. There was a small settlement there with a store and a shabby hotel owned by Fry McGee. Fry was sitting on the porch of his small toll booth drinking a bottle of beer and reading an old newspaper. Eli asked from his saddle, "You don't look so good, McGee, what's wrong?"

"Hello, Eli. I get pains in my chest almost every day. I think my time is getting short."

"Sorry to hear that. I have a government script for a supply train I took over from Armstrong, but I will pay you in gold if you give me a slight discount and some information."   Fry nodded his head, yes. "Have you seen four men, one of them a Mexican with a large sombrero and a yellow kerchief?"

"I've seen 'em. That gang looked rough and wouldn't pay to cross the bridge, so they forded the stream a little further down. I think the four of them camped there the night before last. For an extra dollar, I'll tell you about the Mexican."

Eli slid off the horse without using the stirrup and looped the reins of his horse over the hitching post in front of the porch. He paid McGee with a ten-dollar gold piece and a greenback and sat down next to Fry.

McGee had quite a tale to tell. "The Mexican is known as *Chico del Diablo*. He is ruthless and very fast with a gun. I'm quite surprised that there isn't a price on his head. There might be farther out west. He is a killer, and the men riding with him are no better. He passed through here about two weeks ago heading east. There were about twenty men with him then, only three when he came back. They camped down by the ford. My son-in-law and I stayed up all night on guard while they were down there. Stay away from him, Eli, if you want to stay alive."

Eli thanked him and offered him the government script for his extra benefit. Fry tore it up and said, "Those are next to worthless. It takes months to get paid if you get paid at all. The greenback you paid me may be just as bad. Have you been keeping up with the verbal war between the North and South? We are going to be at war soon, Eli. You should be back with your family, not out here on the trail."

Sadly, Eli related the events in Independence that turned him and his siblings west. Suzette was approaching riding down the middle of the trail, her blond hair streaming out in the morning breeze. The wagon train was right behind her. Fry laughed, "Now I have seen it all, a woman Wagon Mistress. I think I'm ready to meet my maker."

Suzette and the twins stopped and walked over to the porch. Eli introduced them to Fry. "My sister here shot a gun out of Chico's hand a few nights ago. We're going to travel on, but Suzette is a pretty good doctor. Suzette, would you stay and look Mr. Fry over and tell him what happened to the rest of the Mexican's men and the other renegades? Please don't let the end of the train pass you. I don't want you alone on the trail until we finish with Chico del Diablo."

Suzette reached around her brother's neck and kissed him on the cheek. "Thanks for asking me and not ordering me." Eli had to wonder for a moment what she meant, and then it slowly sunk into his burgeoning masculine mind. Suzette wasn't one of his men. Over and above being his sister, she didn't sign a contract with the Army. She was a volunteer, and he had to treat her accordingly.

Eli mounted up, and the twins got back up on their wagons. It was still eight miles to Burlingame, and they would make it there by early afternoon. They had to get there before the blacksmiths cooled down their forges for the night. He crossed the bridge and could hear the creaking of the logs and timbers under the heavy weight of the freight wagon behind him. Roland heard it too and hung back until Jacques cleared the bridge. Horatio got the hint and hung back until Roland cleared. When Horatio crossed, he saw a cross-bracing come loose as the post it was attached to swayed out under his heavy load. He passed safely but got down and stopped Hans before he got to the damaged bent. Eli rode back. Hans was getting a block and tackle out of his stores and was summoning the rest of the German's to help pull the post back into place and secure it.

Eli had to ford the creek with Han's wagon blocking the bridge. He found a spot a little way upstream where he could safely get down and up the steep banks of the creek, and then rode back to the toll booth and joked with Fry. "I'm not going to charge you for fixing your bridge." He dismounted and tied his horse off again.

Suzette was lecturing Fry on the evils of drink and the havoc it caused the human body when taken to excess. "Mr. McGee, your pulse is irregular, and you are at least forty pounds overweight. If you don't taper off, eat right and get some exercise – you're not going to last much longer."

"Girly, my wife and daughter tell me the same thing all the time, but I have lived longer than most out here, and I would rather die happy and content than live another few years lean and miserable. I appreciate your concern, though." Fry tipped up his bottle and drained it.

Suzette put her hand on Fry's shoulder and said, "Goodbye, Mr. McGee. I doubt I'll see you again." She untied Patches and mounted up. Eli wanted to ride down the creek and see where Chico forded and camped.

The banks of the ford to the south was easier than where Eli had crossed north of the bridge, but the bottom was soft. Easy enough for horses, but impassable for wagons. On the west side of the creek, they found a littered campsite. Among the trash were some empty money belts and pouches and a broken strongbox from Wells Fargo & Company. These looked like the remnants of a stage holdup, petty theft, and trail robberies. Eli asked Suzette, "Do you think the massacre was Chico's idea or the renegades that he joined up with?"

"I don't think it was his idea even though Mr. McGee told me Chico is a cold-blooded killer. He was on the most western outpost of the ambush. If he were leading, you would think he would be south of the trail with most of the men. Too bad he wasn't; we could have killed him there."

Eli was trying to get into the mind of the outlaw. "I think we are going to see him again. You hurt him and embarrassed him, and we killed most of his men. He is out ahead of us now, and if I were him, I would wait until we are in a town, feeling safe letting our guard down. He would be a fool to attack us on the trail again with only three men, and he's no fool, or he wouldn't still be alive."

Suzette said, "We're not in the open prairie yet. What about a sniper attack from the trees or the rushes? He could pick off one of us and ride out fast."

Eli answered, "Roland didn't see any rifles on them when they rode past him back at the bathhouse. What worries me was his parting words, *Not today amigo*. In his mind, he has not finished with us."

Suzette said, "He was getting his beard shaved off to change his appearance. Cleaned up, he could hide in plain sight in a crowd. What's the next town?"

"Burlingame, we'll hold up there to take care of the mules. There's a hotel there; we can get you a room for the night if you want?"

Suzette considered that and answered, "I'll think about that one after we look it over. Hans is moving again. Let's get going and stay close to the wagons until this plays out."

They covered the eight miles to Burlingame in less than two hours. Main Street was more of a service center for wagon trains than a town. There were more than a dozen blacksmiths with corrals for lame animals and large lots around them for parking wagons. Eli's supply train filled all the corrals, and there were still some wagons that would spend the night in the street. Eli made the rounds of the blacksmith shops to assure payment, and by the time he was back to the one block that looked like a town, hammers were ringing up and down the street.

The hotel was two stories with a restaurant, bar, general store downstairs. It advertised eight rooms up above, but no running water and no bathhouse. A row of outhouses behind the hotel served the patrons, and they smelled pretty rank in the summer sun. Suzette said, "I would rather sleep in the wagon." Eli had the three supply wagons and the Germans in a half-circle behind a rock wall that was built around the town well across the street from the hotel. The well itself was a well-known watering spot for the trail. The well wasn't deep but served as a shallow portal to an underground river. You could see water running through the bottom of the well. Several hand pumps served to fill the buckets of thirsty travelers.

There was an older man in a rocking chair on the porch of the hotel. Eli and Suzette walked over to talk to him. They asked about Chico, and the old man, like Fry, had a tale to tell. "They won't come into town anymore; the blacksmiths and their hands will kill him and his men on sight. They robbed a stage a few weeks ago out west of here and killed the driver. They came into town with some money and drank themselves stupid inside at the bar. There must have been twenty or so of them, most of them were out here on the porch. They left in the middle of the night and rode up and down the street, shooting and yelling. They left out and went east; we haven't seen them since. A mail rider found the stage the next day. We have a constable, but he is worthless. He sent word to Council Grove; they could have wanted posters printed up by now. I expect Wells Fargo will post a reward for Chico. The rest of his men are just ne'er-do-well nobodies, troublemakers, and vagrants. One of his men is Mark Richardson, my grandson."

Eli had to tell the old man, "Your grandson might be dead, we killed a large band of renegades east of here two days ago. Your grandson may have been with them."

"No, Mark passed through here last night. He and my wife were close; he stopped to give her some money and then rode out to the west. He's not dead – yet."

Eli took it all in. "Let's go up and look at the rooms. Maybe we can set a trap for him here, but from what you have said, I don't think he will risk coming into this town even though Mark is familiar with it." They went up through the door to the hotel lobby and met the owner behind a sign-in desk. She introduced herself as Mrs. Richardson, wife of the older man out on the front porch.

"We would like to look at the rooms upstairs," Suzette said after introducing herself.

"I don't have a suitable room for the likes of you, honey. But I could put you up in my cabin. I live a block out the back with the only painted cabin on the avenue. I'll stay here tonight, and you can have my little shack all to yourself."

Eli broke in. "No, she is going to stay across the street with us. We want to make it look like she is up there by herself. Chico del Diablo is looking for her. We want to draw him into a trap."

"Oh God, my grandson is with him, I don't want him killed," Mrs. Richardson said with desperation in her voice on the verge of tears.

Eli understood the woman's fears. "Where are his parents?"

"They're somewhere in California digging for gold. That's all they ever wanted – easy money. For all I know, they're dead or in some opium den in San Francisco. We haven't heard from them in years. They never paid much attention to Mark when they were here except when they thought the boy needed another black eye. He is a troubled lad, but I still want him back. Please, please don't kill him."

"I promise we will try our best to take him alive, but that may be out of our control. He could get killed somewhere else. How old is he?"

"He's only thirteen, big for his age but smaller than Chico and the other two whites. He wasn't armed when they passed through here the other night. Here are the keys to Rooms Six and Seven. They're at the end of the hall upstairs across from one another. I hope and pray you can make good on your promise, Eli."

The twins had come over, and the four of them went upstairs to check out the rooms. Mrs. Richardson was right; the rooms weren't much: a simple dirty cot, a slatted chair, a crude table, and a water pitcher and a chamber pot. The smell wasn't much better than the outhouses out back. Eli made the call, "We'll set up the ploy, but I can't ask anyone to stay up here and watch the door."

Roland had an opinion and voiced it. "I don't think that is a good idea. If Chico thinks Suzette is up here and doesn't find her, he will know that we tricked him, and he'll be wary of the next trap. I would rather he searched and didn't find her. We can watch the hotel from across the street. We can even watch the back if we stay upwind from the privies, but I don't think anyone in their right mind with a nose that works would come in that way."

Eli thought about it and agreed. "We will enter the hotel before dark and have a beer in the bar. After dark, we will sneak out the back and take Suzette up to Mrs. Richardson's cabin and stay up there to guard her. Jacques, you could stay with the Germans and post the guards at the hotel. Let's get out of here and organize Hans and his men."

The hammers rang into the night and well into the morning with lanterns and campfires and the pale light of the new moon casting Main Street into dim shadows. All was in place by dark, and Suzette and her brothers played out the charade hoping Chico had a watcher posted somewhere. Despite their preparations, Chico nor any of his men showed up. It suddenly dawned on Suzette as to why as she, Eli, and Roland walked back to the hotel. "He is waiting for his hand to heal. The bandage I saw in the barbershop was red with blood. It's going to be a while before he has his confidence back before he makes his move."

Eli was skeptical, but Roland agreed with her. "I want you to practice your fast draw every day. Even if we never see Chico again, there will be more men like him as we get farther west."

Eli thought, *Granddaughter, fugitive, Wagon Mistress, and now Gun Slinger. Where's this going to end?*

Mrs. Richardson had strong coffee and a hearty breakfast for the men who were up most of the night. Mr. Sue brought Maria to the hotel; she was walking on a set of wooden crutches he had made for her. As they left the hotel, Eli was surprised to see a wagon that wasn't his across the street with the Germans. It was a blacksmith wagon, and there were eight healthy mules hitched to it. Hans started talking to Suzette in German.

Suzette translated, "The furrier wants to come with us. He is homosexual and shunned by the German coal miners. They don't want him around up there because he is different. If you feed him and buy him four sacks of coal for his forge, he will shoe mules every night for his safe passage to Santa Fe."

Eli didn't need to think this one over. "Tell him he's with us. He'll have the seventh position in the train where Hans can take care of him, and you are handy to translate. I wonder what our father would have thought about a homosexual blacksmith?" Everyone laughed, but there were teams to hitch up and the two horses to saddle.

Suzette turned to Mr. Sue and Maria. "Make sure she doesn't put any weight on the leg for at least another week and then only as little as possible. Thank you, Mr. Sue." And to Maria, "Ser un poco cuidadoso." (Be careful little one.)

It was only a half-hour after dawn, and Jacques had the lead wagon heading out of the west end of Main Street. There weren't any stragglers this morning. Everyone was looking forward to a record-setting day, and if the weather held, this could be it.

TWENTY MILE DAYS

The weather was clear, and the trail was dry. Eli and Suzette rode out ahead of the wagons and stopped on the rise north of the trail where they could see the whole length of the supply train. Towns and settlements were sparser the farther west they went, but Eli told Suzette that there was a sizable burg called Wilmington, about six miles from Burlingame. There were some doctors there, and she could have them look at Maria's leg. From the rise, they looked out to the northeast, where a heavy plume of dust on the horizon held their attention. Eli explained, "That's the second military road coming down from Fort Leavenworth. That must be a large column from the looks of the dust, and with the speed they're traveling, it must be cavalry. We're going to have some company soon."

They rode down to *Dragoon Crossing* and waited for Jacques to arrive with the lead wagon. Eli rode down through the ford and was pleased with the rocky bottom and the low water level. The creek was a problem for him previously when it was high with rain; he had to wait two days before it was safe to cross. Today the wagons would drive through the crossing like any other part of the trail. It was going to be a very fine day. He was setting his goal to make it as far as Allen for the night. If they made it that far, this would be the first of what he hoped to be many twenty-mile days on the way to Santa Fe.

After the last wagon crossed the creek, Eli and Suzette rode at a gallop back to the head of the column. They turned south off the trail to stop by the Hayanna Stage Stop. The proprietor here was a bit grouchy, and while Eli never had a problem with the man before, he was in a particularly bad mood today. Suzette thought she could charm him into answering a few questions. She asked if the man had seen Chico and his men.

The man exploded. "That bastard passed through and stayed in the hotel two nights ago. That young shit with him broke into the store and stole some supplies, and they left before dawn without paying. I don't think he's coming back this way, or he wouldn't be burning his bridges. All for the better if he's gone forever."

Eli said, "He will be gone forever if we find him."

"You'll never find him if he doesn't want you to see him."

"That's just the point; he's going to be looking for us."

Suzette asked, "Did you notice his hand? Was it bandaged?"

The Bellyacher, the only name Eli knew the man by, scratched his head before answering, "Yes, he had a bandage on his right hand, and he asked about a doctor when he first arrived here. I told him about the doctors in Wilmington. I don't think they are very good, but they have a lot of experience putting people back together that get hurt on the trail. I would bet he stopped there."

Suzette thanked the man kindly, and they turned to leave. When they got to the door, the man yelled out to them, "Hey, if you catch up with him, tell him he owes me – Monty J. Cook – money before you kill him."

Eli turned back and asked, "How much?"

"Five bucks."

Eli took out his money roll and peeled off five greenbacks and laid them on the counter. "For your information, thanks." Cook couldn't believe that he was just made well, and he watched silently as Eli and Suzette left.

Eli and Suzette rode west on the loop road back to the trail and met the train at its midpoint and galloped up to the front. As they rode into Wilmington, Suzette stopped at the first doctor's office and waited for Mr. Sue to pass with Maria. Eli rode over to the second doctor's office but returned to Suzette after finding out that Chico didn't stop there. Suzette stopped Mr. Sue's wagon and pointed at the doctor's office. Mr. Sue helped Maria down, and they followed Maria into the office of Jacob E. Firth, M.D. Suzette hoped he was a good doctor as she looked up at his weathered shingle hanging above his door.

The office was empty, not a good sign. Good doctors always had patients waiting. The doctor was a small man, and he walked up from a row of examining rooms that lined a hall leading to the back door. He was clean, and the office was spotless. He introduced himself as Doctor Firth and looked at Maria. Firth's nurse came in from the examining rooms and introduced herself as the doctor's wife. She led Maria back and helped her up onto a table.

Suzette commented, "You don't have many patients."

Firth answered, "We have only been here a week. Mostly we have been cleaning the place up and trying to recover some of the last doctor's patients."

"What happened to the last doctor?"

"Firth looked grim and answered, "The town lynched him."

Suzette was startled and asked, "What for?"

"Malpractice, he killed a young woman in childbirth. Tragic, but the story goes, he cut her to relieve the birth canal and couldn't stop the bleeding. We came here from Dodge City to take over the practice."

That explained the weathered sign. Suzette wanted to know about Chico, but she would wait until the doctor finished with Maria.

Out in the street, Eli was waiting for the last wagon to pass. He could see the cavalry riding into town. There were about fifty soldiers and two chuckwagons, pulled by horses. The captain was Major Barnes. Eli had met him several times at Leavenworth.   Barnes greeted Eli, "We got word that Armstrong was dead and that you took over the supply train. We are heading to Council Grove. There is trouble there with Comanche moving down from the plains up north. They aren't peaceful; we are going to find them and calm them down. Here, I have a requisition for some of your rifles and ammo. We'll lighten you up a bit when you get to Council Grove. It looks like you are making good time."

Eli told Captain Barnes about the delay on The Narrows and the massacre on the trail, and Barnes was impressed with the fact that they had killed so many renegades and only lost one man. "You're going to be famous if you keep this up. I'll be sending a report back to Leavenworth. Your Quartermaster is going to be very pleased with you. Keep up the good work." With that, he turned up the street and led his soldiers out of town.

Suzette came out of the doctor's office with a smiling Maria with the stick of a hard candy sucker sticking out of her mouth. "She's going to be fine; Dr. Firth said the leg is straight, and the bones have already knitted together. She must stay on the crutches for another three weeks and in the splint for another five. Maria told me in the doctor's office that she has grandparents in Bernalillo. Where's that?"

Eli answered, "I don't know. Council Grove is the farthest west I've ever been on the trail. What about Chico?"

"Dr. Firth's first patient; he stitched up a wound from a bullet fragment between his thumb and forefinger. The doctor and his wife felt intimidated by the two men with Chico. There was a young man out in the street with the horses, and he was looking up and down the street as if he was watching for something or someone. Dr. Firth didn't ask for a payment, but his wife did. Chico paid her, but she noted, with some reluctance."

"How long before he heals up?"

"A week and the stitches come out. Doc said he would be sore for a month, and the man wasn't clean; there is bound to be an infection. He won't be a fast gun for a while, maybe never again. I won't have that problem." With that, Suzette drew her revolver out in one blindingly quick move and said, "Bang, you're dead, Chico."

Eli was glad that she was practicing but said, "Remember its bang, bang – bang. There are three of them. Don't shoot the shortest one."

Mr. Sue helped Maria up into the wagon, and as he climbed up into the driver's seat, he told the driver, "Chop Chop!" The universal Chinese slang for hurry up.

They left town at a fast gallop. The mules were comfortable inside the wagon train, but they weren't comfortable being out on their own. Suzette could see the dust from the train in the distance. The day was warming up, and Jacques would be slowing his pace not to stress his mules. It only took twenty minutes to catch up to the last wagon. Mr. Sue would have to be satisfied with his position back in the worst of the dust until they set out again the next morning. Eli and Suzette rode back up to the front of the column. Other than discarded trash and household items along the trail, the prairie was empty of farms and buildings as far as they could see. Eli stopped them halfway to Allen to water the teams and enjoy some lunch. Even with an hour's break, they would reach Allen well before five in the afternoon. Twenty miles was in reach; that would be their daily goal from then on.

Allen wasn't much to look at and even less desirable for a stay. It did have a store, a saloon, and a blacksmith shop, and a toll bridge over 142 Mile Creek. The proprietor of all the businesses in Allen was a man named Wethington, a slaver. His blacksmith shop was headed up by a white man who ran a thriving business fixing wagons, but at every one of the forges, black men labored. Wethington and his slaves were not a happy content group. Everything the man owned had been burned to the ground several years ago by abolitionists. Eli figured that it would probably be burned down again since the Territorial Legislature passed an anti-slavery bill over the governor's veto several months ago. Wethington claimed his wagon repair works was on thin ice; it couldn't run at a profit without slave labor. He was trying to keep the slaves he had working as if they were indentured, but more than half his crew had already slipped away.

Wethington wanted to raise the toll on his bridge to make up for the loss. Eli wasn't sympathetic, and as he handed Wethington the Army script for the toll, he said, "Take up your rates with the paymaster. If you ran your businesses with a little more common sense and paid your workers fairly, you wouldn't be having any problems." Wethington didn't like Eli. They had been around and around on this issue every time Eli passed through. Eli crossed to the west side of the creek and passed a good camping spot on the north side of the trail. He would go on another two miles, just far enough to make it inconvenient for any of his men to spend their money in the slaver's saloon or store.

When they reached a rise covered with the high grass that gave its name to this area of the west known as the Tall Grass Prairie, Eli circled his arm in the air giving Jacques the signal to circle the wagons and set up camp for the night. The wind was just strong enough to make waves in the grass, giving one the impression of waves on the ocean. Jacques drove in a huge circle, easily a hundred yards in diameter. When he returned to where he started, Mr. Sue was pulling in off the trail. The blacksmith had stayed on the bare earth of the trail and was already setting up his forge. Eli watched the supply train as it made the transition from its long column on the trail into a makeshift fort. Teams were being unhitched and staked out or hobbled in the center of the circle. Hooves were being inspected and cleaned, and the men were looking for sores to dress where the harnesses rubbed on the shoulders. The cooks were busy chopping patches of grass to make fire breaks around their wood stoves and fire pits.

Suzette helped Maria down from Mr. Sue's wagon, and they walked a short way out into the deep grass. In places, the tallest stems were more than six feet high. There were patches of *Texas Bluebells* and *Prairie Larkspur,* but mostly the tall grass dominated the landscape as far as they could see. There were trees and shrubs along the creek bottoms, but the groves that provided shade and shelter were now miles behind them. When they returned to the wagons, Eli was writing in his journal. They had made more than twenty miles that day, their best mileage since they left Olathe, still more than four-hundred-twenty miles to Santa Fe. Eli wondered what the record time was for a crossing, or if anyone had ever kept track.

He was still deep in thought when Mr. Sue rang the dinner bell; by then, he was more asleep than thinking. His days were longer than anyone else's, but he would fight off the fatigue and stay vigilant. He could easily see how a man like Armstrong could slip into alcoholism after so many years, crossing back and forth across the endless grassland wilderness.

Paul Hayman showed up after the evening meal and played until dark. Roland kept a close eye on his sister. She didn't encourage Paul, but the young musician was becoming a more frequent visitor, and the only person he seemed to care to speak to was Suzette. Roland was going to run him off as the sun fell below the horizon, but Eli beat him to it.

Eli waited until Paul finished a song and then said, "Paul, it's been a long day, and we are turning in. I suggest that you do the same, we'll see you tomorrow and I'll bet that they invite you to play a concert in Council Grove. Paul took the hint, and his disappointment at not having a private moment with Suzette before he left for the night was as palpable as the light of the waxing moon on the prairie.

Eli, Suzette, and the twins walked over to the blacksmith's wagon. He had repaired the hooves on four mules that night. He was drowning the fire in the forge, and Eli thought the blacksmith was probably the only man in the wagon train that was more tired than him. Suzette chatted with the man in German. He assured her that he was fine and could handle the long day on the trail and then the work of the forge until nightfall. Hans was already guarding Eli's wagon as Suzette climbed up to her bed. Eli and the twins stretched their hammocks between the wagons. Eli couldn't remember falling asleep, his brothers let him rest and stood his watch for him when it rolled around in the last hours of the morning before the sun rose to wake them for yet another day.

The camp still had a way to go to be a well-oiled machine, but it was improving daily. The mules were still the biggest problem to the green handlers, and despite Eli and the twins' constant teaching and example, hitching up was still the most arduous task of the day. But there was an improvement to note; five minutes were shaved off from when the men were first rousted around four AM, till they were pulling out onto the trail. Eli and Suzette rode out ahead of the column. With the rising sun behind them, they saw some trampled grass leading off the trail a short way from the camp. They followed it to a spot that had been trampled down by some animals. Eli assumed they were horses, and a group of men had ridden up quietly, dismounted, and walked close enough in the tall grass to survey the camp. Back out on the trail, there were shoed hoof prints in the dust leading onto the trampled trail. Eli said, "I think Chico has been looking us over. We will be in Council Grove by this afternoon, weather permitting. We may see him there."

Suzette knew Eli was worried about her. She tried to reassure him. "Don't worry about me Eli, if he comes after me, I promise you I will kill him this time."

The day wore on; everyone was starting to experience the tedium that crossing the prairie was going to bring on. At least when they got toward Santa Fe, there would be mountains. Here there was only the rolling grassland and the occasional creek lined by trees and brush. Suzette spent her days either on Patches or next to Eli on the driver's seat reading the trail guide that they inherited from Armstrong. She felt that she could find her way to Santa Fe by herself. There were only a handful of landmarks on the prairie portion of the trail. One notable stop she had read about was the *Post Office Oak* in Council Grove. She asked Eli about it, and he said he would show it to her.

Thunderheads were building up to the southeast as the supply train neared Council Grove. Eli and Suzette rode out ahead to take up accommodations in the Hays Inn. He would have to find Captain Barnes and arrange to offload some rifles and supplies. If Barnes took enough, Eli could give up some wagons. He already knew who he would be leaving behind if the opportunity arose. He would send some of the slower drivers back to Leavenworth, or perhaps they would stay with Barnes. As they approached the Neosho River, Eli guided Suzette over to a large oak at the side of the road. There was a crevasse in the trunk of the tree, and travelers heading west could leave messages there for returning caravans to pick up and carry east. There was a wanted poster on top of several other pieces of mail. Suzette took it out of the tree and held it up for Eli to read.

WANTED DEAD OR ALIVE
CHICO DEL DIABLO
ONE THOUSAND DOLLAR REWARD
WALDO, HALL & COMPANY

Under the headline appeared a picture of a heavily bearded Mexican with a large sombrero. Scrawled under that was a message; a personal message for Suzette in badly spelled words.

CE YO SON CHICA

Suzette set her lips in a grim narrow line and put the poster up on a nail on the tree trunk. She backed off ten feet and then, in a blur, drew her revolver and shot the picture of Chico between the eyes.

COUNCIL GROVE

As Suzette crossed the rocky bottom ford of the Neosho River, she was thinking about where and when a confrontation with Chico might occur. Eli walked his horse to the Hays Hostelry and paid a boy from the livery stable out back to put their mounts up. Suzette removed her Henry rifle from the scabbard and slung it over her shoulder. Eli walked into the lobby to get rooms for the four of them, but Suzette trailed behind looking up and down the street, thinking how easy it would be to get ambushed here from a rooftop or in a back alley. Eli was talking to Seth Hays about the rooms. There were only three left. Captain Barnes and his lieutenants and some travelers waiting for the eastbound stage had taken up all the rest of the accommodations. Eli took the remaining three rooms and wanted to go back out into the street to secure the closest stables and corrals for their wagons.

Captain Barnes was seated at a table in the restaurant and called to Eli as he passed the door. Eli and Suzette sat down at his table. Army communications and orders from Barnes's commanding officer at Fort Leavenworth were spread out on the table. The captain stood up and shook Eli's hand and greeted Suzette. "Welcome to Council Grove, Miss Callahan. The trail must suit you; you are looking more beautiful than ever." Suzette returned a smile that shone as bright as the late afternoon sun, and she took the Henry off her shoulder and leaned it against the table as she sat down. Like the perfect officer/gentleman that reflected his West Point training, Captain Barnes tended to her chair.

Barnes sat down and went on to deliver some disturbing news. "Eli, there is Indian trouble out west and north of here. The Comanche tribe is on the warpath, and I have been commanded to build a fort here and patrol fifty miles east and west on the trail. It's only thirty-two miles from Fort Riley to here, but there may never be a road connecting Council Grove directly to Junction City. The railroad is only interested in the east-west right of way for their train, and the Army and the government are pouring their resources into fortifying that route. That leaves this portion of the trail relatively open. By the way, your attack on the renegades was brilliant, and you're going to be offered a commission in the Army if you want it."

Eli's head was swimming. A delay, a commission, both unwanted, but this man had the power of life and death over all military matters here in Council Grove as the commanding officer of the outpost. Eli answered the only way possible, "We will help with your fort, but I must decline on the commission."

Captain Barnes went on, "There's a small hill that overlooks the cemetery on the west side of town. My men are out there building an earth revetment. I need your drivers and crews for a few days to set up out there and help with the earthworks. For now, there will be only an armory, a headquarters building, and some officer quarters inside the fortification. I expect it will be temporary and abandoned as fast as it goes up after this trouble is over. I'll make up for the delay. I'm going to lighten your load stocking the armory, and I'll keep six of the supply wagons and one chuck wagon. Choose your six slowest teams and leave them here."

"Six supply wagons will leave us short on provisions to reach Santa Fe."

"I'll give you a letter that will get you resupplied at Fort Larned. You won't run short, and you'll travel faster. Miss Callahan, that's a very interesting rifle you have there. May I see it?"

Suzette handed over the rifle with a caution, "Careful; it's loaded."

Barnes cradled the weapon like a newborn child. He didn't hold it to his shoulder, and he didn't work the mechanism. He handed it back and said, "I've heard about these. Lots of firepower at close range, but the Army isn't interested in them – as of yet. While you're here in town, could you write me an account of your attack on the renegades and emphasize the role the repeaters played in that encounter? Maybe it could help sway some opinions in Washington."

Eli stood up; Jacques was pulling up with the first of the wagons. Eli excused himself and went out to issue his orders for making camp out by *Fort Barnes*. He walked over to the corral across the street and made arrangements for the Germans to stay there for several nights. He stopped Mr. Sue and had him pull into the stable next to the corral. He would divvy up the rooms. He and Jacques would take one, Roland and Mr. Sue another and Suzette and Maria would take the third. Eli would have the buckboard from the hotel pick up his brothers and the Germans and take them out to the fort for the workday. The buckboard would return them to town at the end of the day. He crossed the street and walked back into the restaurant. Suzette was telling Barnes about Chico.

Barnes was asking, "Why is he after you?"

"I shot a gun out of his hand and injured him. There was a wanted poster for him at the Post Office Oak. He scrawled a message on it that said he would see me soon. We expect him to try to attack us here in Council Grove. There was another poster out front, but these aren't going to keep him out of town. He shaved off his beard, and if he's smart, he probably ditched the sombrero by now. No one would recognize him if he walked into town in broad daylight."

As Eli sat down, the wind outside was picking up, and dust started blowing in the stronger gusts as a thunderstorm neared. Lightning flashed, and the thunder rolled a few seconds later. Their good weather and dry trails were ending for a while. Only Barnes was pleased, "This will make the digging easier."

Eli wanted to set a trap for Chico and his men. He sat and discussed that with Captain Barnes. Mr. Sue entered with Maria. Suzette excused herself and went to the desk for a room key. She was going to settle Maria into their room and arrange for a hot bath for the girl. Maria smelled the aroma from freshly baked bread wafting out of the kitchen. She looked at Suzette and said, "Tengo hambre."

"Después de su baño," Suzette answered. She was hungry, but first, she needed a bathroom. Eli was going to send the buckboard from the hotel to fetch their brothers and the Germans back from the Army camp. They were going to have a feast in the restaurant early in the evening. Suzette helped Maria up the stairs and sent one of the maids out with some money to find some new clothes for both of them. Suzette was looking forward to her bath, maybe the last one for a month or more.   As the maids were drawing the bath, Suzette familiarized herself with the hotel. There was the main hall at the top of the stairs that paralleled the street, and a smaller hallway that led off the back of the landing that exited onto a stairway on the back of the hotel that went down to the back alley. Her room was at the end of the west hall on the front of the building. She didn't know where the other rooms were, but she hoped that her brothers and Mr. Sue would be close.

Later that afternoon, Suzette and Maria made their way down the stairs. Suzette supported her young charge on her right side and told her to sit down if she thought she was going to fall. Climbing the stairs was a lot easier than going down. Suzette's older siblings were seated at a table with Captain Barnes. Two lieutenants sat with Mr. Sue at an adjoining table. Suzette helped Maria to a seat next to Mr. Sue and was going to sit down herself when Captain Barnes took her by the elbow and ushered her to a seat next to his. We have a plan, and we need to discuss it with you over dinner."

Hans and his men came into the restaurant from the stable across the street. They were clean, and they even looked like they had gotten haircuts for the occasion. Suzette wondered if Eli had invited Paul Hayman, but she was surprised when Mrs. Hays showed up with Paul, a violin player and a young woman who Mrs. Hays introduced as entertainment for the evening. The trio played and sang like they had been together all their lives. Dinner was buffalo brisket with rich brown gravy, baked potatoes, and an assortment of fresh vegetables. The music was loud, and there was no opportunity to talk over dinner. Dessert arrived, fresh apple pie topped heavily with sugar and cinnamon. Everyone drank coffee, but Maria drank fresh milk, and Mr. Sue had tea. Dinner wound down, and Captain Barnes ordered three bottles of whiskey for the tables. He asked Paul and his trio to leave them alone now and thanked them for the wonderful entertainment. A waitress brought out the whiskey; the Callahans were pleased to see that it was their father's blend, but all of them wondered how much longer that brand would be available.

Captain Barnes got everyone's attention ringing his glass with a spoon. He laid out his plan. They were going to lure Chico and his men into a trap. Suzette was going to establish a pattern of visiting the Catholic Church several times a day. Chico was certain to have watchers waiting for an opportunity to inform him when it would be safe to attack. The church was a block west of the Hays Hotel and across the street. It was a stone structure with only two entrances, one in the front and one on the sacristy. Both doors were visible from the windows of the southwest room of the hotel, Suzette's and Maria's room. The lieutenants were both crack shots, and one would be on the roof of the hotel and the other inside the church dressed as a priest. Each time Suzette went to the church, her brothers would be watching from positions up and down the street and behind the church. There were empty lots on both sides and behind the church; there was nowhere left to hide. The charade would start immediately with everyone getting into position before Suzette made her first visit to the church.

Suzette translated all the details of the plan to the Germans, and the men dispersed. Suzette waited five minutes then walked out of the hotel and down to the church. It was a lovely building of moderate size, built out of the local limestone. It was called Christ's Church of the Trails, and Suzette felt a little strange pulling open the heavy oak door and stepping inside. Her family wasn't religious, and if there was a Christian God,

Suzette wondered why He allowed the carnage out on the trails. There were three women in the church, cleaning and tidying up the altar. There was some light still streaming from the windows from the dim light of dusk, and the nearly full moon lit the east windows. There was a red candle to the right of the altar in an ornate stand. Suzette knew enough about the Catholics to understand that was their symbolic light indicating that Christ in the form of the Eucharist was in the tabernacle on the altar. She remembered that the red candle was called the Sanctuary Lamp. Most of the light came from two racks of candles, one on each side of the Church. A statue of the blessed virgin was on the right, and St. Joseph was on the left; the racks of candles blazed at their feet, offerings of the faithful sending their prayers up to God. Holy water fountains stood at each side of the inner doors. A wide aisle ran down the center of the Church with rows of pews on each side. A low railing separated the pews from the altar area.

The lieutenant who was going to play the role of the priest was sitting in the front pew. It was obvious that the man was praying. Suzette sat down next to him, and he made the sign of the cross and turned to her and spoke, "I'm Lieutenant Frank Lindsay, please call me Frank. I'm going to be your confessor." He pointed at a heavy wooden cabinet at the back of the church. There were three doors. Frank pointed out that the center one was for the priest. The two side doors were for the penitents. Frank pointed out that the cabinet was called a confessional.   The confessional sported a heavy oak construction, a stout-soundproof cabinet where the sins of the faithful were shrouded in secrecy and darkness. A side benefit; the bottoms were bulletproof if you sat down on the floor. Frank said, "That may come in handy if the shooting starts."

Suzette thanked the young soldier for the tour and left the church to walk back to the hotel. Her brothers stepped out from their hiding places, and so did the Germans — nine men with Henry rifles, more firepower than Captain Barnes's entire company. Suzette's hand went instinctively to her hip; she needed to feel the confidence the Lefaucheux gave her. Horatio was at her window in the hotel. He signaled her, waving a white cleaning rag to indicate that the street was clear. Tomorrow she would repeat the visit once every three hours to establish a pattern. If Chico had a man watching, they wanted it completely clear that Suzette would be in the church every three hours. When she got to the hotel, Suzette went into the bar. It took five more minutes for her brothers to arrive. Each had taken a circuitous path to and from their hiding places. Main Street wasn't busy. There was nobody in sight but Suzette and a few townsfolk, not even the Germans, as they made their way to the back door of the stable. Barnes was pleased with the drill and told them to sleep lightly. Eli assured them that one of them would be on watch up in the hall, and two Germans would be watching the front and back doors through the night. Suzette finished off the evening with a simple statement, "If I kill Chico, I want the reward money to go to Maria. By the way, Captain Barnes, where is Bernalillio?

"It's in New Mexico on the other side of Santa Fe."

"If something happens to me – please see that Maria's grandparents get the reward money."

Captain Barnes was reassuring, "Nothing is going to happen to you, little lady."

As they ascended the stairs, Eli turned to Barnes, "There's always the unexpected."

Captain Barnes was resolute, "Let's hope not."

The next day was set to establish the routine; Eli and the twins left with the Germans to the worksite. In an hour, the hotel buckboard would retrieve them and return them to the north side of town. They would walk down to the back of the hotel. The Germans walked down the river bottom and stole into the back of the stable across the street. At eleven in the morning, Suzette set out on her first trip to the church. The street was busy with people coming and going from the shops on each side of the street. Suzette took her time and stopped now and then to look in the store windows. She didn't see anyone taking an interest in her until she got to the door of the church. There was a young man about a block to the west watching her. She went into the church and stayed a quarter of an hour. Frank was there dressed in a black cassock with a white Roman collar. "He whispered to her, "I'll be sitting in the confessional from now on when you arrive."

She left the church and walked back to the hotel. As the night before, her brothers came in about five minutes later. Suzette asked, "Did you see him?"

Roland said, "I was close enough I could have touched him. That must have been the young Mark Richardson. I don't think we are going to have to wait long."

Captain Barnes came down. He had been on the roof with binoculars. "The watcher rode out of town and then headed south. He'll report into Chico, and then he'll be back. Lieutenant Ingersoll is staying on the roof and will wait and see if and when he returns. That could give us an idea of where they are holding up."

Suzette set out again for the church at 2:00 PM. Richardson had returned at noon. He probably spent twenty minutes riding back and forth and maybe five minutes at Chico's camp. This time he was sweeping the porch of a saddle shop only a half-block away. Suzette spent her fifteen minutes sitting in the confessional booth talking quietly to Father Frank. She left after fifteen minutes, and Richardson was still at the saddle shop. He had stopped sweeping and then made a conspicuous clumsy effort to start again when Suzette looked over at him. Suzette walked back to the hotel on the south side of the street. She hoped Richardson kept his attention on her and didn't see Horatio's all-clear signal from her window. This time when she got to the hotel, her brothers didn't arrive. Something was going on, or they would have come back by now.

Captain Barnes came down the stairs. He saw the watcher ride down to the south side of town and join three men who turned and rode down the west bank of the river. They are watching and planning. Captain Barnes looked at Suzette and said, "It's going to happen, maybe tonight. Are you sure you still want to go through with this?"

Suzette set her lips in the same thin line as for when she shot Chico's poster and nodded her head yes.

Richardson was in front of the stable across the street for her five o'clock visit and sitting boldly on the front porch of the Hays Hotel at eight o'clock, pretending to read a book. Suzette wanted to cuff him by the ear and tell him to go home to his grandmother, but she didn't want to spoil the trap. Hans sat in front of the stable across the street, his Henry resting comfortably in his lap watching the men and women of Council Grove having a stroll in the twilight after a hot, humid day. Hans looked like he didn't even notice the young man, but had young Mark made a move toward Suzette, Hans would have shot him dead. Young Mark had no idea that his life was hanging by a thin thread.

Nothing happened that night. When Suzette returned to the hotel after her eight o'clock visit, the watcher was gone. Captain Barnes and her brother's meeting in the bar was now as routine as Suzettes visits to the Church. She could tell the tension was building. So could Captain Barnes. He spoke to that issue. "Gents, it is common for the tension to build when waiting in ambush for an enemy. Don't let it get to you; nervous trigger fingers never do well in battle. Stay focused; this will come to an end soon enough."

Suzette went up to her room. Mr. Sue and Maria were playing checkers. Now there was a way to relax. Suzette put her hand on Mr. Sue's shoulder and said, "You're a good man, Mr. Sue." Mr. Sue excused himself for the evening, and Suzette played several games of checkers before they blew out the lantern and went to sleep. Suzette lay awake with a gentle breeze blowing the curtains in the windows, and the light of the full moon streaming in. She wondered what the next day would bring. *The plan is simple*; she thought, *never let Chico into the church*. With any luck, it would all be over out in the street. If Chico got into the church, she or Father Frank would have to kill him. The last thought before she fell asleep was Eli's comment to Captain Barnes, "There's always the unexpected."

Dawn came the next morning with thunder clouds covering the eastern sky. It was clear to the southwest, so maybe the weather would hold. Around ten o'clock, a funeral procession was entering town from the south. Several large Mexican families were escorting a pine coffin on the back of an ox cart. They came up the road by the river and turned onto Main Street. Captain Barnes watched the procession, and his chest clutched as the mourners stopped in front of the Church of the Trails and carried the casket into the church. He went down to confer with Eli and the twins. "It could be a ruse," Barnes stated. "We could storm the church, but if it is a real funeral, that would just blow the trap."

Roland spoke up first, "Suzette, what do you want to do?"

"Is the watcher out there?" she asked. Barnes shook his head no. Suzette wondered what Frank would do with a funeral to conduct. Could he pull that off? Could he delay the funeral party? She made her decision. "I'm going to church at 11:00. Let's get everyone in place early."

Suzette stepped out on the porch at 11:00 sharp. She looked around as if assessing the clouds in the east. The watcher had to be here somewhere, but where; and where was Chico? She took her time as casual as ever and walked down to the church. "Father Frank was out front trying to explain to several of the older men in the funeral party that Father Dominic was out of town and he was standing in for a few days. Suzette translated, and Frank was much relieved. The family of the dead man was insisting a requiem mass be said immediately, but Suzette came up with an idea and asked the Señors if they had dug the grave yet. They said they hadn't, and Suzette suggested that they go down to the cemetery and get that done. Father Frank would hear confessions and say the mass when they got back. The Señors seemed reluctant to leave their families in the church, but after talking quietly among themselves, they finally agreed to go down to the cemetery and make arrangements for their dead friend. As they were leaving, the most elderly of the men whispered to Suzette, "Mucho peligro, señorita. En el ataúd, el hombre no está muerto." Suzette nodded her understanding. She told Frank to go into the confessional as if he was going to hear confessions. Suzette looked across the street. Young Mark was there in an alley holding four horses. She knew the dead man in the coffin was Chico, but where were the other two? With grim determination, she stepped into the vestibule, her hand on the Lafourche.

Frank sat down in the center of the confessional and closed the door. He parted the curtains and then slid the small door to the compartment on his left open. That side was empty. As he slid the door on the right opened, a man intoned in a gruff voice, "Bless me, father, for I have sinned." Frank heard the hammer of a gun click as the penitent cocked his weapon. "Just stay quiet, and you may still get to say mass for your amiga." Frank slid the door to the right side closed and quietly slid down in his seat. He had a .44 caliber Colt under his cassock. He took it out and waited in the darkness with his feet pressed tight against the heavy oak door.

Suzette entered the church and walked a short way up the aisle, keeping her eye on the casket. As if on cue, the lid flew off, and the women and children in the pews screamed. Chico smiled and said, "We meet again, chica."

"The only person you're going to meet today is Jesus. How appropriate you came to church to do it."

Chico started to raise a gun from his side. Suzette drew and fired her Lefaucheux dead center into Chico's chest. There was a loud clunk instead of the dull thud she expected. Chico fired; maybe his hand was still sore, or maybe Suzette's round turned him slightly because his shot grazed her left side. She fired again and shot Chico between the eyes. It took less than a second for the three shots. Chico was dead, and Suzette was wounded.

There was a muffled report of a gun behind her. The man in the confessional had fired over the top of Father Frank's head, who was in the fetal position on the seat of the priest's cubical. The man crashed his door open and was raising his gun to shoot Suzette in the back as Frank kicked his door open with both feet and sent the man spinning over the last pew. Frank shot the man three times through the back of the pew. There was more shooting at the front of the church as Roland burst onto the altar from the sacristy. He put two more rounds into a man hiding behind the altar, then took several steps toward the communion rail and vaulted it. He looked down at Chico in the coffin. He pulled the shirt open on the dead man and saw that Chico had a steel plate under his shirt. Roland put the lid back on the coffin and said, "Now we can have a real funeral."

Only seconds had passed. The church was heavy with gun smoke and the coppery smell of blood. Eli came crashing in the front door. He saw the blood on Suzette's shirt and was terrified until she smiled at him and told him to get Father Dominic. She walked out of the church. The Germans were running in from their positions up the street. Jacques had Mark Richardson by the front of the shirt backed up against a wall with the barrel of his revolver pressed against his forehead.

"Let him go," she told her brother. The young man turned toward her, and Suzette delivered a crippling right to his solar plexus. As the boy struggled to breathe again, she said, "Go home to your grandmother. If I ever see you again, I will kill you." She backed up a step and then knocked the young man out with a roundhouse kick to his head. "Leave him," she told Jacques. Her side was burning; she needed to get to her medical kit. Jacques took her back to the hotel. He asked Mr. Sue to get the medical kit from Eli's wagon across the street. Suzette sat in the dining room and rolled up her shirt. The wound wasn't deep and was only about two inches long. The hot bullet had done a good job of cauterizing the wound, and there wasn't a lot of blood for a wound that size.

Mr. Sue came rushing in with the medical kit. Suzette took out her curved stitching needle and the sharpening stone. She gave the point of the needle some strokes with the stone and then handed it to Mr. Sue to thread. His hands were shaking, and he couldn't get it done. Maria took the needle and thread and stabbed the eye on the first try. She handed it back to Suzette and held Suzette's shirt out of the way. Suzette applied some antiseptic salve and started stitching herself up. Mr. Sue took the needle from her and finished closing the wound. The rest of the men just stood around, useless, and amazed. Suzette helped finish the last stitch, then passed out as she tied off the end of the thread. Maria clipped off the extra suture and put the medical kit back in order. Eli picked Suzette up and carried her up to her room.

Captain Barnes said, "Damn, that's one tough woman."

I'll drink to that," Father Frank said then added as a respectful afterthought, "Sir."

Roland asked both men how old they thought Suzette was. Captain Barnes offered, "Early twenty's, maybe twenty-two."

Roland laughed and told the two officers that Suzette was only fourteen.

Barnes commented, "I'm going to stay on her good side. I can't imagine what she will be like when she grows up."

The men went into the bar, and the telling and retelling of the story of the shooting carried on until the early evening. Father Dominic had calmed the Mexican families, and the albuelo who tipped Suzette to Chico hiding in the coffin, came to the hotel to thank everyone for freeing them from the tyranny of Chico and his partners. He wanted to see Suzette, but Roland told him with some struggle with the Spanish, that he would have to wait till morning.

For the first night, since Chico intruded on their lives, everyone slept soundly. The Germans relaxed their guard. Eli and his brothers slept as soundly as the dead men in the church. The Mexicans were having a fiesta behind the stable across the street. The noise didn't keep anyone awake. Mr. Sue just sat down in front of the girls' room and fell asleep with his legs crossed and his back to the door. He wasn't quite ready to let down his guard, or maybe he felt a little guilty about not being able to help Suzette when she needed him. He finally fell asleep; it wasn't a concern for what Suzette thought of him that kept him awake. It was old memories and trauma from war and battles in China in his younger days. He wondered as he drifted off if Suzette would have the same kind of problems when she got older.

COMANCHE CONTACT

The rooster crows, the dogs start barking, and Suzette wakes up to her final day in Council Grove. She listens to Maria's soft breathing beside her and quietly lays semiconscious in the graying light of dawn. The dull ache in her side brings her back from a feeling that she was at home in the Great House, to the harsh reality of yesterday. She had killed another man; even though in self-defense, it didn't soften the thought that killing was a way of life out here, and it was getting easier and easier. She had read stories about gunslingers that carved notches in the handles of their pistols for every man they killed. She wondered if she did that, would she have any handle left on her Lefaucheux by the time she reached Los Angeles. A silly thought, she put it out of her mind and readied to start her day. When she came down to the dining room, Eli and the twins were sitting over a map, mugs of hot coffee cradled in their hands. She could see Mr. Sue back in the kitchen, fussing over the stove. This breakfast would be their last meal in a hotel for months to come.

Eli had the manifest from the Quartermaster and had marked all the delivery locations on the map. Most of them were forts and outposts on the northern route of the Santa Fe Trail. Captain Barnes had marked all the freshwater springs on the map between Council Grove and Fort Bent, Colorado. The first spring west of Council Grove was Diamond Springs. Suzette sat down and counted the dots; more than twenty days on the trail to reach Fort Bent, a little over four hundred miles. Eli had marked which camps would be dry and would ration the water sparingly. Captain Barnes was explaining that this was a strange weather year. Eli already knew that; the weather had killed their father and mother less than a month ago, and the prairie was already dry enough that the renegades had used prairie fires to scatter wagon trains. Captain Barnes didn't think the Indians would be that organized, but he wanted to discuss tactics none-the-less.

"You people have already demonstrated that you can take care of yourselves, but you have never fought the Indians before. I have been thinking of your firepower, and I have some suggestions on how you might best use it against the Comanche and Cheyenne. First, I'm going to give you more horses and a couple more drivers to free up all four of you for scouting. I would always keep two scouts out ahead of the wagon train. Both these tribes have horses but not many guns. They also travel in small bands, and the ambushes that have occurred on the trail, have been carried off by only a dozen to twenty braves at a time. The women and children stay in camps five miles or so from the trail. You must scout ahead, two of you at a time, and about a quarter-mile north and south of the trail. If you encounter a war party, it will give chase. Their tactic is to ride you down. There will be another war party somewhere out ahead. Their tactic is to let you ride past the first party and then attack with the second. If you passed the first without noticing it, it would either cut you off or take up the chase on fresh horses. You have to get back to your lead wagons where the firepower is."

"I suggest that you split your firepower. Put three of your German wagons at the rear to protect that flank. At the first sign of trouble, pull the three wagons with the repeaters abreast on the trail, there is usually room for that. Have your drivers pull off to both sides of the trail to form a long rectangular box with the mules facing in. Wait for the scout to lead the war party back to the train. The most important thing is to keep the wagons together. Mules like to bolt at the sound of gunfire. If a wagon breaks away, the Indians will ride it down and sack it. Stop and practice the move and have all your men fire over the heads of their mules after every wagon is in position. I guarantee that some will bolt. Drill them until they will form the rectangle and stand. I don't care how much ammunition it takes, but get the training done as quickly as you can. I'm fond of you people, and I don't want you to wind up lost at the hands of hostiles."

The Germans came in from their quarters across the street. Mr. Sue arrived with several of the kitchen help carrying platters of fried potatoes, bacon, and scrambled eggs. It would be the last meal they would eat in a comfortable dining room for four hundred miles to Fort Bent. Everyone ate their fill and drank their coffee with fresh milk. Suzette envied the pioneers that traveled with oxen. They could have milk cows with them, but a fast-moving mule train couldn't give up their speed for the luxury of fresh milk.

Barnes got around to asking Suzette about her wound. "I'm fine," she replied. "I had an excellent doctor stitch me up, and there is no infection."

Barnes commented, "They are lucky to have you along. Don't let the Indians catch you, or you will suffer a fate worse than death." Suzette had no intention to be taken at all, let alone taken alive. She excused herself from the table and went across the street to the stable and saddled up Patches. She rode over to the *Last Chance Store* to see what they had in the way of medical supplies. As she rode up, there was a boy on the steps catching sunlight with a mirror and casting his reflected beam up and down the street. He could spook horses with it, and he was having some fun with the animals along the road. It gave Suzette an idea for the scouts. She knew the Army was experimenting with signaling mirrors, and she knew they needed a way for the scouts to stay in touch with the wagon train and each other. The store only had four of the little mirrors left. She bought all of them, along with a small sack of hard candy. As she left the store, she handed the candy to the boy and said, "Thanks." She was thinking of signals the scouts could use to stay in touch with each other and the lead wagon as she rode out to *Fort Barnes*.

Somber with the last warnings from Barnes, Eli, and his crew loaded into the hotel buckboards and made the short journey out to the wagon train. The rest of the men were ready to get back on the trail. Working as ditch diggers for the Army didn't appeal to them. Eli explained what was going to happen next.

Eli read out the names of six drivers that would be offloading with Captain Barnes and then returning to Leavenworth. All but one of the six were relieved that their contract would terminate early. One was indignant, he had signed on to go to California and wanted to stay with the train. He asked if he could downgrade to a drover's helper and switch places with another man who might want to return to Leavenworth. One helper stepped forward. He told Eli that he was no coward but had a wife and five children in Freeport. He wanted to stay closer to home. Eli allowed the switch, and they got to unloading four crates of rifles, a keg of shot, and four kegs of powder off his wagon and into the newly constructed armory.

Captain Barnes had six good horses brought from the corral. Each was saddled and had an empty rifle scabbard, and an Army Colt 0.44 revolver in a belt and holster looped over and tied to the pommel. He had a dozen extra Colt revolvers, and these went to the Germans and six other men who claimed they knew how to use them and were good shots. Lieutenant Frank came out of the armory carrying a footlocker labeled Surgeons Medical Kit and had it loaded into Eli's wagon. "We have two of these and no doctor. You might need this more than us." Suzette thanked him with an affectionate hug and kissed his cheek; a kiss he would remember the rest of his life.

Barnes shook hands with Eli, the twins, and the Germans and said, "Godspeed and safe journey." Turning to Suzette, he said, "Be careful, young lady," and offered his hand.

"I won't depart on a handshake Captain Barnes." She pulled him into a hug, held him longer than she held Frank, and kissed him farewell. "Thank you for everything." Before Eli could protest, she slid her Henry rifle out of the back of the cargo wagon, mounted Patches in one graceful move, and rode out to the trail. She was determined to play her role scouting before Eli had the chance to stop her.

Captain Barnes and his officers watched from the top of their parapet on the wall of the earthen fort as Jacques and Suzette waited for the wagon train to pull out to the trail. Frank was a bit jealous that the Captain got a long embrace from Suzette, but quickly passed it off. Rank has its privileges. They all agreed when Barnes said, "That's one young woman who is going to change history." Sadly, they watched the wagon train pull out of sight. "Let's get the patrols organized men; we still have the Army's work to do."

Eli was down to thirty-six wagons and seventy-six men counting himself, the two drivers from Captain Barnes and two young women. He could see Suzette on the rise about a quarter-mile ahead. She was scanning the horizon and the creek bottoms out ahead with a pair of binoculars. He waved when he saw her turn to him before riding down the rise to the west and out of sight. She would get a talking to when he and Roland rode out to relieve them. The scouts would trade off every five miles so their horses would always be fresh. He would have to consider very carefully what he would say to her in her new role as Army Scout. Eli knew the little sister in Suzette was gone forever.

Eli had them practice forming the "box" with the wagons three times on the way out from Council Grove. They made Diamond Springs easily that day without incident and passed Lost Spring the next. The third day they came to *Cottonwood Crossing*, noted as a difficult crossing on Eli's map. The Cottonwood River drained a large area to the north and could swell unexpectedly with thunderstorms upstream. That day the river was low, and while the mules labored through the muddy bottom, not a single wagon bogged down; Eli was relieved. They would make twenty miles that day and *Little Arkansas Crossing* in two more days; eighty miles as the crow flies, more than ninety trail miles. Eli was pleased but knew they could do better. There would be soldiers at the Little Arkansas River, and Eli would be offloading more rifles and supplies.

On the afternoon of the fifth day out from Council Grove, Eli followed the trail to the northern crossing on the Little Arkansas River. There were supposed to be soldiers here. He had Jacques and Roland take the wagon train across the ford and told them to work their way down the west side of the river to the second crossing. Eli and Suzette rode down a trail on the east side of the river. It was less than a mile to the south crossing. They found the soldiers at a spring on the east bank. There were about 20 soldiers in the troop; Lieutenant Chet Myrick was in command. Eli rode up to the camp and introduced himself. Eli asked, "Why aren't you at the north crossing?"

"I lost two men up there to cholera, and more than half my men are still sick with it. There is a clean water spring here. We are going to deepen it into a well, and as I am able, there will be a revetment around it. We see bands of Indians almost every day, but so far, they have left us alone."

Eli sent Suzette to fetch their wagons and the Germans. He didn't like bringing wagons back to the east side of the river while the rest of the wagon train would make camp on the west side. He hoped Lieutenant Myrick's report on no hostile Indian activity proved accurate. He would lend what aid he could, perhaps help deepen the well and dig some trenches for defensive positions around it. He could spend a day here, but no more. He didn't envy the soldiers stationed at this isolated outpost; they could easily be overwhelmed by hostiles if the Indians formed up into one consolidated force. He wasn't sure that his heavily armed force could even survive a sustained attack by a large force.

Eli rode around to survey the area. There were few trees outside of the river bottom, and the banks of the river outcropped with limestone here and there. Rock for shelter from arrows and the makings of bulletproof walls were within walking distance of Myrick's camp. Suzette returned with the six wagons of their unit and one more supply wagon. Eli didn't think of the supplies; he was glad Suzette had. Eli had the wagons form a ring around the soldiers' camp. He would have to ask Myrick why he didn't have any horses. It wasn't usual for the Army to send foot soldiers out on the trail. Suzette was looking over the sick men. She was dosing all of them with the quinine pills from the Army medical kit and had several others being cooled down with cold water from the spring. Eli asked the lieutenant, "Where are your horses?"

"Indians stole them when we were too sick with cholera to stop them. We still have our saddles and weapons. We hid the saddles under that stack of brush over there."

"We have an extra horse in our wagon train. You can send a rider back to Council Grove and report to Captain Barnes. He has built a temporary fort there and will have enough horses to get your men back up and riding. In the meantime, we're going to help get you fortified here."

Eli waited until Suzette was finished doctoring the men and then laid out his plans with his brothers and the Germans. Half the men would stay across the river and guard the wagon train. The rest of the men would cross to this side on foot with picks and shovels and start digging trenches for the defensive positions. There would be six trenches, laid out on a circle big enough to keep the horses inside at night. Limestone blocks would be carried up from the outcrops, and each trench would be lined on the side, facing out for extra protection. It wouldn't be much, but it would be better than leaving Myrick and his men without any protection.

The sun was settling in the west, and Eli knew it would be an almost sleepless night with his wagon train split between both sides of the river. The moon would still be bright enough for him to cross back and forth, checking his guards and the fickle Arkansas River. While the river was benign during what was turning out to be a drought year, it could swell in an almost flash-flood reaction to thunderstorms hundreds of miles to the northwest. The only good thing about this location was the buffalo Jacques and Roland pulled into the soldiers' camp. They shot the buffalo on their last patrol west of the river. Those that could sleep tonight would at least sleep with their bellies full of fresh meat.

The evening settled into the dark of night, and there would be only several hours of starlight until the waning moon rose in the east. The river came alive with the sound of insects and owls. It reminded the Callahans of a night in the forest back home. There were numerous campfires in the west camp, and the sound of Paul Hayman's banjo played on the night air along with the ring of the blacksmith's hammer. Suzette and Roland were working out a system of signals that the scouts could use with the mirrors. They wanted to keep the system simple and after much discussion trimmed their list down to just four: One flash — I'm here; two flashes — a sighting; three flashes — join up; four flashes — under attack. They could modify the signals if they saw a need later, but for now, Suzette explained her idea to Eli and Jacques. Jacques, more military-minded than the rest, said, "I doubt you would have time for number four. Gunshots would be more useful, and everyone would hear those and be on alert." Everyone agreed.

Eli hoped for a quiet night, and he turned in early, wanting to get some sleep before the moon rose. That's when he suspected they would see Indians if they were going to be any looking to attack or steal something from the camp. Hans would be on watch rotation when the moon rose. Eli asked Suzette to tell Hans to wake him then. He stretched his bedroll out under his wagon and fell asleep in minutes. The rest of the camp joked about his snoring when it got loud enough to compete with the sounds from across the river.

The moon rose just three short hours after dark, and Hans woke Eli against his better judgment. He handed Eli a mug of strong coffee, and as they sat around the small fire, Hans tried in his best English to tell Eli that he was pushing too hard. Eli shrugged it off; his responsibilities weighed heavily on his mind. His horse remained saddled through the night, ready for any emergency. He finished his coffee and rode off in the light of the rising moon. He would circle each camp, check on his guards, and make sure that their perimeter was secure. When he crossed the river, Jacques was waiting for him on the west side of the crossing. Jacques said, "All is quiet, but the men are tense. I think it is finally dawning on them that they are out on the prairie in hostile territory, and while you have whipped them into a quasi-military unit, the training has kept Indians constantly in their thoughts. It isn't the passage they thought it would be when they signed on, but it is what it is. They need to kick some hostile ass to gain some confidence. Rumors are going around that there are bands of four hundred or so ready to attack, and that makes them nervous."

Eli thought over his brother's comments and just responded, "Let's hope Captain Barnes is right about the small bands. We could handle fifty or maybe even more, but four hundred could easily take us down. Their casualties would be severe, but they would probably win. We will keep up the training when we get back on the trail. Tomorrow will be a workday, and we'll probably still be camped here tomorrow night. I don't like sitting in one spot too long; it gives the Indians time to gather their forces. Let's try to finish with Myrick early and move five or ten miles if we can."

Jacques had a suggestion, "Why don't we increase the workforce to three-quarters of the men and have all four of us riding patrol? We could be done with Myrick by two or so and then travel till dark."

"Good idea, I'll put the word out at sunrise." The brothers rode the perimeter of the larger camp and told the guards that they would be riding a larger circle, several hundred yards out. They didn't want nervous trigger fingers wondering what was out there in the semi-darkness. They started their sweep on the south side of the camp. They circled to the west and then back to the river on the north. As they approached the river, they heard a horse riding out on the east bank. They couldn't see the rider through the thick cottonwoods and willows that choked the river bottom, but they knew it was a watcher. Eli said, "Tomorrow, let's keep the patrols paired up. I don't want anyone caught out there alone."

The rest of the night passed quietly, and as the cooks rousted the camps at dawn, Eli briefed the men on how they would handle the work of fortifying Myrick and his men. "It won't be an elaborate fort, but it will give them some cover until reinforcements arrive. There will be an empty supply wagon in Myrick's camp. I want at least twenty men loading and hauling limestone blocks over to the camp. The rest of you can be digging the six trenches and lining the tops with the limestone. Hans will supervise the work at the camp. Myrick's men will help with the work, but more than half his troops are still weak from cholera. They are strong enough, though, to stand guard on the east side of the river. I want fifteen men to stand guard on this side of the river. Let's eat up and get to work."

Hans pulled a roll of rope from one of the supply wagons and stretched it across the river on the downstream side of the ford. The river wasn't that fast over the wide crossing, but the water was more than knee-deep. If someone stumbled, he didn't want them winding up in New Orleans, and there was always the chance that the river could rise while the bulk of the men were on the east side of the river.

Eli and his siblings mounted up to patrol out to the west. Eli and Suzette were on the north side of the trail, and Jacques and Roland on the south. They flashed their signals back and forth, and Eli was very pleased with his sister and her ingenuity. They adopted some stealth for their scouting routine. They would ride up behind one of the endless rises out to the west and then slowly walk to the top scanning all around as the next draw came into view in front of them. When they got to the top of the rise, they would signal the other pair of scouts, and they would move ahead while the first pair waited and watched for them to crest the next rise.

Coordinating was working well, but on the third rise, Eli held up his hand and stopped Suzette before she reached the top of the low hill. He could see a herd of horses in the draw about a half-mile to the north. They counted twelve braves as they rode out to the west. Through his binoculars, Eli could see that most of the Indians were armed with spears and wore headdresses made of buffalo horns. "Comanche," he said. Suzette flashed two times to indicate a sighting. Roland acknowledged with one. Then she flashed three times for them to join up. As Roland and Jacques turned toward them and broke into a gallop, Suzette turned back down the east side of the rise. She didn't want her brothers to ride up the rise announcing their presence.

Eli rode down from the rise and joined his siblings. "There is a herd of horses in the next draw about a half-mile to the north. I think they are Myrick's horses. We counted a dozen Indians riding out to the west. They looked like Comanche. We'll ride north up this draw and look over their camp. They must have left a guard, but if Barnes is right about the tactics, the band out west will split into two groups and spread out along the trail. If we can, let's get Myrick's horses back. Suzette, I want you to herd the horses back to the camp. We will ride a rearguard, you just run that herd like hell and get them into the wagon ring. I don't think the horses will cross the river; if they do, we're going to have a hard time rounding them up. Let's go." They rode up the draw and topped the rise a half-mile up. A young boy was guarding the camp. He wasn't armed but played with a stick and a ball of prairie grass trying to keep it up in the air. His eyes were as big as dinner plates when the four riders came sweeping down the hill.

Suzette backed the boy up to the trunk of a cottonwood tree and held her Henry steady on the young man's chest. Her brothers cut the horses loose, and Roland led two over to Suzette that had halters and lead ropes. "Ride," he said as Eli and Jacques pulled the hitching ropes through the rings on the bottom of the bridles on the rest of the herd. Suzette was riding up the rise going southeast to meet the trail with her men fanned out and riding south to protect her flank. It was about two miles back to the camp. Suzette kept nudging Patches to go faster and was talking encouragement to her.

"Come on, girl, only five minutes, and we'll be back in camp. Get me there, girl; get me there." She heard shots to her rear, that couldn't be good, then more shots in rapid succession. Her brothers were in a firefight; she wanted to turn back, but Eli had ordered her to ride to the camp, and that is what she did. As she neared the wagon ring, all the guards were waiting, rifles raised. One of them shouted, "It's Suzette, hold your fire. Suzette thundered through the ring with the herd of horses. She turned the two lead horses around the inner circle and pulled up to a stop. She was afraid the mules were going to bolt in the ruckus, but their stays and hobbles held them in check. The rest of the horses turned at the river and circled the mules again before they slowed and stopped. There was more shooting out west. Suzette dismounted with her Henry and took up a position behind the closest crate barrier. The men there asked her what was going on. "We stole Myrick's horses back from the Indians; I think they are pissed."

Eli and her brothers came into view on the trail. There were more than twenty Comanche whooping war cries and taking occasional shots with pistols and arrows. Her brothers were shooting back, but their aim wasn't the best facing backward and holding the rifles in one hand. Nonetheless, they dropped three braves before they came within the range of the wagon ring. The Indians intent on the chase and angered by the loss of their comrades, didn't notice how close they were to the camp. A volley from the men who had a clear shot at the Indians dropped three more braves and five horses. Each man had two rifles and got ready for the next volley. If they could hit them at two hundred yards, the next volley at closer range could end this battle in a few moments. Eli and the twins were only a hundred yards out.

Suzette and almost every man on the line had a clear shot. She fired and dropped the lead Indian with a bullet in the middle of his chest. The rest of the men fired, and the devastation was almost complete. Eli bolted into the ring with his brothers and leaped off his horse before he could stop it.

He ran back to the barricade and drew his colt. There were only six braves left when he rode through the ring, and only three by the time he was ready to fire. Suzette was dropping them with every round she levered into the chamber of her Henry. Then, there was only one Indian left. He lay to the side of his horse for cover and turned out of the melee. Suzette was going to shoot him in the back, but Roland pushed the barrel to the side and said, "Let him go, news of this massacre needs to make it back to the rest of his people."

Eli wasn't concerned about the brave; he was concerned that the men were standing in awe with mouths agape, looking at the carnage. "Reload, **NOW, God damn it!** There could be fifty more coming!" Eli turned to Suzette and his brothers. After you reload, let's get lead ropes on Myrick's horses and take them across the river.

The men across the river had attacked the work with a vengeance that morning. Maybe they just wanted to get their minds off the Indians, or maybe they were just bored with the trail; either way, the work was good therapy. As the trenches deepened, Myrick and his men took up positions checking their fields of fire and stocking in what few possessions they had. A load of limestone was arriving every hour. It took a full load to build a parapet around one pit. All work stopped at the first sound of gunfire, and every man was in the trenches armed and waiting for targets. Lieutenant Myrick commanded, "Hold your fire until you are sure of your target. We don't' know what is happening over there." There was a hell of a ruckus across the river, but their side was quiet. They stayed on guard after the shooting stopped until they saw Suzette lead a herd of horses down to the crossing. They cheered when Suzette brought the herd into the camp. The soldiers jumped out of the trenches and took charge of the mounts.

One soldier that didn't get out of his trench yelled at Mr. Sue, "Hey, *chink*, bring me some water."

Mr. Sue dropped the limestone block he was carrying and said politely, "My name is not Chink, it is Sue. Mr. Sue, if you please. If you want water, show some respect."

The sorry excuse for a soldier pulled himself out of his trench. "I'll show you respect, Chink." He approached Mr. Sue and tried to connect with a right cross, a roundhouse punch that only found thin air. Mr. Sue stepped to the man's right, forcing him to turn to throw another punch. The man tried a jab with his right. Mr. Sue swatted it to the side like it was a bothersome horsefly. He stepped to the right again, forcing the soldier to turn again. The soldier rushed Mr. Sue; he stepped to the side and kicked the raging bull of a man in the ass as he passed. The soldier fell on his face. The rest of the soldiers and men from the wagon train had formed a circle to watch, and they laughed as the big man struggled to get up.

The soldier was red in the face, and he was winded. It wasn't that hot, but sweat was soaking his shirt that only made his rank odor worse. He tried at least a dozen times to hit Mr. Sue. Winded and dizzy from cholera, he finally stood looking at Mr. Sue with a dazed look on his face. Mr. Sue walked up to him and pushed him on his chest. The big man fell on his back without trying to break his fall. He lay where he fell, staring up at the sky. Mr. Sue said, "Cholera can hang on for a long time. I suggest you rest up before you call another Chinese, Chink." Mr. Sue helped the soldier's friends carry him back to the trench. He filled a ladle with cool water and helped the man drink it.

It wasn't noon yet, and the men finished the last load of rock on the east parapet. A double row of limestone blocks lined each trench, and the men from the west camp were stocking the last pit with ammo and supplies. He looked over the work and told the men to get ready for the trail as soon as they were back across the river. It only took ten more minutes, and the Germans had their wagons hitched and ready to go. The cook served up a parting meal of buffalo stew, and everyone ate their fill.

Eli shook Myrick's hand and wished him luck. He left a crate of rifles and a keg of shot and powder. He mounted up and headed his wagons across the river. Suzette joined him, and they rode out ahead to patrol the trail. Eli joked with his sister, "Now in addition to *Gunslinger,* we have to add *Horse Thief* to your title."

Suzette reached over and put her hand on Eli's forearm. "I don't care what you call me, just get me to Los Angeles in one piece." Eli noticed her hand was shaking. They just passed the last dead Indian lying in the trail. Suzette was thinking about the cost. There were going to be many widows and orphans tonight in the Indian camp. At least they were safe for the moment and on their way to Colorado. She couldn't wait to see her first snow-capped mountain.

FORT LARNED

Drivers and their helpers wasted no time readying their wagons and pulling out onto the trail. Hans waited with three of his wagons to take the rear position and would rotate each day to lessen the burden of the dusty duty among his men. The trail was dry, and while there were clouds, there was not a single thunderhead within sight to settle the dust. Dust or mud, these seemed to be the only two conditions on the drought-stricken Kansas prairie. Jacques was in the lead wagon, and on Eli's orders, he kept the pace at a lively walk. Despite the late start, they wanted to make it to *Cow Creek Crossing* by nightfall.

Eli and Suzette were north of the trail, Roland, and Horatio to the south. With the wagon train moving along at a fast clip, the scouts didn't have as much time to ascend each rise to surveil the country out ahead. They were galloping through the bottoms of the swales to stay ahead of the train. Ten miles ahead, they came upon a vast herd of buffalo. Eli commented to Suzette, "There must be more than ten thousand of them." The buffalo were grazing and walking slowly to the southeast. There wouldn't be a blade of grass left standing after they passed. "I don't want to get stuck in the middle of that herd less they stampede, they could raise hell with the wagons. Signal the others to join up."

Roland and Horatio came up at a dead run. Suzette thought they probably expected more Indians. They were surprised when they could see the vast-brown sea of animals out ahead. "What do you want to do?" Roland asked.

"I don't want us in the middle of them. The herd is moving southeast; what do you think about us getting behind it and driving the buffalo south of the trail?" They all agreed on this plan, and Eli sent Horatio back to stop Jacques before he got in the path of the buffalo. They rode to the north to circle behind the herd, but they didn't need to stampede the herd as they planned. There was an Indian hunting party that did that for them. Whooping and firing what guns they had, the Indians swept down on the herd from the northwest, and soon the thunder of hooves drowned them with a noise that made their chests vibrate. The horses were spooked and wanted to run with the buffalo, but Eli had them hold back and watch the herd pass. They could only see the first animals on their side of the herd through a solid wall of dust stirred up by the flailing hooves. A young brave was riding at the edge of the herd, his attention on the buffalo he intended to kill. He turned and charged in driving his spear deep into the heart of the two-thousand-pound beast. He didn't notice the three scouts from the wagon train watching, and Eli turned and yelled over the thunder of the hooves, "Let's get back to the trail."

It took five minutes for the herd to cross to the south side of the trail. Eli told the scouts to stay close in, and he gave Jacques the signal to advance. They didn't know if these Indians were hostiles, but caution was the order of the day, as it would be every day until they were well out of the hostile territory. As they moved into the track, the stampede carved out of the prairie grass, they could see that the Indians had made four kills. There were bands of women moving to each kill. They would dress out the meat, tan the hide back at their camp, and make use of every part of the animal. There was a white man with several Indians and a wagon at one of the kills. A bit amazed, Eli and Suzette rode out to meet him. The man was young, perhaps in his early thirties. He introduced himself as Bill Mathewson and assured Eli that the Indians with him were not hostile. They were hunting meat to feed the folks settled around his trading post on Cow Creek. He said it was only eight miles further on. He hoped their wagon train would stop there for the night. He told them there was a fairly large band of Comanche in the area, and they were on the warpath. More visitors, the better, they improved the security of his tiny post.

"Maybe not anymore," Ely replied, and he related his events of the morning. Bill Mathewson took on a degree of respect for the young wagon master and his scouts.

He looked at Suzette and asked, "And how many did you kill, young lady?"

"A lot more than four," she said, casting her glance to each of the dead buffalo.

"You're going to become known as *Dangerous Woman Yellow Hair* among the Indians," Bill told her.

Suzette didn't want another moniker, and she didn't want notoriety for the killings; she wanted to be known as a strong woman who held her own on the trail and survived.

Eli moved the wagon train forward. They crossed *Cow Creek* without incident and set up their camp for the night. Bill had sent one of the mounted Indians ahead, and there were grills full of buffalo steaks sending up their savory vapors by the time the wagons circled for the night. Bill came over to Eli's campfire after dinner and listened to Paul Hayman's banjo. He sat talking with the Callahans long after dark. He had a lot to say about the tribes on the prairie. They were all at war with one another at one time or another. Keeping track was hard. The Cheyenne and Comanche were at the moment working together, and they were trying to stop the western flow of settlers onto their lands. His Indians were second-generation Osage, and while their ancestors were warlike plains Indians, his were domesticated and in tune with the white man invaders. There was a lot of starvation on the prairie due to the drought. He was hunting meat for settlers who were short of supplies due to crop failures in the dry conditions back in the staging areas. Bill finally focused on Suzette and the Henry rifle she was cleaning.

"That's one of the new repeaters?" Bill asked.

"Yes, it's a Henry rifle. Not as powerful as your Springfield, but deadly at a closer range. It holds sixteen rounds and one in the chamber. Be careful; it's loaded." She handed it to Bill for an inspection.

"You take good care of it. How much did it cost?"

"I haven't paid for it yet. It's on loan for the moment from a hardware store in Santa Fe. I'll let you shoot it in the morning."

With that, the camp wound down for the night. Eli reduced the guards to the usual compliment, one per every six wagons. He was nodding off at the fire and was asleep in thirty seconds as soon as he completed the arrangements for the night. All hoped for a peaceful night's rest, but that was not to be so. Around three in the morning, the weather changed. First, a cool breeze carrying the smell of rain blew in from the southwest, welcomed as a relief to the hot, dusty days. But the refreshing breeze was short-lived as a violent thunderstorm followed close behind. Strong winds that threatened to rip the canvas tops off the wagons raked the camp. Lightning lit the raging dust storm, and thunder deafened ears as the men scurried about securing loose items and comforting the mules.

Suzette was terrified, waiting for the roar of a tornado or the weird pressure drop that she experienced in the tornado that killed her parents. She had her arms around Maria and had the girl covered with a poncho underneath Mr. Sue's chuck wagon. A tornado didn't materialize out of the night, but the rain arrived, torrential in its nearly horizontal fury driven by the wind. It started to hail, small pellets that stung like BB's on bare skin. The mules were getting the worst of it, and they strained at their hobbles and tethers trying to break free and run away from the stinging pellets. After a few moments, the mules settled down and tried to herd up with their hindquarters to the wind, heads down, and their eyes closed to protect from the wind-driven hail. The hailstones were getting larger. In a moment, the hailstones were as large as a 0.50 caliber rifle ball. Now the men were like the mules, huddled behind the wagons trying their best to keep from getting pelted to death. Maria was whimpering, and Suzette was struggling to keep them covered up with the poncho. The temperature fell to near freezing. *Amazing,* Suzette thought, *we were sweltering and sweaty trying to sleep, and now we are shivering in the cold.*

The hail turned back into rain, a lot of rain. Cow Creek came alive and was raging, carrying tree limbs on its surface and tumbling rocks along its bottom. Suzette mistook the roar of the creek for the roar of a tornado, and her fear deepened. Maria was praying, and Suzette was inclined to join her. The rain maintained its torrent then stopped abruptly. Suzette crawled through mud and ice to get out from under the wagon and then pulled Maria out and got her up on her feet. Mr. Sue was muttering in Chinese, and from the sound of the words, Suzette figured he was cursing. He lit a lantern and was searching for his pots and pans that had blown away in the wind.

Eli found Suzette and then started walking around the camp, checking on the damage. Here and there, the men were getting fires started to warm up and fix breakfast. The empty wagon that they used to transport the stone for Myrick's fortifications was turned up on its side; Eli helped right it with six other men. The mules settled down regardless of their severe pelting in the storm. His crew was sorting out their mules by lantern light casting small islands of light in the inky darkness.

All in all, they were lucky. There were no injuries and only a few torn canvas tops and some missing odds and ends. The storm was still raging to the northeast, and there was still an occasional flash of lightning that lit up the night sky and gave the impression of flash powder being set off to take pictures of the camp.

By sunrise, everyone was looking forward to a hot meal and an early start on the trail. Eli wanted to make it to *Great Bend.* There were soldiers there and a stage stop. It would have been an easy day's travel in the dust, but he knew it probably wouldn't be possible with the trail offering up its only other option – mud. "Endless prairie and endless mud, that's what the day will bring," Eli said as he got back to his wagon. Mr.

Sue handed Eli his morning tea. "I see your teapot survived the wind, Mr. Sue."

"The teapot is like a treasure; it was in its cupboard. Coffee pot not so lucky; it's on its way back to Missouri or maybe Chicago." Everyone laughed, and Eli was glad to see that the men were in good humor. Today would not be an easy day for them, and like Eli, most were thinking back to their experience in The Narrows. Dust you could live with, the mud would slow them down, and the trail lived up to his lugubrious expectations. The first five miles was a ribbon of mud. The mules were slipping back some for every step they took forward. His drivers and swampers were off their wagons leading their teams, encouraging them, and delivering the frequent curse as they plowed through the mud. The wagons in the back of the train had the worst of it with the wheels of the leading wagons churning the mud deeper and deeper. No one bogged down, and no one stopped, but it was midafternoon when they reached *Plum Buttes.* Here the trail was wet but not soaked. The storm was a big one, and every rill and gully was still running but settling back down into the drought conditions that would prevail despite the storm. Eli decided they would stop for the night. The leading mules were tired, and the teams to the rear of the train were exhausted. The only animals that had an easy time were the scouts' horses. The scouts only had to walk their horses through the grass on the side of the trail, staying out in front of the train. The scouts spent most of the day sitting in their saddles watching the wagon train plow through the mud.

Amazingly, the pioneers that first discovered *Plum Buttes* named them for the plum bushes that grew around them. The buttes themselves were three sand dunes, nearly one hundred feet tall. Suzette tended to her horse and then announced that she was going to climb the highest dune. Roland and Hans accompanied her to the top. They climbed the dune using the stocks of their rifles as a crutch and a break when they would start to slide down. It was warm and humid from the recent rain. Sweat dripped from their brows and soaked their clothes by the time they reached the top, but the view was worth it. In every direction, there was nothing but prairie with the Arkansas River cutting west to east about three miles south of their lofty perch. "I was hoping to see a mountain on the horizon, but I can't even see Great Bend," Suzette said. There was still plenty to see with another great herd of buffalo northeast of the buttes. Roland was a bit worried; where there were buffalo, there would be Indians. All-in-all, the trail stretching to the horizon offered nothing of interest, but the tedium of drying grasslands intersected by the green lines of creeks and the occasional small thickets in the lowlands fed by the streams. Suzette was beginning to understand why some people committed suicide escaping from the endless grass wilderness of the trail. She put the thought out of her head. It was easy enough to die out here; it was tragic that people chose to take their own lives rather than continue west.

When they returned to the camp, the aromas from the cook fires were promising buffalo stew and steaks for those that still had them. The blacksmith was the busiest man in camp with more than a dozen mules ending up missing one or more shoes after the hard pull through the mud. Paul Hayman, as usual, came to Eli's wagons and livened the evening. Roland noticed that Paul was more fixated on Suzette than ever. The young musician was trying his best to charm her with a song into a more favorable frame of mind towards him. Suzette paid him only polite attention whenever Paul made advances toward her. Roland liked Paul, and he wouldn't have minded if Suzette found the young man to her liking. He decided time would tell.

The next day Eli set his sights on Great Bend, where they would meet the Arkansas River. First, he had to make it to the Walnut Creek Crossing and hoped there wasn't a thunderstorm blowing into that drainage to swell the creek. The wagon train was ready to pull out shortly after dawn; it promised to be an easy day of travel. They hadn't moved even a mile after Roland and Suzette took up their scouting positions when Roland was flashing a sighting. Eli rode out to see what was up for himself. There was a small band of Indians about a mile to the north watching them. Eli and Roland watched back, and as the wagon train pulled up next to them, they advanced staying even with the front of the wagon train. The Indians kept their distance but advanced with them. Eli told his brother, "Don't lose sight of them; I'm going to ride down to Suzette and tell her what is going on. I hope these Indians are just curious and not the advanced scouts of a much larger party." He signaled back to the train for Jacques to join up with Roland, his brief time with only two scouts over, as long as these Indians were near.

They made the rest of the distance to the Walnut Creek Crossing in less than three hours. Roland and Jacques lost sight of the Indians as they neared the trading post on the east side of the crossing. Eli and Suzette rode to the trading post by the creek, and Jacques started moving the train through the crossing. The sign over the door said, *George Peacock – Proprietor.* Suzette asked her brother, "Could this be the same Mr. Peacock from Independence? He did business with our father."

They entered the store, and a very surprised Mr. Peacock said, "Well, look at you two!" Standing in front of his counter wasn't two of the Callahan children, but two lean and weathered pioneers. He rushed around the counter and shook Eli's hand and hugged Suzette. He wanted news from home but was deeply saddened to hear about the death of their father and mother and said, "Your father was the best of men."

Suzette broke down and cried, and Eli said, "The best of men; that is the inscription we put on his tombstone. We never found our father, but there is a marker next to our mother's tombstone. Her grave is on the grounds of her school." As the wagon train passed, they stood outside and watched, and Eli commented, "There are some Indians following us."

George responded, "Those are Kiowa. So far, they haven't been hostile, but I don't trust their chief, *Santank*. He has been in here several times, and he never seems happy. I trade supplies for pelts with them, and I hope we stay friends. It's very lonely out here."

Eli and Suzette bid the old friend farewell, saddled up, and rode west to join the front of the train. There were soldiers just west of the crossing. They had made camp five miles further west, and Eli would be leaving them arms and supplies. The soldiers accompanied them back to their camp, and Eli stopped the train there for the night. A Sergeant Apple, was in charge of the small troop. The soldiers seemed to enjoy the strength in numbers the wagon train provided.

The next day would be a long haul to Fort Larned. Eli hoped the supplies promised by Captain Barnes would be available. He wasn't short by any means, but they were still just halfway across Kansas. They were back on the trail as dawn broke, it was twenty-six miles to Fort Larned, which they could make easily by nightfall. However, Eli knew that the extra mileage gained today would be paid back tomorrow with tired animals not up to set any records. They passed Pawnee Rock and then forded Ash Creek by midafternoon. Eli slowed the pace and walked the mules the last nine miles to Fort Larned.

They reached the fort with its low sod buildings as the sun was starting to settle in the west. Early evening was pleasantly cool, and the men were tending to their teams and congratulating themselves on the longest one-day trek yet. Eli rode into the Fort and met Major Frank Lindsay, the post commander. He introduced himself and presented the letter from Captain Barnes. The major was friendly but skeptical that he could provide enough feed to get Eli comfortably to Santa Fe. His men would stock up the supply train the best he could afford in the morning. He invited Eli to join him for dinner, and Eli accepted after the Major included Suzette and his brothers in the invitation. Eli and his family spent a pleasant evening with the Major and his wife. Suzette was glad to have another woman to talk to, if only for a short time.

Major Lindsay offered the brothers rooms in the officer's quarters, but they declined and left to walk back to their wagons for the night. Mrs. Lindsay took Suzette aside and said, "I have something for you." She reached to the hair clip on the back of her head. It was an ornate barrette, iridescent green, and the shape of a scarab beetle, but bigger. Suzette had admired it at dinner and liked the way it complemented Mrs. Lindsay's green eyes and blond hair. She drew it out of her hair, and Suzette could see it was much more than a barrette. It was the handle for a six-inch hairpin, thicker than a knitting needle, and tapered to a sharp point like a stiletto. "I want you to have this. Please take it and wear it when you are around the forts and military camps on the trail."

Suzette tried to refuse. She had her Lefaucheux revolver, the Henry rifle, and her knife. "Those are for Indians and renegades, honey. You didn't bring them to dinner tonight, and there will be other times when you don't have them with you. A girl always can have a piece of jewelry. Don't worry; I make these, and I have more of them, one for every occasion." Suzette suspected that there was more to the older woman's cautions than she put forth. She asked, "Excuse me for being blunt, and please don't think unkindly of me for the asking, but have you ever been raped?"

"Yes, when I was a young wife at Fort Laramie. My husband was a Second Lieutenant then, just out of West Point. He was away on patrols, and four soldiers raped me in my quarters. I've never been unarmed since."

Tears came to Suzette's eyes, and she said, "My grandmother was raped and almost bled to death. She has written many books and articles about rape. If I can find any in Los Angeles, I'll send them to you. Thank you for this, and don't worry about me. I can take care of myself. I don't feel good about it, but I have already killed some renegades, a larger number of Indians, and a Mexican that wanted to do me harm."

"You're already a grown woman, my dear, and I am not going to worry about you. God be with you, and I hope to see you again. Frank is due to be reassigned further west. We never know where we will be tomorrow." Mrs. Lindsay watched her leave for the front gate. Her brothers were waiting for her just off the front porch. The older woman watched them walk to the front gate and thought to herself; *it will take a lot more than four soldiers to get to that girl.*

Suzette went to check on Maria. "Mr. Sue! What have you done?" Maria was practicing with one of the juvenile weapons of mass mischief, a slingshot. Maria was anxious to show Suzette her new skill. Mr. Sue had set up some tin cups up on a board under a wagon, and Maria was busy pelting them with pebbles. Suzette raised an eyebrow and was thinking back to her younger days and all the mischief she and her brothers perpetrated with their slingshots. She thought about the guns she now carried, and the killings on the trail, and wondered if Maria would also make the transition from pebbles to lead bullets before her journey ended. Maria was getting good, and she laughed each time she hit one of the cups. Mr. Sue was egging her on, and with pantomimes and examples, was enjoying teaching Maria the art of marksmanship. It wouldn't be long; Maria would be out of her splint, and Suzette looked forward to taking Maria rabbit hunting. She laughed at the thought of putting Maria on guard duty; they could all sleep easier with a slingshot added to the armaments.

Before dawn, the soldiers were busy unloading rifle crates from Eli's wagons. Crates of uniforms, kitchen utensils, and sundry supplies were unloaded from the other wagons and marked off the manifest. The soldiers filled the empty spaces with bags of oats and grain, as many as the Quartermaster would allow. Major Lindsay oversaw the provisioning and shook hands with Eli, the twins, and Hans. Turning to Suzette, touched the barrette holding her ponytail and gave her an affectionate hug. He said, "If we could have had children, I would want them to be just like the four of you." He turned and called his men to attention and saluted Eli as he signaled for Hans to pull out with the lead wagon. They were more than halfway across Kansas, and this would be their twenty-second day on the trail.

ENDLESS PRAIRIE

As Suzette mounted up and walked Patches to the front of the train; she waved to Mrs. Lindsay, who was standing by the gate of the fort; the major's wife waved back, both wished they had more time to spend together. She wondered to herself; *she never mentioned that they had children, and the Major said If we had children. Could the rape have left her barren? Infection or emotional damage both could have the same effect.* She put the unanswered question out of her mind. She had work to do, and with a double-click of her tongue, she galloped Patches forward to take the position of the north scout. Roland was on the south side of the trail, towards Coon Creek. Eli wanted to ford the creek and stay somewhere along the Arkansas River to the west of the ford. It would be a short day after the previous hard push to reach Fort Larned.

Eli stopped the wagon train at a place called Plain Camp on the trail map. There was a pond a short way from the Arkansas River, and he circled the wagons around the pond. He rode around the circle, warning the men that the pond was for stock water only. They would operate as dry camps until they reached the next safe watering hole, *Black Pool*, regardless of the ample water flowing in the river. The area was notorious for cholera, and the river water would be a last resort if the drinking water supply ran short. It was an easy day's travel to *Black Pool*. The mules loved the pond, though, and enriched the light green color with an ample supply of manure. There was green grass down by the river's edge. Jacques and Suzette took the horses down to the low banks to graze. Jacques, ever cautious, kept one saddled just in case an emergency arose.

Suzette lay back in the green grass and looked into the deep blue of the sky. Bald eagles were soaring up and down the river taking fish and flying back to nests full of eaglets, no doubt. Where were their nests? Even the river bottom only had scrub brush along its banks. There had to be trees somewhere, eagles nested in trees. Her thoughts turned to the home she left behind, the security of her grandmother's mansion, the comfort of her parent's house in the forest. Where would she be now if she stayed in Independence? Would her grandmother have sent her off to a girl's school somewhere in New England? She pictured herself in her buckskins with her Lefaucheux on her hip and her Henry leaning against a school desk with French literature books opened and other students around her struggling to read. She closed her eyes and fell into a light sleep. She was startled awake by the snort of a horse. Jacques was up in his saddle, Henry resting on the pommel. He was watching intently across the river. On the other side, watching back with more than passing interest was a small band of Indians. Their intentions were obvious. They wanted the horses. Patches was the only horse that was roaming free; the others grazed, tethered on their separate little areas of grass.

The Indians looked different from any they had seen so far. "Apache," Jacques said with a tone of concern. Suzette picked up her Henry rifle out of the grass and fired three shots in rapid succession into the river in front of the band. The Indians were well out of the effective range of the Henry, but behind Suzette and Jacques, some men were running down from the wagon train to join them. The long rifles and bayonets must have inspired the Apaches to greater caution. They turned and rode up the bank to the south and out of sight. "We haven't seen the last of that band," was all that Jacques had to say. They gathered up the horses and returned to the safety of the circle. The caution spread like a wind-driven fire through the rest of the wagon train; Apaches spelled a different kind of trouble, the trouble of the west where settlers, traders, and the US Army was at constant war with the aggressive tribe. Eli put the guards back to double duty. It would be harder on the men, but he would compensate with shorter travel days if necessary, to keep everyone alert.

The night passed with a spectacular half-moon and clear sky full of bright stars lighting the prairie. Eli made the rounds at midnight and told the men on guard to shoot intruders on sight. It would be suicide for the Indians to attack with the visibility of good and clear fields of fire as far as the eye could see. Eli got some rest, feeling confident that there wouldn't be trouble that night. The Apache were known to be fierce warriors. He knew their history from his father's teachings. First, at war with the Mexicans and now with the US Army, the Apache were experienced fighters. Centuries of raiding other Indian tribes, Mexican settlements, and now the white men invading their lands from the east, honed the Apache into a scattered nation of fierce savages. It was a problem he could do nothing about, and he wondered how many military heroes were building their careers using the Apache for their advancement in the military. Too much to think about; he fell asleep thinking ahead to Colorado. Suzette wasn't the only one that wanted to see a mountain.

The next day was hot and dry. The sun beat down relentlessly, and as far as the eye could see, there was nothing but dry grass and an occasional desperate shrub, clinging to life waiting for the next rain. Willows and scrub oak lined the dry creek beds, but these too were clinging to life waiting for water. The tedium of the trail was pressing down hard. Eli would focus on a tree or a different patch of prairie to mark distance but would lose sight of it or forget about it before he focused ahead on the next marker. He stopped the wagon train for lunch along the trail. They could see for miles in every direction, so the wagons just stopped in place, and the cooks took out their wares, ready to serve out what buffalo meat they had left.

Eli was studying the trail map when he looked up and saw six soldiers riding to join up with the trail from the west. "We've got company," he shouted, and some men walked up to the head of the train, checking their rifles and waiting for the cavalry to arrive. Suzette was in the driver's seat next to Eli, and Maria was on the crates behind her, looking out over her shoulder. As the soldiers neared, Eli commented, "They don't look right."

Suzette agreed, chambered a round and opened the tube under the barrel of her Henry, and loaded another bullet into the magazine. The soldiers were riding scattered around their leader, not holding the two-by-two formation of a regular unit. Their weapons were a mismatch of rifles, and only two had the 0.44 caliber Colts that were standard Army issue, and several didn't have sabers or Army issue saddles. As the soldiers drew closer, more discrepancies became apparent. The leader had the epaulets of a first lieutenant, but there were bright patches of blue on both sleeves where corporal stripes used to be in contrast to the faded blue of the tunic. "Deserters," Eli murmured and signaled for the box formation. Suzette was in the shade of the canopy and wasn't able to flash for Roland and Jacques to join up from their scouting positions. She had Maria get down behind the crates behind her. Horatio pulled up close to the left, and Hans did the same to the right. The box was forming behind them.

Hans was looking at Suzette for an explanation; these were soldiers, why the defensive position? The leader was walking his horse between the mule teams close enough to overhear her, so she said in German, "Schlechte soldaten." The word for a deserter in German sounded too much like the English word so she didn't use it for fear it would tip off the deserters that their charade wasn't working. Hans got the idea; he levered a round into the chamber of his Henry and leveled it at the leader's chest.

"Whoa, wait a minute. There is no need for that; we're soldiers, and I am a First Lieutenant in the United States Army." He was trying to act nonchalant, but his hand instinctively went to the butt of his Colt. His men were out in front of the mule teams, but they too were reaching for their weapons.

"What post are you out of?" Eli asked.

"Fort Larned," was the leader's reply.

"We were there two days ago. Major Barnes treated us well, and we offloaded supplies. How long have you been stationed under Major Barnes?"

"Ahhh, four months, he's a good man," the leader relaxed in the half hope that his sham was still holding water.

"When did you make First Lieutenant?"

Now impatient, the man pressed on with his simple-minded goal, "Look, I am an Army Officer, and you are an Army Supply Train. We'll be taking supplies, and I want one of those fancy rifles. You are obligated to hand over what we need."

Eli was cold as polar ice, and his tone was no longer friendly. "I, my friend, have no obligations to deserters. Tell your men to drop their weapons and dismount. You are going back to Fort Larned to stand Court Marshalls for desertion and impersonating an officer.   Major Frank Lindsay, the commanding officer, is going to be very pleased to welcome you back."

It was dead silent; even the mules sensed the change in the tone of the conversation. Some even laid their ears back and put their heads down. The leader of the deserters was trying to back his horse, "Looks like we've got ourselves a standoff here."

Eli was loath to kill white men, but the situation was deteriorating quickly. He needed something to break the deadlock, and it came from behind him. Suzette had whispered to Maria, and Eli heard the snap of Maria's slingshot as a well-placed pebble smacked into the flank of the leader's horse. It bolted forward, and as it passed between the driver's seats of the two wagons, Hans knocked the man off the back of his saddle with the end of his rifle. One of the deserters raised his rifle to shoot, but Horatio was faster and shot the man in the head. Eli and Suzette opened up on the other four men who were on a dead run trying to escape. The mules were dancing in place, but none ran. The leader was on his back between the wagons and was trying to draw his Colt. Hans jumped off his wagon and landed with both feet on the man's head. The noise of his head crushing was drowned out by a shot from the Colt that went wild. The four remaining deserters rode off hard toward Roland. Roland swung his leg over the pommel and slid to the ground. He lay down with the Henry, and when the riders were in range, he opened up.

The man in the lead fell backward off his horse with a bullet in his chest. The other three turned and took some wild shots in Roland's direction, and one of them hit his horse in the neck. The horse went down beside him, and Roland rolled up and used him for cover. He dropped two more of the riders as they turned in for the kill and then winged the last. The outlaw lowered to the right side of his saddle for cover and rode like hell to get away from the deadly hail of bullets. Jacques was riding up hard and turned to give chase. He was at least fifty yards behind the other rider and was pumping rounds at him as the man furtively shot back with his sidearm. The chase didn't last long; the deserter's horse put a front hoof into a prairie dog hole and fell forward head first, breaking his leg and throwing his rider through the air. The outlaw tried to break his fall with his hands out in front, but the momentum was too great. His head hit the ground, and his neck snapped as he rolled over more than several times before stopping. Jacques heard a shot behind him. He turned to look, and Roland was standing over his horse, lowering his rifle. Jacques rode up to the deserter's horse that was withering in agony on the ground. He did the same and put a round in the downed animal's head. He rode back and picked up his brother.

Jacques started walking his horse to return to the wagon train, but Roland stopped him and said they had to go back and search the dead men for ID and collect their weapons, or the Indians would have them. Two of the men had their names scratched on the back of their belt buckles, and the third had a scrap of paper in his shirt pocket with his name on it. The note also said that in the event of his death, he asked for burial in Tennessee. They gathered up all the guns, sabers, and knives. There were saddlebags on the dead horse; one contained a mail pouch filled with greenbacks and coins and jewelry, robber's loot. They stripped the saddles and piled their gatherings. Hans was driving up and had the leader's horse tied to the back of his wagon. Roland switched the saddles and rode off to gather the other horses. Hans and Jacques loaded the weapons and saddles and headed back to the trail; Eli was already moving on. That night would be a dry camp, and the next day, they arrived at the freshwater spring called Black Pool. The spring was the last safe water on the way to Fort Wise, and everyone drank heavily, and the water barrels were topped off.

Just after nightfall, the sound of wagons could be heard down by the river. The supply train was alert and waiting for them, the cracks of whips and the lowing oxen announcing their arrival long before they pulled into the light from the fires of the wagon train. The drivers pulled up to the small stream running down to the river from the spring and fell face-down into the clean water to drink. The oxen weren't interested; the animals must have drunk at the crossing several miles to the west where the trail branched on the Cimarron route to Santa Fe. Eli walked over to meet the leader of the wagon train. He was an Englishman; his name was Cornelius Jones. Eli brought him and his drivers back to his camp, knowing there would be leftovers from the evening meal.

Jones and his men were thankful for the food, and after they ate, the drivers headed back to their wagons to take care of the oxen. Cornelius stayed and had a woeful tale to tell about their crossing from Cimarron. The drought was horrendous. They lost oxen on the way and were attacked by Indians several times. They had lost several men and two wagons to the attacks and more than a dozen oxen to the drought. Two more men died of cholera, and they were without clean drinking water for two days. Cornelius knew some of his men must have drunk at the Arkansas River crossing, and he hoped the river was clean and didn't carry cholera or yellow fever. Suzette went to her medical supplies and retrieved enough quinine pills for Cornelius and his men. She handed them over with instructions and said to be sure to get more when they reached Fort Larned.

Eli and Cornelius talked into the night. Cornelius was full of news. Indian activity west of Santa Fe was increasing steadily. The route up from Cimarron was now treacherous. He didn't know why the Apache were this far east. He figured this might be his last trip. He would look for work on the trails farther north or even get a job with the railroad. He had been back and forth on the trail many times, and this was the first time he lost men, and it bothered him deeply. He finished up his dissertation with, "Son, If you stay out here long enough, the trail is going to get you. It is as harsh as it is long. Take my advice, finish your contract with the Army and find other work." As Cornelius walked back over to his camp, the Callahans sat in agreement. They already experienced enough violence on the trail to know the older man was right. They were going on to other work. They didn't know just what the other work would be. They were headed west to the land of opportunity. Roland joked, "Maybe I'll retire to San Francisco where I can lay naked in the cool fog every morning and eat fish for breakfast instead of buffalo. That's it! I'll buy a fishing boat." Everyone laughed.

Jacques and Roland took the girls up to the spring, where they could bathe in the dark. Most of the men were already naked at one time or another and had washed up with water from the stock barrels. The spring water was cold, but no one cared. It would be a long time going west with only the river water for quite a few more days. Eli gathered up his men and told them that until they reached the mountains, they would be boiling water every night to replenish the drinking water supply. No one was to drink from the river unless they boiled the water. It would take time, and it would slow them down a bit, but care had to be taken, or cholera or yellow fever would be stalking around, taking down his men. Eli finished up, "Indians, renegades, and deserters are bad enough. Let's keep it that way; we handle them routinely." The men laughed as they returned to their wagons. Everyone was glad they were on the "wet route" and not heading down to Cimarron on the shortcut.

Seven more days moving west and the tedium of the trail grew deeper with every mile. They passed the ruins of Fort Mann and Fort Atkinson, wishing the forts were still active. Army patrols weren't frequent but were welcome as they passed and shared whatever news they had. Keep moving, was the advice from every troop they encountered. An Overland Stage passed them on the twenty- seventh day and offered nothing more than a hello from the driver. Fort Wise would be their next contact with an Army post, and while Eli was averaging more than eighteen miles a day, it still seemed impossibly far to the Colorado border. The full moon came and passed, and the comfort of nights lit by moonlight was gone again. The tedium of the scenery weighed heavily on the morale of the drivers and their helpers. Every rise, every bend of the river, everything looked hopelessly the same. Eli knew everything came to an end. He just wanted to maintain his sanity until they finally reached the west end of the prairie.

The morning of the tenth day out from Fort Larned Eli announced, "We'll be in Colorado today. It won't be the end of the prairie, but it won't be Kansas anymore." Cheers went up from the men as the news circulated through the camp. The travels had been good. They saw small bands of Indians, but none resulted in armed conflicts. The day before, they took in an Army patrol who had been badly mauled by the Arapaho. The young lieutenant didn't lose any men, but he had seven seriously wounded. Eli had more than several empty supply wagons now, and Suzette turned them into hospitals and cared for the wounded. She extracted some arrow points and one musket ball and stitched wounds. All the men would live if the threat of infection didn't take them. The young lieutenant was Cody Barringer. He had a cut on his arm and waited to the last for Suzette's care. He was from the New Mexico Territory.

Suzette had a thousand questions about his home and how he came to be a lieutenant. The young man was quite taken with her and couldn't believe the good medical care he was getting in the improvised field hospital.

By noon, Eli knew they were in Colorado. They had crossed Kansas in thirty-two days. *Not a record but not bad for his first time as the wagon master*, he thought. Two more days and they would be in Fort Wise. He hoped they could keep up the pace and make it there as quickly as possible for the sake of the injured soldiers. The prairie still looked the same, but there was hope. They surely would see the mountains soon. Mountains meant no buffalo, and no buffalo meant no Indians, at least not the Plains Indians. He hoped his Indian troubles were over, at least till they got back into the Apache territory south and west of Santa Fe.

It was the middle of July; if all went well, he would be pulling into Fort Moore on the west coast by October. For now, he was anxious to get to Fort Wise. He knew reaching a destination would greatly bolster the morale of his supply train. He was already feeling uplifted, seeing the trace of green in the prairie grass. It wouldn't be long before the tedium of the Short Grass Prairie would be over, and the new challenge would be the mountains. He knew it would be different and more difficult. He was looking forward to the challenge. It couldn't be any harder than what they had already experienced. He hoped he was right as he fell asleep under the stars in eastern Colorado.

The next morning it was clear, and the sun rose bright and blinding on the eastern horizon. It had rained during the night, and while there were still clouds to the east, the western sky stretched out before them as far as the eye could see. The supply train was on the move early as usual, and by midday, they had already moved about fifteen miles. Suzette was riding scout on the north side of the trail away from the river. The land was nearly flat, but she was on the rise no more than twenty feet higher than the trail itself. She had Patches standing stock still and had her binoculars up to her eyes, scanning the horizon. Eli was watching her from the trail, concerned that she was farther out than she should be. He spurred his horse to an all-out run as Suzette flashed three times for a sighting and then two times to join up. She must have signaled to Jacques first because he was already riding hard to the north. Roland was in the middle of the train, checking the drivers when one of them pointed out at Eli riding away. Roland didn't see the signal but knew Eli was riding out to join up with Suzette. He spurred his horse and bolted out from the trail. Suzette kept flashing the signals like she was desperate to get their attention. Jacques reached her first, and Eli pulled up a moment later. "What's up?" Eli demanded.

"Let's wait for Roland; he'll be here in another minute." Roland rode up and pulled up short.

Suzette pointed to the northwest and said, "A mountaintop."

"No way," said Eli incredulous. Suzette handed him the binoculars, and Eli's jaw dropped open as he spotted the snowcapped peak in the distance. The base was blue, but the top was distinctively white; it was, without doubt, a mountain. They passed around the binoculars, and Eli said, "It has to be *Pikes Peak*. We are at least one hundred fifty miles from it, but it is a crystal clear day. We're not far from Fort Wise, but we won't get there today. Nobody cared they had seen a mountain; they had made it across the grassland wilderness of western Kansas; they were true pioneers, and they were unstoppable, Colorado was in sight.

Eli had Jacques and Suzette ride forward to find a campsite. They did just that and settled the supply train above a meander of the river where the water was running fast, and there was white water on rapids and the sound of the Arkansas River coming alive, fresh from the mountains. *The mountains* thought Suzette; *I have seen a mountain*. It was new, and it promised the long-awaited change of scenery after the endless pull across Kansas. Her last thought before falling asleep that night was wondering if she would be as tired of the mountains by the time they reached Los Angeles as she was of the prairie that seemed never to end. As sure as the sun would rise in the morning, she knew that all she had to do to find out was to keep going.

FORT WISE

Morning of the thirty-fifth day on the trail promised rain. Black thunderheads, already dropping rain, loomed to the southwest and were moving north into their track as the wagon train started onto the trail. Flashes of lightning brightened the dim light of the sunrise, and the wind kicked up and smelled like wet prairie grass. It was only a short way to Fort Wise, and all were excited to get there even if they had to slog through mud the last few miles. The closer they got to the mountains, the less the impact from the draught. The grass was trying to sprout, and the bushes along the rushes looked green and alive.

Roland was riding scout to the south, and Suzette was in the north position. They could see the thunderstorm was already crossing the trail, and lightning was hitting the ground at an alarming frequency. They stayed off the high ground and joined up on the trail as the first of the rain started to pelt them. They were both in ponchos and were looking back to the wide-eyed mules on the lead wagon. Eli was climbing into the driver's seat and taking the reins. Horatio had both hands on the brake ready to pull and hold it at the first sign of runaway mules. In less than a minute, the trail turned into their old enemy – mud. By the time the last wagon pulled through the wet trail, the mud would be more than a foot deep, churned into soup by the heavy wheels. It didn't matter; the fort was only a few miles ahead. They had spent days on end in the mud; this would be an easy go.

Roland and Suzette saw a large stone building up ahead. Visibility was poor, and they rode for the portal, thinking it was Fort Wise. The stone building looked more like a Scottish Castle with walls sixteen feet high. A sign over the portal read *Bent's New Fort,* and they could see that the stone wall was four feet thick as they rode through the portal into the yard and up to a hitching post in front of what appeared to be the headquarters of the fort. They knew they were in the wrong fort, but were already inside and wanted to look around. The rain was letting up, and a burly man walked out of a lean-to along the wall that was a blacksmith's shop by the look of it. The man wasn't nearly as large as their Uncle Rufus back home, but he had shoulders like a bull, and his nose was flattened, and teeth were missing. His appearance announced his professions; the big man was a blacksmith and a boxer. He didn't look or act friendly. He was staring at Suzette as she shucked off the poncho. His stare was lascivious, and he kept his eyes on Suzette as she and Roland dismounted and walked their horses to a hitching post in front of the headquarters.

"Well, look at the pretty vixen that fell out of the thunderhead," the big man said as he walked across the yard.

Roland stepped into his path, "Looking is fine, touching is dangerous. She has killed men for a lot less."

"And who are you?" The big man slurred, having difficulty articulating through broken teeth and scarred lips.

"I'm Roland Callahan, and this is my sister, Suzette." Roland's manner was easy, trying to open up a friendly dialog to sidetrack the blacksmith's lustful advance. The big man tried to step around, and Roland stepped into the big man's path again. Roland noticed that he was more battered up than he first appeared. He walked with a limp, and his jaw wasn't symmetrical like it had been broken one or more times and set poorly. His nose was even worse.

"I want to talk to the woman," the big man growled, acting like he was going to push Roland out of the way.

Suzette tried to diffuse what was shaping up to be a confrontation and said, "I can hear you just fine from where you are." She dropped her poncho to the ground and stood feet slightly apart and her hand on her revolver; the big man took a half step and pushed Roland out of the way. Suzette drew her Lefaucheux and raised it ready to shoot the big man between the eyes. "Best back off," Roland said quietly. "I told you she killed the last man who went after her."

The big man stopped but stood his ground, a hateful look spreading on his face, his fists clenching and unclenching at his sides. A weathered-looking man in his early fifties stepped out of the office behind them and stopped just under the porch out of the rain. He quickly summed up the situation and said, "Stand down, Jim. Save yourself for the fights tomorrow." He walked down into the mud and offered his hand to Roland, "I'm William Bent. That's Jim Swindlehurst. He is pretty good at shoeing horses, mules, and oxen, and fixing wagons, but his real love is fighting and molesting women. I've kept him out of jail since he was a teenager. There's a reward to anyone who can take him in the ring. I add twenty dollars to it every time he fights. It's up to over four-thousand dollars; he's been undefeated for a long time."

"I'm Roland Callahan, and this is my sister Suzette. You can see for yourself that she is dangerous. If Jim kept coming at her, she would have killed him. You better keep him on a leash if you want to keep him alive." Swindlehurst snarled, and he turned red in the face and then purple. Roland thought he was going to foam at the mouth, but then Bent stepped between him and Suzette, and the blacksmith backed down.

Bent pursed his lips, "He has that problem. That's why I keep him here. Notice there aren't any Indian women inside the fort. That's because of Jim. I would send him back east to fight before he is too old, but he would be in jail in a heartbeat or even dead. They call him *Bent's Brawler*. You're a big lad; you interested in a fight? I would pay in gold if you could beat him, but I warn you, the fighting is bare knuckles, and it is brutal. There are matches over at Fort Wise tomorrow. There is a signup roster over there on the door of the fort, and my agent, Chester Landstrom, should be in the yard, putting up the ring and taking bets. The prize money is substantial."

"I'll think about it." The supply train was passing the front of Bent's Fort. "We have a delivery for Fort Wise. Maybe we'll stay around for some repairs and the fights."

Roland rolled up and stowed their ponchos in the saddlebags, but Suzette stood stock still with her gun held steady, pointed at Swindlehurst. She kept her gun out as she deftly mounted her horse and rode out of the portal. All the while, *Big Jim, Bent's Brawler*, stared at Suzette. Bent was admonishing the big man as Roland rode out behind his sister. They joined Eli at the lead wagon, and Roland told him they had met the legendary William Bent and his blacksmith. "It seems there might be another problem with a Suzette admirer. The blacksmith has a problem controlling himself around women. He's big and looks like he's been in the ring a long time."

"We need to stop for repairs, and there is always a passel of mules to shoe after a mud bath. I'll send some work up there. That will keep them busy for a while."

The post commander was Colonel Herman D. Schultz. He was glad to see the supply train. He commented that Eli was young to be a wagon master, but when Eli told him that Armstrong had drunk himself to death, he huffed and said, "Well, you must be a good replacement because you're here two days ahead of schedule. Have your drivers form up their camp out there below the trail. You'll see some Indians, but they are peaceful and tend our gardens. Others come and go all the time to trade with Bent; they are also friendly for the most part. By the way, the Army has made Bent an offer to lease his fort. We are waiting for him to make up his mind, but I hope to take over his castle here shortly. I don't know what the Army will do with it, but I will have to arm a garrison up there to keep it secure till the powers-to-be make up their mind. Did Bent ask you about taking freight to Santa Fe?"

"No, he didn't, but I haven't talked to him yet. Roland and Suzette pulled in there by mistake during the heavy rain. They met Bent and his blacksmith. They left in a hurry because the blacksmith seemed to fixate on Suzette."

"Humph! The blacksmith, he's a bad 'un. He fancies himself a boxer, but the truth is he is just big, tough, and mean. He has a problem controlling himself around women. My men try to whip Swindelherst every time Bent sponsors a fight. He claims he'll pay the man who can beat his *Brawler* in gold. I imagine he could; he has made a fortune out here trading for buffalo hides with the Indians and selling them back east for a healthy profit. Some say his *castle* is full of gold and silver. I suppose he is looking for safe transport to send it east or down into Mexico so he can retire. I see him from time to time, mostly when he comes to get his boxer out of the stockade."

"I'll have some wagons sent up there for repairs, and while we are here, we'll keep a guard on Suzette. We have had this problem before. If the blacksmith attacks her, she will kill him. It might be hard doing business with Bent if that happens."

Schultz smiled sadly, "It wouldn't be a bad thing if Swindlehurst were dead. My wife won't live here with me because of him. There's a history there; I'll tell you more tonight after dinner. Let's go over the manifest. I'm anxious to get the rifles into the armory, and I'm sure that by now, you are ready to lighten your load."

Fort Wise was big, but it wasn't much for appearance. Most of the soldier's barracks were crude adobe buildings, side by side with the tops fortified as revetments to make an outer line of defense around the east, north, and west sides of the fort. The south side faced the river. The interior yard was nearly a hundred yards square, and there was a more substantial fortification on the north side where the headquarters, armory, and storehouses were laid out around a small courtyard. There was a well at the edge of the parade field with a windmill lifting water to a tank on a tower. A track of the Santa Fe Trail cut through the north end in front of the fortification. There were some Indian teepees outside the lines of adobe soldier's quarters. Compared to Bent's Fort, Fort Wise looked shabby like only a temporary site, built with haste, and with only local materials and a skimpy budget.

Eli and his brothers walked around the fort after the wagon train set up camp across the trail from the fort. There was an open flat there above the river. They could look across well-tended gardens and see Bent's fort, less than a mile away. Soldiers with some Indian workers were putting up a boxing ring in the middle of the parade field. There was a notice for the fight on the heavy doors of the fortification. Bent's prize money for anyone who could take his *Brawler* was up to over four thousand dollars. Eli commented that there would be a lot of takers with a pot so large. There were five soldiers already signed up to fight. There was a huckster out on the parade field taking bets and making odds on the prospective challengers. Roland commented, "That must be Landstrom, Bent's agent." Landstrom had a chalkboard next to the ring, where he posted odds and a safe where bet money was locked up until time for the payouts. A big soldier was working on the ring. He was an easterner talking with a Boston accent and looked like he had been in the ring before. He was the Army favorite; odds on him were a low two-to-one. Odds on the other entrants ranged from five to twenty-to-one. It seemed that Bent knew how to maximize his profits for the trouble of keeping his *Brawler* in hand.

Suzette didn't care that the fort wasn't fancy. She was offered a room in the officer's quarters and guaranteed the privacy of a hot bath in her room. She couldn't wait. She went out to collect up Maria, neither of them had a decent bath since the swim in the Black Pool. That seemed like hundreds of miles and ages ago. She would keep Maria with her until they were well out of the reach of Swindlehurst. As Mr. Sue walked them back through the parade field, Suzette was explaining the ring and the odds board to Maria in Spanish. There were some Mexicans in the parade field that overheard Suzette speaking Spanish, and they tried to enlist Suzette as their translator. They had issues with the post commander and didn't trust the Army interpreter. She put them off till later when she and Colonel Schultz would be available.

When they reached the doors of the fortification, Suzette was shocked to see her mild-mannered brother Roland's name on the bottom of the signup roster for the fight. There was room on the roster for seven fighters, Roland would be number six. Roland was a good boxer, and he was undefeated back at the school in Independence and up at Fort Leavenworth. However, there they fought with gloves, very strict rules, and a referee with authority to punish transgressions. She felt terrified for her brother. *What was he thinking? He doesn't need the money*, was raging through her head as she looked for him around the parade field. Hans was nearby and told her that Roland took six wagons up to Bent's Fort for repairs. Suzette would talk to him later. The allure of hot water and clean clothes was calling. She shook her head and put her arm around Maria and went into the fortification to find her room in the officer's quarters. On the way, she explained to Maria in Spanish the foolishness of men and their raging hormones. It was time Maria understood everything about men and women for her protection. She would loan Maria her barrette until they were well away from Fort Wise.

Roland rode over to Fort Bent and hitched his horse to the rail in front of the office. He walked inside and saw Bent sitting behind his desk, negotiating with two Arapaho. Bent was haggling over buffalo hides that were stacked next to a hide-press outside, waiting for word that the deal was final. Bent was rattling on in the Indian's native language. It was obvious he had issues with what they were demanding for payment. Back and forth, the bickering went on for more than ten minutes. Finally finished, the Indians both nodded their heads, and Bent filled out a script for credit at his store and pushed it across the desk. The Indians left, but their body odor stayed behind, and Roland suggested that Bent go out and look at the wagons he brought for repair. Bent signaled his blacksmith to join him as they walked to the portal.

All six wagons needed minor repairs to the iron parts of the wheel brakes, and there were over a dozen wheels loaded into the wagons that needed new steel rims. Bent drove a hard bargain, but Roland had the upper hand in that they had a blacksmith in their wagon train. The work he brought Bent was a backlog, and they would like to complete it before leaving out on the trail, but it wasn't urgent. Bent conferred with *Big Jim* and finally settled on completing all the work for sixty dollars. He wanted payment in advance, but Roland refused and wouldn't pay until he could see that Swindlehurst completed the work to his satisfaction. Bent relented, but his blacksmith was angry that Roland had raised a challenge to the quality of his work. Bent walked back into his fort, but the blacksmith stayed. The drivers were unhitching the mules and would walk them back to their camp.

Swindlehurst directed his anger in a different direction. "Where is your sister?" He snarled his question.

"Well out of your reach," Roland answered. "By the way, I signed up on the roster for the fight. You'll get the chance to whip up on me tomorrow. Suzette is sure to be there, you can impress her with your prowess, but I doubt you will win."

"I'll smash you," was all the big man had to offer, and he held up a clenched fist the size of a ham to emphasize his point. Roland smiled at him; his fist wasn't much smaller. He walked back into the fort to retrieve his horse and ride back to the camp. Swindlehurst was yelling at some Indians to unload the wagon wheels and take them into the forge. He was pulling the first wagon for repairs into the fort by himself, obviously trying to impress the younger man with his shear strength. "I'll kill you," was his parting remark.

"Make sure you do a good job on the wagons, asshole," Roland said, touching his hat brim with two fingers and then flicking them out forward in a gesture of dismissal. Roland wanted to ire the big man as much as possible. The madder he was stepping into the ring, the better. Rage alone seldom won a fight. His father had taught his boys well. A fistfight was the last of Roland's worries; he too was undefeated in the ring, and he had fought experienced men from Fort Leavenworth and their sons. He was willing to take a beating to teach the blacksmith a lesson, and he would give the prize money to Maria's grandparents if he won. He hoped Suzette wouldn't think he was fighting to protect her virtue. However, that would be an extra benefit to winning. He was sure his siblings would think he was crazy as he rode the short distance back to his camp. He was right; Eli and Jacques were waiting for him, and it was obvious that a lecture from his brothers was imminent.

"Roland, you're the best boxer of the three of us, but what if you get hurt beyond repair?"

"You know I can take care of myself. This man is old for a boxer, and he's more than just past his prime; he's banged up pretty bad. I may not win, but I am going to hurt him a good deal before I go down."

Eli said, "He was ready to attack Suzette right in front of you over at Bent's. You told me she held her revolver on him all the time she was there."

Roland added, "*Bent's Brawler* is a berserker. He can't control himself; he should be no problem in the ring."

"Nonetheless, he is famous for putting men down with one punch. Remember Uncle Rufus's story of killing the man in Kingston with one punch that broke the man's neck?"

"All the time, Rufus and I sparred; he was never able to land one of those devastating punches. Big men can be strong, but they are slower and easier to hit. Look, he may have forty or more pounds on me, but I have more than twenty years to his better, and I know I am twice as fast. I am going to teach that son-of-a-bitch a lesson he won't forget, and if I win, Bent will probably disown him. He wouldn't last a minute out in the world. He would be hung or killed for his sexual aggression."

Eli could see that his brother was determined. "I am going to spread some rumors over at the fort that you just lost your mind when you signed up to fight. I'll let a few soldiers know that you are not very good at it at all. You just thought the money would be nice to spend on harlots in San Francisco or something. It should increase the odds. I'll bet a hundred dollars on you."

They laughed to lighten the mood. Jacques put his arm around his twin and said, "I know you can beat him but watch out; he'll probably fight dirty if he thinks he's about to lose. You won't be wearing a cup and a helmet like back at mom's school."

"There weren't cups and helmets at Leavenworth, and I did good enough there too." They walked over to the fort to check the odds on Roland. They stood at four-to-one, but after another hour, they were up to twelve, and another hour after that, they were up to twenty. The power of gossip in an Army Camp was useful when needed.

Suzette and Maria were in the courtyard of the fortification in front of Colonel Schultz's office. Suzette had taken off Maria's splint before her bath, and the young girl was walking carefully without it. Maria had Suzette's barrette and was practicing on a bayonet dummy, thrusting the stiletto end of the barrette up through the bottom of the dummy's chin. Suzette was instructing in Spanish, "I want you to stand like this and strike with enough force to knock this dummy's head off. Stab like you're throwing a punch; lead with your hip. Remember, if you fail, you will be raped or even killed. It won't be a time to be girl-like. Push that pin into his brain like an angry-grown woman, and you will survive." Maria did just that. She jabbed upward as if landing an uppercut to the chin. The stiletto penetrated just in front of the throat, and the head flew off and rolled to a stop ten feet behind the dummy.

"That's more like it," said Colonel Schultz from the porch of the headquarters. "The trail is no place for an unarmed girl."

Roland and Jacques walked the women out through the doors of the fortification. Suzette looked over at the sign-up roster and moaned. "Look what you started." She punched Roland in the arm and pointed at the roster. Mr. Sue had signed up in the seventh spot. They walked over to the odds board. Roland was up to twenty-five. Odds didn't appear yet for Mr. Sue. Roland asked Bent's agent why there was nothing on Mr. Sue. Landstrom was a small thin man and looked like a badger sitting while wearing a brown leather vest and a brown derby on his head. "Haven't met him yet," the badger replied in a high voice. He took off his hat to wipe his brow, and his bald head shined like a mirror sweating in the hot, humid air.

Roland said, "We'll send him over – that is if we can't talk him out of it. He's a little twerp; I have beat the crap out of him several times myself to keep the *little chink* in line." Mr. Sue wasn't that small, but he was at least eighty pounds lighter than *The Brawler*. Roland was doing his best to up the odds. Eli chuckled, but he hoped Swindlehurst wouldn't make it as far as Mr. Sue. They walked the short distance to their camp, to talk to Mr. Sue, but Mr. Sue wasn't in the camp. The driver of his chuckwagon told them that Mr. Sue was down by the river. Roland walked over and looked down the bluff. Mr. Sue was sitting cross-legged on a rock in the river. He was naked, just staring at the water, the very picture of calm and serenity. Roland decided to wait until he came back up to the camp rather than disturb his meditation.

Horatio came running up to him, excited, "Mr. Sue signed up for the fight, and the odds are already up to forty-to-one. Should I put my money on you or him?"

"I would bet on me. I intend to win. I don't want Mr. Sue to fight, and I will do everything I can to whip that big bastard, so he doesn't have to." Horatio hurried off to put five dollars down on Roland before the bookmaker closed up shop for the day.

The Callahans and Maria sat with Colonel Schultz and his officers for dinner. There were fresh venison tenderloins and fresh vegetables from the fort's gardens. Schultz had a bottle of light red wine for the ladies and a quart bottle of Callahan whiskey for the men. The conversation was light but finally got around to two subjects that had to be brought up, which seemingly everyone was reluctant to discuss. Eli asked what had happened between Swindlehurst and the Colonel's wife.

"My wife's name is Martha; she is a doctor in her own right. Swindlehurst was constantly harassing her for sex and even came close to raping her several times. I had him in the stockade on many occasions and came close to hanging him once. Jailing him was all the law, and the military code would allow. It made me look weak in front of the men. They expected me to kill him. Martha finally took the stage back to Independence so that no more incidents would occur. The men sorely miss having a doctor at the fort. I miss her too. Say, speaking of Independence, I suspect that you are the Callahans of *Callahan Meadows*." Schultz was holding up the whiskey bottle, pointing at the label. "What are you doing on the trail?" It was obvious the Colonel wanted to change the subject.

Eli took the lead, "The commander at Leavenworth convinced our mother that we should be in the Army Supply Service and far out west when war with the southern states breaks out. From what we have seen on the trail, it would probably be safer somewhere on the front lines in Virginia." The Army men laughed in agreement. "Suzette here is just running away from our grandmother. Our father and mother died in a tornado just before we left. That was tragic, but the trail looked a lot better than staying behind. None of us are interested in making whiskey, and Missouri is going to be ripped apart when the war starts. Roland wants to go to San Francisco and buy a fishing boat, or maybe he will go back east and become the heavyweight bare-knuckles champ. Jacques is going to join the Army when we get to Fort Moore, and I suspect Suzette will join up with a wild-west show; that is if she survives meeting up with her grandmother again. Grandma is probably on a clipper headed around the horn by now. She'll be waiting for us in California."

"I salute you," Schultz and his officers stood for the toast. "You could sit out the war in Europe on a warm beach. But you are out here in the Supply Service helping to preserve the Union. To the Callahans."

"To the Callahans."

The bottle was empty, but Roland said, "Not to worry, I have a keg of Callahan's finest over in Mr. Sue's chuck wagon. I was thinking of sending it up to Bent's fort to see if Swindlehurst would show up tomorrow afternoon with a hangover, but you can put it to much better use."

The dinner wound down; the Army officers left for their evening rounds, and Suzette and Maria retired to their room. Eli and his brothers walked back to their camp, and Roland had some hands take the keg of whiskey over to the fort. Eli reduced the guards to just two, one on the east and one on the west to guard the approaches from the trail. Colonel Schultz extended his guard perimeter to include the supply train, and everyone slept easy that night, everyone but Roland and Mr. Sue.

Roland was exercising and dancing around a fire pit, jabbing at imaginary opponents in the empty air. Mr. Sue had on what looked like black pajamas with light slippers on his feet. His exercise was the same set of movements he did every morning, but at the end of each move his arms or a foot would strike out lightning fast, so fast that the arms of his light tunic would make swishing noises in the air. After a while, both men were satisfied that they were ready for tomorrow and what it would bring. Jacques encouraged them to rest. *Bent's Brawler* was big and strong, and he wouldn't go down easy, "You won't be any good if you are sleepy." The two contestants agreed and turned in. They still didn't sleep as easy as the rest of the camp.

THE FIGHT

The next morning, the camp awoke to the smell of bacon wafting through the air. Eli thought, *a sure sign of civilization. We are getting there.* Roland and Mr. Sue were up with the cooks and sat around their fire ring, discussing the fight and their opponent. Eli joined them and opted for a cup of strong coffee before Mr. Sue's Chinese cup of soup. He needed to wake up and clear his head. Bent had something on his mind to ship and had sent Eli a note the night before asking to see him early that morning. Mr. Sue's helper was cooking pancakes, and Eli wouldn't go up to Bent's fort until he ate his fill.

Over in the fort, Suzette and Maria were up early and joined Colonel Schultz in the officer's mess for breakfast. Suzette asked the Colonel about the fight, the rules, and if there was a doctor to take care of the injured. "We don't have a doctor per se. We have a vet for the horses, and he serves as the "*cut man*" for both opponents.

Suzette was translating for Maria, and then she asked, "What's a *cut man*?"

"It's just how it sounds. The cut man is there to stop the bleeding when a boxer gets cut. If he can't stop it within three minutes, the referees stop the fight, and the referees award the fight to the cut boxer's opponent."

"Can I be Roland's *cutman*?"

"You can be that and more. You can come to the weigh-in and do the physical examinations. Your brother told me you stitched yourself up after a gunfight in Council Grove. Is that true?"

"I'm not going to show you my scar to prove it, but yes, it's true."

Colonel Schultz asked how old Suzette was. Suzette didn't have to lie about her age. She told Colonel Schultz that she was fourteen. She hoped that the major didn't put it together that Roland wasn't eighteen. It would be an easy way to get him out of the fight, but it also might get the twins ousted from the Army Supply Service. The Colonel let it pass. If he knew, he wasn't saying anything, and he had a growing admiration and respect for Suzette. It was obvious that he missed his wife.

Schultz went over the rest of the rules. Like a teacher, he carried on, "There are three rounds per bout, each three minutes long. There is a one-minute rest in between rounds. There are two referees. One is always Bent's accountant, a shill named Vincent Ronkainen. The other will be an Army Sergeant named Steve Brady. They alternate between rounds. The one in the ring has the final word, but he can confer with the other referee to clarify an issue if he missed something. Both referees name the winner of a round after each round is over; two out of three rounds and the bout awards to the winning boxer. The rest of the rules are pretty straightforward; no hitting below the belt, no rabbit punching, no kicking, biting or scraping with the nails, and a few other items like no elbow smashes or head butts. Most of Swindlehurst's fights are over in one round, sometimes in seconds with one massive blow. That's why Bent puts up the roster with room for seven opponents. With luck, my men will do better this time around, and Swindlehurst will tire by the time he gets to your brother. By the way, who is this Mr. Sue from the supply train?"

Suzette remembered the soldier at the Little Arkansas Crossing. She thought it best to portray Mr. Sue as a weakling rather than a secret weapon. "He's a cook!" Suzette said incredulously. "I hope he has sense enough to walk into the ring and lay down to end the fight. Swindlehurst could kill him."

Colonel Schultz just muttered a humph, but several of the lower-ranking officers dwelt on every word Suzette said. Nothing was more important that day than intel about the pugilists, especially the two from the Army Supply Train. After breakfast, Jacques was waiting for Suzette and Maria at the doors of the fortification. They walked over to the ring. It was impressive, built out of one-inch ropes held fast to four steel posts buried in the ground. The ring was twenty-four feet square, just like the regulation rings back east, but there were only two ropes instead of four. The top one was four feet off the ground, and the bottom one was one foot below that. Suzette told Maria that a regulation ring would have four ropes. Like the fort, the ring suffered a skimpy budget. Soldiers were carrying over some makeshift bleachers and setting them down ten feet outside of the ropes. On the west side, a platoon of soldiers was putting up a reviewing stand. Suzette assumed that was for the Post Commander and his officers. Landstrom was setting up his odds board and getting ready to open shop. There was still a lot of money out there in the Army payroll. These men didn't have anywhere to spend it; most just had the paymaster keep their money for them. The fights were a big attraction and good for their morale, not to mention a pathway to a fortune if someone could beat *Bent's Brawler*.

Suzette walked up to the bookmaker. "Mr. Landstrom ----."

Landstrom cut her off, "Honey, you can call me Chester; what can I do for you?"

Suzette ignored the comment even though she wanted to knock the little weasel on his ass. "I want to put down a bet on my brother." Maria heard the word brother and turned Suzette away from the little man and shook her head no. She had two silver dollars of her own money, and she put them down on Mr. Sue's square. Suzette looked over to make sure Jacques was far enough away not to see what she was about to do. Suzette felt a lot of loyalty to Roland, but she took five gold double eagles out of a pouch on the back of her holster and put them down on Mr. Sue.

Landstrom laughed and said, "You ladies must be new to this game. I will be more than happy to take your money." He noted the bets in his logbook and wrote out and signed two chits and handed them over to Suzette. Suzette gave Maria hers and then read her own. It had Mr. Sue – one hundred dollars, and Chester W. Landstrom's signature appeared at the bottom. Landstrom was opening the safe to deposit their money as the girls turned and walked away. There was a grin on his face; there had never been a one hundred dollar bet in all the years Big Jim had been fighting. Suzette wasn't going to tell her brothers she bet on Mr. Sue. Maria was exuberant, though; she expected to be rich beyond her wildest dreams. Suzette hoped that was true, even though that meant Roland would have to lose his fight. She put the chit in the pocket of her trousers; she thought it best to keep the bet to herself for if and when it would be time to collect.

The morning wore on. Eli went over to Bent's fort to see what Bent wanted to talk about before the fights. Swindlehurst was at his forge, hammering and cursing. It looked like he was on the last of the wagon wheels, and having a hard time starting the steel rim over the wooden rim. *Far too impatient,* Eli thought, *the rim isn't hot enough.* Eli hoped the big man's inpatients carried over into the ring. It would be good for Roland if Swindlehurst joined the fight eager for a quick knockout.

Eli walked into Bent's office. "I'm glad you're here; I have a problem." Eli waited for the man to go on. "I have over eight hundred pounds of silver and another three tons of high-grade silver ore. I want you to take it to Santa Fe and deposit it there in the Territorial Bank. "

Eli would have room in the wagons since his men were unloading more than half of the remaining arms into the Fort Wise armory. He wasn't sure about the regulations concerning him carrying such a valuable shipment for a civilian. He paused as if he was thinking for some effect and asked, "How much will you pay?"

"Ten percent for the full delivery to the bank. I'll send Landstrom with you, and he will pay you in Santa Fe."

"I'll ask Colonel Schultz about this. If he approves, I will be back up with my wagon."

Bent wasn't keen on the Colonel knowing how much silver he had, but he agreed. Eli left the office and looked over the wagon wheels. He told Swindlehurst, "My brother will be up to inspect the wagons, but the wheels look good." With that, Eli rode down to Fort Wise, hoping that the Colonel was free to see him. He found the Colonel in his office with Suzette and three Mexicans locked in a heated argument. A Hispanic corporal was standing to the side of the desk; *he must be the Colonel's interpreter,* Eli thought to himself as he stood against the back wall to wait his turn. Suzette was sitting with the Mexicans. He heard Bent's name several times as the Mexicans became more agitated and impatient.

Suzette finally turned to Schultz and said, "They are going to kill Bent if he doesn't pay up. Bent owes them more than a hundred dollars on silver bars that they brought down here to trade. Bent says the bars aren't pure and that he paid them fairly for the silver content. These men say the bars are pure, and they want payment in full. There is some other problem with the payment I don't quite understand."

Schultz was quiet and considered his dilemma before he spoke. "This isn't my problem, but they can't kill Bent, or I will hunt them down and hang them." He fell silent again and sat looking at his hands on the top of his desk while Suzette translated. When she finished with the last sentence, Schultz looked up at his translator, who nodded that Suzette translated accurately. The Mexicans sat quietly, waiting, but they were extremely unhappy. Finally, Colonel Schultz gave his corporal an order, "Send for Bent and have him bring the silver in question with him." Suzette told the three men what the Colonel had said, and they nodded in approval.

The corporal hurried off to send a rider up to get Bent, and Eli stepped forward and asked, "Could I have a minute of your time?" Schultz seemed eager for a reason to ask the three men waiting for Bent to leave for a while and made a shooing motion with his hand to get them to wait outside the door. Suzette explained in Spanish that her brother had some private business with the Colonel, and the three men got up, nodded respectfully to the Colonel and Suzette, and left.

Eli laid out Bent's proposal and asked if he could transport Bent's silver within Army Regulations. Schultz was quick to answer. "Not normally, but I can and will authorize it. Maybe if Bent can get his money out of here, he will finally vacate the fort so we can take over. I'll tell him that you can do it; don't mention your payment to the manager at the Territorial Bank. That will be between you, me, and Bent."

Eli thanked the Colonel and gathered up Suzette for a stroll around the parade field. Maria was waiting at the door of the fortification. She was excited with a look of anticipation on her face like something was about to happen. "What's going on?" Suzette asked.

Maria smiled and pointed. Mr. Sue and the Germans were walking onto the parade field. Mr. Sue was in his black pajamas with the light slippers on his feet. He looked comical in the middle of the rough-looking Germans. They were obviously up to something. Hans smiled at Suzette and held a finger up to his lips and raised his eyebrows with a boyish look that said it all; they were up to some mischief. Mr. Sue and the Germans walked over where they were sure Bent's weasel would see them, but not close enough to grab his attention too easily. Mr. Sue started yelling in Chinese at Hans. The Germans formed a circle around Mr. Sue and started pushing him back and forth between them. Mr. Sue yelled louder, now everyone on the parade field was looking at the confrontation. Finally, Hans yelled something at Mr. Sue in German and pushed him down into the dust. All six of the Germans laughed, and one of them even spat on Mr. Sue as they walked off. Mr. Sue got up and was barking in Chinese. From the tone of his voice, everyone could tell he was cursing as he brushed the dirt off his clothes.

Mr. Sue walked over to Landstrom's table and put down two silver dollars on his square. He poked his thumb into his chest and grunted, "Sue." Landstrom wrote out his chit for the bet and handed it to Mr. Sue, who looked at it, then he started talking in Chinese, first calmly them more excitedly. He started waving his arms around and yelling at Landstrom. When he leaned over the table to yell right in Landstrom's face, Landstrom snapped. He got up and pushed Mr. Sue back against the ropes. Mr. Sue kept yelling and shaking his fist in Landstrom's face. Finally, the weasel had enough. He hit Mr. Sue in the jaw with a right cross, and Mr. Sue went down. Suzette started to run over, but Maria grabbed her arm and held her back. Mr. Sue stayed down for more than a minute like he was knocked out. Landstrom was standing over him with his fists doubled up on his hips. Mr. Sue came to and pulled himself up the ropes and just stood there for another minute hanging over the top rope before he staggered off back to the camp, not saying another word. Landstrom was shaking his head in disbelief with a look of disgust on his face, then he opened a drawer in his table and took out a piece of chalk and wrote 100 after Mr. Sue's name on the odds board.

Maria giggled, and Eli and Suzette were astounded that Mr. Sue and the Germans could pull this off considering the language barrier between them. Either the Germans were doing better on their English lessons than Suzette thought, or Mr. Sue was hiding the fact that he could speak German. Maria was happier than Suzette had ever seen her, and the young girl said, "Vamos a ser muy rico."

"What did she say?" Eli asked.

"We're going to be very rich." Eli felt like the dumbest man in town. A lot was going on here, and he didn't understand any of it.

"Are you telling me that Maria bet on Mr. Sue?"

"She did, and so did I. You got a couple of dollars?" Eli had two greenbacks in his pocket; he gave them to Suzette. Suzette gave them to Maria and told her to wait a while before upping her bet. They could see Bent driving over on a buckboard pulled by a grey dapple mare. "Let's go back to the office," she said as she took Eli's arm to turn him back to the fortification.

"How much did you bet on Mr. Sue?"

Suzette stopped and answered with righteous indignation in her voice, "None of your business."

"Well, it doesn't matter. If Roland beats Swindlehurst, Mr. Sue won't have to fight. You will get your money back. There's Bent, and he's got his blacksmith with him; let's get back over to the office."

They walked into Colonel Schultz's office, and this time, they sat in the chairs in front of the desk. The three Mexicans were standing to the right side with their backs to the wall. Eli thought that was odd, but then he saw one of the Mexicans remove the strap that held his sidearm in place in its holster. They wanted to be ready with their weapons just in case things went south with Bent. The Colonel also noticed the small but significant move and looked at Suzette and told her, "Tell them there will be no gunplay."

Bent came in with Swindlehurst, who had a small wood crate that looked heavy but which he handled easily. Swindlehurst put the crate down on the desk and then fixed his gaze on Suzette. Now it was Suzette's turn to be cautious. She drew her Lefaucheux and laid it across her lap, cocked it, and met Swindlehurst's gaze until he backed down. The blacksmith took the lid off the crate and withdrew four silver bars. Each one was perfectly shaped and stamped 1,000, with the numbers perfectly centered on the top of the bar. The bars didn't bear a smelter stamp, a lot number, or a bar number, but it was obvious they were poured by a professional, and their beautiful sheen and rich silver color spoke well of their purity.

One of the Mexicans stepped forward with a pouch and took out three bundles of twenty-dollar bills and one of Bent's notes that gave credit in his store for an additional eight hundred dollars. Two of the bundles of the twenties were bills issued by *The Bank of the United States,* and the third was bills issued by *The Mississippi and Alabama Railroad Company*. He placed the bundles neatly next to the stack of silver bars but held up the note and showed it to the Colonel and then turned and showed it to Eli and Suzette. Bent sat down in the third chair, and *Big Jim* leaned to the side against the wall opposite the Mexicans.

Eli and Suzette sized up the problem immediately. The amount paid by Bent seemed fair, but the Mexicans had no use for the eight hundred credits at Bent's store. They wanted their payment in money they could spend in Colorado, and didn't want to travel to the bank in Santa Fe to convert the bars to currency. Eli had Suzette confirm that they were correct, which she did after a short apology for not understanding the issue in the first place. The Mexicans were shaking their heads yes, enthusiastically, and with a degree of relief.

Eli spoke up, "I have a suggestion. These men don't want the eight hundred dollars of credit. They want to go back to Colorado with money they can spend there, not here. Bent, you should give them back their silver, they will give you back your money, and I will buy the silver and pay them right now with double eagles."

"Where would you come up with thirty-eight hundred dollars in gold?"

"That's not any of your business, Mr. Bent. Do you want to end this or not?"

Bent considered for a moment and then stood up and took his money off the table. He turned to leave, but Colonel Schultz asked him to wait a moment. Suzette explained the deal to the Mexicans, and they left with their silver and Ely to go over to the supply train for payment. Schultz explained to Bent, "This young woman is the closest we have for a doctor at this moment. She is going to examine the boxers before the fight and confirm that they are fit and ready to fight. Since your man is already here, I want him examined now. There will be several guards on him to make sure he behaves, and he better. I understand that she is deadly, and Jim will die if he touches her."

Jim let out a loud guffaw, grabbed his crouch, and slurred, "I'm readier than you could ever imagine."

Suzette was ready to raise her gun, but she didn't have to. Colonel Schultz had been holding his Colt .44 under his desk all through the negotiation with the Mexicans. Now he was holding it on the boxer with a cold, steely look and a steady hand. Schultz said, "Take him to the clinic, and if he gets himself killed and can't make the scratch, I'll make you forfeit and pay all the bets. Also, I authorized Callahan to take your silver to Santa Fe. Now get out of here."

Bent led his man out and over to the infirmary. When Suzette and Schultz stepped out, Hans and the rest of the Germans fell in around her and followed them to the clinic. They went in first and leveled their rifles at Bent and Swindlehurst. Suzette entered with Schultz and said, "They don't speak English, so they will shoot at the first sign of trouble. You," she said, pointing at Jim, "take off your shirt and sit down here." She pushed a straight back chair into the middle of the floor. The big man obeyed, looking from barrel to barrel, probably wondering which one would kill him if he touched the girl.

"Is this necessary?" Bent asked with impatience.

"Yes," Schultz answered. "Yes, if it was the exam you are referring to or the guns."

Suzette stood in front of Jim and had him turn his head to the right. She swung her left hand up as if she was going to slap him in the face, and the big man didn't flinch. She had him turn his head to the left and repeated the feigned slap with her right hand, and Jim flinched. "As I thought, you are blind in your right eye." She listened to his heart, "You also have a heart murmur. Are you sure you want to fight?"

"Fighting is my life." Suzette didn't quite know all that he meant by that statement but, looked at Bent and wondered if the merchant would pull Jim out if she declared him unfit to fight. The rest of Jim, reflexes, and muscle tone, checked out fine. She weighed him, two hundred fifty-five pounds. She figured he had thirty-five pounds on Roland and a lot more than that on Mr. Sue.

"I recommend that you quit fighting, Jim, and save your other eye for the rest of your life. You'll need that eye to learn another trade. Your heart could get worse, and you won't be able to work as a blacksmith anymore. I can only recommend; I don't have the authority to stop you or I would." Suzette looked at Schultz. He had never been faced with this problem before, and he just shrugged. Suzette finished up, "You can get your shirt back on and go." Hans and his men followed Jim out of the clinic.

Bent stayed behind and had some questions. "What causes a heart murmur, and how serious is it?"

"I don't know what caused it; it could have been a fight injury or an infection that attacked his heart valves. A murmur occurs when one of the heart valves doesn't seal completely and leaks as the heart contracts. It isn't usually fatal in itself, but it could be the forerunner of a much more serious problem. I know you make a lot of money on the fights, but if you want to keep him alive, you should back off and get him to quit."

"He probably would like nothing better than to die in a championship fight and truth be told; the world would be better off if he were gone. He'll make the scratch; if you are smart, you will get your brother to back off." With that, Bent donned his bowler and left the clinic. He headed back to his fort to load up the silver in Eli's wagon.

The rest of the boxers were lined up outside of the clinic, Roland and Mr. Sue joined the line well after Jim had left through the doors of the fortification. One by one, Suzette examined the young men. All of them were in excellent physical condition as compared to Jim. Roland weighed in at two hundred twenty pounds on the dot. He hadn't gained or lost even an ounce since his last fight in Independence. Mr. Sue was a different story. He was older, of course, but his body was all well-toned muscle and sinew like wire. "How old are you?" Suzette asked as she listened to his heart.

"Forty-Six," was his quiet reply.

From his physique, it was obvious he wasn't past his prime. Suzette said, "You're good to go." She wrote his weight down on the chart for the fight statistics, one hundred eighty pounds. She checked him off in the *passed* column. The only one she failed was Jim Swindlehurst. She didn't think Bent or Jim would pay any attention to her findings. After all, she wasn't a real doctor, and she was the sister of one of the opponents. She knew everyone would look upon her exam result as biased.

The afternoon wore on. Eli returned from Bent's Fort with his wagon heavily loaded with silver bars and bags of high-grade silver ore. Bent, Big Jim, and a man Suzette hadn't seen before rode down on Bent's buckboard behind him. Bent pulled up close to the ring, and Eli drove through the doors of the fortification to secure his load for the night.

There were over two hundred men in the Parade Field. Most of them were soldiers, a contingent of cavalry had ridden in just for the fight. Indians were gathering to watch, and even some Indian women were at the back of the ring of spectators. Landstrom was at his table still taking bets, and the man that rode down with Bent joined him. Suzette walked over to check the odds board. Landstrom snickered at her and asked, "Are you here to say goodbye to your money?" When Suzette just looked at him and smiled, Landstrom introduced the new man in the picture. "This is Suzette Callahan, the *doctor,* who tried to fail Jim on his physical. Miss Callahan – Vincent Ronkainen, Bent's accountant and one of the referees for the fights."

Ronkainen wore in a checkered topcoat tailored from light linen for the hot summer months. The buttons of his coat were stretched tight over his potbelly. He had a green Derby on his head and was sweating profusely in the bright sun. It was over ninety degrees. That was one authority Suzette did have. She could call off the fight if the temperature rose over one hundred. She was glad to get into the shade under the cover of the reviewing stand and glad to get away from Landstrom and Ronkainen. She didn't like either one of them, and Ronkainen repulsed her with the stench of his sweat and fat belly.

The first fight was due to start in ten minutes. Swindlehurst and the Army favorite were already in the ring stretching and throwing punches into the air. The Army cheered heartily as their man danced around the ring. They and the Indians all booed whenever Swindlehurst made a move. Landstrom and Ronkainen were in the ring now along with the soldier's *second* and the vet, his *cutman*. The Army referee entered the ring and quieted the crowd. He introduced himself as Master Sargent Jesse Smith and then introduced Vincent Ronkainen as the alternate referee. There was a coin toss and Jim as the reigning champion called "Heads." He won the toss and chose the far corner of the ring with the sun to his back.

Smith was ready to start the first fight. He called the boxers to toe up to the scratch line – just two lines in the dirt four feet apart in the center of the ring. He introduced Swindlehurst as the reigning champion from Big Timber, Colorado, weighing in at two hundred fifty-five pounds. The soldiers in the crowd went wild hissing and booing and shaking their fists in the air as Big Jim held his fists above his head and flexed his massive biceps like a weightlifter. The Army favorite was Jack Thompson from Syracuse, New York, weighing in at two hundred thirty-five pounds. Now the crowd cheered much louder than the boos they leveled before and broke into a chant that went on for a full minute – Jack, Jack, Jack. Ronkainen finally raised his hands to quiet them so he could go over the rules with the two men. Ronkainen stepped back when he was finished and yelled, "Let the fight begin." Landstrom was the timekeeper and rang a bell on his table with a steel hammer. The two men in the ring squared off and went at it.

Colonel Schultz arrived as the fight started and sat down next to Suzette on the reviewing stand. "I see Swindlehurst didn't take your advice."

Thompson was good; he was landing a lot of punches, but so was Swindlehurst. The sound of bare-knuckles hitting soft flesh was sickening to Suzette. After one round, Jack had a cut over his right eye; other than that, he didn't seem hurt. The cutman stopped the bleeding with pressure on the wound, and Thompson was back on the scratch line after the minute break between the rounds. The referees each scored the first round a draw, Ronkainen awarded the round to Swindlehurst and Smith awarded the round to Thompson. Round two was the same, but this time it was Swindlehurst who had a cut on his chin and another above his left eye. Smith was the referee for this round, and he looked Swindlehurst over and then let the round proceed. When the bell sounded, it took longer for Swindlehurst's cutman to stop the bleeding, but the big man was back up on the scratch line well ahead of the three-minute limit before his opponent would be named the winner. It was obvious that Swindlehurst was tiring. He would usually finish with a fight by now. The second round was awarded to Thompson by both referees.

Landstrom rang the bell, and the men went at it again for the third and final round. For the first minute, it looked like it would be another draw, but then Swindlehurst caught Thompson looking away for a moment and landed his signature knockout left haymaker on Thompson's jaw. The young man went down but wasn't out. He rolled around and struggled to his feet by the count of eight. The crowd cheered their encouragement. Swindlehurst, however, pressed his advantage and had Thompson on the ropes delivering blow after blow to his opponent's midsection. Then he stepped back and delivered the second haymaker. This time Thompson went down and stayed down, not moving for the full count of ten. A moan went up from the Army and then boos as Swindlehurst left the ring. There would be a fifteen-minute break between fights. Suzette went down to check on Jack. He was coming around, and his second was helping him out of the ring. "I thought I had him," the young man was saying over and over. He was trying to apologize to his Army buddies for losing the fight.

Suzette found her brothers in the crowd. Indian women were selling fry bread and corn fritters. Everyone was sweating, and the aroma of unwashed soldiers was strong. There would be four more fights before Roland was up, but

Suzette was determined to tell her brother that Big Jim was blind in his right eye. She delivered her message and kissed Roland on the cheek and wished him good luck. She hurried back to the reviewing stand and the fresher air it offered above the sweaty crowd.

The second fight started, and it was Smith's turn to be the ring referee. The round lasted only one minute, and the crowd moaned as the second opponent counted out at ten. From the reaction of the crowd, no one expected him to win. It was the same with the third and fourth opponents. Jim had only one good punch, but he used it very effectively. The fifth opponent was a different story. He was an experienced fighter and took one of Swindlehurst's left hooks and stayed on his feet. When the big man thought he should have gone down, the man hit Swindlehurst hard in his left eye with a lightning-fast jab. The big man bellowed and came back like a maniac using his weight and reach to his advantage. He landed blow after blow and then in the second round connected with his left hook. His opponent went down on one knee, and blood covered the right side of his face. Blood was gushing out of a long tear from his right temple to below his cheekbone. His fight was over. He stayed down on one knee, and Smith awarded the bout to Swindlehurst. Suzette felt sick. She went down to help the vet stitch up the wounded man. She needed to do something to get her mind off of Roland. She climbed the stairs back up to the reviewing stand, and Colonel Schultz was surprised to see her covered with blood. An Indian woman who she hadn't noticed before handed her a wet towel and a bottle of cool water. Suzette thanked her graciously and sat down. The bell rang for the first round of Roland's fight.

Ronkainen was the referee. Swindlehurst's left eye, his good eye, was swelling shut, but Ronkainen let the fight go on. Roland was quick and skillful, moving in and out and landing blow after blow to the big man's stomach and face. Swindlehurst wasn't able to land a blow in the first round and didn't want to stop fighting at the sound of the bell. Roland knew he was going to win. He returned to his corner, and his brothers wiped him down with a damp towel and gave him some water. "You're doing good, but be careful, he's getting desperate," sage advice from Eli.

Round two was much the same. The big man was tired, and he was red in the face, angry that he couldn't land a blow. Roland kept the pressure up, two quick blows to the stomach, and then a jab to the face over and over again. By the end of round two, both referees had scored both rounds to Roland. Big Jim was in trouble, and he knew it. Bent was in the first row of the bleachers sitting behind Landstrom, and he looked worried. His man was taking a beating; the worst Bent had ever seen. There was a lot of money at stake. Ronkainen would be the referee in the ring for the third round. Bent was praying his man could do something to hand Swindlehurst a win.

Big Jim was slow to make it to the scratch line for the third round. Landstrom sounded the bell, and Swindlehurst threw his left hook, and the crowd laughed and cheered when Roland stepped out of the way. Roland came back strong and knocked Swindlehurst back against the ropes. The referee should have called the fight. Big Jim could hardly defend himself, and Roland kept up the pounding on the stomach, and the jabs to the face. But the big man didn't go down; raw instinct kept him standing. Roland backed up; it was time for his signature move. He faked with a left jab to Jim's stomach. Jim dropped his hands to protect himself, and Roland put everything he had behind a devastating uppercut with his right. Jim's knees buckled, and he went down on his knees. As he sagged down to the ground, he lashed out with a hard-left jab and hit Roland square in the crouch. Roland whipped forward at the waist in pain. Jim was already down on his hands and knees, and Roland connected with his forehead to the top of Jim's skull.

The crack of heads colliding was loud, and both men were down. The crowd was wild, booing and shouting **FOUL, FOUL, FOUL**. Ronkainen called the fight, and when the crowd settled down, he announced that the fight was a draw. Both men fouled out. Swindlehurst hit below the belt, and Callahan headbutted. Roland was back on his feet but dizzy. Eli and Jacques were in the ring, yelling in Ronkainen's face. From the booing and angry shouts, it would be a miracle if Ronkainen would live another day. Bent was sitting quiet, relief apparent on his face. Several soldiers were carrying Swindlehurst to his corner. Landstrom doused the big man with a bucket of water, and he regained consciousness. Suzette hurried down from the viewing stand to check Roland for a cracked skull or concussion.

A ring of soldiers with their bayoneted rifles leveled at the rest of the crowd brought order to what could soon turn into a mob lynching. The crowd resorted to throwing tomatoes and vegetables of all kinds into the ring. Most of the soldiers had been through this with Ronkainen before. Along with the tomatoes, wadded-up claim chits were a favorite projectile. Mr. Sue just stood quietly at the back of the crowd taking it all in. He caught Suzette's eye and smiled and waved. Landstrom and Ronkainen were in the ring, doctoring Swindlehurst. The clock was running down; if Swindlehurst didn't make the scratch line, Mr. Sue would be the winner by default, and Landstrom was regretting posting the one hundred to one odds on Mr. Sue. Mr. Sue walked through the crowd and stepped through the ropes. When he entered the ring, Ronkainen derided him, "Hey Chink, you here to clean up this mess?" Eli and Jacques climbed into the ring to act as Mr. Sue's second and cutman. Eli thought to himself, *it's not smart to call Mr. Sue a chink, Buddy.*

Mr. Sue just stood there in his black outfit and slippers, but now he wore a white sash with three embroidered red dragons on the wide end hanging down to his knees. "No, I'm here to fight." Two soldiers showed up with brooms and made a hasty effort to clean up the litter before the intermission ended. They didn't quite make it and left a few tomatoes broken open and slippery, already rotting in the hot sun. Smith would be the referee for the first round. He called for Swindlehurst to step up to the scratch line. The big man rose and walked forward, stooped slightly with his head down. It was obvious he couldn't see very well. He toed up to the line. Mr. Sue bowed and removed the sash, his long black shirt, and the slippers, and handed them to Eli. He stepped up to the scratch line standing confidently in his black trousers. He was ready. Swindlehurst made his first big mistake, he underestimated the smaller-older man and snarled derisively under his breath and uttered, "I'm going to kill you, Chink."

   The bell rang, and Swindlehurst raised his arm in the air and brought it down with his massive fist clenched like a club. Mr. Sue stepped to the side, and as the big man stepped forward to keep from falling, he slipped on a tomato and fell hard. The crowd laughed and cheered Mr. Sue. Even though none of the soldiers bet on Mr. Sue, they wanted to see an end to *Bent's Brawler's* undefeated years. Smith was quick to start the count, but Jim was up by seven. Smith signaled for them to start again. Desperate to end it, Jim threw his left hook. It swished through the air in front of Mr. Sue's face. He didn't move; he didn't even flinch; he just stepped to his right, and Swindlehurst stumbled forward several steps, looking like he would fall again. Mr. Sue gave his opponent time to recover. Jim was red in the face when he threw the punch, and after he turned around to face Mr. Sue, he was purple. The crowd was up on their feet but quiet, not knowing what to expect. Jim lashed out with a left and right jab. Again Mr. Sue didn't move; just leaned left then right to avoid the blows. In frustration, Jim rushed forward, trying to drive Mr. Sue back against the ropes. Mr. Sue moved to the side, and as Jim passed, he hit the big man in the muscle on the side of his cheek with his fist doubled and his thumb under the first two fingers. His index finger made a point, and it penetrated deep. Swindlehurst howled out in pain, and the crowd finally realized it was time to cheer. It would have been easy for Mr. Sue to hit the big man repeatedly as Roland had done, but he dodged more feeble blows and waited for his chance to hit his opponent in the same spot again. This time Swindlehurst not only bellowed, but he also staggered and held his hand to the side of his face.

The round was not going well for Jim; there were still two minutes left in the round, and Swindlehurst was backing up, avoiding another blow from Mr. Sue. The tactic did little good; the next blow came right behind Big Jim's jawbone right under the ear. Swindlehurst swung wildly, and Mr. Sue backed up but kept moving to his side, causing his opponent to turn in a circle to follow him. The bell finally sounded, and Swindlehurst staggered back to his corner. Only three blows and Smith awarded the round to Mr. Sue. Ronkainen was reluctant but also gave Mr. Sue the first round. He knew full well that one more shenanigan on his part, and his life would be over. The crowd saw Mr. Sue as their new hero. They were on their feet, cheering and clapping. Mr. Sue acknowledged them with a serious look of concern on his face and a small bow. Mr. Sue refused the water Jacques offered; he wasn't even sweating. He said, "This will not be a victory I will be proud of."

Two soldiers had scurried into the ring to throw out the last of the trash. They dove through the ropes as the bell rang. Mr. Sue walked into the center of the ring. Mr. Sue addressed Ronkainen, who was in the center of the ring, "You should forfeit the bout now."

Swindlehurst looked like he was willing to do that, but Ronkainen replied, "Sorry, too much at stake." He motioned the big man up to the scratch line and signaled the two men to fight as the bell rang to start the second round.

Swindlehurst just stood there with his arms down for at least thirty seconds. Mr. Sue stood quietly in front of him. The soldiers were chanting, "Call the match! Call the match! Call the match!"

Mr. Sue backed up and kicked up with his foot, not connecting but making the big man flinch. Jim had rocked his head back, and Mr. Sue followed through with a straight arm punch that was a blur and didn't slow down when it connected with the end of Swindlehurst's chin. The big man fell to his knees, and Ronkainen was slow to start the count. The crowd did it for him, yelling out the numbers. Big Jim got to his feet by nine. He stood up and took his stance with his hands up, fists clenched, ready to fight out of habit. Again Mr. Sue told Ronkainen he should forfeit the bout. Ronkainen shook his head *no* and leaned in as if to check out Swindlehurst. In a quiet voice, he said, "You got to take him now, or you are going to lose."

With one last burst of energy, Swindlehurst rushed forward and threw his left hook. Mr. Sue ducked under the blow and again struck out like lightning and hit Big Jim on the end of his left-short rib. There was a moan of agony as the big man went down again. The crowd started to count again, but Landstrom interrupted at the count of six, ringing the bell furiously to end the round. Again, both referees awarded the round to Mr. Sue. This time Mr. Sue didn't go to his corner; he stood at the scratch line in the middle of the ring and waited for the bell. Swindlehurst was up off his stool, standing with his back to the ring, leaning with his hands on the ropes. He was still in a lot of pain. From the viewing stand, Suzette yelled out, "Stop the fight." She was holding onto Maria and was looking imploringly at Colonel Schultz to do something. The Colonel just shook his head slightly in a *no*. He wouldn't interfere.

The bell rang, and Swindlehurst staggered back into the center of the ring. He threw some wild punches, and Mr. Sue hardly had to move to avoid them. As Swindlehurst was readying for his next flurry of punches, Mr. Sue let out a blood-curdling yell and hit the big man in his solar plexus with a straight arm punch, his entire body weight behind the blow. Jim doubled over and held his stomach. He fell to the side, and this time, he didn't get up; he lay in the dust moaning and clutching his stomach. With dread, Ronkainen started to count him out. The crowd went wild. As one, the soldiers in the bleachers to the right of the viewing stand jumped up with a cheer; as they came down as one, the wooden bleacher collapsed. Suzette closed her eyes; she knew there were going to be a lot of bones to set. Bent was lucky, he had been on the bottom row, and he didn't jump up. He and Landstrom sat there on the collapsed seat, unbelieving as the crowd counted out their man. Bent was getting up out of the dust. Men were rushing in to sort out the wounded. Colonel Schultz walked down and pulled Bent up the rest of the way and said, "Open the safe." Bent was reluctant, but he signaled Landstrom to open the safe. Schultz said, "By my count, you owe Mr. Sue here four-thousand three hundred and sixty dollars."

Suzette stepped forward and slapped two claim checks down on Landstrom's table. "And you owe Maria four hundred and me another ten thousand, and we won't take any funny money."

Mr. Sue took his chit out of a pocket in the back of his sash and handed it to Maria. "Make that six hundred for Maria." He walked over to the table with the safe as the soldiers around the ring backed up, making a corridor for Mr. Sue to walk through.

Ronkainen started to tremble and said, "We don't have that kind of money down here. We can pay you up at the fort in the morning."

Suzette drew her revolver and put it under Ronkainen's chin with the hammer cocked. "Now," was all she said.

Colonel Schultz motioned to two of his soldiers, "Lock Bent and Landstrom up in the stockade. Ronkainen, you better have Mr. Sue's prize money in that safe, or you're going into the stockade with them. Under the circumstances, I could keep you in there for your safety till next year sometime."

Ronkainen opened the safe and pulled out a leather bag from the back of a shelf. It contained the prize money, two-hundred-sixty-eight double eagles. He counted out six-hundred more dollars in Federal Banknotes and handed the total to Mr. Sue. Mr. Sue handed his winnings to Maria and said, "Yours," and walked off without saying a word. Ronkainen looked at Suzette and said, "I can pay you over at the fort." Suzette looked over to see Swindlehurst finally roll onto his back. She was relieved, the big man would live, but she hoped he would give up on his fighting career. Maria stood frozen, looking into the top of the bag. She had never seen more than one double eagle at a time, and now she had a whole bag full. Suzette took the heavy bag from Maria and handed it to Eli for safekeeping.

Ronkainen closed the safe, and Jacques spun him around and patted him down. "Well, Vince, what do you have here." He removed a derringer from the man's inside pocket.

Eli walked Maria back to the camp. He was anxious to find his friend. Suzette and the twins went up to Bent's Fort in the buckboard. It took over two hours for Suzette to sort through a wide variety of twenty-dollar bills, rejecting counterfeits and notes issued from unknown banks. Finally satisfied, they left Ronkainen sitting dumbfounded inside his walk-in safe. Suzette had half the amount in double eagles and the rest in Federal Banknotes. She left Ronkainen in a state of shock and was humming to herself on her way back to the supply train camp. Eli was sitting around a cold fire pit, drinking tea with Mr. Sue. Mr. Sue was glad to see Suzette and the twins. Hans and his men started to clap as they walked up to the small circle. The drivers and helpers had gathered around. Suzette had kept six hundred dollars separate from her winnings and added it to Maria's bag of gold. She put her arm around Mr. Sue and said, "I love you, Mr. Sue. You have a bit of psycho and liar in you. Not enough to be callous and dishonest, but enough to get the job done. What do the three dragons on your sash signify?"

"My family in China has held the championship of our province for three centuries. I am the last survivor of that family line, the last dragon; all the others perished in the wars with Peking. This sash is very precious to me, and it represents hundreds of years of my family's honor. I wouldn't have fought a helpless man, and I feel ashamed for that, but I did it for Maria."

Suzette started weeping quietly. Big tears ran down her dusty face. A soldier came running over from the Fort. "Swindlehurst has collapsed, and they can't wake him up. The Colonel sent me to ask for you to come to look at him."

Suzette gathered up her medical kit and started to leave with the soldier. Hans and his Germans went with her. Mr. Sue sat down and hung his head between his knees. "What have I done?" was all he had to say as Eli put his arm around his friend to comfort him. Maria cuddled Mr. Sue from the other side. They sat that way well into the night.

Suzette returned after midnight and told them that Swindlehurst would live, but his heart murmur was considerably worse. She didn't think he would ever fully recover this time around. Mr. Sue was relieved, but he said he would carry this guilt for the rest of his life. Roland, the philosopher, reflected and said, "Guilt is a possession of one's soul. However, shame is worse. It comes from everyone around you, and that is what Swindlehurst will have to face. You will never have that from any of us. It would be an honor if you would teach me how to fight as you do. Let's get some sleep; we're back on the trail tomorrow."

ABDUCTION

s usual per their routine on a travel day, the camp rose and ate before sunrise. Eli gathered his mule team and walked them over to Fort Wise. His wagon was inside the fortification, Jacques and Roland had slept there on top of Bent's mountain of silver, only their bedrolls to cushion them against the unforgiving pile. Colonel Schultz had six of his horse soldiers assigned to guard the wagon on the way to Santa Fe. A young lieutenant introduced himself as Henry Barksdale. His colonel made it clear that Barksdale was to provide escort and security for Bent's silver. He was to defer to Eli's command in all matters concerning the supply train. After they pushed the heavy wagon out of the doors of the fortification, Colonel Schultz took Eli aside and told him to look after the lieutenant. He was as green as prairie grass in the spring. The six men, though, were seasoned soldiers; Eli thought the young lieutenant was in for some training by the older men. The colonel went on, "I'm going to keep Bent and Landstrom in the stockade till the end of the day. Sergeant Baxter, who is our jailer, reports that Landstrom was raving mad and carried on all night about the ten grand he lost to your sister. I wouldn't be surprised if he attempted to take it back. It would take an army to attack you directly, and he doesn't have one. It will be something devious if there is any attempt at all."

"Don't worry," Eli assured him, "he would die trying anything."

Eli and the colonel shook hands, and Schultz, in a fatherly manner, said, "Take care, son." For all his years in the military, he had been sending young men out in the way of danger. Eli was far from the first, and even farther from the last that he would bid farewell to before he finished his Army career. Eli hitched his mule team to the wagon. With a click of his tongue, he was back to leading his wagon train forever west. They would cross the Arkansas River at La Junta; then, there would be two days of dry camps until they reached Iron Spring. That would be the last wet camp before they entered the mountains. There was a garrison of soldiers there building a fortification, and Eli would be offloading rifles and ammunition. Lieutenant Barksdale was familiar with the trail as far as the mountains, but Santa Fe would be the first time for him as well as everyone else.

At first light, they were ready to pull out. Paul Hayman and the blacksmith walked up to Suzette as she was tightening the cinch on Patches. Paul was a bit bashful as usual, "Suzette, I hope you don't think this is too pretentious, but I had Adalwolf help me make this for you." It was a replica of the barrette she had given Maria. The handle of the barrette was an elongated arc made from a silver eight-reales Mexican coin. The six-inch stiletto spike was steel along with the clasp.

Adalwolf, the blacksmith, was apologetic. In German, he said in English, "I'm sorry, Miss Suzette. This burette is the best I could do out here on the trail."

Suzette accepted the gift graciously and kissed them both fondly. Paul's heart, as well as other parts of his body, was pounding. "It's beautiful, Adalwolf; there is no need to apologize. Thank you. Thank you." Then it hit her; she had never heard the blacksmith utter a word of English up till then. Grabbing Adalwolf by the arm as he started to walk away, she said playfully, "I'm on to you. You're the translator that set up that bit of monkey business with Mr. Sue and the rest of the Germans, aren't you?"

"Guilty, as charged Missy. I am sorry I misled you. Sometimes it is good not to be able to speak English. You hear all kinds of things that people would rather keep to themselves thinking you don't understand."

"Really, like what?"

"Yesterday before the fight, I went up to pick up the wheels from Bent's blacksmith. That fat man who was the referee was telling Bent about your bet. He said that if Landstrom lost that money, he was going to get it back. There were two rough-looking gents there. The fat man talked to them quietly, away from where I could hear, then the men left and rode out hard to the west. I suspect that they will be up to no good. By the way, Swindlehurst could speak a little German; I didn't have any trouble with him. I'm sorry he got hurt bad, but I can't feel sorry for him. It will be a week before Roland will be able to sit his saddle again."

Suzette thanked Warner again and reaching behind her head, slid the stiletto into her thick braid, and fastened the clasp. "It's perfect, thanks, Paul." With that, Paul received a peck on the cheek, and she mounted up and rode to the front of the train to join up with Eli. She and Jacques would be the first scouts. The Army patrol seemed a little confused as to what to do at first, but then the seasoned soldiers took up positions, three in front and three behind Eli's wagon. They didn't need to be told by Lieutenant Barksdale; he was riding forward with Jacques on the riverside of the trail. Giving orders to his men had never crossed his mind.

That night, their thirty-seventh on the trail, they camped at the confluence of the Purgatory with the Arkansas River. The moon was waning but was still half full. Shortly after midnight, with a half-moon to light the trail, a buckboard passed the camp. Two horses pulled it and two more followed with lead ropes tied to the rear. Hans had the guard duty and reported to Eli in the morning with Suzette translating. The two men in the buckboard looked like Ronkainen and Landstrom, but it was too dark to be certain, and they were traveling fast. Eli nodded his affirmation, "Bent's old fort is about twenty miles ahead. We are going to see them again soon. Be careful, Suzette; thanks, Hans."

Eli was sure they were going to see Landstrom and Ronkainen on the trail that day but was somewhat disappointed when they didn't show up. He didn't want them to have time to rally a larger force. He wasn't worried about the two hucksters, but the men that Adalwolf overheard at Bent's Fort were a different matter. He wouldn't let up on his precautions until they were well out of reach of Bent's henchmen. He pulled the supply train into the field in front of Bent's Old Fort for the night. There were some teepees across the river, but the remains of the old fort were charred timbers and busted down adobe walls. Eli was hoping to find some trace of Bent's men, but the ruins were bereft of any sign of recent habitation.   The broken-down wall offered little security, so he put his wagon with Bent's silver in the center of the ring for the night. He would double the guards for several more nights unless Landstrom and Ronkainen made their play sooner. He knew they couldn't stay out on the trail for long without supplies, and a buckboard couldn't carry much for four horses and four men. The next day they would cross the Arkansas River, and it would be two more days of dry travel before they would reach Iron Springs. He knew his pursuers couldn't leave the water supply of the river. They would be out of reach soon.

As evening fell, Paul Hayman was back into his routine of playing and singing until one by one, the drivers and their helpers turned in. Suzette and Maria had been outside the ring, taking care of their business earlier in the evening. Suzette went out again to relieve herself before turning in. A soldier went out with her to keep watch for trouble. Suzette was walking back and thanked the soldier for standing guard, but as she passed him, he swung his rifle and hit her at the base of her skull and knocked her out. Two men appeared from the shadows and carried her off. The soldier walked back to the camp, making sure no one saw the kidnapping. Most of the men were already asleep, but Eli was walking toward the soldier and asked about his sister. The soldier told him she was already up in his wagon bedding down for the night with the young Mexican girl. Eli had no reason to suspect that the young man was lying, so he walked over to the fire pit by Mr. Sue's chuckwagon and finished the evening talking with him. Mr. Sue was finally talking about his life in China before migrating to Europe and eventually to the east coast of the United States. Mr. Sue had quite a history: in China, he was a general of an army of over fifty thousand men and survived several huge battles before he gave up his command and left his homeland. Eli asked, "Why are you traveling as a cook?"

Mr. Sue shrugged his shoulders as if the question wasn't relevant and said, "I like to cook, and it is an easy way to see the world." Eli was impressed with the depth of his friend's experiences and made a mental note not to take the harmless-looking Mr. Sue for granted anymore. They turned in for some rest. Eli would be up to check the guards after midnight, and morning would come soon enough. As he was drifting off to sleep, he heard a horse riding off in the dark of night. He thought he dreamed it and fell off into the deep sleep of the exhausted. Hans woke him at midnight, and he made a round of the camp. As he got back to his wagon, Maria was walking around from fire pit to fire pit, calling softly for Suzette. Eli stopped her and asked, "Where is Suzette?" Maria shrugged with a frightened look on her face.

Eli panicked, "How could she be gone?" Then he remembered the soldier who told him she was up in his wagon and the horse that he thought he dreamed of riding off in the middle of the night. He drew his Colt and fired three rounds into the air to roust the camp. Within seconds everyone was up, and in another instant, the men were searching every wagon for Suzette. Lt. Barksdale reported that one of his men was missing too. Some of the men speculated that Suzette ran off with the soldier but then shook their heads in disbelief. There was no way Suzette ran off with someone she didn't even know.

With lanterns to light their way, Eli had everyone walking out from the wagon train circle looking for any sign or clue to Suzette's disappearance. Some men came running back from the ruins, waving a note at Eli. They found the note pegged to a crack in the wall with a wooden wedge. Eli read the note to himself with dread. He called the men together, and when everyone was within earshot, Eli read it out loud.

Callahan
*If you want the girl back
alive, leave my ten- thousand
dollars and a hundred pounds
of silver at the door of the fort
and leave out of here. We will
return her tomorrow night,
provided I have my money,
and you are on the south side
of the river by then.*
Landstrom

Hans came running from the southwest corner of the ruins. "Come," he said, beckoning urgently. Eli followed him back around the fort. There were wagon tracks on a road that led from there back to the trail. They were narrow and not deep enough for a heavy wagon. Bending down close to the tracks and holding his lantern close, Hans said, "Buckboard." He couldn't elaborate in English, but it wasn't necessary. He was doing fine getting his point across with his one-word sentences.

Eli had a tough decision to make. He could leave the ransom demand and go west in the morning, but that meant he would have to trust that Landstrom would live up to his word and deliver Suzette back to him. There were other options; his favorite was hunting down the little worm and killing him. Roland had a better idea. He said, "It is very likely Suzette will escape. We can leave a dummy ransom at the fort. They must be close. We need to have everyone with a horse up and scouting. We'll follow the track of the buckboard at first light. We'll either find Landstrom's camp or Suzette out on foot. Let's get back to the camp. We have to be ready for first light."

They weren't the only ones making plans. Suzette had come to with a pounding headache and found herself in a dimly lit cave chained to a peg high up on the wall. A handcuff held her left wrist, but her right hand was free. She heard men talking; one of them sounded like the weasel. She quietly took stock of her situation. They had taken her revolver along with the knife from the scabbard on her calf. She reached behind her head. They hadn't taken her barrette. She wasn't helpless. At least one of these assholes was going to die. Landstrom was the first on her list. The soldier that knocked her out was second. She reached around and felt the lump under her left ear. It was low enough that concussion wouldn't be a problem, but it hurt like hell. The handcuff was tight, too tight for her to slip her hand through. There wasn't much she could do but wait for an opportunity.

She couldn't see the men talking out in the front of the cave. They were planning something, and Suzette could only hear every other word or so, but she got the gist of the conversation. Ronkainen and one of the men would circle back with the buckboard and watch for the supply train to leave. Landstrom and the other man would stay here. Their horses had to be close. That was good; she hoped that she would need one soon. The cave quieted down; then, she heard the crack of a whip and the rattle of wheels over rock. *Good*, she thought, *now there were only two men left to guard her*. She laid back to rest and wait; it couldn't be long to first light. Eli and her brothers would find out she was missing, and they wouldn't rest until they found her.

Eli and the twins were walking their horses following the buckboard tracks long before first light by lantern light. The track they were on led back to the trail about a mile west of the old fort. In another three miles, the dirt of the trail changed into a rocky trail. They were on a large span of rock that had been scoured of all its topsoil by floodwaters from the river. There were two miles of the rocky trail, and no tracks were leading off it on the west side. The river was too deep to cross from the rocky trail, so somewhere on the rock, the buckboard had left the trail. When the supply train passed here, Eli would have the driver's helpers fan out and walk the perimeter of the rock formation. He would keep the supply train moving in the event they were being watched. He hoped to find tracks leaving out from the expanse of rock. If they didn't, it would narrow the search area to the rock formation, maybe an area of four to six square miles. A lot of ground to cover, but he had an army of angry men at his disposal, and they would look in every nook and cranny. They would find her, and the men responsible for taking her were going to pay with their lives.

Eli rode back to the head of the supply train. Jacques left the trail and rode up to the east side of the rocky outcrop. It was almost three miles to the northernmost tip farthest from the river. There, he found the tracks of the buckboard leading off to the northeast. There was another rocky outcrop about a mile away, and he spurred his horse and covered the ground to the first of the rocks in less than two minutes. He looked back down to the south and couldn't see the buckboard, but he did see a dust trail. He turned toward the river and pushed his horse again to catch up. It was more dust than a single horse would make, and they were traveling fast. He was sure that when he caught up to the dust, he would find the buckboard. Hope against hope if his sister was there, he was going to have a hard time fighting five men. His options would be limited if they held Suzette hostage at gunpoint.

When he was a mile from the fort, he could see the tail end of the supply train off to the west. He could stop and try to flash a signal, or he could fire his rifle and try to get their attention. He decided to do neither and kept riding to the fort. The buckboard was already there. Only two men were carrying the ransom crate to the buckboard. One of them was the missing soldier. Ronkainen was at the reins. He was alone on the buckboard, Suzette wasn't there. Jacques pulled his Henry out of the scabbard on his saddle and levered a shell into the chamber. He was still a hundred yards away when he started firing at them. The men on the ground threw the heavy crate onto the back of the buckboard and bolted for their horses. Jacques dropped the soldier with his third shot. The other man rode hell-bent for the river. Ronkainen whipped the team and headed out on the trail to the east. Neither of these men was important to Jacques, and now his horse was lathered up and winded. He leaped down and in one sweeping move, vaulted into the saddle of the soldier's horse. He didn't even look down to see if the man was dead; he just turned and rode out to the west. He didn't have to go far. Eli, Lt. Barksdale, and his remaining five soldiers had heard the shooting and were riding hard to meet him. He pulled up short and told Eli that Suzette wasn't in the rock pile by the river. She was further north, and they should be able to backtrack on the buckboard's trail to wherever it led. Lt. Barksdale sent one man back to make sure the rest of the men didn't waste time searching the wrong pile of rocks.

It was a while after Ronkainen and the other men left that Suzette decided she had to do something. She had only two things: her barrette and her female wiles. She called out to Landstrom and the other man, "I need to pee, and I need water." She had tried to make her voice as commanding as possible. Landstrom was annoyed. She figured he didn't want to interrupt his card game; she had heard them shuffling cards and cursing occasionally. "Did you hear me? I need to pee you bastards."

Finally, one of the men came to the back of the cave. Light from the lantern and the entrance of the cave framed his silhouette, and she could see that the man was too big to be Landstrom. It was brighter than when she woke up; it had to be early morning. The man approached her and said, "You can pee right there. We're not letting you lose."

"Are you going to watch, or are you going to give me my privacy?" Suzette was struggling one-handed with her belt buckle.

"I'm going to watch," was the reply. Suzette was trying hard not to act afraid or shy. She dropped her trousers and undergarment and moved as far as the chain would allow away from where she had been laying. She really did need to pee, and she squatted down and did so as the man looked on lasciviously.

She got up but didn't pull up her pants. She asked with a slight smile, "You want some of this?" She returned to the wall and lay down and watched as her jailer walked to her feet and started to drop his pants. She hoped her acting was good enough. She spread her legs and let out a surprised gasp as the man knelt and exposed himself. He leaned forward on his hands and knees, ready to move up and thrust himself inside of her. Suzette struggled to keep the smile from turning to a look of abomination and fear. It was time. She put her hands behind her head and closed her eyes. The idiot was even more encouraged as he pulled open her shirt, but his eyes bulged, and he sucked in a breath as if to scream when Suzette plunged the stiletto just under his left ear deep into his brain stem. He didn't move or make a sound. His head sagged, and then he just settled down on top of her. Suzette lay still and put her fingers to the man's jugular vein to feel for a pulse. She knew he was dead after a couple of minutes. She rolled him off and arranged him in a fetal position before she searched him. She found a knife in his boot then cradled into the dead man as if they just finished sex.

Landstrom was getting impatient, and he called out. When he didn't get a response, he got up, unhooked the lantern and walked the short distance to the back of the cave. He saw his partner with the girl cradled to him with a hand on her breast inside her shirt. "God damn it, you idiot." He rushed in to pull the man away from Suzette, not realizing that he was dead. He lifted the man's hand off Suzette's breast, and in a blur as fast as her draw, Suzette slashed Landstrom's throat. Blood gushed out of the severed arteries and blinded her. Landstrom had his hands at his throat for a moment and then fell forward, covering his dead partner and Suzette. She just lay there as he bled out. The blood was running down across her bare breasts. It was hot and sticky, and the coppery smell was strong enough to drown out the rancid odor of both men. It was almost sensual, but Suzette put the thought out of her mind as she struggled to get out from under her victim. Landstrom had her

Lefaucheux tucked under his belt. There was a small key in his vest pocket. She unlocked herself and hurled the chain from her wrist then got up to pull her bloody clothes back on. She put the barrette back into her braid, picked up the lantern, and walked to the front of the cave. She picked up a canteen and drank, then poured the remainder of the water over her face to clear her eyes. There was a fire ring just inside the portal with a frying pan set up to cook bacon. She lit the fire, hoping there would be clouds of smoke, but the wood was bone dry. There was hardly any smoke. In a minute, the bacon sizzled, and Suzette's mouth watered with hunger.

She looked around; the cave was in a small depression; she was surrounded by rock on three sides. There were two horses on a tagline and saddles on the ground. She started to saddle one up when she heard the fall of hooves on the rocks above. Eli and Jacques looked down from above. Suzette looked up, squinting into the bright sun behind them. "You guys hungry?" She asked as she finished cinching up the saddle. "Breakfast will be ready in a few minutes."

Eli laughed with relief and slid down the rock face. He took his blood-soaked sister in his arms and said, "You look like you just slaughtered the pig for breakfast."

"Two of them, in fact! One hardly bled at all; he died of a cerebral hemorrhage. The other one died of a serious throat laceration." That reminded her, she had to go back to the cave and find her knife. Jacques rode in with Eli's horse. He followed his siblings into the cave.

Eli said, "We smelled the bacon, or we would have ridden right past here and never seen this cave." He was trying to avoid asking why Suzette was bloody and if she was hurt, but it was all too apparent as to what had happened when they found Landstrom and his dead partner with his pants down around his ankles.

Roland put his arm around his sister and asked, "Did he .....?"

"No, but he got close. I hope neither of them carried any diseases. I want to go down to the river and clean up."

Eli was looking over the front of the cave. It was obvious that the men had used the cave before. It must have been their private hideout back in the days of Bent's Old Fort. Suzette hadn't noticed before in the dim light, but with the lantern, she could see that there were at least a dozen names scratched in the wall next to the chain. She found her knife in a scabbard on the rapist's belt. She slipped it into her boot and said, "Let's get out of here."

As they walked out of the cave, Jacques speared a piece of bacon with his knife and smiled at his sister. "This bacon is pretty good; you better not tell Mr. Sue that you can cook." Suzette picked up the pan and poured the bacon grease onto the fire. She let the bacon cool a bit, then scooped up a handful to eat as she rode down to the river. They mounted up and rode up and out of the cleft in the rock. Suzette was rubbing her bruised wrist and was uncomfortable on the strange mount. The sun was warm, and by the time Lt. Barksdale and his men joined them, she was dry and only faintly smelled of blood. They rode down to a place on the river west of the fort. Willows surrounded it, and it was a good swimming hole with a rock at the side for diving. Suzette didn't wait for the men to withdraw, she started undressing as soon as she got to the rock. She dove into the water, and a red trail flowed off her and down the river. She would have to clean her clothes, but for the moment, the cold water felt good. She would be clean, but never the same again.

Eli asked Jacques about Ronkainen and the other man who got away. The other man had crossed the river. Dealing with the Indians on the other side would be his problem. Ronkainen was headed back to Bent's New Fort. They both laughed, hoping that he wouldn't look in the ransom crate until he got there. It was full of metal but not silver. Through the night, Adalwolf had melted down a hundred pounds of bullets and poured them into neat one-hundred-ounce bars. There were a few twenty-dollar bills under the lead bars with their ends sticking out, just enough to make the rest of the layer of paper look like the ten grand Landstrom wanted. They could hear Suzette beating her bloody clothes against the diving rock. Jacques commented, "I don't know what it is, but she seems different."

Eli agreed; he didn't know what it was either, but somehow, the killings were changing their sister. He put it off as nothing to be overly concerned over. Another month or so, they would be back in civilization. He knew that they had all changed coming through the violence of the trail. He didn't know what it would mean or how they would fit in when they got to Santa Fe or farther on to Los Angeles. All he cared about for the moment was that they were together again and safe. New Mexico was waiting; he could have them there in just a few more days.

Later than he wanted, Eli led the supply train down to the north bank of the Arkansas River. The crossing was noted as not particularly difficult, but the river was on the rise despite the drought on the prairie. Eli judged that there was enough daylight left to get everyone across and rode down into the river to get a feel for the bottom. It was solid enough, but at the deepest part of the river, the water was nearly four feet deep. He rode back to the north side and passed the word that foodstuffs and feed bags would have to be stored high. Wagons that carried cargo that didn't matter if it got wet were to start crossing immediately. He rode back along the supply train with more instructions. "Form a ring on the other side; we will be in Apache territory from now on, so don't let your guard down."

More than twenty wagons pulled forward to cross. Roland was the first and traversed the deep water without incident. When he pulled up the other bank, Lt. Barksdale and his five soldiers rode up with him. There were Indians; a lot of them sitting on their horses and watching, probably trying to decide if an attack on such a large wagon train would be worth the loss of life it would entail. When the second and third wagon joined Roland, he moved forward, expanding his defensive ring on the south bank. The Indians pulled back, keeping their distance. As more wagons crossed the river, they kept expanding the circle. If the Indians wanted to attack, they had lost their advantage. Their best opportunity was when Roland first pulled up out of the river. Now the wagons on the south side of the river were a formidable-well-armed force, and more wagons followed to swell the circle but at a slower pace. Eli rode across and had several of the supply wagons that didn't carry perishables return to move more of those supplies to the south side of the river. He rode out ahead of Roland's wagon and signaled Lt. Barksdale and his men to join him. They walked their horses toward the Indians, trying to act as non-threatening as possible.

One of the Indians, in a more elaborate headdress than the rest, walked his horse forward with several braves on either side. He pulled up just short of Eli and asked in Comanche, "Doctor?" Lt. Barksdale turned to his translator, Corporal O'Riley, and asked what the Indian said.

Hearing *doctor,* Eli told the translator, "Tell them yes, but ask where they need *him*. Don't let on that our doctor is a woman."

"In our camp" was the reply.

"How far away?" was the next question.

Not far was the answer.

Eli wasn't in any way going to let Suzette leave his sight with so many Indians so close at hand. He made up his mind, "Bring your sick here. Make camp with us by the river. Our doctor will take care of your sick or wounded." It took several attempts for O'Riley to make the points clear, but he finally got the full message across. The leader of the Indians carried on a heated conversation with his braves, and then he nodded at Eli, and he motioned for the whole troop to follow him back to their camp. Eli was relieved, but at the same time, he thought that they wouldn't sleep easily that night with so many potential hostiles so close at hand.

By twilight, all but a few wagons were across the river. Jacques with Hans and his men got the last of them across when Eli came riding down to the crossing. "You better come to see this."

They went up the bank and to the outer ring of wagons and looked down to the south. It looked like there were more than five hundred men, women, and children making their way down to the camp. They turned downriver a short way, and much like seasoned trail travelers started putting up teepees and building fire rings, an exercise that they no doubt did several times a week. Everyone was busy, even the children. The Indian that spoke for the group earlier had a litter tethered to his horse, and he turned toward the wagon ring instead of the Indian camp. There was a woman on the litter, and she was in bad shape. Eli had the German's untie the litter from the back of the horse, and they carried it into the wagon ring. The man who first spoke for the group sought out the translator and told him that his name was Quanah. O'Riley learned that he wasn't the chief of the band, but that his father was.

The two men followed the litter to Eli's wagon. Suzette had the medical kit spread out on a table with another table set up for the patient. She first examined the young woman on the litter and then had her gently transferred to the table. Quanah asked O'Riley, "Where is the doctor?"

The soldier pointed at Suzette, and a look of concern spread across Quanah's face. Some of his men arrived, pulling two slaughtered buffalo into the wagon ring. Eli looked and Quanah and said, "Thank you."

O'Riley asked, "How did this happen?"

Quanah answered, "Apache at the waterhole." Eli assumed he was talking about Iron Spring because it was the only water on the trail down to the mountain pass that would take them to Santa Fe.

Suzette gave them a summary of the woman's condition. "She has lost a lot of blood. Trampled by a horse would be my guess. She has a compound fracture of her left femur, several broken ribs on her left side, and these bruises on her face are not life-threatening, but the inside of her mouth has a bad cut, and there are several loose teeth. I can patch her up, but I can't guarantee she will live. There may be internal injuries beyond my capabilities." Eli motioned for the translator and Quanah to move away from the table.

Eli told O'Riley to relay the woman's condition and that Suzette would try her best, but let the brave know that the woman might still die. O'Riley tried his best, but again it took several attempts to get all the points across. Quanah called to one of his men that were helping carve up one of the buffalos and sent him to the Indian camp to retrieve something. The man returned with an older man and woman who he introduced as the woman's parents. He also told O'Riley that the woman was one of his wives, one that he treasured over and above all the rest. When Suzette learned that the older couple were the woman's parents, she went back to the footlocker that was the medical kit and dug out a transfusion tube. It was about six feet long and had a needle at both ends. The rubber tube was the same kind of rubber-like Maria's slingshot. She kept it in a sealed bag and would boil it out after using it and seal it in the bag again. She had Hans lift the medical footlocker to the top of the table full of instruments. It was difficult for O'Riley to explain to the older man that they wanted him to sit on top of the footlocker.   The man was babbling on to O'Riley with a look of fear in his eyes as Suzette swabbed his arm with alcohol and inserted the needle on one end of the tube into a vein. She held the tube up until it filled with blood displacing the air, and then inserted the other end into a vein in the crook of the woman's elbow. Suzette had never done this before, but she had watched Jessica do it in the surgery in Independence. Sometimes the transfusions saved lives, and sometimes the patients died anyway. She wished she had paid more attention back then. O'Riley told her that the older Indian was trying to tell them that he wasn't sick.

It was time to go to work on the wounds. Suzette judged that the broken ribs had to come first. She probed the ribs under the bruise and found two that were simple breaks, but the one in between them was more complicated. She would need to cut the skin opened and pull the rib up into place. She hoped the lung underneath was not pierced or collapsed. As she sterilized a scalpel with alcohol, the woman's mother started to tremble. Suzette looked up to O'Riley and told him to calm her down. She made her first cut parallel over the sunken rib and pulled the incision opened. Maria was there with sterile gauze, and Suzette had her mopping the blood from the wound. Suzette could see the rib, and there wasn't air bubbling up from underneath it. The broken rib had not pierced the lung. Suzette took a pair of dental pliers off the table of instruments, and holding the incision opened with one hand took hold of the rib with the pliers and maneuvered it up into place. There was one small vein that was a bleeder, and she closed it off with a stitch. Then she started to close the incision. The mother pushed her hands away and sprinkled some brown powder in the wound from a leather bag she had drawn out of her serape. Mom backed off and motioned for Suzette to continue. It only took a few more minutes for Suzette to finish stitching the incision. Suzette was relieved to see that it wasn't bleeding.

The leg was much more difficult. The piece of bone sticking out of the side of the trampled thigh was only the start of the problem. Suzette worked several hours into the night and asked for more lanterns as she was trying to put the puzzle of the shattered bone back together. It was cooling down, but Suzette was sweating profusely, and Maria kept wiping her brow to keep Suzette from dripping sweat into the wound. She finally had the pieces of the bone back in place and started to close the wound. The woman's mother insisted that she sprinkle the wound with the brown powder before Suzette close it. It still took an hour to finish. The injured woman moaned and lolled her head. Suzette had O'Riley and Maria hold her up, and she had the woman drink a small dose of laudanum. Her eyes glazed over, and she lay back with a sigh of relief. There was still the cut inside the mouth to suture. She removed the transfusion tube from the woman first and then her father and laid it aside. The woman's father sat stoically through the whole procedure. The older man was pale, and a little dizzy from his loss of blood, and O'Riley had to help him down from the table. Suzette had forgotten about the older man; she hoped that he still had enough blood to function. The older man was tough, though, from his hard life on the prairie. He looked on with wonder and stood with pride, having helped save his daughter's life.

It was after two in the morning when Suzette finished. She was exhausted but had to eat before she turned in. Now aware of the gnawing hunger in her stomach, she realized that she hadn't eaten for a full day, other than some jerky when she first returned from the cave to the wagon train. Mr. Sue was standing by and ready to take care of her. He started her out with a cup of his hot soup. She had made fun of Eli for adopting it as his drink of choice in the morning, but she had to admit that it tasted good, and it was soothing. He followed up with a hearty bowl of buffalo stew. Besides potatoes, the stew had fresh carrots; the man was a magician. She ate and fell asleep sitting by the fire pit. Mr. Sue picked her up and carried her to Eli's wagon. He thought as he carried her of his own family that he lost to the wars in China. Suzette woke as he lifted her onto the back of the wagon. She had her arm around his neck, and she pulled him to her and kissed him on his cheek. She climbed onto her bedroll and collapsed, instantly asleep. Maria covered her up, and Mr. Sue thanked the young girl. He would stay up, as were most of the men in the camp. They were uneasy with such a large band of Indians within a stone's throw of them. Eli was uneasy too. He had tripled the guards and stayed up himself watching for the first sign of trouble.

But there wasn't trouble that night, and like the drivers and their helpers, the Indians were up before first light. The only two people still asleep in both camps were Suzette and Maria. They deserved some rest, but Eli would have to get her up soon to pack up the medical kit and check on her patient. He wondered if the Indians would travel with the wounded woman or remain by the river. He didn't have to wait long for an answer, Quanah wanted to talk, and O'Riley was asking him to join them.

Eli and the twins listened to O'Riley as he put forth a proposal from Quanah. The Indians wanted their help to retaliate against the Apache. It would be beneficial to the wagon train because the Apache were blockading the waterhole at Iron Spring. They would need to replenish their drinking water there, and Eli was no fool, he didn't want to fight a large band of Apache alone. Quanah and his braves would travel along with the wagon train. His women and children would stay here. The older men and boys of the camp would keep them safe while he and his braves were away. It didn't take long for Eli to consult his brothers and Hans. They all agreed it was a good plan. One thing, though, Eli would drill the Indians to fit into his defensive position with the wagon train. They had only a few guns among them. Spears, bows and arrows, and an infinite amount of courage were their best weapons. Eli agreed to the arrangement, and he and Quanah shook hands. Roland wondered where Quanah learned that white man's custom, but then Bent's Old Fort was just a little way down the river. "Eli kept hold of the Indian's hand and said, "Let's go check on your wife."

The woman was awake and smiled at her husband when he got close to the operating table. Eli needed for Suzette to look her over before they moved her, and he regretted that he would have to wake her. She wasn't easy to roust, but he persisted, and she finally rolled out of the back of the wagon. Mr. Sue handed her a cup of strong coffee and said, "Doctor's hours are tough." Suzette thanked him and walked over to the operating table. She pulled the blankets back and first checked on the leg. There had been some seeping during the night but no serious bleeding. The wound wasn't infected, and Suzette was pleasantly surprised. She would have to find out what the brown powder contained. She removed the bandage from the wound on the woman's rib cage, and as the leg, there was no infection. Suzette got out her stethoscope and listened to her lungs; they were clear. She moved the stethoscope to listen to her heart, and it too was beating as normal. She wanted to make sure that the woman's bowels were working after two doses of laudanum the night before, and moving the stethoscope to her lower stomach, was surprised to hear a small-second heartbeat. The woman was pregnant. It was hard to tell in the dim light the night before, but in the morning sun, it was obvious that her stomach was starting to stretch a little with a baby. Suzette was glad that the dose of laudanum she administered the night before was small. It didn't take much to put the injured woman out for the surgery on her mouth, and as evidenced by the healthy heartbeat of the baby, it didn't hurt the child.

Suzette looked at Quanah and motioned him over. She put the earpieces of the stethoscope in his ears and first held the bell on the woman's heart, and then moved it to her stomach. A beautiful smile spread across Quanah's face, and tears welled up in his eyes. He took a talisman from his neck and carefully put it over Suzette's golden head of hair. She lifted her braid out from under the leather thong herself; she didn't want the Indian to discover the stiletto attached to the barrette. Maria was up, and Suzette asked her to find O'Riley. She wanted to talk to the woman's mother and find out what was in the brown powder that she applied to her daughter's wounds. They also needed to move Quanah's wife back to the Indian Camp.

The supply train was ready to head out. Lt. Barksdale's soldiers transferred the woman back onto the litter she was carried in on, and they walked with Suzette over to the Indian camp. The mother and father hurried over and made a fuss over settling their daughter in their teepee. Suzette had O'Riley ask the older woman about the brown powder. He learned that she made it from the dried petals of a yellow flower. The older woman indicated that it came from a long way away, and she pointed to the southeast. Suzette surmised that she was pointing at Texas. She was getting ready to ask if she could have some, but the woman went digging in a crude buffalo skin pack and withdrew another leather pouch and handed it to Suzette. The discovery of the brown powder was amazing, an ancient cure for infection, and no one ever got close enough to the Comanche to discover it. She left instructions that the cast that she fashioned on the wounded leg was to stay on for two moons — no walking on the leg till after the first full moon turned dark again. The woman hugged Suzette, and as she left the teepee, most all the other women and children looked on her with reverence and awe. Suzette asked O'Riley, "Why are we always at war with these people?"

Mr. Sue had her medical kit put back together and was removing her surgical instruments and the transfusion tube from a pot of boiling water on his fire. He handed her a dish of scrambled eggs and potatoes. Suzette gave him the leather pouch and asked him if he knew what the brown powder was. Mr. Sue smelled it but shook his head *no* with a frown. Then he drew a tin cup of hot water from his tea kettle and mixed in a pinch of the brown powder. Mr. Sue smelled the tea and raised his eyebrows with a look of recognition and then tasted it. "Ahh-ha! I know what this is, but I don't know the name in English. I will look for it as we travel." Suzette looked at Mr. Sue in awe. Her respect and wonder at her cook's depth of knowledge continued to amaze. She wondered quietly to herself if she would ever be as knowledgeable, but in good Callahan fashion, she accepted that as a challenge, one she would pursue with all the vigor her young mind could bring to bear.

Suzette finished packing up, and the supply train was ready to pull out. It would take two days to reach Iron Spring, and everyone was hoping that the Apache would have moved away by then. They were more vigilant on the trail than usual. Eli increased the scouts to pairs of riders and pulled them in closer to the trail. He didn't want a repeat of their last experience with a hostile band. The scouts were to signal as soon as there was a sighting and then ride like hell back to the protection of the wagon train. He practiced forming the box twice along the trail and had O'Riley explaining to Quanah where they wanted his braves in the formation. Eli didn't want his men shooting the wrong Indians if the Apache attacked. Each of Quanah's men was given a yellow Army bandana to wear around his neck. They donned their uniforms with a degree of pride. The

Army wouldn't miss a crate or two of bandanas, and the simple measure would save lives in a battle with the Apache.

The first day passed with no incident: no sightings and no troubles with the wagons. The trail was heavy with dust from the drought and drinking water was rationed carefully regardless of the spring up ahead. They couldn't make it to the mountains without replenishing their water supply, especially the stock water. Even though the summer was cooling off, the dust of the trail was insufferable for the animals as well as the men. There wasn't a blade of green grass anywhere, and even the few bushes were drying up and near death. By the time Eli circled to make camp, parched throats and dehydration were taking a toll on the animals. Nonetheless, all drank sparingly, and the bare minimum was rationed out to the horses and mules from the stock tanks. Quanah and his braves were an extra comfort for security, but they were also an extra liability to the water supply.

Lt. Barksdale was incredulous. It was only eight or so miles farther to the spring. He wanted to water the animals and push on. Eli backed him down. "If we must fight the Apache for the water, I want to finish that early in the day. If we get there tonight, we will be fighting in the dark, and even though the moon will be full in three more days, we can't fight at night without killing Quanah's men too. We stay here, Lieutenant. We'll be at the spring early tomorrow." The Lieutenant wasn't happy being usurped on tactics by the younger man, but O'Riley and his sergeant took him aside and calmed him down. They respected Eli's leadership despite their commanding officer having to be straightened out on every decision.

The next morning was the same as the last, not a cloud in the sky and only the promise of another choking-dusty day. The morning was cool, however, and Eli wanted to make some good time before the day warmed up to fatigue the animals. He wanted to put the wagon train through one more drill mostly for the sake of Quanah and his men, but he didn't have to. They were only a few miles from their camp when they came over a rise and saw more than two hundred Apache blocking the trail. Eli formed the box for real. Quanah and his men were inside the box; they would take on any Apache that broke through the perimeter with spears, arrows, and tomahawks. Eli and his brothers, along with Hans and the Army contingent, formed a line in front of the three leading wagons. The Apache were walking their horses forward; the tension was electric and filling the air between the two groups. The Apache were no match for the firepower of Eli and his men, but they had the advantage in numbers and were intent on stopping the supply train short of the spring.

O'Riley addressed the chief in a mix of Apache, Comanche, and some Shawnee words. All he could relate to Eli and his Lieutenant was that the Apache wanted them to turn around and go home. Eli shook his head *no* and stood his ground. Then he walked his horse forward, and the rest of the line followed his lead. He pressed the chief back, cradling the Henry across his saddle. The chief wasn't afraid. His horse was. The horse nickered and snorted and took a step back and then another. Eli wanted the chief to throw his spear, point down, in the trail to show he wasn't going to attack. The chief raised his arm probably to do just that, but Lt. Barksdale, thinking the Indian was going to throw the spear at Eli, shot him in the head with his Colt Dragoon 0.44 revolver and the spear fell from his hand as he tumbled backward off his horse.

The rest of the Indians couldn't believe what just happened and were drawing arrows from their quivers and fitting them into their bows. Eli, Jacques, and Hans charged forward, their Henry rifles blazing. Indians were falling with every volley; there was total pandemonium in their ranks. They were turning and trying to ride out of range of the deadly hail of bullets. They just lost more than forty braves, and they hadn't even attacked yet. Eli turned his men back to the wagon train. It was time to reload and be ready for whatever came next. The Indians rode out of sight back towards the spring. Quanah and his men numbered only thirty, but he rode out to scout the retreat of the Apache. He returned in five minutes and reported to O'Riley that the Apache band was still riding towards the spring. Eli decided to move the wagon train forward.

Lt. Barksdale was getting a severe dressing down from his sergeant. He deserved it, and Eli would back up the sergeant if Lt. Barksdale brought charges against him for the insubordination. Now Eli could see clearly why the war with the Apache had been going on for a hundred years. A chief just was shot down without provocation, and many lay dead on the trail with him. Lt. Barksdale and the likes of him were probably the cause of many disputes between white settlers and the Indians. Eli was out ahead of the wagon train as before, but now he and Jacques carried an extra Henry in their scabbards. He moved the wagon train a mile, and then Quanah rode back in again and reported that the Apache were leaving the spring. Eli could see their dust trail moving down to the southeast. Quanah and his men were rounding up the Apache horses that strayed away from the main troop and were standing listlessly around the battlefield.

As Eli neared the spring, he could see that something was wrong. Turkey vultures were circling over where the pond should be at the head end of a narrow green gulch. He looked around, the spring was a half-mile south of the trail, and it wasn't a good place to camp. There were some low hills behind the spring, and if the Apache were going to attack at night, they could use the cover of the hills and the gulch beyond to get close before launching their attack. Jacques rode back from the spring and was the bearer of bad news. "The Apache pulled several rotten buffalo carcasses into the spring. The water is unfit for drinking; even my horse would have nothing to do with it. The flow out of the pool is meager. Even if we clean out the pool, it will be days before the water will be clean again."

Eli had to make a hard decision. "Let's clean out the pool. We will rest the mules here and wait as long as possible and replenish the stock water barrels just before dark. It's only a couple of days till the full moon. We'll travel by night. The Apache went to the southeast, and we are heading southwest. I don't think they would have poisoned the spring if they intended to return, but if we travel tonight, they won't know where we are by morning. Let's get to cleaning out that spring; I want the stock tanks topped off by sunset. Let's make a temporary camp up on the trail. I don't like the lay of the land there behind the spring." Word traveled around the supply train as if every driver had a personal telegraph. O'Riley was explaining to Quanah what they were going to do. Quanah conferred with his men, and they decided that they would also travel at night, but they were going back to their wives and children on the Arkansas River. They would stand guard on the high ground behind the spring and leave out at the same time as the supply train. Even if the Apache came back, there would be a confusion of trails to follow. Quanah doubted that the Apache would go west; there were no buffalo between here and the mountains, and water and wood were scarce, if not impossible for a large band.

Roland was in the spring. He helped pull the carcasses out of the small pond and then had an idea. With the manpower he had, he could bail out the pond and then even shovel out the contaminated mud from the banks and bottom. He sent word over to Eli that he needed twenty men, each with a bucket and a shovel. They may not get completely clean water by nightfall, but at least they would have water that the horses and mules would drink. There wasn't a single tree within sight as far as he could see, so boiling water to replenish their drinking supply was out of the question for this site. Eli returned with the twenty men and stationed Lt. Barksdale and his men on the higher ground with Quanah behind the spring to guard the work party. He could see in the distance with his binoculars that the Apache had stopped. They were at least ten miles away judging from the last he saw of their dust, and that was still close enough that they could stage an attack. If an attack was coming, he was sure it would come at nightfall or shortly before dark. With Roland cleaning the spring, he hoped they would be leaving before then.

The men in the pond were working with a purpose. As they bailed and the water level dropped, the mud was removed from the top rim of the pond and carried away. The pond itself was only fifteen feet in diameter and about four feet deep when they started. It would only take an hour for them to reach the bottom. Eli watched warily with the soldiers for any sign of the Apache. By the time the men got down to the bottom of the pond, he could see a small band of Apache riding slowly to the spring. Roland walked up to the rise with some good news, "We've got about ten gallons a minute, and the horses are drinking it. I'm going to rotate the wagons around a couple at a time, and we will top off the stock tanks first. I'm going to transfer all the drinking water to fill what barrels we have left and then load the empties onto several of our empty wagons. We'll fill those last and mark them. We should probably boil those before we drink, and there should be wood when we get closer to the mountains. We need about another three hours, and then we can head west again." Eli nodded his approval; his mind was on a plan to ambush the Apache approaching the spring.

Roland had knocked the bottom out of a barrel and put it over the source of the water in the bottom of the spring were the incoming water was roiling the sand. He had the men fill in around it so the water would rise in the barrel. Now they could walk into the pond without muddying the freshwater. He was rotating the wagons through what was now called *Roland's Well*. He doubted that the name would stick. O'Riley rode down from the rise to talk to Quanah. Eli was putting a plan into action. Quanah split his men in two; one group walked their horses south, and the other went east. O'Riley brought Roland up to speed on the planned ambush. Eli had already moved everyone down off the top of the rise, out of sight from the east side of the hill. Quanah was moving to hide up and down the wash on the east side of the rise. They were going to cut the scouting party off from any escape to the east. It would take at least an hour for the scouting party to reach the rise. Eli was hoping that the spring would appear deserted and that the Apache would ride in close before they realized that they were trapped.

The filling operation was going smoothly. By the time the Apache were within a quarter-mile of the wash on the east side, twenty wagons and their mules were topped off and watered. Eli had twenty men with their long rifles up behind the rise, and he couldn't see Quanah and his men, but he knew they were out there in position. There were only twelve Apache in the scouting party. Two of them rode forward into the wash. They stopped east of the rise, and one of them pointed to the circling vultures and then waved the rest of the party down. This time Lt. Barksdale's sergeant was coaching him, whispering to his lieutenant to wait. The two Apache, who had scouted ahead of their party, split up and started around the rise. When one of the scouts spotted the wagons at the spring, the sergeant yelled, "Fire!" Twenty guns boomed, and all but two off the Apache fell. Those two turned to flee to the east, only to be stopped by Quanah and his men. They threw down their spears and surrendered. Quanah was walking them back to the spring.

When Quanah walked the two Apache behind the rise, he called out to O'Riley to translate for Eli. One of the Apache was the brave who had trampled his wife. It was Quanah's right to kill him, but the execution would be in the Indian way. The brave would be staked out on the east side of the rise and left to die. The other one would carry a message back to his people. Quanah wanted the Apache to leave his territory. If they didn't move on by dawn, Quanah would attack, and Quanah would spare no one. Eli didn't approve of the method of execution, but it wasn't time to interfere with the Comanche; for the time being, Quanah was an ally of the white man. It was important to keep it that way.

By nightfall, there were only two supply wagons left to water, and three wagons stood by with empty drinking water barrels. It would take another three hours to fill the barrels, but there was no sign of the Apache to the east. Eli turned to Roland and said, "Don't leave until every barrel is full." Roland stayed in the spring with the soldiers and Quanah and his men. Roland pulled out before midnight with every barrel topped off, leaving Quanah's band and their prisoner in the moonlight. Roland had a strange thought as he topped off the last water barrel. He told O'Riley that the white men are going to defeat the Indians because the Indian tribes kill one another instead of banding together to fight a common enemy. Tribal instincts don't serve them well. O'Riley agreed. There were over a million Apache scattered over the southwest, and everywhere they were, they were at war with white men, Mexicans, or other Indians.

Eli was studying his trail map by lantern light, as Roland and the soldiers rejoined the wagon train. There was another spring up ahead called *Hole in the Rock.* He doubted that they would be able to find it in the dark, but it was purported to have good water. The map indicated it wasn't big enough to water a large wagon train. None the less, he would look for it along the way. The moon was two days away from being full, and it would be easy to see the spring if there were trees around it. Four hours later, they were in the vicinity of the spring. Eli thought that what he needed was a thirsty horse. Well, maybe his horse was thirsty enough to lead him to the water. Suzette rode with Eli on the edge of a low swale that had to be Timpas Creek. The creek was dry; even the few deciduous trees and grass that grew in the creek bottom were dry.

They were sure they had passed the spring, but then they heard a sharp but faint bark. Surprised, Suzette said, "A dog?" They rode back along the edge of the creek, and there was another bark, sharper this time. Suzette whistled; this time, there were a series of barks, louder and more excited. The spring was nothing more than a hole in the rock in the creek bottom. Scoured out and no doubt dug deeper by thirsty pioneers, the hole was about eight feet deep, and there was a dog trapped in the bottom. There was a meager puddle of water, so the dog wasn't dying of thirst, but it had to be hungry. Suzette got down and lay at the edge of the hole and reached down as far as she could to let the dog smell her hand. The dog was a medium-sized mutt and standing on its back legs with his front paws on the wall; it licked Suzette's hand.

Eli jumped down into the hole and picked the dog up and boosted it up the wall. Suzette pulled it up the rest of the way. The dog was crazy happy and licked her face with a good bit of slobber but then smelled the bag of jerky tied to her gun belt. Suzette untied it and shook out the last few pieces of jerky out on the ground. The dog pounced on the food, and Suzette wondered how long it had been in the hole. Eli called up from the bottom, "Hey, how about you throw me a rope?"

The dog looked like it was an Irish setter, but in the moonlight, it was difficult to tell. Suzette, ever the doctor checked out the dog and pronounced her female. "Can we keep her? We could give her to Maria to look after. She has been brooding about her parents again, and I can't fault her for that. The dog would be good for her. It could get her mind onto other things."

Eli could see tears well up in Suzette's eyes at the mention of Maria's parents. The Callahan wounds were still fresh. "Yes, that's a good idea. Let's ride over to the wagons and see if she follows." The dog did follow, and when Eli handed her to Maria, the girl hugged the dog like a long-lost friend. "Yours," was all that Eli said. Mr. Sue raised an eyebrow but smiled and could see that the girl and the dog were going to be best friends. Maria also had some jerky left that sealed the bond.

By dawn, the supply train had moved almost twenty miles west. Eli saw a grove of cottonwoods in a low-lying depression and pulled the wagons into the shade of the trees for the day. He thought there should be a waterhole here, but with so many cottonwoods soaking up the water below, only a deep well could reach the valuable resource. Everyone was tired, and the mules fagged, but guards were more important now than ever, and animals still needed tending. Nonetheless, all slept well through the heat of the day. They would be at the entrance to Ratón Pass in three more days. There would be water there in the headwaters of the Purgatory River. Ratón Pass would be a challenge with the heavy wagons, but he was looking forward to a challenge that didn't involve killing more Indians. Later in the day, he fell asleep for a well-deserved rest. By evening everyone was looking to move on in the cool air of the night.

Suzette fell asleep under the wagon, wondering what it would have been like had she let the man in the cave follow through with his rape. However, sex with that man was out of the question. His fetid breath and the stench of his body were overwhelming, and disease wasn't just a risk; with a derelict of the trail, it would be a certainty. Then there was the risk of pregnancy to consider. She had all these things on her mind when she fell asleep and was dreaming of Paul Hayman when the barking of the dog woke her. She was perplexed to have woken up sexually aroused. Letting Paul start a sexual relationship on the trail would be a complicated mistake, and she would have to wait and keep him at arm's length until the time was right.

She wondered about her brothers. They were older and certainly had women who wanted to be with them, along with plenty of opportunities during their trips to Fort Leavenworth. She couldn't talk to them about sex. She missed her mother and even Jessica or Lily. They were women, and she could talk to them. Then she thought about Hannah and what Hannah would say, "You're young. There is plenty of time. Wait for the right man. Wait till you are married." She bolted out of her slumbering dream to more barking and a piercing scream from Maria.

Maria was pushed up tight against her with the dog held tight in her arms. There was a large rattlesnake curled up under the back of the wagon. The dog was getting more agitated. Suzette was wide awake in an instant. She was taking her Lefaucheux out of its holster to shoot the snake, but it wasn't necessary. A shovel flashed down from the back of the wagon and cut the snake into several pieces. Mr. Sue said, "Time to get up, ladies. We have fresh meat for our breakfast.

Maria and Suzette climbed out from under the wagon. Their hearts were still racing, and Maria was shaking from the adrenaline rush. She patted the dog on the head and said, "Eres una buen perro."

Mr. Sue was gutting and skinning the snake. With the skill he approached the job, it was apparent he had done this before. Suzette asked Maria in Spanish what she would name the dog. The girl reflected on this a while and said, "Huérfana," the Spanish word for an orphan, like herself. Suzette thought *Ojos de serpiente* would be a better name, but the dog wasn't hers to name. Mr. Sue had skinned and cut the snake into sections and had it skewered on a spit, cooking at the side of the fire pit. A skillet with the last of his potatoes was cooking on the grate next to it. It was strange eating breakfast in the late afternoon, but with a little luck, they would reach the Purgatory River east of Ratón Pass by morning, and there, they would find water and be traveling during the day again.

Suzette and her brothers each had a large piece of the rattlesnake. Maria refused to eat it despite the alluring smell and the offer of something different than the hardtack and salt pork that they were down to in their food supplies. Eli was also hoping that when they reached the Purgatory River that there would be clean water. It was dry from the drought where it joined the Arkansas River, but there should be water in it upstream and closer to the mountains. One more night on the trail, and they would reach the river by dawn. The drivers and their helpers were hitching up their teams. The cooks packed up the chuck wagons; it was time to resume their journey.

The full moon rose in the east with a spectacular sunset in the west. The heat of the day ebbed, and a cool breeze greeted the travelers as they pulled out onto the trail. They weren't alone on the trail. Shortly after dark, a lone rider was coming at them from the south. He was pushing hard, but he pulled up at Eli's wagon. He was with the Pony Express. He was a small lean man no older than Eli. He had good news; there was water where the trail met the Purgatory. He was riding to the station at Iron Springs. Eli told him there wasn't a station at Iron Springs. There was a large band of Apache in the area when they came through. No doubt, they burned the station to the ground and scattered its rock walls; there was no sign left of a station. Eli told the rider he better conserve his horse, and he offered him one of their spares and a water skin to see him over the miles to Fort Bent. The rider stayed only a few minutes, and then he was on his way riding hell-bent on his mission to deliver the mail to Independence; there was an Indian pony on a halter trailing behind him.

Before dawn, Suzette and Roland could smell the river. They were scouting at least a mile ahead of the wagons, and Roland wanted some fresh venison. Suzette stayed on the trail, and Roland rode down to the river. Ten minutes passed, and the wagons were approaching. Suzette thought that if Roland was going to get a deer, he better bag it soon, or the wagons would spook whatever game was down there. She was about to ride forward again when a single shot rang out; then, after a pause, there was a second. Jacques rode up to join her. Suzette said, "Roland, our mighty hunter, is putting meat on the table again. It's time to make camp."

"Eli sent me ahead to find a spot. He wants to stop for a day and repair wagons and shoe mules. The men will be happy with some fresh meat. You go help Roland with the game, and I'll locate a good spot." He didn't have to go far. There was a grassy bottom about a half mile further on. Large cottonwood trees lined the river, and there were more on the flat. He rode to one close to the river and stopped and built a fire. There were numerous fire rings on the flat. The grassy flat was a popular campsite on the trail. Roland and Suzette rode up to the fire pit. Each was dragging a deer with a halter rope tethered to their saddle horns. Eli was pulling in with the first of the wagons. He took the best spot under a cottonwood tree and had the rest of the drivers circling the flat. They would eat, have a short rest, and then use the rest of the day to make ready for the crossing over Ratón Pass. Mr. Sue and the rest of the cooks were dressing out the deer. Many of the men commented on the size of the deer. Most of the men were from the east coast and had never seen a mule deer before. Mr. Sue assured them that elk were even bigger; it would only take one to feed everyone, and they tasted a lot better than buffalo.

Maria was playing with her dog, teaching her to fetch. Suzette spread a blanket in the shade of the cottonwood and fell into a deep sleep. She asked Mr. Sue to wake her when it was time to eat. Everyone was looking forward to a good meal. Paul was turning a hind quarter on a spit. Suzette hadn't noticed before, but Paul was watching her every move as she unsaddled Patches and arranged her saddle and panniers for a pillow. Patches was happily grazing on the lush grass and the munching sounds of the horse grazing, the ring of the blacksmith's hammer and songs some of the men were singing as they worked, lulled Suzette into a deep, dreamless sleep. After a while, Maria curled up beside her with the dog in between them. Mr. Sue woke them after a while. He had a plate of venison with biscuits and gravy for each of them. He tossed the dog a meaty bone, and she pounced on it like it was the first meal she had ever eaten.

The day passed quickly with much to do. Eli's wagon was too heavy, and there was excessive wear on the axles; the axles needed replacement. The Germans unloaded the wagon, and the silver was divvied up among three of the empty supply wagons. Hans oversaw the shifting of the silver and kept a precise tally of what went into each wagon. Only his most trusted drivers would be transporting the silver.

While they were loading the last of the silver, a mountain man walked into the camp. Eli wondered why mountain men traveled on foot, but then, they could go places and comb the mountains looking for gold where no animal could follow. The man introduced himself as Richens Wooton. Eli noted that the man was as ugly as a mud fence with layers of dirt and grease on his clothes and hands; the parts of his face that showed around his thick matted beard looked like it would be unhealthy to eat without first washing. Wooton very badly needed a trip down to the river to clean up. Everyone he got near to moved upwind. He had a heavy pack on this back and carried a Hawken rifle slung across his chest. His outfit was all buckskin, right down to his high laced up boots. He had a Bowie knife in a scabbard on his right calf. He was mesmerized by the huge quantity of silver that Hans's men were handling. He figured Hans to be a precious metals merchant and set his pack down and drew out a piece of quartz about the size of a softball. The quartz was laden with gold. It was a beautiful specimen, and Wooton wanted to sell it. He laid into his pitch, "It came from a Spanish mine up by the pass. The Spanish call it the La Veta de Oro."

Suzette stepped in, "Hans's English is limited, but I can translate. How much do you want for the rock?"

Wooton was surprised to be approached by a beautiful young woman in an Army Supply Train. "Well, for you, little lady, I would sell for a hundred dollars. There are probably more than five ounces of gold in the rock, but as a specimen, it is worth much more. I could also sell the mine if there is an interested buyer here. These men certainly have enough silver to afford it." Eli was looking on with a strong look of caution and skepticism.

Suzette took it as a sign that he wanted her to negotiate for the rock and leave the mine alone. "I can offer you sixty dollars for the rock. That will be in gold."

"It's worth at least three times that much!" Wooton burst out.

"Now Mr. Wooton, if I pay you what it is worth, how's a girl to make any money?"

"Maybe you would like to buy the mine instead?"

"Sight unseen; I don't think so."

"Look, I need at least eighty dollars for the rock."

Suzette was going to counter, but she was distracted by a yell or what was more like a cry of anguish from the men's latrine. Eli went over to investigate. Suzette got up to follow, and Mr. Sue joined her; with a look of concern, they walked after Eli. Wooton was flustered. He yelled after them, "Okay! Okay! I'll take the sixty." Rolland dug out three double eagles from his pocket and traded for the rock.

Eli walked back into the wagon circle and said, "We have a problem. That man has the venereal disease, and he says he is not the only one." Suzette was dreading this. She had the treatment for gonorrhea in the medical supplies, but there was no cure for syphilis. The stopover at Fort Wise could cost these men their sanity and eventually their lives if they had contracted the more serious disease.

Mr. Sue rescued her from her worries, "I can examine him. I am familiar with both diseases. They were rampant in the Chinese army." He walked out to the latrine and was back in a few moments. "We're in luck; get the gonorrhea kit out and read me the instructions. I'll take care of this sick call."

Suzette was embarrassed enough just reading the instructions. There were several of a special type of rubber syringe and a bottle of silver nitrate solution. For more serious cases, there was a thick silver wire and instructions for heating it and inserting it into the penis. She hoped they were catching this epidemic in its earliest stages.   The men had no opportunity for sex with an afflicted woman until they had reached Fort Wise, so this could only be the earliest stages of incubation. Eli called all the men together and let them know that Pete, the driver of the seventh wagon, had the *Clap*. Suzette and Mr. Sue were setting up the medical treatment, and any men with painful urination or itching were to get treated immediately. Nine men stepped over to the medical table. One of them was Paul Hayman. Suzette saddened; Paul was the only man in the supply train that she considered as a potential mate.   That wasn't going to be now or ever. Gonorrhea could be cured, but she knew from her grandmother's writings, that the male of the species was constantly thinking of sex, and if one was willing to lower his standards to having sex with an unknown Indian woman or a wag-tail at the fort, he was probably going to pursue that behavior the rest of his life. She hoped this would be a lesson for Paul that would last a lifetime.

Suzette walked back over to Roland. He wanted to hand her the gold specimen, but Suzette was distracted again. Wooton was milling around the camp. Maria asked about what was going on. Suzette took the younger girl aside and explained the dangers of sexually transmitted diseases. When Suzette finished, Maria asked, "And Mr. Paul too?"

"Yes, Mr. Paul too." Masking the disappointment in her answer was impossible. "Let's go swimming and get cleaned up. There is a deep pool a little way down the river. I'll ask Roland to guard us." As they were walking down to the river, Roland put his arm around Suzette in a gesture of understanding. Tears welled up in Suzette's eyes; she didn't talk on the way down to the river. Nothing she could say would lessen her disappointment in Paul. No words were spoken; none were needed. Suzette thought, *Roland, the wise brother, he understands everything*.

The girls stripped down and swam and then washed their clothes. Roland was up on the river bank, Henry Rifle, under his arm, watching the other bank. He thought of a girl back home, one who he didn't want to leave. He wondered if he would ever see her again, and he also wondered which of the young men around Independence she would pick for a mate. There was a lifetime out ahead of them, and there was plenty of time given that they would survive life on the trail. The girls finished in an hour, and the three of them walked back to the camp. Eli told Suzette that three more men came forward for the treatment after she left. Mr. Sue had the medical kit packed up and was cooking venison on the grill over his fire pit. It smelled good, and Suzette was hungry. After dinner, Suzette noticed that Paul was not hanging around as usual. She wondered if he would ever talk to her again. She also had the thought; *would I ever talk to him?*

As the sun was setting, she heard his banjo on the other side of the camp. Tonight, there was a sadder tone to the music.

She accepted that he was going to avoid her. Brooding about the musician, she rolled out her and Maria's bedrolls under Eli's wagon. As darkness fell and the heat of the day gave way to the cold of night, she fell asleep. This night there were no dreams, no unanswered questions. She slept soundly and woke early in the morning to the sound of Mr. Sue chopping wood for the fire.

The routine of the trail was coming to life again. She got up and helped herself to the coffee. Eli was up and having his cup of Mr. Sue's breakfast soup. He was anxious to move. Ratón Pass was only two days away. They would be in New Mexico on the last leg of the trek to Santa Fe. He was looking forward to the challenge of the mountains and getting the heavy wagons up and over Ratón pass. The problems of yesterday were already far from his mind. Today would be their forty-fifth day on the trail.

As they made their way up the river, the crunch of rocks under the wheels of the heavy wagons was a welcome sound compared to the endless miles of dust and mud across the prairie. Even the fish in the river were different from the bass and catfish of the prairie rivers. These fish were trout, and bald eagles were busy fishing and carrying their catch back to hungry eaglets in their many aeries in the tops of the highest cottonwoods in the river bottom. The cottonwoods were starting to turn yellow with the oncoming fall, but the grass in the river bottom and on the benches above the meanders was still green and lush. It was a marvel unto itself after so many miles of drought-parched land. Many of the drivers and their helpers decided on the spot that they would live somewhere where it was green for the rest of their lives as soon as their contracts with the Army were up.

Jacques and Roland were scouting ahead. There wasn't much opportunity to scout north or south of the trail as the valley narrowed as they neared the mountains. They were looking for the Army camp where they were to leave some rifles and supplies. So far, there wasn't any sign of the soldiers.

Where the trail turned south towards the pass, there were six wagons of Mexicans pulled by oxen. Roland rode back to fetch Suzette and Maria to translate. Jacques noted that the wagons carried large lumps of coal. Suzette rode up with Maria behind her in the saddle. Jacques wanted her to ask where the soldiers were. Suzette struck up a conversation with the oldest of the Mexican drivers and his wife, who was the only woman in their small wagon train.

Suzette learned that they were hauling coal to silver mines high in the Colorado Mountains. The soldiers they were looking for, camped at *Cima*. Suzette had to ask Maria what the word meant. Maria peaked her hands like a mountain and then tapped the top of her imaginary mountain with the tip of her left index finger. "Más al sur en el camino." – *Farther south on the trail*. Suzette asked if that was where the coal was from, and the Mexicans said it was. Suzette thanked the man and his wife and rode over to tell Eli what she learned. Eli decided it was too far to travel in what remained of their day; they would camp, water the mules, and fill their barrels from the river before starting up the pass. They would find a suitable campsite for the night and then find the soldiers the next day.

The evening was typical of a night on the trail with the exception that the night air was cooler, cold in fact. Everyone was digging for their extra blankets by morning. The hot coffee and the warmth of the cook fire at sunrise was a welcome friend. Suzette was sipping her morning coffee when Roland handed her the rock he bought from Wooton. As the grey of the predawn gave way to the early light of morning, Suzette fondled the rock and wondered what it would be like to own a pile of gold bars, like Bent's pile of silver. The rock was beautiful, with its veins of gold as busy as a map of the wagon trails around Independence. She didn't know how that thought crept up on her, but she put the rock away in her bedroll in Eli's wagon. She didn't want to let in the sadness and depression brought by her memories of her last day with her parents.

When they set out on the trail, it was obvious that their easy travels were over for a while. The trail steepened, and the mules labored hard to pull the heavy wagons up the grade. They came to a particularly steep slope that pitched to the left, and Eli had to double-team the mules to get the wagons up and over it. It was taking more than three hours to move only two hundred yards. He knew there would be more arduous grades ahead. The *Trail Guide* said that the average time for clearing the Ratón Pass was five days, and that was just for only twenty-seven miles of progress. Lt. Barksdale was anxious to find the soldiers at *Cima*. He rode forward with two of his men and returned after four hours.

Corporal O'Riley, his Platoon Sergeant McNabb, and the rest of the soldiers stayed to help with the arduous task of hitching up and moving the extra teams to get the wagons up the grade. They were relieved that the Lieutenant left for a while. They pulled the lighter wagons up easily, but the heavy ones took considerable doing. In addition to the steep grade, the mules were unfamiliar with being in the mountains and balked at having to pull hard with the rocky trail beneath their hooves. A man was down, having been kicked hard in the stomach. Suzette had him moved up to Eli's wagon. There wasn't much she could do for the man but ease his pain with some laudanum. She hoped that his intestines weren't ruptured, but the bruise was bad, and she knew that such a wound could turn deadly with infection. There was nothing she could do for that. A few days and the man's fate would overtake him if his intestines were ruptured. Surgery to repair a ruptured intestine was well beyond her skills. She had the young man drink a tincture made with the brown powder but doubted it could help if her worst fear was the reality.

Lt. Barksdale returned and reported that the contingent up at the pass was down to only seven out of twelve original soldiers. Out of the five missing, only one died in an attack by Mexican renegades. The rest deserted, drawn to the quest for gold and silver in the Colorado Mountains. Sergeant McNabb wasn't worried about his men; most of them were lifers. He was worried though that more rash acts on the part of his lieutenant could drive away even the most dedicated of soldiers. For the moment, however, they still had eight wagons to pull up the steep grade.

It was a slow process. The heavier wagons had to be double teamed to pull them up. When Eli finally got everyone up to the top of that first steep grade, he called all the men together to lay down some rules for scaling continuing forward. "First and foremost is safety," Eli put forth in his now comfortable command voice. "When we are pulling a wagon up a steep grade, I don't want anyone or any wagon behind it. Most of these wagons were new seven hundred miles ago, but they aren't new anymore. If you stand behind a wagon on a steep grade, you are trusting your life to a bunch of wood, leather, nuts, and bolts that have seen better days. Just don't be in the way if one breaks free. Next, let's talk about security. The first wagon up is alone and exposed; so, Lt. Barksdale, I want you and your men up there with it. Same with the last wagon at the bottom, it becomes exposed. I want you to move down when there are about six or so wagons left below. There aren't any buffalo in the mountains, so I don't expect any Indian trouble, but there will be renegades and outlaws. Let's not let down our guard and let's not get anyone else hurt. Time to move out."

The men climbed back up in the wagons, and Eli moved them up the trail. It was steep, and the mules were laboring hard. They were able to travel a few more miles before it was time to make camp on a relatively level meadow. Water at least wasn't going to be a problem. There were numerous springs and pools in the bottom of the gorge. There were game birds, and more deer than one could count. There were also bugs — annoying flies and mosquitos. The nights were cold but not yet cold enough to kill the pests.

Roland and Suzette were out hunting, and by the time the camp was set up, the report of a single rifle shot was heard echoing down the mountain. About an hour later, Roland and Suzette arrived, pulling a huge-bull-elk between the horses. The animal was hitched up headfirst by the antlers, so he was drug across the grass with his head up between the two horses. The cooks were delighted, this was going to be better than buffalo, and everyone was going to have an elk steak on his dinner plate.

As the evening meal was ready, the Army contingent from *Cima* rode into camp. A young staff sergeant introduced himself as O'Carr. He needed everything for his camp. Food, uniforms, guns, and ammunition, but most of all, he needed winter clothes. The nights were already down in the forties, and soon they would be getting snow at the higher elevations. O'Carr reported to Lt. Barksdale and said he and his men would stay with the wagon train until they cleared the last steep grade. O'Carr was a handsome young man. Suzette could tell that Maria was attracted to him. Suzette put her arm around her shoulders, like the older sister she had become, and shook her head with a commanding, *NO*. Maria laughed and touched the barrette in her hair. Suzette smiled and said, "Esa es mi chica."

The next day was harder than the first on the steep trail. There was a particularly steep grade, more than two hundred feet of it that looked, from a distance, to be nearly straight up. Jacques had an idea. "We could put two teams over the top with a rope and double team the heaviest of the wagons at the bottom." They had four rolls of one-inch rope, and Jacques didn't think that twenty-four mules could break four ropes, and he hoped he was right. He continued, "The rope will wear pulled over the rocks and dirt, so we have to take the heaviest wagons up first." Eli pulled the first rope up over the top of the grade with his horse, and Jacques led two of their teams up to the top. There were parts of a broken block and tackle lying at the edge of the grade. It wasn't hard to imagine that there were a lot of accidents here. Eli's wagon would be the first up.

All the mules were in place, and with a whistle and step by arduous step, the heavy wagon moved up the slope. It would take the rest of the day to get the rest of the wagons up, but the rope worked and was safer and faster than working with block and tackle. Eli inspected the rope after every pull. It was holding up well, but he was still relieved when the last wagon was up. They moved up the trail to another meadow, and as they arrived, Roland and Suzette were pulling in another huge-bull elk. Everyone was exhausted, but there were still animals to tend to and wagons to inspect. The blacksmith was busy; *thank goodness he is stronger than the rest*, Eli thought as he made his rounds. That night the Army would post the guard, and everyone would get a good rest.

Late that night, Suzette woke to a loud eerie scream. It wasn't in the camp, but it wasn't far away either. "Mountain lion," O'Carr said from outside the wagon ring. Suzette rolled over and found her Henry rifle in the dark. The lion sounded close by, and she wanted the security of the rifle close at hand. Later several shots rang out, and the whole camp came awake. Again, O'Carr said, "grizzly bear." Everyone was back asleep as if a grizzly bear visit was a routine occurrence. The next morning the bearskin was stretched on a rack for drying, and Mr. Sue had grizzly bear steaks cooking for breakfast. The supplies to be delivered to Sgt. O'Carr filled a single empty wagon, and two of his soldiers took the wagon to their camp at *Cima*. The soldiers returned later in the morning with the supply wagon, as the wagon train was scaling the next grade, and the wagon carried a load of coal. The blacksmith was elated.

Pulling the wagons up with the ropes became an easy routine. They were on the last steep grade, almost to the summit. Eli had the feeling that things were going too well. That was usually when the unexpected happened, but his premonition served him well when he inspected the last of the heavy wagons laden with silver. He saw that the draw pin wasn't exactly centered in its hole, a sure sign of wear. The blacksmith didn't have another pin, so they switched the pin with another from a wagon that was already up the grade. The heavy wagon came up without incident, and then the empties followed. They were over the top. O'Carr and his soldiers bid farewell and headed back to *Cima*. Another mile and they passed a rock inscribed with *New Mexico Territory*. They traveled easily on the downhill slope on the south side of the pass. There were less-steep grades, but several places still required the ropes to hold the wagons back. A runaway wagon was something they couldn't afford. Eli paid heed to a caution he read in the *Trail Guide* about holding the wagons back, and they descended the steep grades without incident.

When they reached a large flat with a stream on the east side and a spring on the west, Eli signaled to make camp. They had crossed the pass in four days; only twenty-seven miles but four very hard long days and only one serious injury. Eli didn't realize it, but they had set a record for so many wagons crossing the pass in only four days. That record would stand for quite a while and become an interesting page in the history of the pass.

Suzette wasn't concerned with records. She was concerned with Anton, the man with the stomach injury. There was a hard knot at the edge of the bruise, but the man's process of digestion and elimination was working as normal. The knot hurt like hell, and she could administer laudanum for the pain, but if she kept up the treatment, she was sure to turn the man into an addict. She told him that she was going to taper off the laudanum, and he would have to shoulder the pain. That wasn't happy news for Anton. He said he would try his best, though. Mr. Sue had some herbal treatments, and Suzette included a steady dose of tea made with the brown powder she had gotten from the Indian woman. Time would tell. Fort Union was the next stop. She was hoping they had a hospital with a good surgeon. It was another ninety miles to Fort Union. Anton would have to hang on for several more days. That would be his best chance to survive.

They were still in the mountains, and while the trail was smoother, the track was still rocky. Anton was going to suffer from every jolt. Pain or addiction, Suzette was troubled, but Roland reassured her that her decision was correct. If Anton got worse, the addiction wouldn't matter. If he lived till they reached Fort Union, they would turn him over to the hospital with a surgeon who was qualified to open his stomach and remove the knot.

Suzette was still brooding about her decision by the fire pit when Eli came over and said it was time she turned in. It was cold, and she was reluctant to leave the warmth of the fire. "Just a few more cold nights, and we will be back down on the dry prairie and back in the drought. Treasure the cool air because there is a big-hot desert out there ahead of us." Suzette fell asleep wondering what the Pacific Ocean would look like and if they would even make it. There was only one way to find out, and that was by putting one foot in front of the other for at least another month.

Morning came too soon, and she was up and checking on Anton even before the first of the coffee was ready. The next four days were going to be difficult for Anton and difficult for her too. She gave him only half a dose of laudanum before breakfast. They set out to the south, and soon, she was riding scout with Roland. As the day wore on, it was good to be out of earshot of Anton's groans and screams. Fort Union couldn't come soon enough.

By nightfall, they reached Willow Springs. Anton was exhausted and weary from the pain. He was a good soldier, though; he knew he was going to make it. He refused a dose of laudanum before he went to sleep. Mr. Sue was encouraged because the swelling in his stomach was softer than before. The next morning Suzette palpated the knot in Anton's stomach, and it indeed was softer and smaller. The pain had backed off some, and that was also a welcome improvement. She administered only a quarter dose of laudanum, and Anton accepted it greedily. Suzette didn't know if it was out of fear of pain, the anticipation of jarring on the trail, or the hungry craving of withdrawal that accounted for the crazed look of need on Anton's face. There was almost a mystical effect of relief when the laudanum hit his system.

Mr. Sue took Suzette aside and told her it was an addiction; he had seen it many times in China where smoking opium was common amongst his troops. He suggested that they cut him off, and he would prepare a placebo from the ethanol in the medical kit. In the morning, Suzette could dose the placebo, and when Anton hurt, she could tell him that it was the knot in his stomach getting worse. Suzette was beginning to see that a good deal of Mr. Sue's medicine was psychology. Another skill she would have to learn.

The next morning Suzette dosed the placebo. Anton was satisfied, probably with the rush of the strong alcohol, but by noon he was in agony, clutching his stomach and moaning as the wagon swayed back and forth. At least the trail was smoother as they descended out of the mountains. The wagon train was still high enough in the mountains to see out onto prairie more than a hundred miles to the southeast. It did look hot out there.

They reached Cimarron by nightfall. There was a doctor in the small settlement, but he was of little use. He said that Anton was in withdrawal, which Suzette and Mr. Sue already knew. He said that the stomach wound was probably fatal, and they should administer the laudanum to keep him comfortable until he died. Suzette and Mr. Sue sent the doctor back to his shack. Suzette noticed that he didn't have any patients waiting; Jacques returned from a visit to the local bar and had nothing but horror stories to relate about the town doctor's malpractice.

Suzette stuck to Mr. Sue's treatments and dosed Anton that night with the placebo. Anton was shaking and in the throes of cold sweats. Mr. Sue told Suzette that one more day and the addiction would lessen. The knot in his stomach was significantly smaller, but Anton still complained about the pain.

Suzette was suspicious that he was lying about the pain to secure his next fix. They dosed him with Mr. Sue's treatment laden heavily with the last of the brown powder they had gotten from the Indians. "We have to find more of this," Suzette was telling Mr. Sue when a woman from Cimarron came into the camp with two sick children. Cholera, this Suzette could handle. She was glad for the distraction. Anton and her hard decisions were weighing ever more heavily on her mind.

By morning Anton was over the shakes, and the cold sweats and nausea subsided. He refused the placebo and walked to the fire ring and sat down with Eli and Mr. Sue. His stomach still hurt, but he drank Mr. Sue's breakfast soup. Mr. Sue said, "Young man, you have had a hard ride on the dragon. When you get farther out west, particularly to the Chinatowns of Los Angeles and San Francisco, there will be many opium dens. The dragon will be beckoning, and his claw is sharp. He will be hard to resist, but if you want to live out the rest of your life, you must leave him alone. I recommend that you also abstain from heavy drink or anything else you encounter that is addictive. It will be hard, but If you can do this for the rest of your life, there won't be a dragon standing by your grave to welcoming you to an early death." Anton understood Mr. Sue's sage advice and agreed. That day on the trail, Anton was able to sit up on the driver's seat with Jacques, and the day after that, he was able to take the reins.

FORT UNION

When they reached Fort Union, Anton walked from the wagon train camp to the post clinic for an examination. Doctor Robert (Bob) Way was well established with credentials on the wall of the waiting room that attested to years of experience as a Doctor of General Practice and Surgery. He introduced his wife, Dr. Lea Way, who, at the moment, was acting as his nurse. Looking at the credentials hanging on the waiting room wall again, she now understood the meaning of the sign outside. It read *The Doctors Way*.

Suzette immediately liked Dr. Lea Way, who was elegant and kind. Dr. Lea told Suzette that she and her husband married in medical school. Suzette accompanied Anton into the examination room and told the doctor how she and Mr. Sue treated Anton after he developed the knot in his stomach from the mule kick. The doctors could only find a trace of the knot. Suzette only had the empty bag that had held the brown powder, and Doctor Lea recognized it by its unique smell. I think you can buy this from some of the Comanche camped outside the fort. They were amazed that Anton had recovered from what they called a stomach abscess and beat the laudanum addiction to boot. Dr. Bob said, "Young lady, you are going to make a fine doctor one day. There is a medical school in San Francisco, where we studied under the famous surgeon, Dr. Cooper. I'm going to write you a letter of recommendation. The tuition is probably steep, but I am sure you can get someone to pay your way if you need help with that."

As Suzette and Anton were leaving, Doctor Bob stopped her and said, "By the way, there is a complaint against you and your brothers over at the post commander's office. A man named Ronkainen filed it claiming to be Bent's agent. He says you murdered his partner and stole Bent's silver. He wants it back. Check in with the commander, but it is Friday afternoon; you won't be able to see Judge Wilkerson until Monday morning.

From what I have seen, Ronkainen is a snake. I don't think the judge is going to give you any trouble, but you should prepare for the worse."

Suzette left Anton with the doctors. Fort Union was going to be more interesting than she thought. She found Eli and the twins at the quartermaster's office. She brought them up to date with what the doctor had told her. They would have two days to draft up a response to Ronkainen's complaint. There wouldn't be a wasted minute; Suzette was going to hang this bastard once and for all. Suzette asked her brothers about the complaint and wanted to know what they would do on Monday morning in court.

Eli reflected for a moment and then responded, "It would be possible that after Ronkainen had discovered that he made off with a load of lead, he could have gotten some horses and men and made it here before us over the Cimarron Cutoff. I don't expect he will show his face now that we are here. Let's talk to the commander." They walked over and entered the post headquarters. The clerk in the outer office was a young corporal. He wasn't surprised to see four heavily armed, trail-hardened and sun-darkened pioneers. He was surprised that one of them was a girl. They wanted to see the commanding officer, and the corporal could see that they wouldn't be put off. Without asking who they were, he went in and told the colonel that he had visitors.

The colonel came out to the outer office and introduced himself, "I'm the post commander, Colonel Gerald E. Beekman. We have been expecting you, come in and have a seat." Colonel Beekman was a tall man and spoke with a deep voice. His uniform was spotless, and he wore the tall boots of the horse soldier and walked like he had been on a horse many years.

They filed into the office, and the corporal offered them coffee or water. They all opted for the water. Col. Beekman waited till the corporal finished serving the water, and the four youngsters settled in the hard-oak chairs in front of his desk.

Colonel Beekman addressed Suzette, "You, young lady, have become quite famous, and there was a Vincent Ronkainen come by here accusing you of murder.   The four of you have made quite a name for yourselves on your crossing."

He had a copy of a newspaper from Missouri. The headline and lead story were accounts of Suzette's killing of Chico del Diablo in the church in Council Grove. Colonel Beekman rolled the newspaper and held it like a pointer as he went on, "We know about the slaughter of the renegades and the killing of the Apache at Iron Springs. News travels a lot faster than the supply trains out here with the occasional stage and the Pony Express.   The Indians outside are a menagerie of Apache, Comanche, Ute, Kiowa, and even some Navahos from out west. All of the Indians here are peaceful, but don't be surprised if they are afraid of you."

The Callahans sat quietly, and finally, Roland broke the silence, "I would like to read the complaint filed by Ronkainen."

"No problem," said Colonel Beekman. He had several copies on the top of his desk. Each was handwritten. The original was hardly legible, but the copies stood out in a fine flowing hand that was easy to read. "We have a circuit court judge due here from Santa Fe on Monday. I'm going to ask you to stay the weekend and present yourself to the Judge on Monday. We don't have a stockade here, and you are not under arrest.   I don't put much credence in Ronkainen's complaint, and he disappeared yesterday when word came down the trail that you were getting close. He has a lawyer here to make his case in front of the judge."

"Get comfortable around the fort. We are more of a supply depot than a fort. There are no walls or gun emplacements, but be careful. More than half the men here are from the South. If the war breaks out, we may be out there in the streets fighting one another. There is a bar, a dining hall, and a gambling hall. There are some Indian women around, but again, be careful, most of them aren't healthy – if you get what

I mean. Now to another subject – how much silver do you have in Bent's shipment?"

Eli opened his leather pouch and from the back of his logbook, took out Colonel Schultz's letter from Fort Wise, Bent's contract for transport, and Hans Warner's inventory of the silver bars and the bags of ore. There were four tons of bars and three tons of high-grade silver ore. Eli said, "These documents should prove that we didn't steal the silver. I am more concerned about the allegation that Suzette murdered Ronkainen's partner in cold blood. Have you heard the story behind that?"

"No, and I don't want to. Sometimes at a hearing such as this, Judge Wilkerson will call on another senior officer and me to join him on the bench; we act as a tribunal. Talk to young Bill out there. He can tell you all about Ronkainen's case and how the Judge will handle it. In the meantime, enjoy Fort Union." With that, he shook hands with each in turn, and then dismissed them as if they were soldiers under his command.

Outside they sat in the shade of the porch and read the complaint. In essence, it maintained that Suzette was whoring around Fort Wise with her young Mexican friend, and after having sex with Landstrom, she demanded an outrageous price. When Landstrom wouldn't pay, she slit his throat. The complaint made no mention of Landstrom's hired hand that was the one who tried to rape her. Suzette was angrier than her brothers had ever seen her, and her fury reminded them of the lightning in front of the thunderstorms they weathered back on the prairie. Roland offered to be her council on Monday, but she refused. Suzette said, "No, I will handle my defense," and she walked out through the rows of shabby-mud-hut buildings back out to the wagon train. Eli went to see the quartermaster, and Jacques suggested that he and Roland check out the bar.

Eli and the quartermaster made up a schedule for unloading the wagons. The quartermaster had limited space and needed to pack the supplies in the armory and storehouses in the reverse order of how they would be shipped out. Fort Union took more than half of all the supplies Eli had left. The men with empty wagons had three options. They could return east laden with goods from the merchants, join the Army and train as infantry, or continue west with Eli. Some of the men would, no doubt, disappear and head for the mines in Colorado. Others were intent on reaching California. Come Tuesday; they would know exactly how they stood, provided that Judge Wilkerson didn't have them under lock and key by then.

Eli left the quartermaster and saw Suzette leaving the general store with a box under her arm. She told Eli to call the men together. She had a present for them. Eli just scratched his head and wondered, *what now*? He smiled when he saw that it was a box of condoms.

The men finished putting the mules and horses up and were ready for some time off. They knew there was at least warm beer in the bar, and others were anxious to try their luck at the gambling hall. Eli had them all gathered up and was ready to congratulate them on their successful crossing of Ratón Pass, but Suzette stepped in and took control of the meeting. "Gents," she said, standing on the top of her medical trunk. "This box is a happy find for you. It's a box of one-hundred condoms. I'm not going to embarrass you or myself in teaching you how to use them, and I'm not going to pay any attention to who wants them. The box will be here on the back of my wagon. Stop by and take what you need before you go back to the fort." She left the men and her brothers dumbstruck. The men milled around for a while, and then one-by-one started passing by the back of the wagon.

Finished with her speech, she gathered up Maria and walked back to the fort. She made the pretense of taking Maria to the general store, and when she saw some of the men from the wagon train watching her, she did just that and bought Maria a beautiful yellow dress. She also bought some hard candy for Maria and some jerky for Huérfana. They came back out onto the street, and when Suzette was sure no one would notice, she slipped Maria into the doctors' office.

Later that night, the fort turned a little rowdy with the bar and gambling hall doing a landslide business. Paul Hayman was playing in the bar, and the soldiers and men from the wagon train were stomping their feet and singing along drunkenly as Paul played songs they knew. The Callahans, Mr. Sue, Maria, and the Germans were content with the dining hall. There they found some new things available on the menu. Lamb for one; they dined on the leg-of-lamb roast with mint jelly and artichokes, a vegetable no one had ever seen before. Most of the old hands in the dining hall favored eating the lamb rolled in flour tortillas with green chile. Jacques was the first to try the new fair and pronounced it tasty and edible. Suzette stuck with the lamb and mint jelly, but Maria ate voraciously, glad to be back to the cuisine of her homeland.

Colonel Beekman and his clerk came in and joined them for dinner. The clerk was a fine-looking young man, Corporal Bill Smith. He spent a lot of his time looking at Suzette. He didn't know quite what to make of her and figured she was well out of his reach. He did strike up a conversation with her after dinner, though. He told her that there would be something like a county fair the next day. There would be some cowboy events like roping, bronco riding, and a shooting contest. He told her that she should enter the shooting contest. There would be a short-range contest for pistols and marksmanship for long rifles. There also would be some cash prizes. Suzette smiled and took it all in. She asked, "Will there be any boxing matches?"

The colonel joined the conversation and said, "This isn't Fort Wise, and we don't have a champion like Bent's Brawler. Even if we had boxing matches, you wouldn't find any takers here." He looked at Jacques and said, "Roland, right?" Jacques shook his head *no* and pointed at Roland. Col. Beekman turned to Roland and said, "You are famous, son; and Mr. Sue, I can offer you a job as a training officer here at the fort any time you want to join the Army." Mr. Sue thanked him graciously but declined.

They drank some brandy after dinner, and it wasn't half bad. The colonel had been out west for more than fifteen years. He was avid to know about the changes back east and was looking forward to returning to his hometown in Connecticut before long. As always, the looming civil war between the North and the South became the most important topic discussed after dinner. Eli told the Colonel that they were from Missouri, and the Colonel lit up when he finally connected them with the Callahan brewery in Independence. Eli didn't want to bring up the death of their parents and the destruction of *The Complex* but gave the Colonel a summary of what happened.

The Colonel told them that they were a brave family and wished them well. Hans and three of his men excused themselves in perfect English with only a trace of an accent. They had to switch places with the men guarding the silver. The gathering broke up, and as they were walking back to the wagon camp, Roland asked, "I wonder if there is any place in this country that hasn't heard of dad and Callahan Meadows?" They had been on the trail for fifty-three days, and it was August 10th. It had been a long day, and the night air was cooling down. Eli noticed through the evening that Suzette wasn't the least bit worried about the charges against her. She was the first to fall asleep and slept soundly all through the night.

The next day the camp was up before dawn as usual. There were a few stragglers with hangovers, but they joined in the morning's activities despite their groaning. The fort was also up early. There were more than thirty wagons to unload and pack into the armory and storehouses. After breakfast, Eli read off the order in which the wagons would report to the quartermaster. He told the men that after they unloaded and put their mules up for the day, they would be free to do as they pleased until Tuesday morning. Most were looking forward to the competitions, and bets were placed on Suzette for the pistol shoot and Roland for the long-gun marksmanship contest. He let the men know that they would have to tell him by Monday morning if they were going to leave the supply train and exercise any of their other options.

Suzette and Mr. Sue walked over to the Indian camp to search for the brown herb. They took Corporal O'Riley with them to help with translation. At first, the Indians didn't want anything to do with them and shied away. Suzette and O'Riley walked among the Indian women who were working on their crafts. They were trying to find a common language to ask someone about the brown herb. A couple of young Indian girls hit on O'Riley, but he just shook his head *no* and walked on. What a strange trio they made among the Indian women. A sharp-looking horse soldier with his saber strapped to his uniform belt. A Chinaman dressed in his simple black clothes and a blond woman with sky blue eyes, tanned so dark she looked like she could be half Indian herself.

Finally, Suzette saw an older woman, whom she took to be Navaho. The woman was weaving an intricate rug with a pattern that looked like a Spanish saint with the start of a halo over half of a fair face; Suzette guessed that the woman spoke Spanish. "Buenos Dias hermana. Necesito el hombre medicina." The woman understood and must have felt at ease with the endearment. The woman was slow to get to her feet, feeling her years, and led Suzette to a Comanche woman who looked to be a hundred years old.

O'Riley said, "Show her the empty bag and let her smell it." In his best Comanche, he told the woman that they needed more of the brown powder and were willing to pay for it. The older woman smiled and slowly struggled to her feet. She took Suzette by the hand, and they walked down to the river bank. A shrub that had a long bell-shaped flower adorning its branches lined the riverbank. Hummingbirds were busy gathering nectar from the blossoms. The older woman gathered a handful of the blossoms and had Suzette help her back up the riverbank.

They walked to the other side of the Indian camp, and there, the older woman threw the handful of flowers down on a drying mat. There was a younger woman there gathering dried blossoms off the mats, and others were grinding them. She picked up a dry blossom and removed the leaves from a seed pod. She bit the pod open and then peeled back the husk. The pod was full of black seeds. She made a grinding motion with her fist and pointed at several leather pouches next to the women on the mats grinding the blossoms. She picked up one of the bags and gave it to Suzette. She rattled off something that O'Riley couldn't understand. Then Navaho woman said, "Ella dijo ir con Dios."

Suzette took a twenty-dollar gold piece out of her belt and pressed it into the woman's hand. She asked the Navaho woman, "Where are all the men of the tribe?" There were only women and children in the camp. The Navaho shook her head sadly and told Suzette that the braves were out on the prairie, making war with the Apache. Suzette put her arm around the woman and drew her to her side in an affectionate hug and bent down and kissed her on the forehead. They walked back into the fort, and Suzette went into the general store and told the owner that she bought something from the older woman and paid with a double eagle. Suzette added, "If the Indians come in with the gold coin, I wanted you to know they didn't steal it." The store owner just pursed his lips and nodded his head. It was obvious that he didn't approve of giving the Indians money, let alone twenty dollars in gold.

Next, Suzette walked alone over to the doctor's office. Dr. Lea Way was there, the doctor Suzette and Maria saw the previous day. Suzette showed her some of the blossoms and the leather pouch of powder and asked if she or her husband would know its name. Dr. Lea took down a large tome from a shelf in the waiting room. It was a book of herbs and natural remedies. She paged through the front of the book and compared the blossoms to black and white drawings of the herbs. "Ah, ha! I thought so; this is astragalus. It is common in Chinese medicine, and the Indians here use it to control infection. Did you get this from the older woman down by the river? I hope you didn't pay her too much for it."

"Trust me; I didn't pay too much. Thank you. Can I sit and copy the text from that page and also the drawing?"

"Of course, sit here at my desk and make yourself at home." The rodeo had started over at the fort, and young men started showing up in the waiting room with cuts and bruises. Dr. Lea's husband, Robert, was out at a rancher's homestead to deliver a baby, so Dr. Lea was busy stitching up cuts and wrapping up a few broken arms and ribs. Suzette pitched in and stitched up several of the lesser wounds. She wondered why Colonel Beekman allowed what was meant to be a sport that was so hard on his men. By the end of the day, he was going to have a whole platoon on sick call.

By the time the shooting matches started, it was very hot, and Fort Union would have been in the heavy draught if it wasn't for the Mora River and its life-giving water from the Sangre de Christo Mountains to the west. Suzette signed up for the pistol shoot, and she put Roland in for the long rifle competition. The entry fee was five dollars for each event. Every horse soldier had entered the pistol shoot with the Army issue Colt 0.44 revolvers. Every infantryman entered the long rifle contest with their Army issue Mississippi rifles. Roland had an almost new Hawken 0.54 caliber rifle that was his pride and joy for long shots. Suzette only needed her Lefaucheux and was sure she could win the competition.

The judges for the pistol shoot were gathering up the contestants and explaining the rules. There were sixty entries for the contest, and the contest would be double elimination. Two shooters would line up and fire at paper targets twenty feet away. The paper targets had rings starting at ten inches in diameter with smaller rings inside. In the center, there was a black bullseye about an inch in diameter. There was a large slate blackboard from the school set up to the right of the firing line. The names of the contestants stood in a vertical row in the center of the board. Suzette was the only woman, and she was at the bottom of the list. That was fine with her, she was more interested in how the soldiers would perform, and being last, she could watch all of them before it was her turn to shoot. No one from the supply train signed up for the pistol shoot. They knew it would be a waste of money to compete against Suzette.

She walked over to the long rifle competition; the shooters were listed in the center of the board, the same as the pistol contest. Suzette saw all her brothers near the top of the list. She hoped that Eli and Jacques wouldn't be miffed at her for not entering them when she entered Roland. She walked back over to the pistol shoot and watched the startup of the event. The soldiers and cowboys were all geared up for the competition. They were practicing drawing their weapons, pairing up next to each other and sizing each other up. Suzette just watched; she didn't have any male hormones to contribute to the display.

The judges fired a shot in the air, and the first two contestants walked up to the firing line. They were both soldiers, and with the ring of a bell on the judges' table, both fired at their paper target. The lad on the left missed the target, and the board it was mounted on, but the one on the right hit the target within the second ring. The winner moved to the right on the scoreboard, and the loser moved to the left. The crowd wasn't impressed. They were waiting for the better shooters to compete and thinking how they might adjust their bets as the winners moved to the right on the board.

It took some time for the competition to move down to Suzette. Her opponent was a young cowboy, probably half Hispanic, and he looked fit and lean, but his weapon was old, a single-shot flintlock muzzleloader that Suzette didn't recognize. The bell rang, and Suzette aimed and waited for her opponent to shoot. Before the smoke from the flintlock blocked her vision, she aimed and shot her opponent's target dead center. The cowboy was surprised that he hit his target, but he was thrilled to move forward on the scoreboard. He must have been a popular kid because the civilian part of the crowd was cheering wildly. Suzette just smiled and was quite smug to move onto the easier side of the scoreboard. Six more perfect shots and she would win. The men from the wagon train knew she was up to something. The other men that bet on her decided they had made a bad choice. It would be a while before she would have to shoot again; she walked over to check the long rifle scoreboard. So far, her brothers were all on the winning side of the matrix.

Now the pistol competition alternated between the winners and losers. Men from the right were shifted to the left as they lost a round. Suzette beat her first opponent. The soldier missed his target, trying too hard, and Suzette took her time and shot her target in the second ring. The young soldier moaned as if in agony; loath to be out with his second miss and beaten by a woman at that. He would probably have been happier spending his money over at the beer stands. Now the competition was moving faster as more shooters were put out. The men coming over from the right side of the scoreboard were accurate gun hands. As Suzette put another man out with a bullseye, she was getting more and more attention. It wasn't just her tall-shapely body and her blond hair that interested the men. The Lefaucheux revolver was also the center of a lot of discussions. She put out her third opponent and then got a pass on the next rung because there was an odd number of shooters; she had gotten the short straw in the draw to see who would get the pass. *The luck of the Irish*, Suzette thought as she watched the competition move through the matrix.

Each time she had to shoot a little more careful, and after putting the next man out, she had to reload. As she flicked the cylinder opened and slipped in five more rounds, a lot of attention was on the revolver. Questions started up, only a few at first and then a lot flying at her from every direction. The judges called for a break, no doubt, to let the gamblers in the crowd adjust their bets. Eli and Jacques had been put out of the long-gun shoot and were sizing up the odds on their sister. There were three different hucksters with odds boards, and all three had Suzette up at ten to one. They picked out the shadiest looking of the three hucksters, and both put twenty dollars down on Suzette in gold. The huckster snickered and made a big loud deal over the boys who were betting on the dark horse contender.

Suzette let the uproar pass before she stepped up to the firing line. A soldier was her opponent. He looked strong and handled his heavy revolver with ease. The odds on him were only two to one. *No more sandbagging*, Suzette thought to herself as she smiled sweetly at the young man. His revolver was not one of the heavy Colt 0.44 Army issue sidearms. It was a long barrel, custom-made target pistol with a carved styled handle that fit his hand perfectly. The weapon looked heavy, but the Private looked strong enough to wield it accurately with one hand. The bell rang, and both shooters fired at the same time. When the smoke cleared, Suzette could see that her shot was dead center in the bullseye. The soldier was also in the bullseye but a little off-center. A bullseye was a bullseye, though, and they would shoot again. The second round, both were in the bullseye again. The soldier introduced himself as Private Stanley Wilson and told Suzette that he was in a wild west show before he joined the Army. He was confident that he was going to win. The hucksters, though, were getting worried, and Colonel Beekman posted guards on them to make sure none disappeared just before the payoff.

The sun was hot, and everyone was sweating, including Suzette. She undid the top two buttons of her shirt and rolled up her sleeves. She pulled a bandana from her back pocket and wiped her neck and her chest and then raised the dampened cloth to her forehead. She tucked the bandana into the top of her shirt and smiled sweetly at Private Wilson. She told the judges she needed a drink of water, and they agreed to a short break. Men from the wagon train raised their bets on Suzette. Some soldiers bet on Suzette; despite being derided by their comrades. Arguing at the betting table was as hot as the midday sun, and Colonel Beekman stepped forward and raised his arms for silence. Even the long-gun competition was put on hold until this event played out. The judge with the bell hammer called out, "Are you ready?"

Private Wilson said, "No. I have a suggestion. We both can shoot bullseyes all day. What say we move the targets out to thirty feet and fire five rounds each? His revolver held six 0.36 caliber bullets, and he had several extra cylinders on his belt, so he didn't have to reload. He agreed to shoot only five times. The judges agreed, and the targets moved out another ten feet.

The crowd was quiet as both shooters nodded and stepped back to the line. The bell rang, and Suzette's fired her first four shots into her bullseye. She was pacing Stan's rate of fire and took the last shot a little ahead of him. Private Wilson made a mistake. Maybe his arm was getting tired holding up the long gun. Maybe he had sweat running into his eyes. Maybe he was thinking how beautiful his opponent was and how much of her cleavage she was willing to show. Regardless, he didn't wait for the smoke from Suzette's last round to clear. He fired through the smoke. His shot split the side of his bullseye and the next ring out. The crowd was silent as the judges walked down and took down the targets. The silence turned to awe as the judges announced that Suzette had won the competition with all five of her shots clearly in the black, and then the men that bet on Suzette went wild, cheering and rushing to the huckster's tables to collect their winnings.

Suzette congratulated Private Wilson and turned to collect her winnings from the judges. Her brothers were shaking down the huckster that held their bets for their winnings. The huckster was trying to pay up with counterfeit money. The Colonel walked over and told the huckster to pay up for real, or he was going to let these two men take him out behind the barn. Suzette walked over to the huckster's table. She was reloading her revolver and was staring at the man with a look of malice. The man paid up: half in gold, a collection of legitimate greenbacks, and some Spanish silver coins. They had seven hundred dollars more than they had that morning, and the long gun competition still had eight contestants to go.

The long rifle targets were iron buffalos that had to be knocked down with a bullet. The targets started at two-hundred yards and then were moved out fifty more yards after every round of shooting. Each man was allowed two misses, and then he was out. There were eight shooters left, half of them had already missed once, and the targets were now out at four-hundred yards. Hans Warner was still in the competition with one miss, and Roland still had a perfect score, along with four other men. The next round eliminated three shooters, and Roland still had a perfect score; there was only one soldier left that matched him with no misses. They were getting out to the maximum effective range of the rifles. Four-hundred and fifty yards for the next round, Hans was knocked out, and Roland and the other man now had one miss each. Five-hundred yards next and Roland knew that he missed the last target because he didn't compensate enough for the breeze that came up from the west. He aimed three feet to the right and four feet above to compensate for the wind and the bullet drop. The crowd held its breath, and Roland knocked his target down, but so did his opponent. Five hundred fifty yards; this was going to be a real *Hail Mary*. Both shooters reloaded, and this time Roland again adjusted for the wind but also raised his point of aim even higher. He hit the buffalo, and it seemed to balance, teetering backward, and then it fell. His opponent also hit the target but lower down; the target teetered back and forth came to rest, still upright. The crowd cheered, and the Callahan's winnings were another three hundred dollars to the good. One thousand dollars for only a half day's work.

The rest of the day passed quietly. Suzette had a lot of young men visit that were interested mostly in her, but some were genuinely interested in the cartridge loading revolver. Those soldiers quickly became more interested in the Henry rifles. There was an older man who Suzette saw writing a lot of notes at the competitions. He wanted an exclusive interview with her and her brothers and intended to write up a story about them for newspapers back east. They didn't want any part of the publicity but agreed to have dinner with him that night, thinking it better if the man printed facts, rather than the exaggerated rumors of their exploits on the trail. They agreed to meet at the dining hall at 8:00 PM. Roland, always quick to extract an advantage, said, "You'll have to buy dinner, or we won't tell you anything." The writer moaned but agreed. It would be worth it, and his story would feed the eastern frenzy for new tales of the west.

That night the Callahans sat down with the writer. Hans, two of his men, Mr. Sue, and Maria, sat at an adjoining table. There was another man, dressed too slick to be one of the fort's personnel. He wore a black suit with a string tie held with a large blue rock mounted on a silver clasp. His white shirt was pressed and spotless, which was uncommon in itself around an Army post. More remarkably, he had a Lefaucheux revolver, but it was an 1854 12mm model. He struck up a conversation with Suzette, and she quickly learned that he was Ronkainen's lawyer that would present his complaint to the judge on Monday morning. Suzette turned to the writer and told him there were certain things they wouldn't discuss until later on Monday after the hearing. She turned back to the lawyer, James Hobart, Esquire, and asked him where Mr. Ronkainen was in her most charming and seductive voice. He declined to answer and said Ronkainen was close by but wouldn't be at the hearing in person. "Too bad," Suzette intoned, but she would settle for close by. Maybe after the hearing, if she was still free, she could hunt him down and kill him.

Dinner stayed pleasant, and Eli did most of the relating of their stories of the trail. The writer was an ordinary man in his late forties. His name was Edward Sigler, and he worked for the *New York Times*. He assured their stories were going to hit a big market, and he promised not to embellish them. The killing of Chico del Diablo, the renegades, and the massacre of the Apache needed no embellishment. The stories were fantastic enough as they were. He assured the Callahans that all the stories were going to be told and retold far and wide. Hobart was taking it all in. He was deep in thought, refining his arguments that would be put forth in court Monday morning. The evening ended with good brandy, and Roland snuck away from the table and paid the bill. He enjoyed watching Sigler sweat every time they ordered another glass of wine or a dessert. The journalist was as nervous over the bill as a long-tailed cat in a room full of rocking chairs. Roland wanted to leave the reporter owing him one. It could come in useful later on.

Sunday was a much welcome day of rest. Maria wanted to go to church because now that they were farther out west, Catholicism was the dominant faith. Suzette took her to church and was pleased to see Dr. Way and her husband there. Colonel Beekman and some of his officers also attended and were seated in the front pews where important people liked to be noticed. The morning was cool, the all-male choir sang beautifully, and the sermon was in Spanish, the old priest knowing no other language. There was a translator, but Suzette and Maria listened to the Spanish. The old priest lectured his congregation on the evils of human instincts. It covered almost everything that was more or less fun to do around the post. Suzette chuckled to herself. Moderation in drink and condoms were a lot better solution to these sins of humankind than a sermon. She noticed Hans and a few of his men took the advice in earnest and was expecting them to shout "Amen" at any moment. That didn't happen in a Catholic Church, though, and Suzette was pleased that the Ways invited them to lunch after the service. When they walked past Colonel Beekman's office, Sigler was on the front porch, reading a copy of Ronkainen's complaint. He looked at Suzette as if she were of solid gold. Suzette wondered how this was going to play out, but for the moment, she was more interested in discussing medicine with the Ways rather than worrying about her court appearance in the morning.

Monday morning, Suzette opted to take Maria to the post dining hall for breakfast. Soldiers crowded the dining room, and there weren't two seats together anywhere in the room. They went through the serving line, and Maria sat down with a young man who spoke Spanish and was from a settlement close to Bernalillo. Suzette sat down next to a stately looking gentleman and noticed that Hobart was glaring at her from two tables away. Suzette introduced herself all around the table. However, the soldiers already knew who she was. She was surprised to learn that the older gentleman was Judge Wilkerson. He said, "So you are the famous gunslinger woman who allegedly murdered Vincent Ronkainen's partner and his sidekick in cold blood."

Suzette was shocked but kept her head. "I believe we will be discussing this in your courtroom in an hour or so. I'll be defending myself, and my brother Roland will be helping me. After you hear me out, I hope I won't be the one needing to defend myself any longer. I hope you will be issuing a warrant for Ronkainen's arrest."

"We can't discuss that right now, but don't worry, I know Ronkainen's reputation well, and I wouldn't act on hearsay, especially coming from the likes of him. By the way, Sigler is going to be there, and he is out to make you more famous than you already are."

"I'm not looking to be famous, but I won't sit idle while accused so outrageously. I was hoping Mr. Ronkainen would show up for this hearing in person. I would like more than a word or two with him."

"I'm sure you would. Let's see how it unfolds. Hobart over there will go first; the burden of proof rests on him. He is quite sharp, but his problem is greed. He is no doubt working for a percentage of the silver, and from what I have heard about you and your brothers, he won't be trying to take it away from you by force. Well, I'll see you in an hour. I am pleased to meet you."

Hobart was still glaring at her, and when she got up from the table, she saw that Sigler was behind her writing furiously in his notepad. "Famous," she grumbled to herself. She gathered up Maria and headed for the door. She turned and looked back at Hobart. He was still glaring at her. She smiled at him and tipped her head and gestured with two fingers pointing to her eyes and then at him. It could have meant goodbye forever, or I'll see you soon, or I'm watching you. It had the proper effect. Hobart stopped glaring and looked confused.

She went over to the courtroom and found Eli seated in the front row along with Hans and a couple of his hands. She greeted them and then took her seat forward of the banister that separated the judge and jury part of the court from the spectators. Roland was there at the defendant's table. Hobart came in and made a big deal of spreading out his papers and briefs on the plaintiff's table as if there was a prize for the most prepared. *Or maybe*, Suzette thought, *that is what lawyers did when they don't have any real evidence*. Dr. Way and her husband were in the back of the room. Suzette smiled at them and then said quietly to Eli, "We need to strengthen the guard on the silver; that's what this is all about."

Roland said, "Don't worry, sis; here is the contract. Jacques is out there, and he has a nasty surprise for anyone trying to rip us off. He's come up with an ingenious plan to capture Ronkainen." Judge Wilkerson came in, and the bailiff cried out the traditional *all rise*. All conversation ceased as the judge sat down at the bench.

"Please be seated," Wilkerson bellowed. "We are here to hear a complaint filed on behalf of Mr. Vincent Ronkainen against Suzette Callahan and her brothers. Mr. Hobart, you may proceed."

Hobart started right in on Suzette, "Judge Wilkerson, what you see before you here is a cold-blooded killer disguised as this beautiful young woman. She is a prostitute and killed my client's partner in cold blood after he refused to pay an outrageous price for her services. Ronkainen was transporting Bent's silver to Albuquerque, and the Callahans stole that silver and are claiming that they are, in fact, transporting it under contract for Bent. I expect that they are going to show you documents saying that is so, but I assure you, the documents are forgeries."

"This young woman is infamous. The first thing she did when she got to town was to buy a box of one-hundred condoms from the general store. She is a gunslinger to boot, and she proved that at the shooting contest on Saturday. I appeal to your better judgment that you issue a warrant for her arrest, confiscate the silver, and deliver it to my client, Mr. Vincent Ronkainen."

Wilkerson looked at Suzette, "Miss Callahan, what do you have to say for yourself?"

Suzette stood straight and tall; her spine true as the stiletto in her hair. "First, your honor, I would like to address the issue of the *stolen silver*. I have three documents to put into evidence. The first is a letter from Colonel Schultz at Fort Wise, authorizing my brother Eli to transport Bent's silver to the bank in Albuquerque. The next is the contract with Mr. Bent, which also presents an inventory and a provision that Eli Callahan will be paid ten percent of the silver for safe delivery to the bank. The third document is our inventory of the silver, performed by Mr. Hans Warner, a trusted member of our supply train."

Judge Wilkerson looked over the documents and then called on Colonel Beekman to verify that the signature on the letter of authorization was legitimate. Colonel Beekman not only verified that it was indeed legitimate, but he also produced several other letters and orders signed by Col. Schultz for comparison. After several moments of inspection and careful thought, the judge ruled, "I find these documents to be legitimate and your claim that the Callahans stole the silver to be without merit. Miss Callahan, please continue."

"Next, your Honor, I am a doctor in training. After a nasty outbreak of gonorrhea from the stopover at Fort Wise, it seemed prudent to take precautions this time." Several of the men, including Paul, blushed and looked away, and snickers from the crowd added to their embarrassment. Not all of the spectators were convinced, however. All had seen her skill with her revolver the day before. If the gunslinger charge was true, perhaps the other charge was true too.

Suzette waited until the murmurs from the crowd died down. Finally, she said, "I would like to call Doctor Lea Way to the stand."

Dr. Lea walked up from the back of the courtroom. She was dressed in a long-blue western skirt and wor a ruffled-white silk blouse that suited her well. The courtroom was hot, but Dr. Way and Suzette were two of the few people that showed no signs of suffering from the heat. The Bailiff swore her in, and Dr. Lea sat down in the witness stand comfortable and confident. Suzette stood, walked over to the Doctor, and thanked her for coming. Then she asked, "Did you examine Maria Gonzales and me on Saturday morning at your office here in Fort Union?"

"Yes, I did," a simple and direct reply.

"And what was the nature of that examination?"

"You wanted me to confirm that you and Maria Gonzales were still virgins."

"And what were your findings, Dr. Way?"

"You are both as virgin as the day you were born. Mr. Hobart, you bought into Ronkainen's story without checking the facts. That alone makes you a poor lawyer, or maybe you had your eye on a generous fee if you recovered the silver. That, Mr. Hobart, would make you a greedy liar. Either way, what you are accusing Miss Callahan of, is blatantly not true."

The courtroom broke into an uproar; the judge rapped his gavel several times to bring order. Then he said, "Hobart, it seems you have been wasting my time. You only have one choice here. Withdraw the complaint. If you persist, I am going to levy a heavy fine on you for perjury. And, if Miss Callahan here wants to sue for liable, I would be very pleased to hear her case. Dr. Lea, you can step down. Hobart, what say you?"

Deeply chagrined, Hobart replied, "I withdraw the complaint, your honor."

Judge Wilkerson looked at Suzette and asked, "Anything more?"

"Yes. I move that the court issue a warrant for the arrest of Vincent Ronkainen for orchestrating my kidnapping that resulted in the death of Landstrom and his sidekick during my escape."

"I'll take that into consideration." He rapped his gavel and said, "Case dismissed."

Sigler was the last one to leave the courtroom. He was writing as fast as he could while a word-for-word account of the hearing was still fresh in his mind. The Callahans went out, bid farewell to Colonel Beekman and the Doctors Way, and walked to the supply train camp. Jacques was almost giddy with excitement.

He ran over to them, laughing. "Ronkainen's lackeys stole another crate of lead. I can't believe their stupidity. We put it on the top of the pile on the back of one of the silver wagons and left it unguarded for about ten minutes. Lt. Barksdale is tailing them; I expect we will find Ronkainen dead or at least captured by nightfall."

"Let's get back on the trail," was all Eli had to say.

It was going to be a late start, but Eli wanted very much to be back on his way west. The three brothers went to the Quartermaster's office to learn what they would have left of the supply train to make the short distance to Santa Fe. Suzette went to the doctors' office. She had the winnings from the shooting contest with her and was surprised to see Anton waiting there to see one of the doctors. He was pale and shaking but otherwise had no pain in his stomach, and his pulse was strong. Suzette told him he was having a relapse of some of the withdrawal symptoms from the laudanum, but it was smart to have the doctors check him out before they were isolated on the trail again.

Doctor Lea Way came into the waiting room, her white apron was bloody, and she was distraught. She greeted, "Good morning, Suzette, Anton. What can I do for you?"

"Anton has the shakes. I think it is part of the withdrawal from the laudanum, but he wants you to look at him before we are back on the trail. What happened? You are a mess. Dr. Lea, you are covered with blood."

Lea shook her head, "Another stabbing over at the Indian camp. Sadly, they are quite common. This one won't be fatal, but many of them are. Anton, let's have a look at you." The three of them went back to an examining room. Lea confirmed Suzette's diagnosis but also had somewhat of a remedy. She took down a box of tea from a shelf in their kitchen. "This is a willow bark extract. It eases pain and inflammation, and I think it will help. These symptoms can occur for another few weeks. Have him drink several cups a day."

Suzette took the money from the shooting contests out of her pocket and gave it to Lea. "I want you to use this for any of your needs here at the clinic, but also to ease the lot of the women over in the Indian Camp."

Dr. Robert came out of the room they used for surgery as Suzette was handing the money to Lea. "That is a lot of money, young lady. Are you sure you want to part with it?"

"Trust me; we can afford it. By the way, do you have an extra bottle of silver nitrate solution? I'm thinking we are going to need an ample supply to get us all the way to Fort Moore." Dr. Lea went back into the storeroom and came back with two bottles of the gonorrhea cure and was pleased she could do something in return for the generous contribution. Suzette thanked the Ways for all their help and left with Anton. When they walked by the quartermaster's office, there was a heated argument going on inside, and Eli, who seldom raised his voice, could be heard out on the street. He wasn't happy. The Quartermaster was taking the empty wagons out of the supply train and sending them east with a wagon train made up of merchants.

Eli was arguing to keep his supply train together, "Don't you have more freight heading west? Surely you have forts to supply; we could do that. Another problem, most of my drivers and their helpers joined up to emigrate west. I don't think you will find a single one who wants to go back east. We haven't had any breakaways yet, but I think you are going to create a situation here that will bring that on. There has to be something we can do that will keep these men together."

The quartermaster drew somber. "There is, but it is dangerous. I know Colonel Beekman has to send the infantry company down into southern New Mexico Territory to establish posts along the Butterfield Trail. You could take that company down there, but that is in the middle of Chiricahua Apache country. The attacks are frequent and violent. I am loath to send you down there because of your sister traveling with you. I know she is a capable young woman, more so than most, but her life or death would be horrible if she fell into Apache hands. I'll talk to Colonel Beekman, but please consider this carefully. The danger is extreme."

Eli came out of the office and found Suzette standing in the street. "You heard?"

"Yes, and consider this, no matter what trail we take to get to Fort Moore, there will be danger. I don't want to see the men split up either, and especially because of me. Let's see what Colonel Beekman decides."

It was well after lunch when the infantry company came marching out of the Fort. Colonel Beekman was leading them. It was a column of more than a hundred soldiers, sergeants, and several officers. They were all carrying packs ready to march west. It was obvious that he had made his decision. He left the column standing at attention.   Their commanding officer was Captain Poller, a West Point graduate, and an Army officer from his close-cropped hair down to tips of his shiny boots. Colonel Beekman said, "Okay, Captain Poller and his men need to get to Apache Pass. They are going to build camps on the east and west side of the pass. Once you head west from there, you should be safe. Here is a set of orders for Lt. Barksdale. He will accompany you to Fort Moore. Send your empty wagons over to the supply depot. The quartermaster will provision you for the extra men." With that, he offered his hand to Eli and said, "Good luck, and Godspeed, son." He turned to Captain Poller and saluted him in dismissal, then walked back to the fort without another glance back.

Eli turned to Captain Poller and asked, "Does the colonel expect you to walk or ride to Apache Pass?"

"We can walk, but it would be nice to ride if you have the extra room."

"You will be riding, and we will drill your men on our defensive maneuvers when we get out on the trail."

"Very well, but let us march out of sight of the fort. I don't want to give Colonel Beekman the impression that we are getting soft."

"I don't want to make you soft, but a mule can sustain a pace faster than a man on foot. It is practical, and you will see that it will make the defense of the supply train stronger, especially if we have to face a large band of hostiles. We will only go as far as Tiptonville today. That will be an easy march for your column. There we can split up your men among the wagons. By the way, Captain Poller, welcome aboard."

It took until four o'clock to get back on the trail. Tiptonville was only six miles to the south, and it was an easy march for the column. They were fresh and strong and kept the pace almost up to an easy walk for the mule teams. The soldiers sang marching songs from time-to-time, and the songs were strong and boomed out across the chaparral. Tiptonville was at the juncture of the Mountain Route and the Cimarron Cutoff. The Barlow & Sanderson Stage Station was an important gathering point for merchants heading east on the Cimarron Cutoff, and also served as a post office for mail arriving from Independence. William Tipton came out to the supply train when he learned that it was the Callahan train. He had a letter for Eli and his brothers. It was from their grandmother.

Eli opened the letter immediately. As he expected, it was a plea to see Suzette safely across the country. In her words, "Suzette is a strong-minded and clever girl. I know she is with you, and I hope and pray that you will all be safe. I'll be waiting for you in California. God willing, I will see you there." Eli wondered if Denise was turning to God in her golden years; he couldn't remember that she was particularly religious back home. He walked over and gave the letter to Suzette. It wasn't easy for Suzette to read it. When she finished, she turned to Eli and said, "I didn't want to hurt her, but I know I did, and I am sorry for that."

Eli drew her into an affectionate hug. They walked through the camp, looking for the twins. All around them was the hustle and bustle of the men making camp. The soldiers were pitching their tents, and the chuck wagons were busy preparing the evening meal. They were on the east side of the camp when Lt. Barksdale and his horse soldiers came riding in. Lt.

Barksdale was excited. He dismounted and hurried up to Eli and Suzette. "Ronkainen is dead."

"What happened?" Suzette asked.

"When his goons found out that Jacques' crate contained lead, they demanded payment for their services. Ronkainen couldn't pay up, and the goons killed him. We killed all his men, but one lived for a while to tell what happened. I think that is the last of the trouble we will see from Fort Wise. I see we have an infantry company with us now. I will report to the captain."

Suzette smiled at her brother and said, "Life is good." They walked on to find the twins, Eli's arm around her shoulders. *Life was good*, he thought. Harsh and fleeting at times, but good. He was looking forward to getting to Santa Fe and getting Bent's silver into the bank. He was thinking about how he would handle getting the infantry divided up among his drivers. He was also thinking out how to best make use of the soldiers in defense of the supply train. The box defense was extremely effective out on the prairie, but they would be in the mountains for a good deal of the trip to the Colorado River, and other tactics may be necessary. He left Fort Union with sixty-five wagons, the same as when he first took over the wagon train from Armstrong. It would still be workable, and with almost two soldiers per wagon, it would be stronger than before. Jacques and Roland were with Mr. Sue. They had venison again dressed out and cooking on a spit. Suzette gave them the letter. They both read it several times, and then Eli slipped it into the back of his journal.

Roland said, "Grandmother has a long reach. I bet there will be another letter waiting for us in Santa Fe, one sent from the west coast. I'm glad she didn't sound too mad. We should introduce her to the Chiricahua. Then they would know what true wrath was like." They all laughed and went about their chores, wanting to be done with them before the evening meal was ready. Patches needed a shoe reset. Suzette let Maria walk her horse over to the blacksmith. Eli was sitting by Mr. Sue, discussing the new soldiers. Mr. Sue was glad to share his extensive military experience and had some good suggestions as to how the new men should integrate into the supply train. Eli looked relieved; as usual, his ability to listen and learn from the more experienced man would serve him well.

After dinner, Eli called everyone in the camp over to his wagon. He had to lay down the law as to how they would be working together as long as they were on the trail. He had a good plan. Suzette was sure that Mr. Sue had a lot to do with what he was saying. Eli started, "Good evening, men. I was impressed with your march today down from Fort Union. The marching songs were particularly welcome. We have been on the trail now for fifty-six days. We have developed some defensive measures that we will be practicing with you tomorrow. It is paramount that each of you soldiers chooses a wagon that you are going to stay with until we settle you at Apache Pass. We have a defensive maneuver we call *The Box*. When we move into that formation, each of you must be in his appointed place. Our survival can depend on that, and that is why I want you to choose up a driver to stay with throughout the rest of your trip. You will be riding on the wagons and resting through the day. The Apache will probably leave us alone during the day, and then try to steal our animals or murder us at night. On the wagons, you can rest and sleep if you can. At night Captain Poller, I want half your men on guard duty at a time. Our men will also be standing guard on a schedule, one man for every six wagons. At all times, you will be armed and ready to fight, even if you are sleeping during the day. Lastly, it is the job of every man in this supply train to keep the two young women safe at all costs. I don't want any of you coming to me to tell me that one of them has been harmed or killed. I expect nothing less than what we have done since we left Independence, and that is to defend them to the death if necessary. Now socialize a bit. You soldiers pitch your tents with the wagon crew you choose to join. This is how we will camp every night we are out on the trail. If we bed down close to a fort or a town, the procedure might be different but plan on it being the same until Captain Poller tells you otherwise. Any questions?"

One of the soldiers asked from the back of the crowd, "How many Indians and renegades have you killed so far?"

"More than a hundred," Eli replied. "Maybe closer to two hundred."

Another question, "How many of the Henry repeaters do you have?"

"Twelve and they are spread to the front and back of the formation when we go defensive with two in the middle on each side. We will go over all of that as we drill tomorrow. I don't expect any real trouble between here and Santa Fe, but once we get down into the territory of the Chiricahua, all our lives will depend on each man doing his job. For now, socialize a bit and get to know one another. You are going to be together for several weeks. Choose your partners with care. That is all."

"Wait a minute," Suzette shouted as the men started to mill back to their wagons and tents. She got up on top of her medical footlocker so everyone could see her easily and gave the newcomers the lecture on sexually transmitted disease and joked that when they left Fort Wise, there were twelve cases. She told the soldiers that they had the treatment for Gonorrhea and not to hesitate to get treated if they were uncomfortable. "The medical supplies are in Eli's wagon; Mr. Sue will take care of you if you need attention."

With that, the soldiers started to pair off with the teamsters. The drivers, of course, wanted the more seasoned soldiers and the younger recruits who had never seen combat, were having a more difficult time finding a driver that would take them. By nightfall, though, every soldier was settled with a wagon, and most were glad to be relieved of the rigid layout of a military camp. More than thirty soldiers went to Mr. Sue for the gonorrhea cure. Suzette was hoping they would find another General Store that had another case of condoms. Maybe two cases would be in order. They were camped north of some springs with deep cold pools. After dark, Roland and Jacques took Suzette and Maria down to the springs so they could swim and clean up.   The moon was nearly full, and the water was cold. The girls didn't spend much time in the water but felt clean and invigorated after the swim. They walked back to the camp and could hear coyotes in the distance and owls in the trees. Maria pointed up to a small owl that was perfectly back-dropped against the bright moon. "Tecolote," she said. "Igual que en mi casa."

"Same as at her home," Suzette translated. "We are getting close to Bernalillio. Her grandparents probably think she is dead. They are in for quite a surprise. I hope they are ready to be parents again." Suzette and Maria bedded down under one of the silver-laden wagons. The three loaded with silver were inside the circle, along with Mr. Sue's chuck wagon. Mr. Sue had a berry cobbler along with some fresh milk from the cows at Fort Union. Suzette also wondered how Mr. Sue was going to feel handing Maria over to her grandparents. "I hope he is relieved," she muttered to herself as she fell asleep.

Hans quietly brought a crate over to where they were and planted himself along with two of his men around the silver to provide extra security through the night. Hans and his men would work the same schedule as the soldiers, four hours on and four hours off, until the silver was safely in the bank vault in Santa Fe. He was more worried about the soldiers that joined the train than the Indians. He was also worried about the safety of Suzette and Maria. Mr. Sue and the Callahan men all had the same concern. They brought their bedrolls over and surrounded Suzette and Maria. If someone tried to get to them in the night, they would have to trip over Eli's entire contingent to get to the girls.

The extra precautions were not necessary, and the night passed with the changing of the guard and no incidents, Indian or otherwise. Eli and Captain Poller made a round of the camp at 2:00 AM and found all the guards wide awake and alert. Eli said, "Today, we will practice forming up in the defensive position. Out on the prairie, the biggest problem was keeping the Indians from getting to the mules and horses. I'll show you what I think would be a good idea when we do the drills tomorrow."

The camp awoke before dawn. Everyone was anxious to move along. Santa Fe was within reach, and the men and soldiers were looking forward to a break in a major city. Eli was just anxious to get the silver into the bank, but the most anxious of all was Maria. She didn't know what her grandparents would think of her showing up on their doorstep, and she was also dreading Suzette leaving her behind. No matter what the motivation, the supply train was on the trail west before the sun rose above the eastern horizon. Suzette and Roland rode the first scout positions. Eli signaled for the first drill mid-morning. His drivers were well trained in this maneuver and pulled their wagons expertly into position. Eli and Captain Poller walked around the formation, but the drivers already had the soldiers in position at the back of the wagons. Many had stacked crates in the back of the wagon beds for covered shooting positions. Captain Poller had a suggestion, "If we tethered each of the wagons together with a short lanyard between them, an Indian wouldn't be able to ride into the middle of the box to kill the mules."

"Good idea," Eli responded. "We have the rope, and the drivers can make the lanyards tonight. Our weak points are the sides of the rear wagons and the mules exposed at the front.

Cpt. Poller had a suggestion for that, too. "Did you see the Coehoorn mortars the quartermaster loaded you with back at Fort Union? We don't have shells for those, but I think they could be loaded with shot and made into an effective scattergun at short range. Let's look them over tonight."

Satisfied with some good plans afoot, Eli got them back on the trail. Eli posted Suzette and Roland to the south of the trail. Jacques and Hans were on the north side, and Lt. Barksdale was in the middle with his horse soldiers. They practiced forming the box two more times through the day and still made eighteen miles before Eli stopped them in a grassy swale to make camp several miles east of Las Vegas. It was good to see green grass again after the miles and miles of drought-parched prairie. There were no Indian sightings throughout the day, so the camp was relaxed. Eli rode into Las Vegas with Lt. Barksdale and his men. Las Vegas was comfortable with seeing soldiers; it was the first town of any significance west of Fort Union. There was a small garrison there, and Lt. Barksdale wanted whatever reports they had on the Chiricahua. There wasn't much to learn. All the heavy Indian action was to the west of the Rio Grande River. The consensus was that they shouldn't have any trouble on the trail to Santa Fe.

Eli rode back to the camp with the soldiers. The teamsters and their helpers were cutting and splicing lanyards. Captain Poller had one of the Coehoorn mortars out and was loading a shot charge with black powder, 0.54 caliber balls, and a mud plug to hold the load in when they tipped the mortar up to where it would fire horizontally. The mud was reasonably dry after the evening meal, and the soldiers pulled the mortar outside the camp ring to test it. Poller explained, "These mortars are useless unless you want to shoot something on top of a mountain or if you can get an enemy to stand stark still about a quarter-mile away, but they should make a hell of a shotgun." He was right! He pulled a lanyard that tripped the hammer on the percussion cap, and the mortar thundered and peppered the chaparral with lead shot up to a quarter-mile away. "It's only good for one shot during a battle, but it's one hell of a powerful shot." The Captain was pleased. They had six mortars, and he would have them placed strategically in the rear wagons and blocked up so they would fire horizontally. The back of the wagon train would no longer be the weak point of the box.

Mr. Sue had a contribution to the giant scattergun. He asked Cpt. Poller if he could experiment with one of the mortars. He had melted about a quart of tar on his cookstove in an iron pot used for melting lead for casting bullets. Instead of mud, he poured the tar in and let it harden to form the plug for the lead shot. They dragged the mortar over to the side of the camp ring, and this time when they fired it, the mortar barked a blowtorch of flame more than sixty feet long and left droplets of burning tar scattered downrange. Mr. Sue said, "Most effective against horses. If they survive the lead shot, they will buck for an hour or more if they get a burning pellet on their coat, most unpleasant for the rider." Captain Poller was again impressed and ordered the mortars reloaded with the tar plugs.

Captain Poller had drawn a diagram of the defensive formation and marked the wagons where he wanted the mortars placed. He put three in the back wagons covering a field of fire of ninety degrees. There was one at each side of the midpoints of the box, and that left one for the front of the train. The last one was placed in the fourth wagon and would cover the right flank of the box. Eli said, "Captain, it looks like you are well pleased with your handy work and spoiling for a fight."

"I would rather not have to fight, but I want to be ready for four or five hundred Apache in a single attack. That would not be an even fight, even with your firepower and the surprise of the mortars. But we won't go down without taking hundreds with us."

"Let's not think about going down. We're in this to survive, and we can make that survival happen. Once we form the box, you will be in command. We will all be counting on your leadership and seasoned troops to win the day. Please don't let us down."

"Don't worry, lad; as long as my men and I are alive, we will do our best."

Eli was still worried that the Captain was a little fatalistic, but he could be right. Against overwhelming numbers, weapon superiority could ultimately be meaningless. He hoped that if an attack came, the number of hostiles would be small. They were headed to uncharted territories, though, and considering their experiences so far; anything could happen. That night the moon was bright, a few days short of being full. Around 3:00 AM, a single shot rang out, waking the camp and bringing everyone to full alert. A small band of Indians tried sneaking into the camp ring to steal horses. A young soldier had called out a challenge and waited for an answer, then fired his rifle, bringing down the leader. The rest of the Indians fled into the night. Corporal O'Riley identified the Indian as a Comanche. Everyone was relieved. They knew that contact with the Apache was inevitable, but they didn't want to see them until they were well past Santa Fe.

The next day they reached Coruco, which was only a couple of mud huts and a poor excuse for a trading post. But the night was quiet, and the next day after that, they moved on to a spring just east of Glorieta Pass. The spring was a beautiful spot gushing hundreds of gallons a minute of ice-cold water beneath a vermilion colored sandstone face. They had been traveling for fifty-nine days. Not yet two months, but it felt like two years since they left Independence. The moon was nearly full, and as per tradition, the girls swam in the spring after dark. Through the night, a large merchant train passed them heading east on the trail. The wagon master was an older gentleman and rode over to talk to the guards. He had a lot to say about Santa Fe. The city was quiet even though there were hundreds of Mexicans loitering in the streets waiting for news of another big gold or silver strike up in Colorado. Despite the large transient population, crime was relatively scarce. The wagon master was sad to leave there. This crossing was to be his last trip east, and he had a home in St. Louis, where he intended to retire. Eli asked him how many trips he had made on the trail. The older man answered more than sixteen back and forth. Eli intended to make only one and was impressed that the man had chosen to live his whole life traveling east to west, west to east – endlessly back and forth. Eli wished him well and watched as the man rode back to his train in the moonlight. He noted that they weren't the only ones who had traveled at night to take advantage of the cooler weather.

The next morning, they set out early, traveling the easy climb up through Glorieta Pass. It was simple and easy compared to Ratón; in fact, once clear of the summit, the trail stretched arrow straight down a grade that took them to within sight of Santa Fe. Pine trees were left behind, and mountain cedar took their place. Everyone was excited when they reached the outskirts of Santa Fe. They pulled into a marshaling yard on the west side of the plaza. The Bank of New Mexico had closed for the day, but Eli found the bank manager in the cantina next to the bank. They told him what they needed to unload, and he opened the bank. Eli brought the three silver wagons into town, and under the watchful eye of Hans and his men, the silver was unloaded and carried into the bank. It was all inventoried and stored in the vault before anyone in town even realized that a fortune had arrived. Eli presented the letter from Bent and took payment for his fee in gold. There weren't enough gold coins in the vault to pay him, so in addition to several bags of double eagles and Mexican fifty-peso coins, there were several one hundred-ounce gold bars in the payout.

Suzette opened an account for Maria and deposited the four thousand dollars they won betting on Mr. Sue along with the winnings Mr. Sue contributed to Maria's funds. The bank manager said, "This will make the Gonzales's the richest family in Bernalillio. It will change the demographics of that area, but the Gonzales's are already well off. They own one of the wineries and make some of the better wine in the area. They come to town often; I wouldn't be surprised if you run into them out on the streets. Dona Gonzales always goes to the San Miguel Mission for mass when she is in town. If they are here, she will be at the church tomorrow morning."

Suzette thanked the banker and left with Maria. They walked across the plaza and took a room in the La Fonda Hotel. Maria had never been in a building so grand. She and Suzette both had hot baths and donned clean clothes they had purchased while the boys were offloading the silver into the bank. It was the very essence of old-world luxury. They went down to the dining room for a late-night dinner, and Eli, the twins with Hans and his men, joined them for supper. Mr. Sue was in the kitchen, chattering away in Chinese with the cooks and kitchen help. How surprising to find Chinese cooks in Santa Fe? They were expecting Mexican food, but after a while, Mr. Sue led a procession out of the kitchen, and a veritable feast was laid out before them. Santa Fe had an inexhaustible stock of pigs and chickens, and all of Mr. Sue's favorite pork and chicken dishes were laid out before them. Everyone ate their fill and slept well. They had been without the security of a city around them for sixty days. The teamsters and their helpers and the soldiers were making the most of the saloons and gambling halls, and many of them were visiting the ladies of the night. It was good that they were taking a day off tomorrow; Eli expected that very few of the men would be ready for a workday by morning.

Suzette and Maria slept late and returned to the dining room for a sumptuous breakfast. Maria confided that she didn't want to leave Suzette and she wasn't sure her grandparents would take her in. Suzette assured her that they would be lifelong friends and that her grandparents were her flesh and blood relatives. Of course, they would be thrilled to find out she was still alive. They walked the few blocks to the mission after breakfast. The Plaza was teaming with wagons and merchants marshaling to head north to Colorado or east to Independence. The wagons heading to Colorado carried mining supplies: heavy loads of picks, shovels, hand drills, miner's candlesticks, boxes of candles, and black powder. The wagons heading east carried Mexican items: rugs, pottery, statues, maize, tortillas, and barrels of salsa. Suzette mused, there is going to be a lot of heartburn on that wagon train. She saw Epperson's hardware store on a side street, and that reminded her that she still had to make a deal with him to keep the Henry rifles and ammunition.

When they got to the front of the Mission de San Miguel, a Franciscan priest, was sweeping the front steps. Beautiful trees and gardens surrounded the adobe church and stood out as *Old World* elegant. It was amazing what a hundred years of loving care could do for a simple building and the church grounds. Suzette asked the young priest about Señora Gonzales. They were directed into the church and out through a side door into an adjoining garden within adobe walls. The garden was lush with lavender bougainvillea and yellow roses surrounding sandstone walkways. Toward the back of the garden stood a statue of the Madonna within a copse of weeping willows with red roses climbing a trellis shading her from the mid-morning sun. The air was redolent with the smell of the flowers. An older woman knelt in intense prayer before the Madonna. Her eyes were closed tightly in intense concentration, and she was holding a rosary draped over her hands folded in prayer. Maria turned to Suzette, and Maria nodded her head, *Yes*.

Maria walked behind the trellis then quietly stepped in front of her grandmother and touched her on the cheek. Abuela opened her eyes, and her hands flew up to cover her mouth. Her eyes grew wide, already brimming with tears, and then they rolled up and closed. Suzette caught her head before it hit the sandstone and laid her gently on her lap as she knelt to make the woman more comfortable. Maria was clutching her hands to her face in terror that she had killed her. The young priest walked up and put his arm around Maria and said in Spanish, "Your grandmother has been praying for a miracle ever since news arrived that your wagon train perished on the trail. It must have been quite a shock for her to see her prayers answered right before her eyes. Don't worry; she faints during mass sometimes too. She will come around in a few minutes. I'll go get her some cold water."

Suzette said, "Gracias Padre. ¿Cómo te llama?"

The young priest answered in English, "Not Padre yet, call me Samuel. I am a seminarian, not a full priest."

Abuela was still unconscious when Samuel returned with the water. Suzette wet her kerchief, and ever the doctor wiped her patient's forehead. Suzette was relieved when Doña Gonzales opened her eyes and started looking around even though she lay completely still. Abuela said, "La Virgen me ha traído mi nieta."

Maria answered in Spanish, "No abuela, fue la Virgen Suzette."

Samuel laughed and helped Doña Gonzales back to her feet. "Let's go sit down in the church, at least a prayer of thanks is in order, and I will send for Patrón. They sat in the church. Maria and her grandmother sat wrapped in each other's arms. Both were crying, unable to speak. Señor Gonzales came busting in through the front doors. He half-ran down the aisle and stopped in front of the women, a look of wonder and disbelief on his face. He looked at Suzette and Samuel and said in English, "This is not possible; we were told they were all dead."

Maria smiled and said, "I am not dead. Suzette saved my life."

Señor Gonzales looked at Suzette more seriously and saw a strong young woman dressed in buckskins with a sidearm on her hip. He grasped Suzette's hand and pulled her up out of the pew and hugged her. "Thank you," he said, choking back tears. "How can we ever repay you?"

"You owe me nothing, Patrón. Just take care of Maria and see that she has a good life. My brothers and I are heading to Los Angeles, but I might settle at the medical school in San Francisco. Maybe Maria could visit me there someday."

Patrón said, "You have to come to see us in Bernalillo. We are returning there this afternoon."

"Let's go out to the wagon train to get her things, and you can meet the man who has been taking care of her." With that, they left the church; Maria held tightly between her grandparents. Patrón asked about his daughter and her husband. Suzette just shook her head *no*. They walked the few blocks to the wagon train together. Mr. Sue saw them coming and stood stoically with his arms crossed as Suzette introduced the Gonzales family to him and her brothers. Maria gathered up her few possessions from Mr. Sue's wagon, and Roland handed her a leash with Huérfana jumping up and down and barking, happy to be reunited with her owner.

"Mi perro," Maria said. She started crying and hugged Mr. Sue. She couldn't look at Suzette at first and hugged Eli and the twins and then turned to Suzette and said in perfect English through racking sobs, "I don't want to leave you."

"It is time, Maria. These people are your family. I'm just a friend, and I will always be your friend. I will never forget you, and we will see each other again someday." She kissed Maria on the forehead and said, "Vaya con Dios mi amiga."

The family turned to leave, but Suzette stopped Señor Gonzales and slipped the passbook for Maria's bank account into his hand. He opened it and looked at the balance and started to shake his head *no*. Suzette closed his hand over the little book and said, "Take it; the money belongs to Maria. See that she gets the best education possible."

Señor Gonzales couldn't understand how his granddaughter could have four thousand dollars, but he put the book in his pocket and hugged Suzette again with tears welling in his eyes. "She will have the best. You are a beautiful woman, like Maria's mother, but with blond hair. We will never forget you. God bless you and your brothers." He turned and shook Mr. Sue's hand, then walked away with his women. Huérfana was straining at her leash and barking in protest over being pulled away. The dog didn't like leaving her source of table scraps and the bones that Mr. Sue always gave her; she didn't like it one bit. Suzette didn't like it either; she needed a distraction, or she was going to break down and spend the rest of the day mourning the loss of her friend. She asked Eli for fifty double eagles and said she would walk back into town and settle with Epperson for the rifles.

She walked back into the Plaza and took the side street to the hardware store. There was a woman's salon next to Epperson's, and Suzette went inside to find out what she could about Epperson. There were mostly Hispanic women tending other Hispanic women, but an Anglo lady was sitting at a desk toward the back. She had a nameplate on the desk that said her name was Mademoiselle Lynnette. Suzette addressed her in French, "Bonjour Mademoiselle. Pourrais-je vous demander concernant M. Epperson voisine." The woman looked up in surprise; it wasn't very common to hear someone address her in any language other than Spanish in Santa Fe, let alone flawless French with no American twang.

She jumped up and said in English, "Let's go for a walk. I don't want to talk about him in here." Mademoiselle Lynnette was an older woman but still radiated elegant beauty. She wore a dress that rustled with starched petticoats as she stood up. Her hair was piled high on her head and held in place with diamond-studded combs. Beyond looking good, Mademoiselle Lynnette also smelled good. The best you could hope for on the Trail was a woman that didn't smell at all. The elegant woman was the first woman dressed to her station that Suzette had seen since leaving Independence. Suzette let the French woman take her by the hand and lead her out onto the street.

On the boardwalk, Mademoiselle Lynnette told Suzette that her last name was Arseneau; she had been in America for almost twenty years. She came west with her husband, but he was killed here in the streets in a gunfight some years ago. She wanted to know everything about Suzette, where she was from, and where she learned French. They walked away from Epperson's and sat on a bench in the shade of a large cottonwood tree. Mademoiselle Lynnette told Suzette that Epperson was an impotent, lecherous pig. He preyed on young girls and had a collection of pornographic pictures, and that he paid the young girls to pose for him.

"I need to make a deal with him for some rifles. If I play to his weakness, am I going to have to kill him if he tries to rape me?"

"Trust me, honey, I know firsthand that he can't rape anyone. He tried to romance me after my husband died, and he had drunk his pepe to death long before that. He is useless as an octogenarian in a whore house and not much of a human being. He sells the pictures to wealthy men back east. Behind the store, he has a stage, and he has the girls pose nude there. The light is good today; he will probably offer you some money to take off your clothes if you go in there to talk to him."

"I do have to go in because I have to buy some rifles and ammunition. What would you suggest?"

"Let me doll you up a bit. You are a knockout anyway, but a few accents will make you the prettiest girl he has ever seen. He will do anything to get you in front of his camera; you can make the best of that in your negotiations." They walked back to the salon. In an hour, Suzette walked out, looking like a different woman. Her lips were dark red, her eyes subtly shadowed, and she smelled like lilacs. Her hair was coiled up on the top of her head, and she had a jeweled comb holding an elegant wave that swept around her head, held in place over her right ear. The top two of the buttons on her blouse were open, and the tails of a white satin blouse were pulled out of her buckskin skirt and tied together under her breasts. The effect was meant to be devastating on the male libido. Her ample breasts were pushed up, and she showed considerable cleavage for a girl of fourteen. She was without question the most strikingly beautiful woman in Santa Fe that day. She only had to walk next door on the boardwalk, but she got several cat-calls along the way. She just smiled and waved at the soldiers and said, "Later, boys."

She walked into the hardware store and was impressed with the large inventory of weapons behind Epperson's counter. Epperson was impressed too. He couldn't look away and kept ogling Suzette like he couldn't believe his eyes. He stammered, "What can I do for you, young lady?"

"I need to buy some rifles, Henry repeaters if you have them."

"I have some on the way, but they aren't here yet."

Suzette put one elbow on the counter and leaned forward to improve Epperson's view of her young body. Epperson couldn't hide his reaction to her and was staring at her breasts as Suzette said, "They aren't going to arrive, Mr. Epperson. I already have your rifles; what I want to do is pay you for them. I see they go for twenty dollars apiece. There were twelve in the crate, so that would be two hundred forty dollars plus I need to pay you for the crates of ammunition. Would you take four hundred fifty dollars for the lot?"

"I might, especially if you were willing to do something special for me."

Suzette smiled seductively and touched her left breast, "I know all about your photography business, Mr. Epperson. I am not taking off my clothes, but I am otherwise not opposed to you taking my picture."

"Then I need five hundred dollars for the Henry's and the ammunition and at least several pictures of you posing for me out in the sun behind the store."

Suzette had twenty-five double eagles in one pocket and twenty-five in the other. She took out five hundred dollars and put it on the counter and said, "I need a bill-of-sale."

"And you will pose for some pictures?"

"Yes, I'll do that, but no nudity."

Epperson turned to a small desk behind the counter and asking her name, wrote out a bill of sale, signed, and dated it. He handed it to Suzette and then walked to the front of the store and locked the door, and turned his *open* sign over to *closed*. As he walked back to the counter, he took Suzette by the arm and said, "This way, my dear." He led her out a door in the back of the store. The yard behind was walled in on all three sides with tall buildings. Suzette noticed no windows were overlooking the yard. Crates of mining equipment and all types of camping supplies crowded the yard. There was a trail through the amassed hardware, and some open ground and a makeshift stage stood at the back of the yard. There was an expensive-looking camera set up in front of the stage with a stack of plates on a table next to it. Epperson had Suzette stand up on the stage and hold on to a pole. "Lean into it, honey; stick those magnificent breasts out as far as you can."

Epperson was in a hurry to slide a plate into the camera, but he ducked under the heavy black-velvet cover on the back of it and fiddled with the lens on the front. Suzette did as he asked and leaned into the poll holding on up high and arching her back to throw her chest forward. She thought she was wicked to feel aroused, but she was remembering what Landstrom's blood felt like flowing over her and thought she wouldn't mind doing the same to this pig. Epperson closed the shutter on the camera and slid the plate into the back of it and removed the opaque sheet that protected the sensitive emulsion from accidental exposure. He attached a long cable with a plunger at the end to trigger the shutter and walked up behind Suzette. "Look at the camera and smile and don't move." That much would have been passable to Suzette, but he reached over and grabbed the back of her collar and ripped her blouse off as he snapped the picture. "God, you are beautiful when you are mad; how about one more picture?" Suzette turned to him, and before he could protect himself, kicked him hard in his crouch. Epperson went down hard and hit his face on the stage. The sound was a sickening thwack, but Suzette didn't even care if the man was dead. She walked over to the camera and withdrew the plate and exposed it to the sun. She walked back into the store and took a denim shirt off one of the racks and put it on. She walked over to the counter and put down several one-dollar bills for the shirt and then left the store.

She walked back to the wagon camp with every head in town, turning her way. None of the men in the street approached her. She was walking with an angry determination, and her demeanor didn't invite conversation. She got back to the camp and handed Eli the bill-of-sale and the extra money. Her appearance stunned him, and she could tell he wanted to ask her what happened. She held up her hand to stop his question and said, "Don't ask. Sometimes a girl has to do what she has to do." She walked over to a washtub, let down her hair down, and washed her face. She was Suzette again, but she was careful to store the jeweled comb with her few prized possessions. She was ready for one of Mr. Sue's good meals and more than ready to get out of Santa Fe and back on the trail. She spent the evening quietly writing in her journal and missing Maria. Eli told her that they would stop in Bernalillo and see the winery on their way south. She fell asleep under the wagon and dreamed of dressing up again in elegant gowns with her hair up and the jeweled comb fastening the sweep above her ear. Now that was something her grandmother would approve of with a lot of enthusiasm. It wouldn't be that long now before she saw her again.

The next morning when they were ready to leave, Suzette rode back into town and tied her horse up in front of the salon. There was a lantern burning at the back, and Mademoiselle Lynnette walked forward in the dim light to unlock the door. She smiled at Suzette and said, "You did him good, last night he was walking home with a pair of his crutches for support. He had the Holy Grail of a black eye, and his face was black and blue as well. I hope you smashed the camera as well?"

"No, I didn't do any property damage that he could blame on me. I brought back your comb."

"Keep it young lady, and when you get to Los Angeles, where it again to a fancy ball with many young men to charm into marriage. Good luck to you and travel safely." The two women hugged, and Suzette swung up onto Patches' saddle without using the stirrup. She clicked her tongue, and Patches turned instinctively to the noise of wagon wheels on the cobblestone streets. Suzette wondered if Los Angeles could be as wondrous as Santa Fe. She joined up with Eli's wagon, still thinking that someday she was going to be every bit as stately and elegant as Mademoiselle Lynette. It seemed like a funny thought with a rifle in the scabbard at the front of her saddle, a revolver on her hip, and a Bowie knife strapped to her calf. Someday though, she was going to make it happen, but for now, she put it out of her mind as she took her position scouting ahead as they left town. The second leg of their journey, and perhaps the most dangerous, just started.

EL CAMINO REAL

From Santa Fe, it was a short distance to the El Camino Real de Tierra Adentro, the main route between Mexico City some fifteen hundred miles to the south and the San Juan Pueblo northwest of Santa Fe. The differences from the Santa Fe Trail were immediately apparent. The El Camino Real was a road instead of a trail. Even the road leading out of Santa Fe was a well-graded road rather than the myriad of trails one found out on the prairies of Kansas or eastern New Mexico. Eli missed having a guidebook, but he had a map in Spanish that showed all the towns down the Real, all the way to Mexico City. If they were lucky enough to have a road this good and no other problems to deal with, they would be leaving the Rio Grande Valley at La Mesilla and heading west toward Apache Pass within a week. The closer they got to the pass, the greater the risk of attack from the Apache. On the other side of the pass, the Apache threat would reduce the further west they went, and be essentially nonexistent west of the Colorado River.

Another difference was that well-established farms lined the road wherever there was tillable soil. A good number of the larger farms were laid out around walled haciendas. The contrast between the haciendas and the sod or wooden cabins out in the tornado swept areas of Kansas was more dramatic than night and day. There were no storm shelters, so Eli and his siblings assumed that they wouldn't be troubled by tornadoes anymore even though an occasional dust devil could be seen sweeping across the valley floors. The walled haciendas spoke well to the issue of the Apache being at war with the Spanish and Mexican settlers for over one hundred fifty years. Now that the area was a United States Territory, the Apache, who were previously at war with any foreign presence in their lands, now had to embrace war with the US Army. All over the west, the US Army was building up its forces and fortifications to carry on the battle. War with the southern states might give the Apache a temporary truce and maybe even an ally, but the US Army was intent on suppressing the Apache until their violence ended for good.

The Real followed the top of an almost flat mesa with deep ravines on both sides. There were some wagons, riders, and travelers on foot heading north to Santa Fe. Most of the travelers appeared unarmed or at least traveled with their arms within easy reach but out of sight. Eli set his sights on Pueblo San Felipe for their first night on the Real. It would be a thirty-mile trek but easy to make after a day of rest and on such a good road. They would be in Bernalillo by early afternoon the next day. By early evening they pulled up to Pueblo San Felipe, and their summations were confirmed. Eli, nor anyone else for that matter, had any experience with the Pueblo Indians, but it was easy to see that they were not hostile people. The Indians of San Felipe were eager to trade and welcomed soldiers and teamsters alike into the walls of the Pueblo. Eli and Captain Poller both favored a camp of their own making outside of the wall and set up within an easy walking distance of the gate. Most of the men from back east were curious and went over to visit the Pueblo after tending to their teams. The aroma of fry bread, along with costumed dancers in the small plaza of the Pueblo, was an irresistible draw on the easterners. The soldiers were cautious, however. Some went over to the Pueblo; most stayed in the wagon camp outside the walls.

Mr. Sue and Suzette walked into the Pueblo together. There was a spring in the middle of the plaza, and an ancient Catholic Church dominated the south side. All around the square were booths selling a wide variety of Indian wares. Suzette was on the lookout for herbs, but she also wanted to find a treasure to add to her gold sample and the jeweled comb Mademoiselle Lynette gave her in Santa Fe. Most of what the Pueblo Indians had to sell was pottery or woven materials, but there was one elderly couple that was making and selling silver jewelry. Some pieces were similar to the blue gemstone that the lawyer Hobart wore on his tie clasp. Suzette picked up a piece to admire, and Mr. Sue said, "The color of the stone matches your eyes exactly."

Suzette liked the deep blue color of the stone and asked the Indian couple what it was in Spanish. The man started to speak of the legend of the "Sky Stone" and finished up telling Suzette that there were as many names for the gemstone as there were languages among the Indian peoples. He went on to say that the blue gemstone was the stone of the sky, the stone of water, the stone of blessings, good fortune, protection, good health, and long life. Suzette put down the piece and picked up another. She asked, "Is this all you have?"

The elderly silversmith hesitated for a moment then nodded to his wife, and she reached under the table and brought out a black case and opened it with great reverence. Inside was an extraordinary necklace, earrings, and a large broach along with a barrette for a braid. Again, the Sky Stone matched her eyes perfectly; it looked like the deep blue of the gemstones was made just for her coloring. The silver work was also exquisite, several quantum levels above the pieces displayed on the table. Suzette commented to Mr. Sue, "This is beyond just jewelry; it is art!" Mr. Sue agreed and suggested that she ask the price.

¿Cuánto cuesta el precio? She asked politely.

The Indian couple was reluctant to sell, and they said that it took many seasons to collect the stone and craft the intricate silverwork. It was their masterpiece, probably the last of its kind that they would make in their lives. The woman put the necklace on Suzette. She slipped the earrings through her pierced ears and pinned the broach to the front of her vest. She reached up and pulled the barrette from Suzette's braid. Her eyes grew wide, looking at the stiletto, suddenly realizing that the barrette was a weapon. She handed the barrette to her husband, and he looked it over. Even though it was just an iron trinket, he could well appreciate that it was a strong and stealthy weapon of self-defense. Suzette took the barrette from the set and asked if he could add a stiletto spike to his barrette. The old Indian said he could, but it would take the rest of the night. "Quiero comprar el set," Suzette told them. The couple started to talk amongst themselves in their native tongue. Suzette was at a loss to understand a word of what they were saying, but she was certain that they did not want to sell.

The discussion went on for some time. The sun was settling lower in the west, and the shadows were growing long in the plaza. They finally told Suzette that she looked beautiful in the jewelry, and they would sell, but the price had to be substantial. They asked her how much she would offer. Suzette conferred with Mr. Sue. He had some sage advice. "The gemstones are called *turquoise,* which is the French word for Turkey, where traders carried it into Western Europe thousands of years ago. The set is worth at least two hundred dollars. Consider this; if you pass it up, you will hate yourself for the rest of your life. I wouldn't dicker. I would pay them what they want or whatever you think it is worth."

Suzette nodded her head yes and unbuckled her gun belt. From the pouch on the inside of the back, she prized out ten double eagles. From the smaller pouch behind the handle of the revolver, she shook out another five. She told the silversmiths that they had to have the barrette ready by the time she left in the morning. The couple stared at the money on the table. It was more than they had ever gotten for a piece of their work. It was enough money to let them retire if they wanted to. They looked at each other, and then the man reached over and swept the money into his hand. "Amanecer mañana señorita." He kept Suzette's iron barrette, and it was apparent that he was thinking of how he could modify his piece to duplicate the stiletto. Suzette packed the jewelry back into its case and clutched her newly acquired treasure to her breast with both hands as she toured the rest of the Pueblo with Mr. Sue.

When they returned to the wagon camp, Suzette showed the set to her brothers. Roland said, "I'm glad you are still a young woman who can value fine art jewelry and wear it with aplomb. You are going to look great with your hair up, and that necklace draped on your bosom. We have to get you somewhere you can dazzle some young men with your charms. Of course, you will have to leave the revolver out of the ensemble, or it won't matter how good you look." They all laughed, but Hans presented Suzette with a small double-barreled derringer and told her that she could wear it in a garter on her leg when she dressed up in an evening gown. That night they dined on fry bread and roasted goat. All considered it a very interesting meal, nutritious and tasty. They could also see why a good deal of the Pueblo Indians were portlier rather than the lean-muscular form of their cousins on the prairie. Not a single person stopped eating until they were stuffed full and moaning the laments of having overeaten.

The next morning Suzette walked into the Pueblo and went to the booth to collect up the barrette. The elderly couple was very proud of their work. They had fashioned the stiletto from the handle of a heavy sterling silver spoon. It was as strong as the iron stiletto, and the large turquoise stone fit comfortably in the palm of her hand. They hugged Suzette with tears in their eyes thanking her again for the generous purchase and wished her God Speed on the Real. Suzette slid the iron barrette into her braid and put the turquoise one through a buttonhole on the front of her vest. She smiled at the elderly couple, hugged each of them, then turned and walked back to the wagon train. It was forming up and almost ready to move out. She saddled Patches, checked her Henry rifle and the Lefaucheux, and mounted up. She was anxious to get to Bernalillo and see Maria with her family. It was hard to describe how much she missed her young friend already.

The morning air was crisp, and the mules were enjoying a fast pace. Eli's map of the Real showed that they were approaching the Rio Grande River. The Sandia Mountains were spectacular on the east side of the valley, and every mile offered a new panorama as breathtaking as the mountain ranges in Colorado. It wasn't even ten miles to Bernalillo, and they covered the distance in less than an hour and a half. It was still early morning when they pulled up to the little village on the west side of the Rio Grande. Grapevines covered the slopes dipping gently down to the river bottom; the Gonzales Winery was the most prominent building in town. There was a walled courtyard in front of the winery, and the Callahans pulled the wagon train up short of the gates and walked in.

Maria sat on the right shoulder of the biggest man they had ever seen. He was easily seven feet tall and must have weighed near four hundred pounds. Suzette first thought he was a statue because he stood perfectly still. Maria let out a yelp though when she saw Suzette, and the big man slid her down his chest and gently put her on the ground. She ran into Suzette's arms, crying and laughing. It had only been a few days since they parted in Santa Fe, but you would have thought that they had been apart for years. Huérfana came bounding out of the doors of the winery. She went straight to Mr. Sue, probably looking for a bone. Mr. Sue was prepared and slipped the dog a piece of jerky that kept her tail wagging for several minutes.

Maria's grandparents and about a dozen other people came out of the winery to welcome them. Patrón was giving orders in rapid-fire Spanish, and some of the workers were scurrying off to do his bidding. Maria started introducing them to all her relatives. The gargantuan was Uncle Juan, who everyone called Tio, a gentle giant who picked Maria up with one hand under her arm and lifted her back to his shoulder. Then he reached for Suzette, who wanted to jump away but thought it best not to offend her hosts. Uncle Juan bent down and pulled Suzette onto his other shoulder. The man was amazingly strong and walked them around the courtyard. Suzette flashed back to happier times in Missouri, and the pony rides her father would give her, and stories of the giant dog Goliath that Eli was said to have ridden like a horse when he was a toddler. She quickly turned her thoughts away from the sadness and came back to bask in the happiness of the moment.

There was a beautiful young woman half hiding behind the door of the winery. Maria called for her to come out. She introduced her aunt, Lia. She was a little older than Suzette and wore a brightly colored serape, a rainbow of blues, reds, yellows, and greens over a white cotton dress. Knotted white yarn trimmed the edges of the serape and her long-raven-black hair, a long fall almost to the back of her knees, shined in the morning light. The serape was tied at her waist accenting her figure, and the long white dress embroidered with roses down one side, draped loosely over her bare feet. The boys were enthralled, but it was Roland who couldn't take his eyes off her. He lingered there at the door as the introductions moved on. Roland smiled at the young woman, and he was thrilled when she smiled back.

Patrón led everyone into the winery. Behind them, the courtyard was bursting into activity with tables being set up and a makeshift kitchen rolled into place near the door of the winery. Eli sent the word out to the wagon train to make camp. It was obvious they wouldn't be going anywhere any time soon. Patrón was doing the winery tour. Young girls gave everyone a wine glass, and each time they passed a vat, generous samples filled the glasses. Many toasts were put forth honoring Maria's rescuers. More people were gathering outside. The arrival of Maria's savior was cause for a fiesta, and with enthusiasm, the locals embraced it. It looked like Bernalillo hadn't had cause to celebrate in quite some time. Tables were being set up, and the soldiers and teamsters joined the party in the courtyard. There wasn't enough room for everyone, so the party kept building outside the gate. Suzette was half tipsy after two glasses of wine and had to refuse more offerings of Patrón's finest politely. A mariachi band came together out of the crowd with their instruments, and before long, there was dancing and singing. The young Callahans had never been in a happier crowd alive with the spontaneous energy of the fiesta.

It was still morning, but a feast was underway for the midday meal. Most of the men switched from wine to tequila, another of Patrón's specialties. Roland didn't drink heavy. He followed Lia around like a love-sick puppy, and Suzette enjoyed watching him, the wise brother, beguiled by this beautiful Spanish woman. She was going to have a lot of fun teasing him about this later on. But as the morning wore on, Roland wasn't following the young woman anymore. He was leading her by the hand, showing her the wagon train, the horses, and the impressive armaments. For the midday meal, they sat together and later on they spent the afternoon dancing and singing with the mariachis. Paul Hayman was in his element. The mariachis would play one of their tunes, and then Paul would play one of his. It was a contest as to who would run out of songs first. The soldiers were hopelessly drunk. Suzette and Jacques went out to relieve the guards on the wagon train so that they could come in and join the festivities.

The afternoon started to ebb towards evening. With the men from the wagon train and the soldiers, there were at least five hundred people at the fiesta. The entire town turned out and contributed to the occasion. Señora Gonzales walked out to Suzette with a young Dominican Priest. Señora introduced him as Father Ernesto Bond. Suzette was surprised to find a Dominican with an English name and equally surprising, Father Ernesto spoke perfect English. "You are a very famous young woman, Miss Callahan," he said as he held out his hands to greet her.

"Please, Father, I only want to be an ordinary young woman. I didn't do anything beyond what any Good Samaritan would have done. I don't seek to be famous, and I am not necessarily proud of all the things I had to do on the way here."

"Nonetheless, you saved Maria's life." Suzette thought the priest was going to say more, but he paused and drew up the white-knotted rope that served as a belt holding his black cassock tight at the waist. Father Bond fiddled with the knots on the belt for several moments and then drew pensive and said, "Señora Gonzales wants to send Maria to California with you. She wants her to get a good education. Maria has told her that you are already a good doctor. Will you be going to medical school in San Francisco? You could take her with you. No?"

Suzette could see a problem here. She answered, "Yes, I will probably go to the medical college if they accept me. But taking Maria with me is out of the question; it is much too dangerous down through the Apache country. Maria has already come close to death once. I won't put her life at risk again."

Now Father Bond had a knot in each hand and was snapping the rope tight to emphasize each point of his argument. Suzette wondered if the young priest was even aware of the nervous habit. He was arguing a point that if Apache Pass were too dangerous for Maria, it would be too dangerous for her too. "What can we do, Miss Callahan? Señora is adamant, and Maria is begging to go with you."

Suzette gave it a moment before she responded, "I won't leave my brothers, and I can take care of myself. I could send for Maria after I reach San Francisco. She could travel there on a stage from Santa Fe up through Colorado and west to Sacramento and then down the river. She will be safe going that way. Please have the Señora consider that."

Father Ernesto could see that Suzette's concern for Maria's safety was deep and sincere; he promised he would try his best. That difficult point resolved; he gave the rope belt a rest. He looked over to the fiesta and saw Roland and Lia sitting hand-in-hand. Suzette followed his gaze and not only saw Roland and Lia but Señora Gonzoles waiting for the young priest to continue. With respect, Father Bond brought up another subject that Señora Gonzoles wanted him to discuss. "Your brother is quite taken with Lia. Her sister was Maria's mother. She is a Martinez. There are only two families here in Bernalillo, the Gonzales and Martinez clans, both go back to the first settlement of the area by the Spanish. Lia is a very sad young woman. The Apache killed her husband one week after they married. She lives alone, and she is still grieving, but maybe your brother is just the man to rescue her from that lonely grief. She seems much taken with him too."

Now Suzette was incredulous. "Father, what are you suggesting? They have only known each other a few hours, and they don't share a common language; and again, we can't take her with us for the same reasons we can't take Maria."

Father Bond proposed an alternative, "What if we send her with Maria on the stage to San Francisco? I think it would be a good idea for Uncle Juan to accompany them too. Juan, as you have probably noticed, is a gentle giant. He isn't exactly retarded, but he isn't completely normal either. Emotionally, he is the same age as Maria and has assumed the role of her guardian and companion for life. He was sadder than Lia until you brought her back to us. For a while, I feared that he would take his own life!"

"I think that would work, Father. I can see to it that Maria will get the best education possible. I have a grandmother too, waiting in Los Angeles for us. If I go to San Francisco, she will go there too. We can all stay with her until Maria finishes school. Eventually, I will go wherever Eli goes. He is the patriarch of our family now; we all rely on his strength and judgment to get us safely across this country. Maybe Doña Gonzales could find a wife for him too."

Father Ernesto chuckled and then turned and started talking to Señora Gonzales in rapid-fire Spanish. Suzette could follow the conversation, but it was hard. Mr. Sue was there on his chuck wagon. He brought over tea for everyone, and Father Ernesto was glad to have it. Señora wasn't convincing easily. Suzette heard Lia mentioned several times along with San Francisco, school, and the dangers in Apache country. Señora pointed at Suzette several times, and Mr. Sue said, "Señora Gonzales thinks you are invincible, and no harm could befall Maria as long as she is with you."

"How can you possibly know that? I can't even follow the conversation."

Mr. Sue smiled, "Trust me. It is a grandparent kind of thing."

Suzette looked at Mr. Sue and with a startled expression and asked, "You have grandchildren?"

"Yes, I'll tell you more about that when we are better friends. Let's listen to Maria's grandmother." Suzette wondered how many more layers there were to achieve in Mr. Sue's complicated character until she was considered his best friend. But the conversation between Father Bond and Señora Gonzales had turned into a heated argument that demanded her full attention.

Now Señora was arguing more fervently, pounding one fist into her other opened palm to drive home a point. Suzette felt sorry for Father Ernesto; he was back working on the rope belt, twisting it tight, letting it unroll, and twisting it again. He didn't have an easy job here caught in the middle. Finally, Señora settled down, and Father Ernesto explained. "Señora is afraid that if Maria doesn't go now, Patrón won't let her go in the future. He will want to keep her here until she is old enough to marry, and he will want to approve of the husband. She is suggesting what she thinks is an easy solution. Your brother marries Lia, Juan goes along to guard all of you. Everyone goes to San Francisco, and after a while, Patrón and Doña Gonzales take the stage to come to visit."

Suzette sat down by Señora. She put her arm around her holding her close and said, "Abuela, podría morir de camino a Los Ángeles. Entonces, ¿qué sería de Maria? (I could die on the way to Los Angles. Then what would become of Maria?)

Señora clutched Suzette's hand and wouldn't let go. She just sat there thinking. After several long moments with a faraway look as if she could see the future across the valley, she nodded her head yes and said, "Sí, lo entiendo. " She got up and led Suzette back into the courtyard. A lot was going on; the courtyard was alive with the traditions and deep culture of the old world. The sun was setting; the children were trying to break a piñata; men and women were dancing. Paul was singing a sad ballad about a young soldier and his girl back home. Roland was dancing with Lia. He was holding her close, and she was looking up at him with more than just a little affection showing on her face. Señora glanced at the unlikely couple and then looked at Suzette with an expression that pleaded to understand. Suzette was skeptical about love at first sight, but maybe there was something to it after all. Suddenly she felt a pang of fear; what if Roland wouldn't leave without Lia, and he stayed behind to pursue the beautiful woman. Maybe Abuela was right; maybe they should call Father Ernesto over and get them married tonight. Too much to think about, Suzette settled down with a glass of light red wine and watched the fiesta wind down. Roland was old enough to figure this out for himself.

The next morning came early as usual, but the men were slow to rise and shine. Mr. Sue was up on his usual schedule. Suzette noticed that the camp was slow to come around and asked Mr. Sue, "Why aren't you hungover like the rest of the idiots that were trying to drink Patrón under the table?"

"Old trick from China. Tequila is white -- like water. Same as Chinese Moutai. After the boys were about half liquored up, I switched Patrón and myself to water. Nobody noticed, and your brothers went down hard. Don't worry; I have the cure cooking up on the fire. Go roust them and tell them the doctor is ready for sick call."

Suzette went over and kicked Eli in the boot. He was stretched out on top of his bedroll fully clothed. He moaned. Suzette similarly woke Jacques and yelled with a drill sergeant's voice, "Sick call you drunks. Where in the hell is your Irish? You are pathetic. Your father would be ashamed to call you his own. Get on your feet. Get moving. I want to go to Los Angeles – the one in California you wasted sots. **RISE AND SHINE.**" Eli crawled out from under his wagon, and Mr. Sue handed him a cup of the cure.

Halfway through the diatribe, Jacques, had his ears covered and was rolling around moaning. Roland was nowhere in sight. "Oh! Oh! Roland is missing," she muttered loud enough for Mr. Sue to hear.

"I have no cure for what ails him, Missy. He has heart trouble of the worst kind. Look, there he is walking over with the woman."

Hand in hand, Roland walked up to the fire pit with Lia. She wore boots and a buckskin outfit. She had two Colt Patterson 0.36 caliber revolvers, one on each hip, and Roland was carrying a carpetbag. Her hair was braided and wound around her neck in coils draped luxuriously over her shoulders. She carried a sawed-off 12-gauge double-barrel shotgun, and Roland led a large bay mare, an elegant black saddle with silver accents sat atop a bright blue saddle blanket; the bridle and reins matched the saddle. Two saddlebags and a bedroll indicated that this woman was ready to travel. Roland looked at his hung-over brothers and asked Suzette to tell Lia that they would have to wait a while to ask Eli's permission for her to join the wagon train.

The sun was rising above the north crest of the Sandia Mountains, and the soldiers, teamsters, and swampers were up, obviously more used to a night on the town than Eli and Jacques. Eli was up and coherent, and Roland was about ready to ask his permission for Lia to join up with their train when Doña Gonzales came storming out of the winery complex with Father Ernesto in tow. The storm didn't subside as she walked angrily up to Roland and started berating him in rapid Spanish. Suzette could follow her rave easily but was relieved when Father Ernesto stopped her and translated. "Essentially, she approves of Lia going with Roland but insists that they are married first. She is worried that Roland will not stay the course once you reach your destination or that perhaps he will tire of her along the way. Lia is an extremely capable young woman, but she carries vengeance for the Apache, who killed her husband. Roland, in our culture, the matriarchs rule;

you're lucky that Lia's mother and father are away, or there could have been some serious trouble here already for your actions last night."

Eli was finally awake and focused, finally realizing that Roland had spent the night with Lia Martinez. He took a moment to form up his thoughts and then said, "Roland, this is a lifetime decision made in only one day. It's dangerous where we are going. Take a moment and consider your answer wisely." Jacques and Suzette stood shoulder to shoulder with Eli as if to emphasize his point. "You have our blessing whatever you choose."

Suzette offered an alternative, "Lia could go with Maria and Tio on the stage up through Colorado. You know that would be safer." More men and women were arriving from the village, obviously more of the Martinez family. They joined the group, waiting for Roland's reply with a lot of whispering among the women of Lia's family.

Roland looked into Lia's eyes and was decided, "I'll do it, Father."

"Wait!" Suzette rushed to the back of Eli's wagon. She rummaged in the footlocker that held her belongings and her little wood box of treasures. She came back and put a gold ring in Roland's hand. It was their mother's wedding band; she only wished that she had the mate to it, but that remorseful thought pushed out with something much sillier. Lia was still holding her shotgun. Suzette wondered if this was what *Shotgun Wedding* really meant. She took the shotgun from Lia and hugged her. "Bienvinido a mi familia." She stepped back and motioned for Father Ernesto to proceed.

By this time, all the soldiers and men gathered, and Lt. Barksdale and his cavalry formed up on each side of the bride and groom and made an arch over them with their sabers. Paul Hayman played a quiet hymn in the background. Maria arrived riding on the shoulder of her uncle. Patrón and more men and women from the Winery joined the ceremony. Doña Gonzales looked on with a satisfied expression that said she finished her work here, and Lia looked up at Roland with tears of thanks and happiness in her eyes. Father Ernesto recited the vows in Spanish for Lia and in English for Roland. The ring slipped onto Lia's finger, and Father Ernesto pronounced the couple man and wife. A hundred rifles boomed out a salute at Captain Poller's command as Roland kissed his bride. A cheer resounded and echoed off the walls of the winery as the entire population of Bernalillo started to dance and make ready for another fiesta. Eli saw this coming and headed off the fiesta with a command to form up on the Real. They would be leaving in one hour.

With many hugs and well wishes, Bernalillo returned to their jobs and daily routine. Patrón sent for a small chest and presented it to Roland as Lia's dowry. Roland accepted the gift, laden with silver coins, not to hurt anyone's feelings. Roland knew it was important that he allowed Patrón to uphold the traditions of his people. He put the dowry chest on the back of Eli's wagon and took the reins of his big gelding from Jacques. He and Lia mounted up and rode out of the camp down the Real. Patrón shook Eli's hand, and Señora hugged Suzette and whispered in her ear, "Sigues siendo la matriarca de tu familia." (You are still the matriarch of your family). "Via con Dios y proteger a mi nuera." (Go with God and protect my daughter-in-law). Suzette released Doña Gonzales and nodded her head yes. She wondered how it was going to feel having a sister. Suzette held Maria for a long time and assured her they would be together again soon. It broke her heart to leave the girl. Tears streamed down her face as she walked away. Maria also stood crying, held between her grandparents, Tio's giant hand on her shoulder, Huérfana sitting in front of her. Parting was a very difficult moment for the two young women.

Eli knew he could make twenty-five to thirty miles a day on the Real, but he chose to keep the pace down to twenty. Captain Poller wanted his men to walk at least five miles a day with rifles and full packs to stay in shape, and Eli didn't want to arrive at Apache Pass with tired men and exhausted mules. The trip down the Rio Grande was picturesque with the remnants of three volcanic cinder cones on the west side of the Rio Grande and the Sandia escarpment to the east. As they moved south, they saw more and more birds on the river. Some signs read *Peligro - arenas movedizas,* here and there along the river, some of them in spots that beckoned with cool calm water. Suzette passed the word that the signs meant *Danger Quicksand.* Jacques spread the word up and down the column. The last thing they needed would be to lose men and equipment in a treacherous river bottom.

Below Albuquerque, they passed a settlement called Socorro and saw a place on the river with millions of birds. Snow geese, sandhill cranes, whooping cranes, and a literal plethora of ducks of all kinds along with Canadian geese, blue heron, and snowy egrets crowding the marshes along the river. Suzette rode beside Lia now, and Lia knew the names of all the birds and taught them to Suzette as they rode along together in front of the column. Herds of deer were plentiful along the river and provided a steady diet of venison. The only Indians they saw were Pueblos, Lia was constantly watching for Apache, but they saw none. It took nine days to reach La Mesilla and Fort Fillmore. Captain Poller reported to the Post Commander, and Eli reported to the Quartermaster. Both visits yielded valuable intelligence about the recent Apache movements.

Only days before their arrival, news related that several hundred Mescalero Apache passed south of La Mesilla headed west. The commander was sure they were going to join up with the Chiricahua and try to close Apache Pass. They were poorly armed as usual and had some women and children with them. He was more than pleased that Captain Poller's company of Dragoons would be digging in at the pass. It was way too far to the west for him to keep the pass open with his regiment. It was a very dangerous area, and many pioneers and stagecoaches encountered the Indians in recent months, with a total loss of life.

The quartermaster also had good news. He didn't have any Coehorn Mortars, but he had more than two dozen shells for them. Such was the mystery of Army Supply. He issued the shells to Eli along with more Colt 0.44 revolvers, and an ample supply of primers, powder, and shot. He also told Eli to lie over for a day, and the Colonel would send a platoon of cavalry with them as far as the pass. The cavalry platoon, under the command of Lieutenant Miles Preston, was due back that night and would have a day of rest before going out on patrol again. Eli would gladly accept the offer of mounted troops, and he left the quartermaster to find Captain Poller over at the colonel's office. On the way over, he saw Roland and Lia taking a room in a small adobe building that served as an inn. Opportunities and privacy were rare on the trail, and while Eli did all he could to assure their privacy, it was hard in the close living conditions of a wagon camp.

Lt. Colonel John Baylor commanded the post. He had a lot to say about the pass and tactics. He shook Eli's hand when Captain Poller introduced them, and the Commander was quick to make the offer of more troops. Eli accepted just as quickly, and then the three men, along with Lt. Barksdale, sat down around a rough conference table for a long discussion about the pass. It was well after dark by the time the three of them got back to the wagon camp for a late dinner. Eli was dreading leading his men into a battle with what could be over five hundred Apache, but he knew that his men and the soldiers were a formidable force. The fate of all involved would finalize in just one more week. It wasn't easy sleeping on that thought.

APACHE PASS

L t. Colonel John Baylor was expecting Lt. Preston to return from patrol by early afternoon but was pleased when the young Lieutenant led his horse soldiers into Fort Fillmore shortly after dawn. Lt. Preston was eager to report. Apaches mauled his platoon the previous day, and he had several wounded men who needed care. He chose to keep moving through the night rather than risk another encounter. Lt. Col. Baylor sent for Suzette to help with the wounded and sent word for Captain Poller and his officers to report into the headquarters for another briefing. Eli and Jacques came in with the officers to stay abreast of the Army's plans.

"Mr. Callahan, I know you are technically a civilian and a non-combatant. But if you intend to get through the pass, you are going to be involved in the fight. I am going to issue all your teamsters Sharps rifles and ammunition. The breech-loading rifles will increase your firepower tremendously. The Sharps are not as rapid-fire as your Henry rifles, but a trained man can fire ten rounds a minute accurately, and they have an effective range of five hundred yards. Take the best marksmen among your teamsters and swampers to help with training and draw sixty rifles and ammunition from the Armory. Take your men to the firing range for training and stay there until every one of your men is proficient, say out to two-hundred yards."

"Captain Poller, you are of this minute promoted to Major. Your orders are to secure that pass. There will be enough Sharps for about half your men, and we have enough Colt 0.44 revolvers in stores here to arm all of them. Lt. Barksdale, you are now Captain Barksdale; and Miles, you are now First Lieutenant Miles Preston. You will have two platoons of cavalry with Sharps carbines and Colt revolvers. Take plenty of ammunition. You will be out there with Major Poller for a while. Mr. Callahan, you can draw the necessary supplies from the quartermaster. Make sure to take enough to sustain Major Poller's company for a month. We will supply him from here after you leave him on the pass. I have two Pima scouts that will work for Lt. Barksdale. They are familiar with all the camps and water holes between here and the Gila River and speak the Apache language. Good luck to all of you."

Eli gathered up his men and reported to the Armorer for the rifles. He walked over to the little adobe cottage and knocked on Roland's door. The newlyweds were up and about and welcomed him in. It was a neat little room with a privy out back. Eli gave Lia his Henry rifle and beckoned her to follow him. He explained to Roland, "The Army is issuing Sharps rifles to the teamsters, and I want Lia to have my Henry and learn how to use it. Training will start on the rifle range in thirty minutes. I'll have Suzette teach her how to use the rifle. The Army is spoiling for a fight; we will inevitably be drawn into a fight or attacked outright. I don't think we will be able to bluff or negotiate our way through the pass. You could still send Lia by stage up through Colorado, but after we leave here, that option will not be possible. I know she also wants vengeance, but I thought it wise, though, to offer her a safer journey while it is still available." Roland nodded in understanding and agreed to have Suzette train her and explain the Colorado option to her again.

On the rifle range, the men were excited to receive a better weapon gratis the US Army. They practiced shooting at iron targets up to five hundred yards away. The 0.52 caliber bullets were amazingly accurate. Within ten minutes, most of the men were hitting the two and three-hundred-yard targets with ease. Within a half-hour, many were hitting the five-hundred-yard targets. An Army Staff Sergeant named McPherson called the men together and trained them on how to break down the rifles and clean them. Lia was a natural markswoman. Suzette enjoyed teaching her friend how to load and shoot the Henry rifle. Disassembly and cleaning the more complicated mechanism took much longer than the simple task of loading and shooting. After the training session, the two women sat on a blanket in the shade of the adobe cottage, disassembled the weapons, and cleaned them.

Mr. Sue and the rest of the cooks had a midday meal ready with fresh beef, corn, and potatoes. Everyone ate heartily after the morning of training. Rumors of Apache movements and their warlike nature pervaded the conversations around every fire pit. Suzette spent a long time talking to Lia in Spanish. The young bride was shaking her head "no" many times, and it was apparent she wasn't going to leave the wagon train. Mr. Sue finally put his hand on Suzette's shoulder and said, "Leave her alone now; her mind is made up, and her fate is bound to ours and will be that way as long as we are all alive."

Eli asked Mr. Sue, "You didn't want a new rifle?"

Mr. Sue answered, "If I need one, there will be plenty laying around. But look, I have a new weapon." He drew a long hardwood staff out of the back of the chuck wagon. Iron covered both ends, and the wood was aged and extremely strong. Eli hefted the weapon; it weighed about twelve pounds, longer and heavier than an Irish cudgel. He made a mental note for Mr. Sue to give him some training with it when they had a little spare time. For the rest of the day, they would be inspecting and repairing wagons. The men were rearranging their loads to provide shielded firing positions within the wagon beds. The blacksmith was shoeing mules as usual, but he also had the furrier from the fort helping him. Hans Warner sat stoically watching the activities and studying an Army map of the trail from Fort Fillmore to the Gila River. By the end of the day, everyone was as prepared as they could be. Roland and Lia went back to the adobe cottage, and the camp settled down for a last night's sleep within the security of the fort.

They left the next morning on the usual schedule for the wagon train just after dawn. There would be a full moon for the next few days, so the odds of a nighttime visit by the Apache were high. Lt. Preston was extremely wary. Apache scouts could be sighted from time to time on the tops of the hillocks and mountain ridges. The Apache would disappear as soon as they sighted the wagon train, riding ahead to watch and report the progress to their chiefs. The Apache parties were small until they crossed the Mimbres River on the third day. The farther west they got, the larger the Apache bands grew. They were making twenty miles a day, and Major Poller still marched with his troops the last five miles of every trek. In a week, they passed a burned-out stage stop that was named Steins after an Army Major who camped there a few years back. The bodies of the station master and his hands had been scalped and left in the sun to rot. Lt. Preston pointed out that the murders were for the singular purpose of intimidating their column. The stage stop had operated for years unmolested. The Apache were sending a message. He proposed to Major Poller that they send one of their own.

Lia stopped her horse and looked at the bodies for a long time. She pointed at one of the young Mexican hands and said, "Frank Azavedo de Pueblo San Carlos." Roland could see that her horror was palpable, but as she turned away, her face set with grim determination for vengeance. To Roland, she was still beautiful, but he was seeing a side of his new wife that overshadowed the beauty and reflected a deadly-all business attitude. The contrast was dramatic, but even though Roland vowed never to make her mad at him, he knew that the attitude would serve well to keep her safe in the days ahead.

The next morning, Lt. Preston left out in the dark with his men to get well ahead of the wagon train. Eli was on the lookout for the Apache band and saw them about an hour after they broke camp. The Indian band was larger, forty braves, or more; they were on a small hillock about a mile away. As the wagon train approached, Capt. Barksdale broke off from the column and rode hard at the Indian band. Just as the Apaches were going to break and ride away, Lt. Preston attacked from behind with his platoon, killing more than a dozen with the first volley from their carbines. Taken by surprise from behind and faced with Capt. Barksdale's charge in front of them, the rest of the Indians scattered. Many more Apache died, and Capt.

Barksdale rode down the stragglers and killed them. They gathered up the ponies, more than forty, and herded them back to the column. Lt. Preston rode back with the war lance of the leader of the band. He let more than a half-dozen Apache escape to tell the tale of their demise. The Pima scouts identified the Apache as Chiricahua, a tribe they were not expecting till the west side of Apache Pass.

For the next two days, they didn't see any more Indians. If they were there, they were much more careful than before. The Apache tactics were well known. They would not attack unless they were confident that they could win. When they saw the Indian scouts again, the Indians kept their distance and never again made the mistake of being ambushed by surprise. Suzette and Lia rode alongside the wagons. There was no need to ride scout on the trail with the cavalry riding ahead and on both sides of the trail in numbers. Major Poller wanted to fire the Coehorn mortar in the front of the train so that he could switch to the shells they acquired at Fort Fillmore. He had Suzette quizzing the Pima scouts as to where they might set up an ambush. The Pimas tole Suzette there was a spot famous for Indian attack about another day west, less than ten miles from Apache Pass. As she translated for Major Poller, Jacques listened. "The waterhole is in a small valley on the north end of the range where Apache Pass threads west through the mountains. Behind the small valley, there is a slope up to a saddle where the Apache can approach undetected to within a few hundred yards of the campsite below. If they stay there, Major Poller can set the mortars up to bear on the slope, and deploy the cavalry to either side." Jacques and Major Poller were discussing tactics. Eli planned their next day's travel to reach the waterhole early to plan and set the ambush in place well before nightfall.

Shortly after they turned toward the south, and just a few short miles north of Apache Pass, the Pima scouts indicated a waterhole in bedrock in front of a sandy wash that came down from the foothills of the mountains to the south. They pointed up a slope to a saddle towards the southeast and said that the Apache would attack in force from that direction. A second raiding party would be waiting to attack on horseback from the east around the point of rocks that jutted down into the plain of the valley floor. There was a waterfall on the point of rocks fed by a spring about halfway up the slope. The wreckage of many wagons and evidence of past slaughters of pioneers littered the floor of the little flat at the mouth of the wash on the west side of the point of rocks. Further up the wash, the stream bottom was wet, and a slow trickle of water was working its way downhill before disappearing in the sandy bottom of the flat valley floor.

Major Poller looked over the setting and agreed that it would be a good place to set up an ambush. Half his troops would climb the point of rocks and take up positions on a rocky butte overlooking the saddle from the north. The Pimas said that the bulk of the Apache force would attack from the saddle. Three Coehorn mortars would be set up at the bottom of the slope. The troops at the top were to lay in hiding and let the main force of the Apache pass through the saddle where they would be under the guns on the butte. Jacques opted to be on the butte with the soldiers. Capt. Barksdale would keep his cavalry west of the camp but be ready to mount up and ride around the point of rocks to pursue any attackers that would come from that direction. Lt. Preston would be spending the night at least a mile and a half to the east out on the valley floor and would ride in to intercept any warriors lucky enough to escape over the saddle to make their retreat. Eli liked the plan but wanted to wait till after dark to move everyone into place. Major Poller agreed, Apache scouts had to be up there someplace watching. He wanted everyone to look as naïve as possible. While it was still light, the soldiers would only have a picket line across the mouth of the valley. That made the flank facing the slope look vulnerable. Eli said, "Let's set up the camp, feed everyone, tend to the animals, and get some rest. I doubt anyone will be sleeping tonight."

The evening passed quickly, and as darkness fell, everyone sprang into action. Half the Dragoons started up the slope with Jacques to scale the butte. Lt. Preston rode out to take up his position in the valley. The Coehorn mortars were moved into place and camouflaged with branches cut from the brush along the creek bottom. The rest of the soldiers dug into firing positions to each side of the mortars. The chill of the night set in, and the waning moon rose in the eastern sky well after midnight. Half the men slept at a time, but most were too keyed up to get any sleep at all. Their vigilance was well rewarded. Around two in the morning, the men on the top of the butte signaled with a lamp that they had contact. More than two hundred braves were walking their ponies quietly up the east side of the saddle.

Fifty of them stayed mounted behind the saddle, but the rest dropped down on foot and stealthily crossed through the saddle without making a sound. There were another hundred braves down in the wash east of the point of rocks. Sgt. O'Riley thought to himself that he couldn't have choreographed a better ambush if he tried. The Apache were overconfident and had read the wagon camp as poorly organized for defense. They had performed this sortie with great success too many times in the past to be careful of a trap. The Apache would work their way down the slope to hide in a position as close to the camp as they could get undetected. Typically, they were loath to attack in the dark, and they would wait until the first light of dawn to attack.

Everyone was afraid even to breathe as the Indians worked their way down the slope. Fingers rested on triggers; blood pounded in their veins, driven by a mix of fear and excitement. The first of the braves stopped fifty feet in front of the mortars, and the rest crept down behind them. All was quiet for two nerve-wracking hours. Darkness was slipping into the dim light of dawn as the Indians stood as one, fired a volley of arrows, yelled a war-whoop, and charged. Major Poller fired the first mortar, and the effect was devastating. The mounted braves who were waiting on the east side of the saddle crested the ridge and charged down the slope. Every bush and a good many of the Apache were on fire. The second mortar roared, and braves and ponies crashed to the earth. The horses that weren't hit by lead shot were sprinkled with burning tar and soon bucked the remaining braves off. The Indians on foot made easy targets for the soldiers on the butte, backlit by the fires. Some braves in retreat made it over the top of the saddle and took to the horses under withering fire from the top of the butte. They found Lt. Preston to cut them down as they reached the bottom of the east slope.

The Indians in the wash east of the point of rocks attacked when the first mortar fired. They couldn't see the devastation of their main force and could only assume that their fellow braves were carrying on the attack successfully. A blast from one of the rear mortars killed many and scattered the rest. Capt. Barksdale rode into their midst with sabers drawn to cut them down. Suzette and Lia were guarding the wash bottom to the southeast. Twenty or more braves came rushing toward the camp on foot. The women were shielded behind crates and opened up with the Henrys and methodically shot every single Indian before they reached the perimeter of the camp. Roland knelt at Lia's side as a backup, but let the women do the work sweeping the narrow field of fire with their deadly aim. He hoped this encounter would purge the vengeance out of Lia's spirit and allow her to lay her thoughts of her first husband to rest.

Several Indians ran in from the northwest. Mr. Sue was there with several teamsters and caved in the forehead of the first one with a powerful blow from his staff. The next, he killed with a devastating thrust to the solar plexus, and the last turned to run. Mr. Sue felled him, throwing the staff like a javelin and striking him in the back of the skull. The Indian went down hard and then came to and rolled over but froze as a rifle pressed to his forehead. Mr. Sue said, "This one will live to tell the tale of this massacre."

The entire battle was over in less than five minutes. Major Poller called out in a commanding voice, "Everyone, reload and hold your positions." The fires burned down, and the glow left the little valley bathed in the light of breaking of dawn. Capt. Barksdale rode back in from the east. He had several wounded men, one with an arrow in his chest. Suzette had her medical station set up inside a tent within the wagon circle. Lanterns lit her examination table, and she went to work removing the arrow, checking that the lung was not pierced and then cleaning and closing the wound. The man was unconscious but came around as she worked on the others with minor injuries. Lia stood guard just in case an Apache was lucky enough to get into the camp and lay in wait for an opportunity to attack. The light of the rising sun drove the last of the darkness away, and the carnage of the night's work lay up the slope, in the washes, and everywhere one looked out from the camp. Major Poller wanted a body count, and Lt. Preston rode in from his position out in the valley. There were no Indians left alive anywhere on the slope, in the wash to the east of the rocks, nor the creek bottom to the southwest. Lt. Preston had gotten his revenge. Soldiers from the butte were putting down the last of the injured Indian ponies and making sure that all the Indians on the slope were indeed dead.

Not a single teamster or swamper was injured, but the first fusillade of arrows had felled several mules. The remaining horses and mules were jumpy from the smell of blood on the morning breeze. Eli made the rounds and then gave the order to break camp and continue back over to the road to Apache Pass. He made a special attempt to reward the two Pima scouts, but seeing so many of their enemies and abusers dead, was reward enough for them.

As they were hitched up and got ready to leave, three mounted Indians were spotted up on the saddle. Roland got down off Eli's wagon and rested his Sharps rifle on the footboard. He took the shot, more than five hundred yards to the top of the saddle. He didn't hit the Indian he was aiming at, but he did shoot the pony out from under him. The brave quickly swung up behind one of the other riders, and they disappeared over the saddle. Major Poller commended him on a good shot but was sorry Roland missed the Indian. One more dead Indian would have made the body count an even three hundred. Eli wondered how many were left up at Apache Pass. They left the little valley and got back on the road south. It was only nine short miles down to the mouth of the pass. They would be there in about two hours, but as soon as they rounded the mountains and turned south, considerable dust could be seen up at the pass. They had won the first battle, but they were still far from getting through the pass. He hoped they could avoid a fight, but Major Poller assured him that the Apache would never forget the defeat they took last night, and vengeance would be their credo, carried to the grave of the entire Apache Nation.

As they pulled within sight of the pass, Eli could see that Major Poller was right. There were more than five hundred mounted Apache standing in the mouth of the pass and on the hills to both sides. They stopped a mile from the mouth of the pass, and even though the Indians were not moving, Eli signaled to form up the defensive position while they contemplated their options. Major Poller called his captain and lieutenant in, and one of the Pima scouts was riding in from the south. His report was in excited rapid Spanish, and Eli called over for Suzette and Lia to help with the translation. The scout had stumbled onto the camp of the Mescalero about a mile south of the pass. There was water there, and it was a logical place for the Apache from out east to bivouac. Many women and children were there virtually defenseless.

Jacques and Major Poller had their military minds busy with a plan. Major Poller took the lead. "If we make a feint toward the Indian camp, the Mescalero will break ranks and leave the pass to defend their women and children. If we can separate the main body, the dragoons can attack from over that low hill to the north of the main road. There are even wagon tracks up that way, so their charge can be fast. We have three empty mortars, and I have loaded them with shells. They won't do much damage, but the Indian ponies have never been around artillery fire before. They will bolt. We need to move the column up to within a quarter-mile of the main force with the mortars in front. We will hold there and try to negotiate our way through this. If that doesn't work, Lt. Preston, I want you to take only six of your men and make the feint towards the Indian camp. If the Mescalero come down and chase you, I want you to circle and lead them back to the rear of the column. The mortars loaded with the shot will be back there and can open up on them after you ride past and join up with Capt. Barksdale. The two of you will ride up the hill to the right of the pass and attack as soon as the first shells fall on the main body of the Apache. You press your attack until you have to reload, and then turn and ride back to the column. Have a dozen of the men hold back on using their rifles so they can guard the rear of your retreat. The point is to get the main body to move down to within easy range of the infantry. If I can, I will be dropping shells behind you. Get to the back of the column where you can reload, and then rejoin the fight as per your best judgment."

"Remember, most all plans-of-attack fail after the first shot. Don't be afraid to make your own decisions and act accordingly. Any wounded -- you need to bring into the middle of the formation. Miss Suzette, I know you will want to fight, but there is no way we can take on such a large force without serious injuries, and we will lose some men in this fight. When it is time, put down your rifle and take care of the wounded. Mrs. Callahan can guard you; I don't want either of you on the front lines. Understood?" The women nodded their acquiescence, and Major Poller ended the briefing with, "Let's move forward."

Eli rode around the box formation, reassuring the men and making sure everyone was locked and loaded. When he was sure everyone was ready, he moved the column forward and reformed the box within three hundred yards of the Apache. A gutsy move, but he saw a chief in an elaborate headdress sitting on a magnificent black horse with several other braves a hundred yards in front of his force. The chief was extending an open invitation to negotiate. Eli and the Major rode forward alone, guns holstered without worry. They had more than a hundred marksmen at their backs with sights trained on the Indian party and the Indians in the first ranks behind them. The chief was elderly and spoke in Spanish with a heavy Apache accent.

Eli called for Suzette and Lia to join them. As Lia pulled up next to the Major, she said in Spanish, "We meet again, Mangas Coloradas. Do you remember me? You killed my husband over by Socorro last year."

Recognition finally dawned on the chief. "You are the woman with long hair. This time I am going to enjoy making you my wife, and your friend, the yellow one, she too."

Lia smiled at him like the grim reaper and said, "First, you will have to win a battle you cannot afford to fight. Even though you are many, we will kill many of your brave warriors, their families left in sorrow. Still, we will go through the pass, and more and more Americans will come every day for the rest of your days. You cannot stop us. If you live through this battle, you will be hunted down and killed like a dog in the streets. That is if I don't kill you first." Lia levered a shell into the barrel of her Henry and leveled it at Mangas' chest and held steady. Suzette levered a shell into her Henry to back her up. They had the old warrior's attention. No Indian dared to make a move at the expense of their chief.

Roland rode up with the young Apache captive led on a tether behind his horse. His hands were bound, and his head hung in shame. Roland slid to the ground and cut the young brave loose and pushed him forward to the chief. Lia said, "The only one left from your attack last night. You cannot win this Mangas, turn around and go back to Santa Rita de Cobre. Send the Mescalero home. Send the Chiricahua home. Live to fight another day. Go away and dream about making some other women your wives. You are probably too old to sire more children anyway."

Suzette shook her head in disapproval and talked to Lia quietly, "Don't challenge his manhood again, or he will fight to prove himself in front of his braves. Let him make his decision now. I know you want to kill him, but there is a lot more at stake here besides your vengeance." Lia listened but sat stoically with her rifle held steady on the chief and her other hand resting on the handle of her Colt Patterson.

Mangas also sat quietly, contemplating his options. His braves were armed mostly with bows and arrows and a light scattering of various rifles and revolvers pilfered from pioneers they had slaughtered. Ammunition was hard to come by, and never in the kind of supply that a battle of this magnitude would demand. Three hundred dead weighed heavily on his mind. He turned and reluctantly rode back to his line. Major Poller waited a few more minutes and then also turned back with the rest of his party. They waited. They could see that Mangas was in heated discussions with his war chiefs. Lia, along with Lt. Preston, was hoping they would attack. It was too early for the Indians to wait for nightfall to press their attack. Eli could press the situation by advancing the column, but Roland was all restraint. "Let's wait it out. Let Mangas decide his fate. We can stay here two days before we will have to move back to the spring for water. Let's feed the troops. That will be a message in itself that we are not leaving."

"Good idea," said Mr. Sue. He went back and got the cooks breaking out cold rations for everyone. Eli was watching the Indians through his spyglass. There was a lot of discussion going on. The Mescalero, he assumed, were not happy to fight and die for Mangas; they could care less about a pass to the west. The Chiricahua had more at stake. All of what they considered their lands lay to the west of the pass. Mangas was no fool. He didn't live this long, making two bad decisions in as many days. His heavy losses the night before served as a hard lesson. Finally, as the cool of the morning was turning to the heat of the day, Mangas rode back alone. Eli and Major Poller met him with Lia and Suzette to translate.

Mangas spoke first. "My war chiefs think you are weak because you have women to speak for you. They think I am weak to listen to you. We outnumber you more than two to one, but you have better weapons and big guns that bark death and fire to many at one time. The Mescalero have no belly for this fight. What remains of my Mimbreño want to go back home. The Chiricahua won't fight you as long as you don't try to settle in their lands. Long hair, you win the day with your Army. We will go home, but we want our ponies back. You have no use for our horses, and they are our lifeblood. Let me save some honor here and return to my braves with the horses."

Eli made this decision. He didn't have the supplies to feed the herd of Indian ponies they rounded up the night before. He turned back to Jacques and Roland and yelled, "Bring up the ponies; we're giving them back." Roland had two wagons back out of the side of the box, and soldiers herded the ponies out from the middle of the formation. Roland had a halter on the lead pony, and he led the herd over and handed the halter to Mangas. Eli told Suzette to tell the chief to go in peace; he had made a good decision. Lia wasn't happy to let Mangas live but wouldn't destroy the negotiation by shooting the chief in the back.

It took another hour for the last Indian to leave the pass, and then the cavalry led the wagon train forward. The infantry walked in single files on both sides of the wagon train, and Eli entered the pass. It was unremarkable compared to Ratón with an established road all the way through. There was a spring a short way up on the south of the road. Eli left six supply wagons just west of the spring, and Major Poller set up a perimeter with his mortars trained on two high prominences overlooking the spring. Eli left enough water barrels to fill two wagons that would act to supply a camp that the Major would establish on the west side of the pass. He made the rounds of his men and wagons and asked the teamsters and swampers if any of them wanted to stay with Major Poller. None wanted to stay; they had signed on to go to California, and moving on was all that any of them wanted. The Army would have to manage on their own with the wagons and mules that Eli left behind.

Eli shook Major Poller's hand and then gave the order to move out. Lt. Preston would see them through to the west side of the pass, where he would choose a position to build a fortified revetment. Apache Pass was now secure under the control of the US Army. More and more Americans would be flooding the lands of the New Mexico Territory. Lia's prediction that Mangas would never see the end of white men in his lands during his lifetime was going to come true. Eli wondered, though, about the other young war chiefs and the other Apache tribes between him and the Colorado Crossing. He doubted that their battles with the Apache were over.

When they came down from the west side of the pass, the broad plain of the San Pedro Valley stretched out before them. It was easy to forget about Indians and attacks looking at the spectacular panorama that every turn of the road offered. But Eli heeded Major Poller's warning that the Apache would not attack as long as they maintained their constant vigilance and kept his guard up and posted scouts ahead as he did back on the Kansas grasslands. One more day and they would come to the San Pedro River, which they would follow to its intersection with the Gila River to the north. The Gila would take them to the Colorado River and Yuma.

RIO de SAN PEDRO

Coming down the west side of Apache Pass was a gradual slope that left the high rocky slopes behind and immersed them in the grassy valleys of southern New Mexico Territory. Suzette and Lia rode close to the wagon train. Eli wouldn't relax his vigilance over the women until they were well out of the Apache lands, and that wouldn't be until they were well west of the Colorado River. Suzette and Lia made use of their time learning more of each other's languages. Lia wanted to learn English so her husband would be more comfortable with her, and Suzette, ever the doctor wanted to be fluent in the Spanish names for all the parts of the human anatomy. Like any young woman, Suzette wanted to know more about sex, and Lia was open and shared her experiences with her first husband but held back about her relationship with Roland.   With three weeks of traveling together and sharing the hardships women faced in wagon life, the two women were forming a strong lifetime bond.

Lia was amazed at learning the Callahan family history. It was hard for her to understand why they were here. Most of the pioneers that passed through New Mexico were simple common folk, not wealthy. Most were able to make their way west with only enough supplies, weapons, and wagons for the passage. The Callahan's were indeed unique. From Suzette's ramblings about the homestead in Missouri, her mother and grandmother, Lia garnered some of the same dread of meeting up with Denise that Suzette carried with her like the hot desert sun on her back. Lia wanted to reach California, where she and Roland could have some children. She did not want to become pregnant while traveling on the trail, and Suzette helped her with that with condoms from her medical supplies. Lia wanted to be as comfortable with Eli and Jacques as she was with Suzette. Suzette assured her that it would come, and it would be easier when Eli and Jacques shed the burden of the responsibility for the wagon train.

The scenery was spectacular. The mountain valleys were mostly grasslands sprinkled with the occasional scrub cactus and mesquite trees with cottonwood and willows in the wet river bottoms. The highest mountains were already snowcapped, and the nights were uncomfortably cold. They had traveled on strict water rations for three days before they reached the Rio San Pedro River. There were numerous trails, same as out on the Kansas prairie, but almost all of them established roads, that spoke well of Mexican stewardship of this part of the Territory for more than one hundred fifty years. There were lone adobe farmhouses, larger facilities on a few cattle ranches, but no towns larger than one or two buildings. It was simply a vast, spectacular empty countryside in need of settlement. Lia was the only one who looked at it as an already settled land. She agreed that it was still quite empty, but the Spanish had been here since the fifteen hundreds; the Indians for many millennia before that.   Lia opened Suzette's eyes, gently informing her that Horace Greeley's "Go west young man, go west," was an exclusively eastern concept. She was already a westerner and didn't suffer the infection of Manifest Destiny.

Eli had put the wagon train on strict water rations as they made their way westward across a broad flat dry lake. On the eighty-fifth day of travel, they reached the Rio San Pedro. At the river crossing, there stood a sign that read Presidio de Tucson -- 65 K. *Deep Rivers*, the older Pima scout, stood at the sign and motioned with his hand toward Tucson and said, "No agua, no Apache." Then he motioned downstream and said, "Agua y Apache."

Eli had Suzette ask the scout which way was best; he replied again with hand motions, "Mui mula morta," pointing to the west. "Mucha agua, muchos Apaches," pointing downstream on San Pedro.

"Ask him if there is a trail if we go down the river."

"Sí, viajó durante muchos años." Suzette translated, and Eli made up his mind that they would be better off traveling with water and defending themselves from the Indians rather than losing mules on the hot-dry desert to the west. He was beginning to think that leaving water barrels behind on Apache Pass with the Army was the right decision at the time, but possibly a mistake in the long run.

"We will stay here for a day of rest and repairs, and then head north on the river. Let's make camp." Roland was pulling in a large mule deer; Mr. Sue was sharpening his knives and setting up the chuck wagon. That would be another advantage of traveling on the river route – fresh game, and from the looks of the river banks and terraced benches above the river, there would be ample grass to supplement the feed for the livestock. There was a beaver dam just above the ford to Tucson, and Suzette was looking forward to a swim in the river, but that would have to wait till dark. In the meantime, there were new species of birds, reptiles, and bugs to put into her language base.

The camp was busy tending to mules and weapons. The air smelled of smoke from the blacksmith's forge and gun oil. Capt. Barksdale was having half the men clean their rifles and revolvers while the other half remained at the ready. He inspected the finished weapons personally to ensure every single soldier assembled his weapon correctly and that it would fire when needed. As the first half of the men finished, the second half started disassembly and cleaning. Capt. Barksdale didn't take time to clean and inspect the weapons since they left La Mesilla. Dirt from the trail and the gunpowder residue from the battle at Chicken Springs would eventually render the weapons unreliable. The smell and feel of a clean and oiled weapon were an ancient source of comfort and confidence from the lowest private to the highest commander. Captain Barksdale had learned a lot since his blunder back at the Arkansas River. His platoon sergeant even admitted that he was starting to gain some respect for him.

Suzette and Lia sat on a blanket and disassembled and cleaned all the Henry rifles. The drivers finished chores by the evening meal, and Mr. Sue and the cooks served up a hearty meal of venison stew with potatoes and carrots. As the chill of the night started to settle in, it tasted like the best meal they ever had. It had been nearly three months since they left Missouri and almost that long since they sat down to a dinner in a restaurant instead of an Army mess hall; Santa Fe and the fiesta at Bernalillo being the only exceptions.

Roland was ready to take the women down to the river for a swim when a commotion stirred up on the trail from the south. They waited as a calliope of lowing oxen, the bray of mules, and the grunting of pigs approached the camp. A single wagon with some children and about twenty animals lumbered into sight. In the dim light of the sunset, they could see a lone Spaniard urging the oxen on with an occasional crack of the whip accompanied by the constant serenade of the teamster's cursing. It seemed that no wagon could move without the constant invective leveled at the draft animals. The Spaniard pulled up on the south side of the camp and climbed down to introduce himself. A handsome young man also left the saddle of a beautiful black stallion and walked over with the older man; he carried two revolvers in holsters and two more tucked into his belt. A Harper's Ferry muzzleloader rifle was carried comfortably in his right hand; the older man carried a double-barreled shotgun. Lia elbowed Suzette in the side when she caught her young friend staring with a little too much concentration at the handsome young man. As he walked into the campfire light, they could see that he was indeed handsome with fine Castilian features, broad shoulders, and a tall frame.

The older man took the lead in the introductions. First, he excused himself for having poor English, and Lia set him to ease, saying that he could speak in Spanish. His name was Juan Emilio de Francisco Escobar, and his nieto was Juan Pedro de Francisco Gomez. They were going to wait at the crossing to join a wagon train heading to California. He considered it providence that they met up at the river crossing just when he was prepared to wait weeks if necessary, to not go on alone through Apache country. He doffed his hat and asked with great respect if he and his children could join up with them. Suzette asked, "How many children do you have?"

"There are seven in the wagon; they are all orphans. The Apache killed their parents in raids below the border. I gathered them up on our way up from Hermosillo. Six are boys, and one is a young girl of about three; she doesn't talk."

Suzette asked, "Why so many boys and only one girl?"

"The Apache take all the girls and kill all the boys if they can catch them. The boys who survive run away or hide."

"Is Juan Pedro an orphan?"

"No, he is an immigrant from Madrid, like me. His parents are still in Spain."

Eli caught the drift of the conversation and asked his brothers what they thought. The oxen wouldn't be a problem. If they held them back, they would eat them, but they would probably be useful in the river bottoms. The children posed a different problem, but Señor Francisco seemed to have them well in hand. They all agreed that they couldn't leave them here. Eli extended his hand and welcomed the Spaniard and his menagerie into the train. Suzette told Senór Francisco, "Give me the girl. We are going down to the river to clean up. After Lia and I finish, I want you to go down to the river and bathe all the rest of the children and yourself. The rest of the men will be doing the same. I am the doctor here, and I will be examining all of you after you clean up. Are any of the children wounded?"

The answer was, "Yes, one of the boys has a stab wound in his leg. The Apache thought he was dead because he was under a beam that was pulled down from the stable of his parent's hacienda. I don't expect him to live. The infection is bad, and he is wasting away."

"Bring him here, but take the rest of the boys down to the river." I'll do what I can."

Juan Pedro went over to their wagon and fetched the boy. He was about four or five years old and was badly emaciated. The stab wound was badly infected, but that was far from his only problem. Malnutrition was eating him alive. Juan Pedro was hanging back, but Suzette dispatched him with a stern command pointing at the river. Capt. Barksdale set up a perimeter around the waterhole above the beaver dam. Señor Francisco and the rest of the boys were frolicking in the cold water but didn't stay long. One by one, he washed the children's hair. He knew they had lice; he had them himself and would be glad to be rid of them. While the Spaniard was down at the river with his orphans, Eli and the twins unloaded every piece of bedding from their wagon and burned it. They had plenty of blankets to replace the bedding and some cots. They pulled the wagon into their perimeter and unhitched the oxen. Eli got the blacksmith to go over the wagon; there were needed repairs before they could trust the wagon not to break down on the trail. The oxen were fed some oats but were just as happy with the grama grass under their feet.

Señor Francisco returned from the river with the rest of the boys. Suzette had Lia dusting them down with lice powder, and Mr. Sue was feeding them with the leftover stew. The children weren't familiar with stew as such, but were hungry and ate like there would be no tomorrow. Suzette tended to the wounded boy, cleaning and treating the wound with her brown powder. Stitches were not possible in the swollen flesh, so she bound the wound so the sides would knit together and then had Mr. Sue feed the urchin. He wouldn't eat the meat or the vegetables but would drink the broth. Mr. Sue said he would take over feeding the boy. He mashed up the meat and vegetables and fed them a small spoonful at a time until the boy would eat no more.

Suzette and Lia took the girl and went down to the river for their swim. Lia was careful to look all-around before stripping down. The soldiers were respectfully keeping their distance, and Suzette stripped-down and undressed the girl and then playfully threw her into the cold water. The girl yelped and started to thrash around, but Suzette was quickly at her side to hold her up and belay her fears of drowning. That settled the issue of talking; the girl wasn't the least bit mute. Suzette knew that, like Maria, she would eventually talk. When the girl got over her fear of drowning, she discovered she could stand on the bottom. Lia brushed out the girl's hair with a nit comb and dunked her repeatedly to kill the lice. They got out and dried off quickly and got back into their warm clothes. Suzette wrapped the girl in a blanket and carried her back up to the camp. She dusted the girl down with pyrethrum powder and then put her to bed in her bedroll. The girl held on to her for a few moments and then was sound asleep. Lia had gathered up the girl's clothes and was preparing to boil them in a cooking pot on Mr. Sue's fire.

As the men returned from the river, the camp settled in for a good night's sleep. Tomorrow would be a workday, and then their journey west would resume. The night sounds were different, and Suzette would ask Lia about a noise that sounded like a small dog barking. She fell asleep with her arm around the young girl, wondering what her name was. Would it be another Maria? *Not likely*, she thought as she faded into a deep, dreamless sleep. Juan Pedro didn't find a night's rest easy to come by. He couldn't get his mind off the young blond woman, and his young manhood was interfering with his ability to get comfortable. That he was going to learn to speak English to get closer to the young woman was his last conscious thought before falling asleep.

The next morning the camp awoke to the cawing of a rooster. Funny Eli thought, he didn't remember seeing any chickens in the Francisco zoo. He crawled out of his bedroll and braced against the chill. The high mountain air was streaming down the low riverbed of the San Pedro. There was a wagon load of soogans for the horse soldiers, and Eli thought it was time to put them to use against the cold night air. Suzette was stirring and had the young girl wrapped tightly in a blanket. She came out of the wagon and went over to the fire, where she had strung the girl's clothes for drying the night before. She dressed the girl but kept her wrapped in the blanket. Mr. Sue was busy sewing up a coat cut from a wool Army blanket. Eli was drinking his morning brew, and Roland was already heading out with the two Pima scouts to survey the path ahead and hunt. They were only gone for about ten minutes when a rifle shot rang out across the valley floor. *More venison for dinner,* everyone thought as the echoes of the gunshot died away. Now everyone was up and awake. The cooks were serving up pancakes and bacon and eying some of Señor Francisco's pigs with plans for more bacon and pork roasts soon.

Señor Francisco and his children came over to join in for breakfast at Mr. Sue's invitation. Suzette was sitting opposite Francisco at the fire pit, holding the little girl in her arms still wrapped in the blanket. All the children were barefooted; that wouldn't do out in the desert, but there wasn't a trading post within two hundred miles so they would have to improvise along the way. Suzette asked Señor Francisco about the rooster. "No gallo," he replied and put his fingers to his lips and let out a high-pitched, piercing whistle. A huge green, red, and blue bird burst forth from the front of his wagon and flew over to land on Francisco's shoulder. Everyone noticed for the first time that the shoulders of Francisco's coat had heavy leather patches sowed on to accommodate the bird's heavy claws. Francisco smiled and gave the bird a nut from his pocket and said, "Madrugada Felipe." The bird let out an exact imitation of a rooster crowing and then was strutting back and forth on Francisco's shoulder as if proud of himself. Filipe was the first Macaw parrot that anyone in the wagon train had ever seen. His bright colors were astounding. Francisco explained Felipe was a young-hyacinth macaw and only knew about fifty words; of course, they were all Spanish words. The young girl in Suzette's arms giggled, and Felipe said, "Buenos Dias, chica."

Everyone thought that was amazing, but Felipe wasn't finished displaying his talents. He suddenly flared his wings, hunched his back, and screamed, "Apache, Apache!" He took flight and flew around in a circle over the camp and kept screaming, "Apache, Apache!" Men all around took up arms ready to defend against an attack. Eli looked down the river. Roland and the Pima scouts were dragging two deer in, but they were about a mile away, and Eli could hardly make them out. Francisco said in Spanish, "A very useful bird indeed." Felipe wasn't getting a rifle volley to his alarm, and he settled back down on Francisco's shoulder but never took his eyes off Roland and the Pimas. It was obvious he never was around any friendly Indians before. He kept up his strutting and kept muttering, "Apache, Apache," but in a whisper compared to the scream of alarm.

Suzette got up and went over to Eli's wagon. The wounded boy was awake and looking a little better. Mr. Sue had a breakfast of broth with mashed meat and vegetables. He wanted Suzette to check the wound. They unwound the bandage and saw that it was soaked. The wound was draining, and that was a good sign. His head was still hot, and Suzette didn't like that. Mr. Sue was helping the boy drink one of his herbal concoctions that were supposed to help with the fever. They were glad that they wouldn't be on the trail so the boy could have another day of rest before the never-ending jostling started again. Suzette rewrapped the wound and noted that despite the swelling, the ends of the slash were starting to mend. She didn't want it to heal over until the tissue underneath was healed, but she could open it back up if she had to.

The day passed quickly with repairs and busy work of all kinds. Several of the men were cutting and stitching leather into sturdy moccasins for the youngsters. Mr. Sue finished the coat and put it on the little girl. By early afternoon she was presented with a pair of boots that covered her legs up to above her knees, not a fashion statement for a New York haberdashery but functional, warm, and most important – snake proof. Paul Hayman delighted the children with songs that he sang and played on the banjo. Felipe loved the music and bobbed his head up and down in time. A boy of eight sat at Paul's side and would occasionally touch the soundbox, hearing and feeling the vibration at the same time. When Paul quit playing and walked off to his chuckwagon for a cup of coffee, the boy went with him.

Eli moved the oxen out to a fresh stand of grass and let them eat their fill. He could see why so many pioneers chose the animals for the trip across America. The little girl followed Suzette and Lia around the camp. Lia told Suzette she would give her a few days to get more comfortable and then coax her into telling them her name. All of the other children took up with one or another of the teamsters. Competition for the children was rampant, and the men who were the cleverest were becoming the foster fathers the kids needed. One swamper could make a coin disappear right before their eyes and then pull it out from behind the ear of an amazed child. He had a boy of six join up with him. Juan Pedro was glad to see this happening. His work of watching and protecting the children when they traveled was going to be much easier, and he wanted to spend his time concentrating on Suzette anyway.

The rest of the afternoon passed quickly. Juan Pedro moved Felipe's perch to the side of the fire pit, and the bird was constantly rattling off words in Spanish as if he was on a mental review of his vocabulary. When darkness finally drowned out the last rays of a brilliant sunset, Felipe started hooting like an owl. After a while, he was making sounds like crickets, and then he let out a yip like a small dog. Suzette exclaimed, "We won't need to get another dog!" Lia corrected her, though. The little bark wasn't a dog but a frog. Usually, the small frogs were out in force after a rainstorm, but some were always living along the rivers. More amazement came their way every day.

Eli was the only one that commented on Felipe. "I wonder if that bird is going to talk all night." Felipe quit talking after a while and settled into hooting like an owl and chirping like the crickets. Before long, everyone was asleep except for the guards who kept the fires burning and the coffee hot. Eli had all the children wrapped in soogans for the night. The sky was crystal clear, and despite the almost full moon, the nighttime panorama was replete with stars. The Milky Way stretched across the heavens, and the high desert animals and insects filled the darkness with their resplendent serenade. Suzette stirred when coyotes howled in the distance. Lia corrected her again; it wasn't coyotes this time but wolves.

The long night shifted towards the day, the darkness receded, and there was a slight rise in the wind. Horses whickered, and the oxen lowed. Felipe crowed like a rooster to officially welcome the day. Huddled around the campfire, the women watched the sunrise change from the pink of dawn into a purple sky. Lia held the girl and said in Spanish, "I bet I can guess your name." The little girl was wrapped in her arms and just shook her head no in a challenge. "John," Lia offered as her first guess. The little girl pursed her lips in annoyance but still said nothing. "Pedro?" Suzette could see where this was going as the girl became more and more disgruntled. "¿Lo sé, Jorge?"

The girl turned and whispered in Lia's ear, "Adriana." Lia hugged the girl, kissed her on the forehead, and told her that she would keep the name secret until she wanted everyone to know. Adriana leaned over and whispered her name in Suzette's ear.

Suzette was thrilled, and she lowered her voice to a conspiratorial whisper and told Adriana, "No one will know, but the two of us." Adriana pointed at Mr. Sue. Suzette shook her head yes in understanding, then got up and walked over to Mr. Sue. She made a big show of looking around to see that no one was close enough to hear and then whispered in his ear. Mr. Sue was busy making love to his morning pots and pans but raised a soapy hand and waved hello to the little girl. A big smile lit up on her face, and Suzette walked off very pleased. *That was a lot sooner than I expected,* she thought to herself as she made ready to saddle Patches. Lia had a nice touch with children; Suzette was looking forward to being an aunt and hoped that Roland and Lia would give her many nephews and nieces. She surprised herself, thinking she wouldn't be the youngest of their family before long. She had never thought ahead until then that there would someday be another generation of Callahans.

As soon as they set out on the road down the river, Eli could see a problem. Trees choked the river bottom, and in many places, branches were rubbing on the sides of the wagons as they passed. It made for a lot of cover if any hostiles wanted to get close. He put Capt. Barksdale and his dragoons out ahead to flush out the brush on either side of the road. There were clear areas on top of the terraces that lined each side of the river, but mostly they were in brush and trees that cut the visibility to a few feet. In places, the road was in the river bottom, and the sandy bottom made pulling difficult for the mules. The oxen, with their wider hooves, had an easier time of it. Despite the sand and having to thread their way carefully through the brush, they made eighteen miles the first day on the river.

With the brush and trees so close, many of the men were experiencing a healthy mix of claustrophobia and paranoia. Eli got some good advice from Jacques. "When we camp, let's set up tripwires and fires outside the wagon ring and cut as much brush back as possible, so it is at least impossible to sneak in and climb up on a wagon." Eli agreed and also went to half on – half off guard duty. Capt. Barksdale would keep half his men on the ready to respond to any intrusion. The work of preparing the camp went well beyond nightfall. Eight fires burned about one hundred feet off from the wagon ring. Tripwires were set up both beyond the fires and closer to the wagons. They hadn't seen any Apache through the day, but Eli knew they were watching, and if he let his guard down, it would be inevitable that the Apache would attack. One comforting thing was the moon was only a couple of days off from being full, so if any hostiles appeared, the men wouldn't be shooting in the dark.

The night was passing quietly until four in the morning. One of the outer trip wires jingled, and more than thirty guns on that side of the wagon ring swung around to train on the embers of the outer fire pit. The tripwire jingled again and half the men with their guns up fired. Something big was crashing through the brush but wasn't coming at the camp. After a few moments, the crashing stopped; whatever it was had succumbed to the powerful bullets of the Sharps rifles. Some of the men wanted to go out and see what they had killed, but Jacques held them back and said, "Wait until light. Stay on the perimeter until we can see what we are doing."

The men settled back down behind their makeshift barricades.   At dawn, Capt. Barksdale rode out with his dragoons, sabers drawn in one hand, and their revolvers in the other. The animal was bigger than a deer with a magnificent rack of horns. "Wapiti," was the opinion of the Pima scouts. But they had more to show Capt. Barksdale. There was fair evidence that a large band of Indians had quietly herded the big animal into the perimeter. There were numerous moccasin tracks and another hundred yards out; there was a dead Apache with a bullet hole in his chest and an exit wound on his back. The scouts rolled him over and checked out what little clothing and markings the dead Indian had. "Cave People," the older of the two scouts, said, "He only carried a heavy stone club." Capt. Barksdale had his men haul the elk into the camp to butcher. The animal was big enough to provide a couple of meals for everyone.

Roland listened to the scouts telling Suzette and Lia about the moccasin tracks and then asked for a better translation. "Cave People," he harrumphed, *troglodytes*. More stone age than any other Indian tribe. There won't be many of them, and they got a firsthand demonstration of our firepower. With any luck, they won't be back."

Jacques asked, "Do you forget about vengeance, an eye for an eye, and all the rest?"

"No, but they won't attack unless they think they can win. That doesn't rule out an attempt to kill one of us in return. Suzette, ask them about the weapons that the cave people have – any guns?"

"They have a few guns; no ammunition," was the translated reply.

Eli stepped into the conversation with a few orders. "We will stop earlier tonight, so we have the camp set up well before dark. Capt. Barksdale, I want you and your men flushing out the woods out ahead of us. If they are going to try a shot with bow and arrow, they would have to lay close to the trail, take the shot, then run like hell. I want you and your men spread out on a line to sprint out ahead about a hundred yards and then trot back and forth perpendicular to the trail. Don't stop moving unless you are close to the train. Sitting still, you make good targets for an arrow. Moving, they would likely miss, and then their position would be revealed. We'll practice this move when we get moving. Throughout the day, we will switch out the mounts. I don't want any tired men or mounts out front. Let's get everyone fed and get moving."

The second day traveling down the San Pedro was easier than the first. With the cavalry flushing out the woods ahead, everyone was more comfortable but still kept up their vigilance as intense as ever. There was some respite from the trees as the trail found its way across wide terraces that weren't completely open but only sparsely covered with mesquite and high mountain cactus. Some stretches of the river bottom contained only swampy stagnant water. Lia called these *ciénegas*. In places, they stretched across the valley floor. A myriad of birds of more species than Suzette could count was feeding in the shallow waters.

In the afternoon, they met up with a band of Maricopa Indians, allies of the Pima, and another peaceful tribe who also spoke the same language as the Pima. Amazingly, Felipe recognized them as friends, and like the scouts, the Maricopa wore full buckskins made of a combination of deer and other hides. Their weapons were a mixed array of museum-worthy pieces, including a blunderbuss of some ornate design. There were only two percussion cap muzzleloaders among them; the rest of the rifles were ancient flintlocks. A few cap-and-ball revolvers looked like they might fire, but likely would be as dangerous to the owner as to the target. All in all, they were made welcome and guided the wagon train to a wide clear area on top of a river terrace, an excellent place to make camp for the night.

The two Pima scouts sat by a separate cook fire they made to the side of the wagon ring and talked extensively with the band of Maricopa. Their Spanish was excellent, so Suzette and Lia sat amongst them and listened to the saga of their hunt unfold. They had been on the river for two moons. They first came downstream hunting Apache, who had raided and stolen a young woman from them. They found the band that had stolen the woman and killed them to a man. Half their band had returned north to take the young woman home, and they stayed on to find and kill more Apache. In that endeavor, they had only been moderately successful. The Apache were clever and lived in small groups. They could go for days without food or water and never build a fire to give away their position if they thought enemies were nearby. The Maricopa, though, had been at war with the Apache for centuries and were masters at hunting them. On this sortie, they had killed more than a dozen over and above the band that they wiped out to recover the woman. Suzette left the circle to return to Eli and report what they had learned.

Eli had an inspirational idea, "Let's ask the leader of the Maricopa if they would agree to accompany us down the river as far as their homelands. We could offer them some better rifles for payment and make it worth their while in gold and silver if that's what it takes."

Suzette said she would try to broker the deal. She walked back into the midst of the Maricopa and addressed their leader in Spanish. "My chief, the big man over by the wagon, wants to know if you would consider escorting us as far as the Gila? We could pay for your services, and if our payment is sufficient, you could see us all the way through to the western edge of your territory. We can feed you, so you won't have to hunt, and we need you to scout ahead, so our route is safe. "

Skilled at negotiation and trade himself, the Maricopa leader asked, "What will you offer for payment?"

Suzette herself, not a neophyte to dealing with the Indians in Kansas, asked, "What do you want?"

That was an easy question for the Maricopa, "Better rifles and ammunition."

"We can spare one rifle and have much ammunition. We can also offer you some money, Spanish silver coins; good for trade with white settlers."

The chief put on a show of discontent and countered, "Four rifles and five silver."

"Two rifles and ten silver."

It was going to happen; the leader started talking among his men. He turned back to converse with Suzette. "Agreed, but I want the rifles now."

Suzette extended her hand and said, "The rifles now, the silver when we reach the western border of your territory."

The leader nodded his acceptance, and Eli, who had been listening in to the conversation, walked over with two Sharps rifles and two ammunition belts. The leader took one of the rifles and looked like Eli just handed him the keys to the US Treasury. The other rifle went to his son, a tall, strong young man with chiseled Indian features. Suzette told the two men that they would train them to shoot and care for the rifles. She asked, "Do you like Wapiti? We have plenty." The rest of the Maricopa honored their leader thinking he had made a good deal. They must have thought that the deal included the food, and they were hungry and ate the rest of all that Mr. Sue prepared. The cooks served the evening meal at the chuck wagons, and Lia split the band up among the different fire pits. There was going to be plenty for all. The Maricopa were amazed at Felipe, who flew around the camp, saying *Amigos, Amigos* in his loudest parrot voice, just shy of a screech.

Lia had Adrianna by the hand; the little girl was afraid of the newcomers and cowered behind Lia's legs. She warmed up, though when one of the older Maricopas pulled a small Katina doll from his pocket and offered it to Adrianna. Lia thanked the man kindly, but he replied, "It is nothing, the Hopi pass them out to everyone who passes through. By the time you reach the Colorado, you can have a whole collection if you want them." Adrianna took the doll and coveted it the same as the young Maricopa coveted the rifle. Lia wondered if he would even put it down to eat. After dinner, she and Suzette were going to teach him and his father how to use their new weapons. While they were eating, a lone Maricopa male accompanied by four women carrying the makings of their camp arrived from the north side of the clearing. They started laying out sleeping mats and unpacked their meager supplies. Suzette brought them into the camp so that they could eat. The women looked more well-fed than the men, but they were hungry.

After dinner, Suzette and Lia had the leader and his son shooting at a large rock on the hillside above the camp about two hundred yards away. To their surprise, an Apache broke cover from behind the rock and started to run up the hill. Felipe started screaming, "Apache, Apache!" behind her. Suzette took the elder's rifle, inserted a new cartridge, and lay down to steady the rifle across the log they were using for a gun rest. By now, the Apache was nearly three hundred yards out and uphill. Suzette took her time and elevated the gun sight. She took a deep breath and let it half out, took aim, and squeezed the trigger. At first, the Maricopas thought she had missed in the full second it took for the round to plow into the back of the Apache. He flew forward, his stone tomahawk flying high up in the air as if he threw it before he died. Unlikely, he was dead before he hit the ground, center shot through the upper chest. The Maricopas were awed. The elder asked with great respect, "Miss Suzette, could I have a lock of your golden hair to adorn my rifle?"

Suzette was amused and not a bit distressed that she had just murdered a man in cold blood. "Yes, however, could I have a lock of your hair in return to remember you by?" The man took a knife from a sheath on his calf and cut a generous lock of his hair, then removed a turquoise bead from his pocket and threaded the lock of hair through. He pushed a light leather thong down through the bead and tied a knot in it and then pulled it back up to the bottom of the bead where it wedged the lock of hair in place. He took a smaller bead and made a noose that could be tightened to hold the lock of hair hanging like a bobble. He gave the amulet to Suzette. Suzette's hair was held back in a ponytail. Lia asked for the man's knife and with a finger, scooped out a lock of hair from above Suzette's ear. Suzette was alarmed but let Lia cut the lock of hair and pulled it back up through the ponytail. She gave it to the elder and then fastened the lock of black hair tightly to the end of the cut lock and let it hang down to the side of Suzette's face.

The elder said with great reverence, "You honor me greatly in the eyes of the spirit. The amulet will keep you safe and healthy all your life." He rolled up Suzette's hair and put it into a little pouch on his belt.

"Time to clean the rifles," Suzette said as she got up to walk back to the camp. She was anxious to see how she looked with her new piece of jewelry. Roland had watched the whole exchange and wondered if when they reached the west coast, Suzette would be more Indian than a white girl. He also wondered if Suzette would ever be the same again. The coldness with which she dismissed the killing of the Apache worried him. She was becoming a hardened woman, and maybe that was a good thing for the trail, as long as it didn't stick with her for the rest of her life. He would worry about that later. It was still more than forty miles of woods and river bottoms to the Gila River. There were a plethora of other concerns; Suzette would have to work out her changing character for herself.

DESIERTO SONORENSE

Even though it was only forty miles to the Gila River, it took four days to traverse the sandy river bottoms and cope with the constant bogging down of the wagons in the soft sand. Here the oxen proved invaluable with their wide hooves carrying them over the softest spots. Each day they encountered at least two places where they had to double team the oxen to the supply wagons to get them through. No one enjoyed the delay because the slow-moving train made for a more opportune target for an Indian attack. The children, however, enjoyed every break in the travels with frolicking in the river or climbing in the trees.

At the mouth of Arivaipa Creek, they were having a particularly hard time of it. They had spent most of a day at the crossing and still had only half of the wagons across. Juan Pedro had exhausted the ox team double hitching and pulling the supply wagons through a hundred yards of deep mud and soft sand. It was time to double team with mules. Juan Pedro was eager to help. When he went to unhitch the first team, he wasn't wary of the rear mule, despite the quivering haunches and wide eyes. A mule-wise teamster would have approached from the other side or spent some time to settle the mule before stepping behind him. Juan Pedro bent down to pull the pin from the drawbar, and the mule struck out with a lightning-fast kick. It caught Juan Pedro just above the elbow of his left arm, and the crack of the breaking bone was sickening loud. He spun out from behind the mule clutching his arm. The fracture was compound; splintering bone protruded from the break, and the pain was murderous. He fell to his knees, trying to catch his breath. His side was severely damaged, as well. He swayed back and forth a few times and then fell forward unconscious.

Suzette was on the north side of the creek and saw the lightning-fast kick and heard the crack of bone. She immediately set about setting up her examining table and unpacking her medical kit. Two men carried Juan Pedro to her on a stretcher. He was still unconscious and looking at the wounds, Suzette thought that was a merciful thing. Lia rode in with Adrianna in front of her in the saddle. The little girl's eyes went wide when she saw her friend and protector stretched out on the table, blood pouring from the wound in his arm. Señor Francisco hurried in and took Adrianna from the saddle and held the frightened girl in his arms. Suzette and Lia set to work. Suzette was washing her hands as Lia fastened a tourniquet above the break to staunch the flow of blood. Suzette would have to find and repair the severed vein before she could work at getting the bone splinters back in place. She was relieved that the bleeder wasn't the brachial artery. If it were, Juan Pedro would have been dead by the time the men got him across the creek to Suzette. The bleeder was a large vein that was cleanly severed, probably by the bone splinter in the wound. Lia was swabbing blood still seeping from the vein on the elbow side of the wound, and Suzette was threading a fine stitching needle with a silk thread.

Juan Pedro moaned and came to only to have Lia pour a dose of Laudanum into his mouth. Suzette pulled the ends of the vein out of the muscle with tweezers and secured the ends of the vein with clamps. She delicately stitched the ends of the vein together and then wrapped it with the thread. When she released the clamps, the patch held, and while it seeped some blood, it was no longer life-threatening. She loosened the tourniquet and concentrated on getting the bones back in place. She had Roland pulling on the arm, and when she was satisfied that everything was in place, she started to close the wound. It took more than an hour to stitch up the torn muscle, close the wound and splint the arm. Lia had cut away Juan Pedro's shirt and shook her head when she saw two pieces of rib broken and pushed inside the rib cage. Suzette was weary, parched from the hot sun. She poured a bucket of water over her head and made ready to open the skin above the broken ribs to inspect the lung underneath and then raise the broken ribs into place. Lia wiped her forehead dry and fanned her with a large-heavy piece of paper.

There was the growing thunder of hooves on the terrace above the south side of the creek. Approaching riders caused a commotion on the south side of the creek; men waiting to cross, reached for their guns. Men down in the creek struggling through the mud and sand stopped and did the same. The riders looked like Spaniards as they broke over the crest of the terrace, and even though more than a hundred guns bore on them, they didn't break stride. The leader carried a banner that was difficult to read as it flapped in the breeze created by the horses at a fast trot. He slowed to a walk and signaled to his men not to draw weapons. The family name *Peralta* appeared below the family crest. A strange animal that looked like the combination of several animals adorned the banner in gold on a red background. It had the body of a lion standing on its rear haunches, but the forelegs and claws looked like chicken legs. The head of the lion was a chicken complete with the blunt beak, but the head had ears like a wolf. The men crossed Arivaipa Creek, wallowing their horses through the mud and sand. They broke back into a trot on the north side raising dust but backed off to a walk when Lia broke into a scathing invective that included references to mothers, fathers, saints, and sinners as she pointed to Suzette's surgery.

The men rode through without stopping or saying a word. Rifles lowered, and revolvers holstered as the men rode out of the north side of the clearing. They resumed the fast trot of soldiers on a mission and quickly rode out of sight. Eli commented to his brothers, "Well, at least they weren't hostile. I wonder who they are and where they were going in such a hurry?"

Roland commented, "They are men from the Peralta family obviously and going somewhere close by or they wouldn't be pushing their horses so hard."

Suzette looked up from the opening on Juan Pedro's side and said, "I'll tell you who they were; they were assholes. I have an open wound here, and now it is full of dust. They didn't give a shit about who we were or what was going on here. If this boy dies of infection, I am going to find them and gun them down." Her outburst silenced everyone.

The silence reigned, but for a few minutes, when a flurry of gunfire was heard echoing down from the north. The sound of the guns died out and then was mute after a minute. "That didn't sound good," Eli said. Let's mount up the cavalry and see what happened. Eli and the twins left the wagon train and rode out with Capt. Barksdale and his men. They didn't gallop off like the Mexicans but picked their way carefully along the trail following the hoof prints of the riders. About a mile and a half away, they came upon a slaughter. All twelve riders were dead along with half the horses. The other half of the horses and all the weapons were missing. Capt. Barksdale stationed his men in a perimeter, and Roland got down, examining the leader and his fallen stallion. There were at least a dozen arrows in the leader and two buried deep in the horse's neck. A gallant steed done in at his prime, everyone regretted the loss. The saddle was magnificent, and Roland wanted it to replace Eli's. He unhitched the saddle, and Eli pulled the dead horse off the cinch with a rope tied to his saddle horn. All the dead men lay stripped of their weapons and valuables but otherwise left alone. Their attackers were nowhere to be seen or heard, probably clearing out of the area as fast as possible, not to be detected or tracked by the superior force of the wagon train. The rest of the saddles and tack were left behind. The drivers and swampers could pick what they wanted out of it when they passed on the morrow.

By the time they returned to the crossing, Suzette had Juan Pedro's ribs back in place, and the wound closed. Señor Francisco was there holding his grandson's hand and looking at Suzette in wonder and respect. He nodded his head stoically when told about the massacre. Señor Francisco said. "Peralta's envoys; they collect gold and silver from the mines between here and California. We will pass the mouth of a canyon shortly after we leave the river valley and go out on the desert floor. One of their mines is up that canyon. The mine is under heavy guard; we should send word up to them when we are near there that their envoys are dead."

Roland was going through the saddlebags, studying the leader's possessions carefully. He unrolled a map on parchment. The map showed the confluence of the San Pedro and the Gila Rivers. There was a large river joining from the northeast further downstream and then another river joining from the north in the western end of a great bend in the river. There was a cataract on the river from the north depicted by a constricted stream surrounded by hills. Above the cataract was an open valley with a hill drawn in red and covered with trees. There was a spring flowing out of the hill into the river and a note that said, *Agua Caliente*. They were passing the map around, and Señor Francisco finally wound up with it. He motioned the Pimas over and showed it to them. The three of them nodded knowingly, and the older Pima, *Deep River*, said, "Mal lugar, no vayas allí."

Suzette asked them why it was a bad place, but the Pima wouldn't or couldn't answer. She studied the map some more and pointed out that there was a Crusader's Cross drawn in over the hill. "Not a Crusader's cross," Francisco corrected. "A Spanish cross, it is used to mark the position of mines so that other explorers who follow can easily find a mineral deposit. Usually, it is a gold or silver mine; that is what the Spanish crave."

Deep River grunted and said in Spanish that there wasn't gold there, just a bad place where no Indian would go. Again, Suzette asked, "Why?" The older man just shrugged and walked away, clearly tired of the questions. Eli rolled up the map and kept it. They still had ten or so wagons to get across the creek. Eli gave the order to circle up to make camp for the night on the north side. Again, with a large band of Indians in the area, he put the men to half on and half off in four-hour shifts to guard the camp. He couldn't get over the feeling that the ambush had been set for them and foiled by the arrival of the Peralta envoy. Maybe the attackers now had what they wanted – horses, guns, ammo, and some money. Eli was hoping they would stay well away from the wagon train. He was tired of Indians, renegades, and outlaws. More than ever, he wanted to move on and tackle the Mojave Desert and face the challenges that nature would hurl at them without hostile humans at every turn. No one slept easy that night, and the next morning, they were anxious to get back on the river road and away from the area. Suzette and Lia slept well, though; they were both exhausted. Señor Francisco sat up all night at his grandson's side.

In two more days of slow going, they reached the Gila River. Here the road was in much better condition, having been traversed by tens of thousands of gold seekers during the rush to California. There were trading caravans heading both east and west made up of every conceivable type of wagon, draft animals, and nationalities. They camped on a flat just downstream from the confluence of the two rivers, and that evening, Suzette was able to converse with visitors and passers-by in every language she knew, including her father's native tongue, Gaelic. Everyone was on their way somewhere. There were traders transporting pottery, rugs, blankets, and woven cloth, along with art items from the Pueblo tribes of the desert. There were pioneers and merchants moving goods and supplies west.   Of a special delight, there were newspapers. The Callahans sat up late reading news items by lantern light, and suddenly Roland flopped a newspaper down and groaned. The headline read, ***Girl from Independence Guns Down Chico del Diablo***. Edward Sigler had done his work well, right down to the last detail of Suzette winning the pistol shoot and the hearing at Fort Union. There was even a pen and ink lithograph of the shooting in the church at Council Corner. "You're famous Suzette," Roland intoned as he elbowed her gently in the ribs.

Suzette punched him hard on the arm, tenfold harder than the tap he gave her. They searched through the rest of the newspapers and found two more accounts of the exploit along with an article about the Callahan *children* that depicted Eli as the *Boy Millionaire Wagon Master*. Now they all groaned, no doubt Denise was getting her fill with the news from the trail. Grandma probably had a scrapbook by now filled with every story about them published in the New York newspapers. Again, the dark cloud of awaiting Denise's wrath enveloped their mood. Suzette translated the articles for Lia, who was more in awe of her sister-in-law than ever before. Lia cut out the articles, rolled them up and put them in Eli's leather pouch with the mysterious map of the hill on the river to the west.

They quickly got back to the sideshow of the Gila Trail. Peddlers came by selling every type of scam ever invented. One had a map of the desert to the west with all the waterholes, and gold mines marked boldly and pitched his ware as, **THE MAP THAT WILL SAVE YOUR LIFE**. Jacques ran him off, but a band of gypsies replaced him before the huckster was even out of sight. The band of gypsies, which was colorful and entertaining, stopped by the wagon train. Among them, there was a lad who could juggle, and the children gathered around him in delight. The gypsies set up a stage and put on a puppet show for the children. The language was eastern European but mixed with words of every culture they encountered in their travels. They were a close-knit group; four colorful wagons hung with copper pots and pans, trinkets of all kinds, and some musical instruments. After the puppet show, where wolves chased children back and forth across the stage of the puppet theater, the men and women took the instruments down from their hangers and more from out of the wagons. They played guitars, violins, balalaikas, and one had a French horn. The least musical of them beat a rhythm on tambourines and small drums. There was an older woman who filled the camp with a voice more suited to an opera house than a forlorn trail. Some of the songs were in German, some in

French, which Suzette translated. They played and sang the national anthem of Spain, and Lia translated that one.

Then the music of the balalaika turned to a serious melody that was distinctly Russian played by a beautiful middle-aged woman with several children of her own clinging to her skirts. Her hair was nearly as long as Lia's, and she wore a colorful blue brocade tunic that she donned just for the performance. Mr. Sue commented that the top coat was Chinese. They doubted that the troop had been to China, but there were large Chinatowns in San Francisco and Los Angeles. The troop was traveling east, Suzette learned speaking German with one of the older gypsy men. She asked Hans about the gypsies, but he was scornful of them and whispered in her ear, "Keep your hand on your wallet and your eyes on your jewelry box." He was standing guard on Eli's wagon and had his men were watching to make sure no gypsies strayed from the troop. Eli paid the gypsies with two double eagles before they even asked for money. The break from the monotony of travel was worth every penny. Before the gypsies left, they made a gallant effort to buy Felipe. Señor Francisco had to refuse many times before the troop gave up and left him alone. The troop moved off to the east to make their camp, but Hans didn't relax his guard through the night.

The next morning Suzette decided not to dose Juan Pedro with the opiate before they traveled. He was lying on his bedroll next to Señor Francisco's wagon, and Suzette and Lia were kneeling to either side, removing the dressings to inspect the wounds. Juan reached up with his good hand and cupped Suzette's breast. She didn't jerk away or admonish him, but after a moment, Lia pulled his hand away and told Juan in no uncertain terms that she would break his other arm if he tried that again. Suzette let it pass, but being honest with herself, she wasn't going to push him away if he tried it again. She was back to pondering what it would be like to make love to the handsome young man. By noon Juan Pedro was in agony again, and Suzette gave him half a dose of the laudanum. Not enough to put him to sleep, but enough to ease his pain for the rest of the day.

Travel down the Gila was easy. The river bottom was much wider than the San Pedro, and the hills to either side of the river were steep. The Gila snaked back and forth on its way to the desert, but generally, it made its way due west along its sinuous track. In two days, they left the mountains and hills behind them and emerged onto the broad valley floors of the Sonoran Desert. Señor Francisco pointed out the majestic Saguaro cacti endemic to the Sonoran Desert and other fauna and flora that they would see along the way; he warned them to stay clear of the cholla. It seemed that everything in the desert was out to stick you or bite you: snakes, scorpions, poisonous lizards, and now cactus. Even though the threat of the Apache was diminishing, there was any number of other dangers taking their place.

Eli, though, was relieved to finally be out of the trees and brush of the river bottoms. Here there was open ground to travel, and from any high prominence, one could see for a hundred miles to the mountain ranges rising from the desert floor to the west. Unlike the Rocky Mountains, there were very few foothills. The desert was amazingly flat right up to the edge of the mountains, which rose steeply to dominate the skyline. There was a Maricopa camp about ten miles west of where the Gila left the mountain gorge. Eli paid two Maricopa scouts to deliver the news of the murdered envoy up to the gold mine. Jacques and Roland wanted to see the gold mine, but Eli wouldn't allow anyone out of sight of the wagon train.

The desert floor was cold at night but still hot in the day. They would reach the Mojave at the start of the winter months and be glad that the cooler temperature would accompany them across the legendary murderous expanse. They still had a long way to go before crossing the Colorado River, but the Apache threat would diminish every mile they moved further west. It was early afternoon when the wind whipped up from the south, and a brown wall of dust bore down on them. Eli halted the wagon train and had the teamsters and swampers pulling off the road so the backs of the animals would be to the oncoming storm. They covered the eyes of the animals both to protect them from the sand but also to keep them from stampeding. They put all the horses on the lee side of the wagons and waited for the front to reach them. They didn't have to wait long, twenty minutes, and the dust storm howled down on them. There was the sound of thunder behind the front, but no flashes appeared in the heavy cloud of dust and sand, and there was no booming of thunder. Very different from the tornados on the prairie.

Suzette thought back to the hail storm and was thankful that the sand was just that – sand and not egg-sized hailstones. The sand permeated everything. There wasn't a single fold of clothing or a nook or cranny in the wagons that didn't fill with sand by the time the storm front passed. They made their way back to the river. The flow from the mountains was quickly disappearing into the sandy bottom, but there were still numerous waterholes where they could wash the sand out of their clothing. Lia had covered her head with a canvas to keep the sand out of her hair. The rest of the travelers weren't so fortunate or as smart as Lia. Eli made sure that all the men cleaned weapons and that the water barrels were topped off before they set out again to the west. For days they were still shaking the sand out of their bedrolls, belongings, and foodstuffs. Everyone was waiting for a good rainstorm, but that wasn't likely until later in the winter months.

Travel west along the Gila was fast; the trail was more like a road than ever before. Years of heavy traffic by Indians, traders, and immigrants had found the easiest ways over the ridges and arroyos of the desert floor. Campsites were plentiful, and Eli reduced the guards to one for every six wagons. The further west they went, the more Maricopa villages they encountered along the river. The Maricopa were farmers and gatherers. They had well-tended fields; some irrigated with water carried in clay pots from the river. The people looked healthy and were experts at making the clay pots and baskets. They gathered the purple fruit of the prickly pear cactus and made wine from that and also a strong drink from the blue agave mescal. Whenever the wagon train encountered a village, numerous people came out to greet them, bearing the full variety of wares to trade. The Pima scouts were respectful but discouraged trade with the Maricopa, especially for the wine and strong amber drink. No doubt they wanted to steer the wealth of the wagon train further west to Pima villages.

Suzette asked the scouts, "What is the difference between you and the Maricopa. You both speak the same language, farm, and gather, and you are both non-hostile tribes?"

The scouts both shrugged, "We bury our dead; Maricopas burn theirs."

Suzette had witnessed some funeral pyres with burning bodies at the edges of the villages along the river. The only wood in abundant supply was mesquite, and it was hardwood and difficult to cut. She was sure the funeral pyres were difficult to build and took valuable fuel away from the cook fires of the people. She thought that the Maricopas must value their traditions with very strong beliefs to continue that custom with the hardship it entailed. She was pondering how the communities functioned when, on the one-hundredth day of their journey, they came to the mouth of the river that led north to the mysterious red hill on the map they recovered from the Peralta envoy. Eli made a mental note of the landmarks around the mouth of the tributary. He was going to return here one day and follow the river up to the red hill. The task at hand, however, was to get the wagon train to Fort Moore in Los Angeles. The Gila River made its turn to the south, and the wagon train turned with it. Villages were prominent, and the Maricopa farms surrounded the villages. The soil in the valley was rich loam instead of sand and gravel. The land was farmed heavily by the Maricopa. Deep River told Eli that when they went through the gap to the south that the river carved through the rocky hills, they would be in Pima lands and not far from his village.

The road through the gap followed the river bottom. It was obvious that in high water during the summer monsoon, the river bottom would be dangerous and impassable. There was an alternate road over the rocky hills to the west, but the scouts guided Eli down the river bottom. Riding ahead, he saw that there was only one spot that could be boggy, but it was much shorter than the soft bottom they encountered on the San Pedro. He had half the wagon train through before double hitching was needed, and by the end of the day, all the wagons were pulled through. They made camp on a wide, flat, open valley floor south of the gap. Venison was plentiful, but that night most of the camp dined on the duck and geese that nested on the ponds above the cataract on the river. One more day and they would be at Deep River's camp.

Travel the next morning was easy, but when they were several miles from Deep River's village, they came upon several people from his village that were sent out to stop anyone traveling the river road. Deep River greeted the people warmly, but then the dreaded news from the village hit him hard. The white man's disease, smallpox, was ravishing his people. He turned to Suzette and asked, "Is there anything you can do?"

"There is no cure, but we can help with quarantine and comforting of the sick. Deep River, I'm not going to lie to you. Smallpox could kill up to half of your people, maybe less, maybe more depending. I'll go there with you, and we can see what we can do."

Eli told Suzette she shouldn't go, but he knew she would. There were gauze masks in the Army medical kits, and Suzette got one out for herself and another for Deep River. It was two miles into the village. They decided to walk to keep the contamination of the virus to a bare minimum. Mr. Sue stopped her, he had a mask of his own made from tightly woven silk, and said, "I'm coming with you. I have fought this kind of epidemic before." He had a bolt of fine white silk cloth under his arm, and he explained, "It's for making masks for those not yet infected. They will be needed to isolate and quarantine the sick."

Suzette asked, "Where did you get that?"

"I bought it from the gypsies. I was saving it for you. For a dress when we got to Fort Moore. Using the silk for masks is more important. Let's go. We are wasting time here."

Lia wanted to come, but Suzette told her to stay back until they were able to assess the status of the village. *Fishing Eagle*, one of the young Pimas, also wanted to come, but Deep River said, "Hold back, for now; I will check on your family." With that, the three of them set off on foot for the village of the Pima. Deep River was stoic, these were his people, but life and death in the desert were daily facts of life. Smallpox was no different than the myriad of perils he faced throughout his lifetime. He knew there would be death. Accepting the onset of a smallpox epidemic without malice toward the white man who brought this disease with them from across the oceans, served more purpose than railing against the source. "It just is what it is," he said with a strong resignation to reality as he shrugged his shoulders and donned his mask. Suzette was impressed that Deep Rivers could accept the death sentence for his people without finding fault with the white immigrants that brought the disease.

They talked as they walked to the village. Mr. Sue knew what they needed as the first measures to save as many people as possible, and was immediately a *general in command*, instead of a cook. "We have to separate the sick from the well. Mr. Deep River, you will have to assemble everyone who is not affected, and I will cut cloth to cover their faces. Suzette, you will have to check the people who come forward for fever. If they are infected, send them back with the sick. We will have the young men who are well, dig a mass grave outside of the village. They can move the dead to the grave, but every day after they touch the dead, they have to wash in the river. That goes for us too. We will have to wash before we return to our camp. Under no circumstances are you to remove the masks. The disease is spread by contact with the sick and their spittle when they cough. Mr. Deep River, the hardest part right at the start, will be to get the uninfected people separated from the sick. Tell them it will only be for a short time. We will make them a mask and have them bathe in the river. They should then move all the sick to one area of the village, and then only people who come forward as caregivers will go in there. Families will be separated, mothers from children, husbands from wives. It must be done, or one third to one-half of your people will die. Understood?" Suzette was translating into Spanish as fast as she could. When she finished, Deep River nodded that he understood.

The village was more the size of a town than a small hamlet. There were more than three hundred of the round mud-huts built from desert brush and covered with adobe for protection from the sun. The people were thrilled to see Deep River. He called for them to bring the leader of the village, and an older woman stepped forward and told him she was now the leader. Her husband had already died of the pox. The sickness was now in the village for one half of a moon. Deep River told her that Suzette and Mr. Sue were great healers, respected doctors that knew how to stop the plague. He had her assemble all of the unaffected people. Suzette estimated that there were three hundred and fifty people that were not yet affected. To date, only twelve people had died, and there were twenty more affected but not yet dead.

Suzette started examining the healthy. Mr. Sue was cutting strips of silk for them to tie around their heads like the bandanas worn by renegades. One-by-one after Suzette's examination, they went down to the river to bathe. She only had to send five back to the village with fever. Several had the first signs of rash that would soon turn to the pustular spotted weals raising bumps on the skin, characteristic of the disease. There were no advanced cases in the healthy group, and the five she sent back to the village only had a fever and the first signs of spots on their faces or extremities. Deep River had twenty young men covered with bandanas, and they walked into the village to find and move the sick to the far western edge of the hamlet. A young mother was clutching the body of a little boy that had been dead for at least two days. Deep River murmured comforting words to her, and she reluctantly gave up the dead boy and walked off to the river to bathe and join the well group. Mr. Sue came to the west side of the village with a dozen women clad in the silk masks with their clothes still wet from washing in the river. Suzette told them not to touch any of the sick until they were completely dry. Deep River translated, and the women stripped naked on the spot and hung their clothes on the closest racks by the hogans to dry.

Fourteen cases were progressing through the final stages. Two looked to be passed the worst of it and would recover. Two more were near death, and the rest looked on her with eyes wide with fear. Deep River told them to relax. They would be fed and cared for until the Great Spirit decided their fate. She moved to the five that she sent back from the initial examination into a hogan by themselves. These were the most contagious, and they were to have no contact with the healthy people in the village other than the caregivers. Suzette sent the naked women down to the river to fill their clay water vessels. When they returned, she had them dress and tie their hair back and set to washing the sick and making them as comfortable as possible. The women caught on quickly, and soon, Suzette and Mr. Sue were standing outside the *hogan hospitals,* wondering how to keep the healthy people away from the sick. Deep River was talking to the older woman who had assumed leadership of the people after her husband died and explained the problem to her. She walked back to the people gathered down by the river and explained the taboo on visiting the sick.

Deep River brought an older woman and a young girl who had joined the caregivers and introduced them as his wife and daughter. Suzette hugged each of them and thanked them for coming forward to care for the sick. Deep River's wife uttered quietly to her husband, and he turned to Suzette and said, "She thanks you for bringing me back to her." Suzette didn't argue that it was the other way around; she was tired and wanted to go down to the river and wash and rejoin her family. Deep River took the young men and went out west of the village with them to dig the mass grave for the dead. Mr. Sue and Suzette walked back to the river and walked into the water and washed thoroughly before removing their masks. Suzette asked, "What do you think?"

"They are lucky we arrived when we did. It is still early, and if the village maintains the quarantine, a week should turn the tide. I know we can't stay here a week, but maybe Eli will agree to a couple of days so we can examine everyone again each morning. Separating the sick at the first sign of symptoms is important. We can teach Deep River to do the examinations, and then we can move on." Suzette nodded in affirmation; what she wanted was a cure, and if that wasn't possible, she at least wanted to understand how the human body could immunize against the disease. She knew that with mumps, the more severe form of measles and smallpox, the body self-immunized itself — people who came down with those once and survived, never caught those infectious diseases again. Somewhere, someone working on medical research had to understand the mechanisms of immunization and how the human body steeled itself against reinfection. That had to be the key.

Suzette had long before decided to become a doctor; now, she was finding more direction in her path forward. She thought back to the Doctors Way back in Fort Union and the letter of reference she carried from them. The Ways suggested that she travel to San Francisco and referred Suzette to a doctor there that was also a medical researcher. More than ever, she wanted to get to the end of this journey and set her sights on formal medical training.

Eli agreed to stay two days, and the next morning, the examination of all the healthy people yielded only two more new cases. The next day there was only one new case, and Eli decided to get back on the road west. Deep River told them that he was going to stay with his family, but Fishing Eagle would see them to the western edge of their territory as agreed. Eli paid Deep River twice what they agreed, and the woman chief of the village came forward and tied another amulet into Suzette's hair. This one was beads of hammered silver, and her lock of black and grey hair complemented the raven black one Deep River gave her back on the San Pedro. The two amulets and the deep tan on her face, shoulders, and arms changed her from an innocent from Independence into a seasoned woman of the west. She looked like she belonged both on and to the desert.

Eli headed them out, skirting the Pima village. They passed another road guard west of the hamlet and bid him farewell. It was time to make some good mileage, and the desert floor was relatively flat, and they didn't encounter a single obstacle to impede their progress. In four more days, they reached Antelope Hill, the western extent of the Pima lands. Fishing Eagle pointed down the river and said the only word he knew in English, "Yuma." Suzette and Lia both hugged the young man even though he didn't smell too good after four days on foot without a bath in the river.

Eli made camp there by Antelope Hill, where the river crowded them close to the hill. Two more days and they would be to the bank of the Colorado River. Across the Colorado lay California, the land of young men's dreams: the Mojave, Los Angeles, Fort Moore, and their grandmother. By this time, one hundred and eight days on the trail, Hans and his Germans were speaking English passably well. Hans offered to deal with "Grandma" at the journey's end. Everyone laughed but then turned to the serious business of staying healthy. Suzette lined up all the men and ran them through the examination for smallpox. There were no fevers and no rashes. Juan Pedro was mending quickly and was back to lusting after Suzette again, a sure sign of health. Eli thought it was amazing; all that way, and they had only lost one man during the attack on the renegades back in the middle of Kansas. It seemed like a year ago instead of five months. In two days, they reached the confluence with the Colorado River. The US Army maintained the barges further downriver that would ferry them across to California.

They were leaving one desert behind only to enter one more dry, hotter, and deadlier than the one they just crossed. The Mojave was a shorter trek to the mountains east of the Los Angeles basin than the Sonoran Desert, but it wasn't to be taken lightly. Many before them had died in the blistering heat and the endless dunes, one more challenge to be taken in stride. They were tough from their hard months on the trail. Maybe they were tougher than the rest. The next two hundred miles would tell.

COLORADO CROSSING

In the two days since they left the lands of the Pima, they had only seen scattered bands of Indians, two or three per group. Technically they were in the territory of the Yuma Apaches, and all Apaches bore the tainted reputation of their eastern brothers. These, though, were not hostile, and the Army garrison at Yuma probably had a lot to do with that. They arrived at the shantytown of Yuma on the east side of the Colorado River and found their way along the few streets to the ferry crossing. Fort Yuma was on the west bank on a prominence above the river. The sun was hot in the late afternoon, and the men and the mules were anxious to get to the water. The Colorado was not a muddy prairie river. With a quarter of a million square miles of drainage, it was deep, cold, and its blue waters flowed past with a determination to reach the Gulf of California as soon as possible. The Colorado wasn't a river with an easy ford.

There was a ferry waiting on the west bank. The operators saw the wagon train arrive and left the bank to cross the river to take the wagon master to the west side. The ferry was a barge that ran on a rope. There were two heavy posts on the east bank of the river spaced about one hundred yards apart. The pioneers looked across the river, and it was easy to see how the ferry worked. There were two more heavy posts directly opposite on the west bank. To send the ferry across the river, mule teams would hitch to an eye in the hawser. First, the mules pulled slack in the hawser so the loop around the post could be lifted off. Then the mules pulled the rope to the post downriver. When the east end of the rope was secure, a mule team on the other side would move its end of the rope to the upstream post. Loops on the end of the heavy hawser dropped over the posts kept the ferry from breaking away and floating down the river. One end of the rope was always secured while the mules moved the other end. With the rope facing downstream, the barge would be released and glide down the rope being pushed by the current to the opposite side. To return, the mule teams would switch the ropes, and the barge would glide back across the river. The Army Garrison was on the west bank of the river, and the Army contracted a private citizen to operate the ferry. The current was strong, and the river was over a hundred yards wide. The barge could only take one wagon across at a time, but there was no crossing the river without the ferry.

Jacques looked over the system and admired its simplicity. The engineering had been worked out long ago and was used all over the world. The US Army had made some improvements, however. The bollards on the barge itself, through which the hawser threaded through, had a braking system that could be used to slow the barge in the strong current. There was a large black man on the barge along with a man dressed like a Mississippi flatboat captain gliding across the river to meet the wagon train. The barge glided to twenty feet of the bank, and then the black man turned a wheel that looked like the helm of a large ship and pulled the barge the rest of the way into the ferry ramp. The flatboat captain got off; the black man stayed behind. The barge captain walked up to the Callahan brothers and said, "Take me to the wagon master."

Eli stepped forward and said, "I am the wagon master; my name is Eli Callahan." He extended his hand to shake.

The barge captain took his hand in return, "I'm Joseph Huntszinger. I collect fees for the Army and run the ferry operation. It's going to cost you some money to cross the river. The big wagons are twenty, the smaller ones fifteen, and the mule teams ten dollars each."

Eli spread his feet and leaned forward in a menacing stance, "I'm not paying a fortune to get an Army supply train across the river on an Army ferry."

Huntszinger harrumphed, "How good are you at swimming?"

"Maybe you should ask yourself the same question." Eli picked the man up by the front of his shirt and carried him down the bank. He stepped onto the barge, walked to the end and flung Huntszinger as far out into the river as he could. The big black man stood stock still with wide eyes but didn't move or say a word to Eli to stop him. Huntszinger was thrashing wildly. The current wasn't that strong near the bank, and the riverman settled into a dog paddle that brought him back to shore about a hundred feet down the river. Eli told the black man to take him across the river.

The big man said, "Yessah," and signaled the muleskinners on the bank with a shrill whistle. A big smile beamed across the barge at Eli. "I be Moses," and he extended his hand. "You might want your horse on the other side." He signaled, and a young black boy led Eli's horse down onto the barge. "This be Lil' Amos. He ain't my son. Huntszinger bought him before we left Georgia. Huntszinger wouldn't buy my wife. When I be free, I's agon back to get her."

Eli realized that all the blacks operating the ferry were slaves. These were the first he encountered since leaving Missouri. The whole ugliness of the Southern States and slavery slid back into his consciousness as they glided into the middle of the river. Eli introduced himself and told Moses that he was from Missouri, and he wasn't a slave owner. Then he asked, "What do you mean, 'When you are free?'"

Moses grew more animated and said, "When da war sets us free."

"What war," Eli asked.

"The war dats comin. The North again the South. De news from back east is full ofs it. The war of emancipatun. No mo slaves. I be gona back to Georgia soon, taken all these niggas back wid me. Get my woman and her mama. Comin back a gona get me some land. Gona raise some hogs and live without a whip at my back."

It was hard for Eli to understand the dialect of the deep South, but the words *whip at my back* were as clear as the blue water of the Colorado. Eli took it all in and was suddenly missing his father and the wisdom of his ways. Eli asked, "Is Huntszinger your owner?"

"Nosa, he be the overseer. Da owner is up in da garrison. His name be Mr. Gordon B. Hughes." It was time to crank the barge ashore.

Eli rode his horse off the barge thanking Moses for the ride. He rode up to the garrison. There was only one wood building with the stars and stripes flying from a short pole and a few others made of adobe. Neat rows of tents housed the soldiers, and a corral made entirely of ocotillo cactus staves held their mounts. Eli walked into the headquarters and was met by an orderly who said the major, who was the post commander, was upriver with Mr. Hughes. Eli asked, "What are the rates for the ferry? I have an Army supply train on the other side of the river, sixty-something wagons and one civilian rig."

The young corporal looked a little confused. "There is no fee for the supply wagons, their crews, or their teams. The civilian wagon and its team are a dollar. Riders are fifty cents each. Didn't you see the sign on the other side? Where was Huntszinger? He should have explained it to you."

"Matter of fact, I didn't see the sign, and Huntszinger went swimming. He must have been hot. Moses brought me across. When will Hughes and the major be back?"

"Less than an hour, they have been up at the Indian camp all morning."

Eli asked directions to the Indian camp and then went down to the river and told Moses to start bringing the wagons across.

Moses asked, "Wadabout Huntszinger?" Eli nodded his understanding and rode back across the river with Moses.

Huntszinger was raving-lunatic mad and was standing on the bank when Eli walked off the barge. Eli listened to him rave, but without saying a word, walked right up to Huntszinger and landed a massive right hook onto the side of his face. The riverman spun around in the air more than a full turn and hit the ground face first, hard like a limp sack of potatoes.

"Load'um up," he said to his brothers, "and get them across." I'm going to go have a little talk with the major and the ferry operator, Mr. Gordon B. Hughes." Eli got back on the ferry with Jacques and the first mule team. It was going to be a slow process. Eli told Jacques to take only half the wagon train across so as not to leave too small of a contingent on the east side of the river so they could guard themselves through the night. Moses now looked on Eli with awe and respect. Eli introduced him to his brother and told him Jacques would be in charge of the river crossing. Eli rode off to find the major, and Mr. Hughes. The Indian camp was not as organized as the Pueblos or the villages along the Gila, but the Indians were healthy and happy. It was hard to believe that they were first cousins to the fierce Apache on the eastern side of the New Mexico Territory.

Hughes had a wagon and was trading with the Indians. The major sat on his horse, watching the proceedings. Eli rode up and introduced himself. The major was Timothy Ellsworth Jenkins. Shaking Eli's hand, he asked, "Are you Aaden Callahan's son?"

Eli was surprised, "Guilty," he answered. "Did you know my father?"

"No, but I met his mother-in-law in Los Angeles. We have been expecting you."

"We? Is Denise here?" Eli asked, thinking he must have missed Denise back at the garrison.

"No, but she is waiting for you over at Fort Moore."

Eli was relieved. "I want to talk to Mr. Hughes about the ferry." Hughes was wrapping up his trades. He told Eli he would meet him back at Major Jenkins' office. Eli rode back to the garrison. He was sitting behind the major's desk, reading the latest newspapers sent over from Fort Moore. The South was convening political conventions, and the fervor for secession was running high. The Republicans were moving to nominate Abraham Lincoln for president, and the south was guaranteeing secession if that were to happen. Some of the

Democrats in the South were looking for calmer and wiser minds to prevail and hoped that the Union would not break in two. The South was steadfast in maintaining their way of life, particularly the institution of slavery that made large-scale plantation farming in the South possible. Eli was well prepared for Hughes when the major ushered him into the office. Eli got up and surrendered the major's chair to him and took one of the hard chairs in front of his desk. Hughes took the other.

Eli opened the discussion with a question, "How is it Mr. Hughes that you can own slaves in California. California is a Free State. By the way, I ran into your overseer down on the ferry, and he decided to take a swim. It must have tired him out pretty good because then he decided to take a nap."

Hughes dropped his pleasant demeanor and waded right into the fray. "Look here, young man, those blacks down there earn wages. They are employees and live on the other side of the river. That is not California. Huntszinger is my manager; he runs the ferry operation."

"I had a good chat with Moses on a couple of trips across the river. If he is an employee, why does he call Huntszinger an overseer, and why does he look forward to freedom if the North and South go to war. And Moses, he tells me you bought him and the boy in Mississippi. I can see that you are exploiting these people. I would bet that you haven't bothered to educate them about their rights out here in the west."

Hughes was turning red with anger. "Look here, Callahan; this is none of your business. Leave my sl…. – employees alone or I will have the major here make you sorry."

"Mr. Hughes, we have crossed this great continent of ours. We have killed hundreds of Indians and renegades. We have endured the storms, the heat, the cold, thirst, and disease on the trail, and I don't think you or Major Jenkins have even fifteen percent of what it would take to make us sorry. You, on the other hand, are nothing more than a strong-minded Southerner with nothing to back you up this far from home. Major, you should arrest this man and set his slaves free. But I am a reasonable lad and a businessman. Hughes, your overseer, tried to bilk me out of hundreds of dollars this afternoon to move my supply train across the river. He didn't fare too well, and neither will you if you persist in your inhuman convictions. How much would you take for your slaves and the ferry operation?"

"I'm not selling, and they are not slaves, they are employees."

"How about Major Jenkins and I go down to the river and ask Moses how much he earns running the ferry? Major?"

Eli got up, and Major Jenkins rose slowly, probably remiss to discover that Hughes was running an illegal operation on the river right under his nose. Hughes was turning purple; he blurted out, "Wait, I'll take ten thousand dollars."

"For what?" Eli asked. "The ferry belongs to the Army; I suspect that the mule teams do too. What exactly are you selling, Mr. Hughes?"

"I need to recover my costs. I brought these niggers here all the way from Mississippi. It wasn't cheap."

"You can get from St. Joseph, Missouri, to Sacramento for one hundred fifty dollars on the Overland Stage. If you had those men walk here, I expect it only took about fifty dollars each in food and a couple of pairs of boots. Sixteen hundred dollars in Independence would get a wagon, supplies, and a whole family across. So again, Mr. Hughes, why exactly was it so expensive?"

Hughes was flummoxed. He couldn't answer.

Eli had him where he wanted him. "Mr. Hughes, I'll offer you two thousand dollars for the operation of the ferry. Major Jenkins, is there a contract involved?"

The major answered, "No, Hughes showed up with his men, and I was happy to let him take over. I don't have a lot of troops here. I needed my men to police the Indian camps on this side of the river."

Hughes could hardly speak, "It's not enough, I – I need more!"

Eli was calm, he smiled and said, "Major Jenkins, I would like to file a complaint against Mr. Hughes and Mr. Huntszinger for owning and using slaves in California. It will be in the best interests of all of us if you carry out your duties. The US Army is commissioned to uphold the laws of the United States, and all of the states it operates in. I can have my brother, Roland, cite the laws of California that pertain to this if that is required."

"Not necessary, Mr. Callahan, I know the law. Mr. Hughes, I'm going to walk down to the river and talk to your *employees*. If they tell me they are slaves, I will be back up here to place you under arrest."

Just then, Huntszinger walked into the office, but he saw Eli there and quietly backed out. Major Jenkins got up and fastened his gun belt around his waist. Then he made an elaborate move and took his saber down from the pegs on the wall behind his desk. He slipped the saber into the sheath on his belt and walked out the door. Eli joined him, and they walked down to the river. Moses was stripped to the waist and glistened with sweat as he was hauling the ferry to shore with the great wheel. Two hands from the wagon he was hauling were helping turn the wheel, straining against the current and the deeper draft of the barge with the heavy load aboard. Eli and Major Jenkins stepped aboard, and Eli introduced the major to Moses. Moses said with respect, "I know who you is, sa."

Major Jenkins asked, "Moses, how much do you get paid for working the ferry for Mr. Hughes?"

"Paid sa? I has never been paid a red cent for all the years of my life. I is a slave, and slaves work for der owners, sa. Mr. Hughes, he owns me and the other blacks with the teams. We eat well, and Huntszinger threatens the whip, but he has never used it." He was quiet then, and when they reached the other side of the river, Eli helped him haul the ferry to shore. Major Jenkins walked over to talk to the two men with the mule team. They were pulling slack in the rope holding the ferry, ready to haul the hawser upriver to the upper piling. The sun was dropping to the horizon, and the dust and clouds in the west promised a spectacular sunset. Moses would have half the wagon train across the river by dark.

Eli asked Moses one more question before he left the barge, "Moses, where do you and the rest of the men who work the ferry live?"

"We live in a mud hogan over back the garrison. We don't live with the Indians, and we gets to eat in the mess hall. Compared to Georgia, it ain't a bad life."

Eli gathered up Suzette and crossed the river with Major Jenkins. "What do you think?" he asked as they neared the west shore.

The major was quiet, but his expression radiated grim determination. "How much did Huntszinger try to charge to take you across?"

"The top end of the scale was twenty dollars for the heavy wagons, and it went down from there."

"I'm going to put Hughes and Huntszinger in a world of trouble when we get back to my office."

Easier said than done, Hughes and his overseer were nowhere in sight when they got back to the garrison. The corporal in the Major's office said that they left and went up the river to the Indian camp in Hughes' wagon. Eli took the lead, "I'm going to act like he took my offer and write out *Affidavits of Freedom* for Moses and the rest of his men. I want them to stay on to run the ferry for at least six more months until you get more soldiers from Fort Moore to take over. I'm going to give you the two thousand dollars I was willing to pay Hughes for the operation, and I am asking you to put Moses and his men on the Army payroll. I also want them to have better housing and transportation back to Georgia when the six months are up. The single men may not choose to go if the country is at war by then, but the married men will want to get back to their families. If they go back to Georgia, I want them to leave here with enough money to buy freedom for their wives and children."

Major Jenkins stood up and said, "I can take care of that." He shook Eli's hand. He took them out behind his office and showed Suzette into one of the adobe shacks that served as a guest house for the garrison. "This isn't much, but it is all we have here. It's a clean place to rest, and the tank up on the water tower is full if you want a cold bath. Well, it isn't cold, the tank is out in the sun all day. In the middle of the summer, the water even gets too hot for a bath.

Suzette thought about Lia, but she was across the river and would be staying there through the night with her husband. "Thank you, Major," she managed, but then the Major invited her to dine with him that evening. "Thanks, but I'll dine with Eli and our German friends. We're celebrating making it to California." As she closed the door, she noticed there was no way to lock it. The door itself was flimsy, built from desert-weathered wood. It could hardly keep out curious onlookers, let alone an intruder. She would have her bath and then be spending the night in Eli's wagon as usual. As she ran the tub full of pleasantly warm water, she couldn't help noticing that other travelers had written messages on the wall. One in Spanish read *El Pueblo de Nuestra Señora la Reina de Los Angeles de Porciuncula-438 kilometers.* Another in French read *Méfiez-vous des grands* – (Beware of the major). Before she stripped down to get in the bath, she moved a chair over to the side of the tub and put her Lefaucheux within easy reach. The Major seemed like a straight-forward Army officer, but she would be careful just the same. She lay back in the water and luxuriously undid her braid and set the barrette alongside the revolver. The soap was brown and rough, but it felt good to be clean just the same.

After dinner, Major Jenkins summoned Moses and the rest of the blacks up to the garrison. They gathered in front of the major's office, and Eli took the floor with Suzette at his side. First, Eli brought them up to understand the laws of California that outlawed slavery, and then he laid out the terms of their freedom. Moses sat with his arms around Amos and, like the rest of the blacks, couldn't believe that they were held here by nothing but their ignorance. Eli had written up six *Affidavits of Freedom* and meticulously wrote the names of each of the black men into the documents. Moses was the first, and when Eli he asked him his full name, Moses told him that he only had one name. That was the way of things in Georgia; he thought that was the way of things the whole world over. "You have to choose a last name, and even a middle one if you want, and that will be your name from this day forward," Suzette explained.

The blacks murmured amongst themselves, and then Moses asked Suzette if she would be offended if they used her family name. She didn't object and said, "My brothers and I would be greatly honored." And with that, there were six new Callahans in the world. She wondered what her parents would have thought of that, but kept the devastating hurt that rushed into her mind pushed well to the back, not letting it intrude on the happiness of the moment. She finished the ceremony by telling Moses and his men to keep the *Affidavits of Freedom* with them at all times. It is a legal document in all courts of the United States.

Moses asked, "What about in the South?"

"Yes, even in the South as long as we are one nation. If war comes, no one can tell how the South will treat freed slaves. I hope you will stay away from there until the nation settles down. I know some of you have families. If they were here, we would free them too, but only time will tell how to work that out for the best. You will know what to do as we write the next chapter of this country's history; for the moment, we want you to keep running the ferry. Major Jenkins will be paying you every week, and you will be safe here on the river."

With that, she stepped off the Major's porch, but Jenkins stopped her before she could walk away. "Would it be alright, Miss Callahan, if I visited over to the guest house later tonight?"

Suzette smiled, "That would be fine, Major." She batted her eyes at him, and the effect was immediate. Jenkins smiled; his eyes wild with anticipation. Suzette knew he was watching her with all the lecherous attention he could muster as she walked over to the wagon camp. In a way, she felt sorry for the men out on these remote posts. She wondered, but knew, that their lives would be turned to a living hell if the South succeeded from the union. She worried about Jacques; he had told her he would join the Army in Fort Moore. Too many worries, she decided as she heard the twang of Paul Hayman's banjo. She stayed the night in Eli's wagon, as usual, and fell asleep wondering just how far 438 kilometers was.

The next morning the ferry operation started well before dawn. Lia was feeding Moses and his men bacon and biscuits as they moved the remainder of the wagons across the river. Señor Francisco was down to only three pigs and had run out of chickens somewhere in the middle of the New Mexico Territory. Finally, there was only one wagon left. Roland had already crossed the river with the last team, and Moses and his men were backing the last wagon down the slope with a mule team and then pushing it by hand the rest of the way over the ferry ramp and onto the barge. The mules pulled the rope upstream, and Moses released the break to glide across the river. The ferry reached the other side, and Roland backed his team down and hitched onto the back axle of the wagon with a stout chain to pull the wagon up the bank. Moses watched as his men switched the hawser around for the return trip. When he reached the east bank, he welcomed Lia aboard with a broad smile and announced himself as Captain Moses Callahan, at her service. Lia had Amos in front of her in the saddle on Juan Pedro's big stallion, and the little boy was terrified and thrilled at the same time for his first time on a horse. Moses bowed deeply and took Amos down from the saddle. They waited until the hawser was in place on the downstream piling on the west side, and with the shrill whistle, he started the team on the east side, pulling the hawser upstream.

Lia was humming a few bars of a Spanish hymn, and they were in the middle of the river when a man on the east bank jumped down from some brush on the top of the bank and cut the hawser with one blow of a heavy ax. Lia could see that the man with the ax was none other than Huntszinger. At the same time, two Indians on the west bank threw a bucket of kerosene onto the downriver piling and lit it on fire. The oiled loop of the hawser burst into flames along with the piling. Moses didn't panic but started hauling on the wheel to keep them moving across the river as long as the west end of the rope held them against the current.

He made it to within forty feet of the bank, but then the burned rope let go, and the three of them and the horse were on their way to Mexico. Roland was waiting for his wife on the west bank and sprang into action. He ran up the bank and flew up onto the back of his horse and rode hard to the wagon camp. He pulled up short and yelled, "Lia is adrift on the river with Moses and Amos." Then he spurred the horse and rode back to the bank of the Colorado to follow his wife down the river. Capt. Barksdale mounted up his troops and followed. Eli went to Hans's wagon and got the long rope they used to cross swift streams and threw it over the back of a mule. Then he and Jacques rode after the soldiers.

The river was swift, and the ferry soon left the Colorado Crossing well out of sight. Amos was scared, Moses was silent watching the river. He told Lia not to worry; in thirty miles, the river broadened, and the current slowed. They would be able to get off the ferry and make it to the west shore, but they would be in Mexico. Just south of the border were several small towns where men who didn't want to deal with the lawmen in the United States spent their days drinking and whoring. Getting off the barge was one problem. Making it back to the safety north of the border would be another. Roland was pushing his horse hard to keep up with the barge.

Lia knew that he couldn't keep pace for much longer in the heat of the day. They would be on their own soon, and it might be days before they made it back to the garrison.

In two hours, Roland had fallen behind out of sight. They knew they had crossed over into Mexico when a settlement of pueblo type houses on the west side of the river loomed into sight. Some men set out in a small boat, much like a whaleboat, to give chase. They caught up to the burnt end of the hawser, and wicked smiles spread across their faces as they started to pull themselves to the barge. Lia handed one of her revolvers to Moses. She took her Henry out of the sheath on the stallion and knelt behind the handrail at the side of the barge. She aimed and shot the sombrero off the head of the Mexican standing in the back of the whaleboat. The rest of the men in the boat must have thought this was going to be an easy chase because only a few of them were armed, and those only with poor looking pistols. Lia worked the lever on the Henry and chambered another round. One of the armed men stood up to shoot at her, but Lia shot him in the chest, and he fell into the river. The rest of the men in the boat were suddenly aware that they were sitting ducks. They threw the hawser back in the water and hauled on the oars to widen the distance between them and the barge. The corpse of their friend was left behind to float down the river with Moses and his crew. The whaleboat put into shore and was soon out of sight.

Another ten miles and the river started to widen. Moses said, "The water will be shallow soon. If you can get the horse into the water, we can swim to the shore." He was right; the barge was caught in a large eddy and was swept slowly toward the west shore. When they were as close as they were going to get to the swampy looking shore, Moses yelled, "Now!" Lia had the Henry tied into the sheath and her colt tied as well into its holster. The last thing she wanted was to be on the west shore unarmed. She dug her heels into the stallion's flanks, and as if he sensed the desperation of their situation, he leaped into the river. Moses took Amos into his arms and jumped into the river after them. Amos was terrified; he didn't know how to swim. Moses held onto him and pushed with strong strokes of his legs to the back of Lia and the horse. She threw him a rope, and Moses let the horse pull him and the boy along. Lia was hunched down, urging the horse on. They only had to swim about a hundred feet, and then the horse was walking up the sandy bottom of the river. They got to the shore, and swarms of mosquitoes descended for their noon meal. "Let's gets ourselves inland, Lady Lia." He handed Amos up into the saddle and ran on ahead to find his way through the rushes to higher ground.

There was a road on the west side of the river, but Moses crossed it and kept going out into the desert. He led them to a hillock about two miles from the river. It was just high enough to hide the stallion behind it. Lia asked, "Now what?"

"We wait till night or till yer husband comes with de troops." Lia had a canteen, and she passed it around. She took some jerky out of her saddlebag. It was wet, but it was something to eat. The desert was hot, and it wasn't long that they were dried out. Lia figured they were thirty or forty miles south of Yuma with a lot of unfriendly country and dangerous men between here and there. She stripped the rounds out of the Colt and reloaded it with dry powder and caps. Moses was lying on the top of the hillock watching the road. Toward evening a dozen Mexicans rode down the road at a fast gallop. They were looking for them further down the river. If the raft hung up and they saw it was empty, they would be circling back, knowing that they passed their quarry. Lia figured that they wanted the horse more than the three of them, but she wasn't giving up the horse. Desperate men would kill them once they had the horse. Being a woman, she expected a lot worse than death if they caught her. After dark, they headed due north; Moses on foot and Lia and Amos on the horse. They moved about five miles and then cut over to the river to water the horse and replenish the canteen. They moved back off to the west of the road, and Moses swept their tracks with a willow bough he cut from the river bank. "We got to keep moving," he said with his voice low knowing sounds would carry a long way in the night air. The moon was half full, and they made good time on the flat desert floor. The moon set sometime after midnight, but they kept moving. The desert floor was like white alkali, and they could make their way slowly by starlight.

At dawn, they held up in a small grove of mesquite. Moses killed a large rattlesnake with a dead tree limb and skinned him out. He cut up the snake into small pieces and had Lia and Amos sucking on the meat for the moisture and nourishment. Lia struggled with the English but kidded him, "I thought black people didn't like snakes."

"I don't, especially de one we calls Huntszinger." Lia laughed; she knew he was trying to lighten the crushing desperation they were facing. Moses was perched up in a tree as the sun reached high noon and called down in a quiet voice, "Riders coming down from the north." In a few more minutes, he could see the blue uniforms of Barksdale's soldiers. He climbed down and told Lia and Amos that they be saved. He took the Henry rifle and walked out of the thicket and fired a shot up in the air. The soldiers didn't hear it, but Eli and Roland were trailing behind with the mule loaded with the rope and away from the thundering hooves of the cavalry; they heard the shot. They turned out into the desert and soon saw Moses out in the open at the edge of the thicket. It only took a couple of minutes, and they pulled up next to Moses. Their horses were fagged, so Eli left Roland in the happy reunion with his wife and rode off on Juan Pedro's stallion to catch up with the soldiers. Roland just held his wife in his arms, and Amos clung to Moses' massive leg. "We be saved," Moses said over and over again to comfort the child.

Eli returned with Capt. Barksdale and his soldiers and they cooked up a meal of salt pork, hardtack, and gravy, waiting for the evening to go back up the river. Eli was loath to leave the rope behind, but he put Moses up on the mule bareback, and they set off across the desert. The moon was just beyond half and provided more than enough light to illuminate the white desert floor. The desert was flat, and when the moon set, they stopped along the river for the rest of the night. The horses needed water, and there was grass along the banks. The soldiers hobbled their horses and settled in to guard their makeshift camp. Lia rolled Amos into a blanket to protect him from the mosquitos and then rolled into one herself. The next day they rode boldly up the road and reached the first of the border towns. Men and women lined the streets and watched them pass through, but only a few men were armed, and they offered no resistance. Lia spotted a cosina and asked Eli if they could stop for a meal. Eli agreed, and the soldiers watered their horses in the trough in front of the restaurant and then sat on the porch as the women of the cosina handed out burros and beans with rice and fresh lettuce and tomatoes from the fields. Everyone ate their fill, and Eli paid their bill with silver reales that he had gathered up for their excursion into Mexico. Capt. Barksdale was studying a map, and he said one more day, and we will be back in Yuma.

They came to the next border town in the dark. Eli had them skirt the town, and they heard the ruckus of hard-drinking men raising hell, enjoying the evening. When the moon went down, they camped on the river again, and Lia told Eli about the man she killed on the boat. He agreed that could mean trouble, but unless there were a lot more of them, one boatload of hostile Mexicans wasn't going to be a threat. They set out at a fast pace the next morning and by late afternoon pulled into the wagon camp next to the garrison. Suzette ran out to greet them and pulled Lia down from the stallion and hugged her and wouldn't let go. She led Lia and Roland up to the guest house behind Major Jenkins' office and left them there. Pointing to the sign on the wall, she asked Roland how long it would take for them to travel 438 kilometers? He told her it was a little less than three hundred miles, and if they didn't encounter any more trouble, they would be at the end of the line in about two weeks.

Suzette was pleased; she walked back to the wagon camp with a prayer of thanks for the safe return of Lia, Moses, and Amos. She told Eli that if they had not returned with Lia, Major Jenkins was going to hang the two Indians he had in the stockade who set fire to the rope. Eli was glad the Indians didn't have to die. Hughes and Huntszinger were the villains here. He wouldn't need an Army major to hang them if he ever saw them again. "Let's get some sleep," he said as they walked to his wagon, "We'll be in the Mojave tomorrow."

THE MOJAVE

ia woke up the next morning with the same contentment she felt every morning after spending the night with Roland. She sensed that the camp was teaming around her with the sound of cursing as teamsters were hitching mules, and all was readied to take to the trail west. She heard the children running and screaming at each other; they must have been playing tag. She gently shook Roland awake and said, "Cuando lleguemos a Los Ángeles, quiero tener a tus hijos." Roland's Spanish was improving rapidly, and while he didn't understand every word, he got the idea. Lia wanted to make him a father before long. He listened to the children playing and thought that couldn't ever be a bad thing.

Roland didn't need a translation, he responded with vigor, "Why don't I try to make you pregnant right now?" Laughing, he pulled her down to the bed for one more time in the privacy of the guest house. They were both smiling when they emerged from the small adobe building a short time later. All around them, the teamsters and swampers were packing their wagons with water barrels, canteens, and any other vessel they could buy or barter that would hold water. Eli was talking with Major Jenkins, who was familiar with the trail as far as the San Diego valley. Suzette was busy with the inventory of her medical kits and scrubbing her examination table. It would be the last time she had the luxury of extra water to keep her medical equipment as clean as possible. Mr. Sue was bartering with some Indians who had brought fresh vegetables to the fort. All in all, there wasn't an idle hand in the camp that wasn't getting ready to make the push through the Mojave Desert. Señor Francisco interrupted the children's game and put them to work.

Eli had decided that they would travel during this first day and then continue at night until they reached the coastal mountains outside of San Diego. Even though it was October, the Mojave was still deadly hot throughout the day, and water for a wagon train as large as theirs was essentially nonexistent. Suzette had one last chore, and that was seeing to Juan Pedro's dressings and comfort before heading out. Juan Pedro was strong, and he was healing rapidly. Suzette and Lia walked over to Señor Francisco's wagon just as he was getting ready to help Juan Pedro up to the top of the cargo for the day's journey. Suzette had him hold up for a moment, and she knelt and unwrapped the bandage around the wound on his arm. The wound had healed completely, and she needed a little extra time to set the arm with a plaster cast. She went back to Eli's wagon for the plaster and cotton wrap for the cast and told Eli what she was going to do. He had her and Lia's horses brought over and told her to stay on the road west until she caught up to the wagon train. He had watched his sister wrap broken limbs before and knew she would not be more than an hour behind.

The wagon train pulled out, and as Suzette was mixing the Plaster of Paris, Lia unwrapped Juan Pedro's rib cage. That wound was also completely healed, and the broken ribs were set hard in place. The ends of the bones knitted together strongly enough that the bandage wrapping around his rib cage was no longer needed. Juan Pedro never took his eyes off Suzette as she was preparing the materials for the cast. Lia could easily see the erection straining to break free of his trousers and nodded at Suzette to direct her gaze to Juan Pedro's condition. Suzette had read up on Juan Pedro's persistent erection and joked with Lia about his condition that she diagnosed as priapism. *Pedro Priapism* was the nickname they gave him and joked about it right out in the open, sure that no one else understood the term.

Suzette told her patient to lay still, and she undid the splint and removed it from his arm. She had his elbow braced up on a block of wood and was patiently wrapping the arm with the soft cotton cloth that would protect it from the plaster. Lia handed her the pot of plaster, and they set to wrapping the arm in the permanent cast that would remain in place for another four weeks. The cast extended down around his elbow. It was still awkward and restraining, but at least now he had use of his left hand. Lia had brought a dose of saltpeter with her from the medical kit and mixed it into a small glass of water and had Juan Pedro drink it before Señor Francisco helped him up into the wagon. By the time they were finished and had the medical kits packed up, the wagon train was out of sight to the west. Jacques and Roland had stayed behind with the wagon, and now Jacques clicked his tongue and shook the reins, and they were off on the last leg of the journey to Los Angeles. Felipe burst from the back of Señor Francisco's wagon and flew in circles out in front of them, ever watchful and ready to scream, "Apache, Apache!" The day was uneventful, and eventually, the big bird was content to settle back on his perch and eat his meal of fruit and nuts.

They caught up to the wagon train shortly after dark. The temperature was still above ninety degrees, and everyone wondered how it would have been to make the desert crossing in the heat of summer. They camped on the edge of a great sea of sand. Rolling dunes stretched north and west as far as they could see. Eli told them that the dunes extended forty miles to the north and was ten to fifteen miles wide at its center. It was hard to imagine that much sand after the endless prairies and rocky desert of the New Mexico Territory. The road west skirted the south edge of the dunes, and there was only a mile or so at some points between the edge of the sand and the Mexican border. In reality, no one could say exactly where the border with Mexico was. There were no demarcations and only a handful of settlements. Some of the residents of the settlements called themselves Mexican, and others called themselves Americans or Californians. Whatever they called themselves, all were eager to sell vegetables and muscatel, a beverage that most of the teamsters and swampers had already learned to avoid.

The next day Eli had the wagon train on the trail before dawn. He said they would make ten miles or so and then break and wait till dark before going on. The mules were holding up well, and the road was either sand or the soft soil of the Colorado River Delta. After fourteen hundred miles of mud, lost shoes, and hoof disease, the blacksmith was finally able to rest when they stopped for the day. The heat was almost unbearable, with the daytime temperature exceeding a hundred degrees with little wind. Most of the teamsters parked their wagons side-by-side and stretched tarps between the ribs of the canopies to shade the animals. The men slept through the heat of the day under the wagons. They were quickly learning why the trail was called the Camino del Diablo by the locals. Suzette was reminded of Chico del Diablo by the name and fell asleep under Eli's wagon, thinking of all that they had been through up till now.

When evening came, it was like no other evening they had ever seen. The sky to the west was draped in brilliant reds and purple hues as the sun rushed to hide below the horizon. As the night grew darker, the heavens put on a spectacular show. Millions of meteors were falling to earth, streaking across the sky from the north to the south. The moon was nearly full, but its brightness couldn't dampen the display. Occasionally a large meteor would fly across the sky, losing sparks as it traveled through the atmosphere to finally burn out. It was easy to imagine that you could hear them tearing through the sky, but Roland, ever the scholar, let them know that was impossible. No sooner had he quit talking that a large meteor made it to the earth. They felt rather than heard the impact, but after some twenty seconds or so passed, there was a thunderous boom from the west. Roland shrugged, as Suzette asked him, "What about that one?"

The meteor shower lasted for several hours, and then the night sky quieted, and only moon and starlight was left to light their trail. They traveled until dawn when Eli signaled to make camp. Breakfast was cooking as the men watered and fed the mules. The tarps were up and the animals sheltered long before the sun rose to its zenith and baked all that was left exposed. Juan Pedro was up and making the rounds. Lia poked Suzette in the side to get her attention as they were sleeping side by side under Eli's wagon. Juan Pedro wasn't suffering from his affliction, probably because the effect of the saltpeter had not yet worn off. Lia wondered if the boy would consider himself sick waking up limp as an older man. He came over to say hello to Suzette and brought her a bottle of fresh lemonade. She thanked him for the gift, but she had her bottle in her saddlebag. Mr. Sue and Hans were busy squeezing all the fresh lemons and making the sugared drink as fast as they could. Mr. Sue knew the lemons prevented scurvy; he was seeing that every man got a fair share of the cool drink before the lemons rotted in the heat.

There were still dunes, but now the endless dunes they passed were more broken up by oases where date palms grew with profusion and shallow ponds, and wells yielded some water. Eli halted the train for rest because Hans was down with severe pain in his side. They made their camp next to an oasis with a small water hole. It was amazing to watch the animals share the water in the oasis throughout the night. The moon was only one day away from full, and the clear desert air allowed the brilliance of the moon's light to shine as bright as some cloudy days. Coyote, deer, rabbits, and owls all made their way to the oasis to drink. At one point, all the wildlife disappeared, and a lone mountain lion slinked stealthily into the oasis. After the large cat drank its fill and left, the wildlife reappeared. First, the rabbits came out of their burrows, and then smaller predators started returning, driving the rabbits back down. The owls, which had been silent while the big cat was in the neighborhood, started calling again, and occasionally, one would swoop down to take a mouse or a small rabbit off for dinner.

Suzette and Lia didn't want to sleep. They stayed up at the side of the oasis to watch the constant stream of wildlife coming to drink. They were particularly thrilled when a bushy red fox appeared and barked a signal to its litter, and eight small pups skittered from the cover of a greasewood bush to drink while the mother watched. In a few minutes, a mother raccoon repeated the signaling of her young, and a half-dozen kits scurried from cover and drank under their mother's watchful eye.

Lia and Suzette finally fell asleep but were awakened before dawn with a bawling animal they had never heard before. Suzette rolled up on her saddle and was dumbfounded, staring at a herd of camels on the oasis. She woke Lia, and they watched the herd as the sun drove away the darkness, bringing the dawn of another blistering day. Eli came and got Suzette; Hans had worsened, and he feared the pain was appendicitis. A quick examination by Suzette's confirmed the diagnosis. The right side of Han's stomach was hard as a rock, but he didn't scream when Suzette pressed on it, but the strain was evident on the stoic German's face. There was still hope that Hans' appendicitis would pass, but if the organ burst, it would surely end her friend's life. She walked a short way from Han's wagon and told Eli, "We have one more day to hope for the best. I have never performed an appendectomy, but I watched Jessica do the procedure many times. If he isn't better by tonight, we will have to risk the surgery out here on the trail. Try to find a good place where we can set up a surgery tent and spend some time.

Eli decided they would travel only through the early dawn, and they broke camp to move west. There were more oases than before, and they came to one with a shallow stream about ten miles from their previous camp. Eli stopped the train, and they made camp on the banks of the small river. The water was warm, but it was clean. Suzette still cautioned the men to boil all the water they needed for cooking and drinking, and then she went to check on Hans. This time the man screamed when she pressed on his side. "That's it, Hans, you are going to have to trust me to remove your appendix. I have never done it before, but if it doesn't come out, it's going to burst, and infection will kill you."

Hans was solemn and said in German, "I have trusted you and your brothers with my life all across this continent. I trust you now. Will you put me out?"

"Yes, I wouldn't open you up without putting you out. You don't have a fever yet, so the organ has not burst, but another day of travel and you will be on your deathbed."

Jacques and the rest of the Germans set up the surgery tent in the shade of a huge cottonwood, and Eli helped Hans over to the makeshift hospital. Lia had a large pot of water boiling, and Suzette and Lia were scrubbing their hands profusely. It was stifling inside the tent, but it was necessary to keep the flies away when Suzette opened Han's stomach. Mr. Sue fumigated the tent with a burning piece of camphor, and the few flies trapped in the tent fled before the sweet-smelling smoke. Eli brought Hans into the tent and laid him out on the operating table. Lia gave him a dose of laudanum, and soon, Hans gave a welcome sigh of relief from the pain, and then he was asleep. Suzette retrieved her scalpels and hemostats from the boiling pot and laid them out on a small stand next to the operating table. Sterile sutures and bandages were ready for the closing of the incisions, and Lia lit three lanterns to drive away the darkness inside the tent. Suzette was already sweating, but she was ready to start.

They opened Hans' shirt and pulled his trousers down to expose his abdomen. He was quite hairy at the site of the incision, and Lia dipped a straight razor into the boiling water and then shaved the area where Suzette would do her work. Suzette palpated the area with her fingers and then made the first incision, about four inches long, from his navel towards the top of his pelvic bone. Then she made the second incision directly over the appendix perpendicular to the first and pulled the layers of skin back to expose the muscles. She had an inane thought as she wondered at the whiteness of Hans' stomach compared to his neck and arms, and wondered if her own body was as darkly tanned. Carefully she cut through the muscle, knowing that nicking any of the intestines would bring on a life-threatening infection. With that done and more hemostats to hold open the incision, she reached down with her index finger to feel the swollen appendix. Now Lia handed her the first of two clamping hemostats to flatten the appendix where she would tie off the red, inflamed organ. With the ties complete, she went after the two major blood vessels attached to the appendix.

Sweat was pouring down her back, but Lia kept her forehead reasonably dry. Suzette struggled for breath under the gauze mask that covered her mouth and nose. Taking a break to breathe and dry off was not an option. With the two blood vessels tied off, she was ready to remove the appendix. A quick slice with her scalpel and she drew the offending organ out of Hans' stomach with a set of tongs. It was time to close but not before they irrigated the open wound with alcohol and sprinkled the brown powder that had proved so effective at preventing infection. She started to suture the layers of muscle and skin back together. By the time she finished, she was wringing wet and about to pass out from the heat. Her vision was starting to close in from the sides as she pulled the last stitch tight. She stood up straight from the operating table and slumped to her knees. Mr. Sue grabbed her under her arms and lifted her to her feet and guided her out of the tent. He walked her down to the river and laid her down in the water. The first signs of heatstroke were already showing on her graying skin. The river was warm but cooler than the air or her body temperature, and she was soon gaining back all her faculties. Her vision cleared, some nausea started to abate, and Mr. Sue poured a healthy glass of cool lemonade down her throat. She thought he was trying to drown her, but as she sat there on the sandy bottom of the river, she started to feel better.

The operation was completely textbook except for the addition of the astragalus powder. Mr. Sue commended her on the work and helped her to her feet. There was a small breeze, and she immediately felt cool with the water evaporating from her skin, hair, and clothes. Jacques came down to help her out of the river and asked, "How do you feel? I think you pushed yourself a little too far that time."

"I'll be okay. Get Hans out of that tent before he comes down with heat stroke too."

Jacques did better than that. He and the Germans took the tent down around the surgery table, and Lia wet Hans down, and the cool breeze quickly brought his body temperature down to normal. Lia had the wound neatly bandaged by the time Suzette got back from the river. Hans lay still on the operating table for several hours before the laudanum wore off to let him regain consciousness. He was still euphoric from the opium, and for the moment, had no pain. He wanted to get up, but Suzette and Lia kept him down. In a little while, he was going to have the mother of all side aches, and they didn't want him moving around without the reminder of pain to keep him from damaging the sutures. It was nightfall before they let him move off the table and then only as far as Mr. Sue's cook fire for some chicken soup. They let him eat, and then Suzette insisted that he go to bed. Hans resisted, trying to be tough, but Suzette knew that the next day could be the hardest of his life. She would give him a small dose of the laudanum to ease the first day of travel.

The next morning, they set out again before dawn, and Eli was expecting to stop when the heat of the day became unbearable. Around ten in the morning, a cool breeze blew in from the west, and he decided to keep going. They made more than twenty-two miles that day, and by the time they made camp, the desert was once again cool with the night air rather than the blistering heat of the day. Suzette wondered if the cool breeze blew in off the ocean, but she had no idea how far away that was, and the air did not smell like a sea breeze. The next day they rounded the southern tip of the Vallecito Mountains, and the landscape started to change. There were still cacti on the desert floor, but there were also grass-covered valley floors and springs along the bottom of the mountains.

The Camino de Diablo turned northwest, and everyone was sure they had put the worst of it behind them. They were steadily climbing in elevation, and within two days they were back up in the mountains. Eli stopped at an alpine lake, and the men were fishing, swimming, and laughing in the middle of water fights, having survived the perilous trek across the desert.

Suzette kept a tight rein on Hans. She wouldn't let him drive his wagon or ride sitting up; she also imposed no swimming and no strenuous exercise. He was upset that they were back in a forest, and he wasn't even allowed to chop firewood. In all, though, he was healing nicely without fever or any sign of infection around the wound. Everyone was excited to see the ocean. Every time they crested a rise or rounded a turn in a valley, they would look as far west as possible, but still no ocean. On the morning of their one hundred twenty-third day, they couldn't see the ocean, but they could see a dense fog bank looking down from the mountains to what had to be a broad coastal plain. They were right because by that afternoon, the fog had burned off, and as they came down the low foothills, the vast Pacific Ocean stretched out before them.

That night, they made it down to a Butterfield Stage Station in the San Diego basin. There was a stage getting ready to head out to the east, and Eli let them know that if they wanted to cross the Colorado River, they would have to go down to the port and buy about two hundred yards of a heavy hawser and take it with them. The stagecoach driver asked what happened to the ferry, and Eli filled him in on the shenanigans of Hughes and Huntszinger. The ferry was somewhere in the Gulf of California or aground somewhere far down in the Colorado River Delta. The crew was still there, but they didn't have a ferry to operate. The driver didn't heed the advice and headed out on his run. The best they could do was hope that there was a westbound stage on the east side of the river when they got there. If one was there, they could use rowboats to exchange baggage, freight, and passengers across the river with little interruption of service. It would be unlikely though that two stages would arrive at the river precisely at the same time. The Butterfield Stage, famous for its rapid and timely trips across the continent, was going to have a little tarnish on its reputation.

Now they were only one hundred and twenty miles from Los Angeles. The reality of completing the journey loomed ahead. Suzette no longer cared about how Denise would treat their arrival. She wasn't the young girl that left Missouri four months ago. She was a trail hardened veteran of a harsh, difficult life who had her future planned out despite the ravings or demands of an angered grandmother. She slept soundly that night as the cool air of the fog bank rolled in and enveloped a very tired wagon train. She awoke completely refreshed, made the rounds of her patients, wolfed down her breakfast, and was up on Patches ready to hit the road north before anyone else. They could be in Fort Moore in six days if all went well.

They reached the coast within hours, and everyone ran down to splash in the breakers on the beach. The water was cold, but no one gave a damn. They had made it to the Pacific. Everything else would be easy going compared to the last four months. They spent an hour on the beach and ate their lunch. Felipe was thrilled to fly up and down a beach full of seagulls and terns. The other birds ignored the colorful intruder, and Felipe was getting bored with the stupid birds that didn't want to play. Roland commented that the gulls smelled like dead fish. He doubted that Felipe would find a friend there.

The cool air from the ocean brought refreshing relief, and Suzette felt like she could ride as far as Oregon if she needed to. The road up the coast wasn't just good; it was a highway beaten down and well maintained as a thoroughfare and trade route for nearly two hundred years. Franciscan missions were spaced up along the coast as far as San Francisco. The US Army was fortifying the ports and building up more Army posts to defend against the threat of the southern states, which were posturing for succession. California was still a vast unsettled country, but it was apparent that the landscape was changing rapidly, and it wouldn't take more than a few decades to flood the state with ranchers and farmers. Already there was not a single piece of open land as they headed up the coast from San Diego.

Along the cliffs by the ocean, condors soared on the sea breeze rising from the waves to crest the bluffs. The birds were majestic in the air with their ten-foot wingspans, but ugly on the ground. Roland explained the condors were survivors and could be traced back by fossil records to prehistoric times. They were birds that relied on soaring for flight and needed the cliffs or slopes of the mountains to take to the air. They were carrion eaters and could soar on the air currents and updrafts for days looking for food. He pointed out that these birds probably smelled like dead meat. Again, Felipe soared with the condors but couldn't find a friend even though the seacoast looked like a huge-bird convention. Roland joked that Felipe was looking for a green, red, and blue bird that was female and also a vegetarian.

Out of San Diego, they made good time. In two days, they camped by the Mission of San Juan Capistrano, and Suzette and Lia walked onto the grounds. Suzette asked Lia what Capistrano meant, but the reply wasn't an exact definition. "In Italian *capi* means understand. *Strano* means strange or different. Hard to tell what Saint Juan was thinking about when he named this place. You will have to decide on your own meaning." Suzette laughed, but she knew the missions were built to convert the Indians to Catholicism, but there weren't any Indians around the mission. The lack of the prime reason for being, however, didn't detract from the charm of the thick adobe walls and the hundred-year-old gardens. Bougainvillea adorned almost every wall, and the rich blooms of azaleas and a hundred other flowers she had never seen before, treated the eye of the observer to a vast array of colors. She was wearing Lia out, asking the names of every new species they saw. An elderly Franciscan friar was sitting on a bench near a high wall devoutly praying in a murmur. Above him on the wall were thousands of mud nests. Lia told Suzette that the nests were the makings of cliff swallows. They watched for a while, but there were no swallows to be seen. They walked back to the wagon camp and settled down for the night. The next day they would be in the Los Angeles basin, and the day after that, they would be at the end of their journey – Fort Moore.

END of the LINE

The morning of the one hundred twenty-seventh day found the Callahans within ten miles of their destination. The US Army believed there was a place called Fort Moore Hill, and that was where Eli was to lead the wagon train. His contact was Captain Winfield Scott Hancock, who was the quartermaster of the post. They were camped on a high rise and could see the tall masts of clipper ships in the San Pedro Harbor to the south. The Los Angeles Basin was a huge grassy plain, peppered with haciendas and farms. The land was rich, and wherever there was water, vegetable farms stretched to the foothills of the mountains to the north. It was a spectacular clear morning, but to the northwest, they could see the smoke rising from Los Angeles; a city now purported to have more than four thousand inhabitants.

Eli had his wagon train on the road early. There was a lot of traffic on the road, mostly wagons filled with produce loaded heavy on their way to the city and empty wagons returning. It only took two hours to reach the outskirts of the city, and Angelinos just shrugged their shoulders when Eli asked directions to Fort Moore Hill. One farmer, though, gave them directions to the house of Captain Hancock, and Eli threaded the wagon train through the dirt streets to the other side of town. The streets were dusty but muddy in spots where open sewers drained sewage toward the ocean. Los Angeles just seemed to be a sprawl of wood shacks with markets and squares scattered here and there haphazardly.

Riding ahead with his siblings and Lia, they finally saw a decent sized adobe house surrounded by wagons with the stars and stripes flying from a tall pole in front. Below the stars and stripes flew the flag of the Republic of California. Eli had his wagons pull in and circle the house. Captain Hancock was standing on the porch, ready to greet him. He wore a crisp Army uniform, starched and pressed from head to toe. His boots gleamed in the morning sun as if keeping them polished might be his only duty throughout the day. Eli thought the captain didn't have much to do commanding a single house rather than a full-fledged fort. Maybe he had a good woman behind him to help maintain his military bearing. He rode to the hitching post in front of the house and slid off his saddle at the end of the line.

Hancock extended his hand as Eli introduced himself, "I'm Eli Callahan. I took over from Armstrong."

"I know who you are. Your wagon train and its exploits against the renegades and Indians on the trail fill the front pages of every newspaper that arrives here from the east. Welcome to Fort Moore and Los Angeles, by the way. See that house up there on that hill? There usually is a woman and her husband up there waiting for you. They have been there a month with your uncle who brought them here on his schooner. They left a few days ago with my wife to sail out to Santa Catalina Island. I'm surprised she isn't back here already. Call in your brothers and that gun-slinging sister of yours, and we will go over what is going to happen to the remainder of your supplies and your men."

Eli put his fingers to his lips and let out an ear-splitting whistle. The twins, Lia, and Suzette walked in to join Eli in the Captain's house. The Captain opened a sideboard cupboard and took out a bottle of Callahan Meadows whiskey. "The last bottle in California," Hancock lamented as he broke the seal and started to pour out a round of drinks. "How about you, ladies?" He asked, gesturing with the bottle.

Suzette and Lia both smiled and pushed their glasses forward. Hancock raised his glass, "Here's to the end of the trail."

"To the end of the trail," they all intoned and downed the whiskey. Lia choked a bit and asked for water. Suzette had been tasting whiskey since she was a toddler in the brewery sneaking sips of whiskey with her older brothers; she laughed as she slapped Lia on the back and slammed her glass down on the table. "Hit us again, Captain, we are definitely off duty now," she said as she held up a glass of water to Lia's lips. Captain Hancock poured left to right, but Lia put her hand over the top of her glass as sweat beaded on her forehead while trying to catch her breath, hoping it would return to normal soon.

Roland didn't feel he had to apologize for his wife, but he chuckled and said, "She's not Irish." Everyone laughed as the trail weariness, and tension faded away in the warming air of a beautiful California morning. Felipe flew in the door and landed on Suzette's shoulder. "No whiskey for the bird," Roland said with an admonishing look to Captain Hancock. Everyone laughed again. The captain put the bottle down and motioned to the chairs. He had business to discuss, and the young family was anxious to hear what the end of their journey was going to entail.

Captain Hancock grew serious. "You and all the men in the wagon train are at this moment released from your contracts. Leavenworth to Los Angeles; that was the legal language. The men who started from St. Louis with the same provision; their contractual service terminates here. But I want to offer them jobs as soldiers if they want that, or teamsters in the Army Supply Service if they don't like the idea of wearing the uniform. I am the last man here representing the US Government. I have the authority to recruit, promote, and run things as I see fit. I need men. There is a problem down in the port. The mayor of San Pedro and his sheriff, are essentially imposing martial law down there. They and a force of about forty longshoremen control the town. There is a navy frigate out in the harbor with a few marines, but they are not enough to set things right ashore, and it is a Southern ship to boot. There is a strong constituent of Southerners here who are not slavers but sympathize with the secessionists. Tension runs high; San Pedro leans to the South. I need that port solidly back in US hands before the war starts. The Callahans noticed the reference to the war. Another Army officer resolute that war was inevitable.

The captain paused and drank some water, then went on. "The sheriff is Wendell P. Hastings. About forty longshoremen are the enforcers who back him up. He is the only one in town allowed to carry a gun. The toughs carry bats, but some of them have arms, and no ship gets unloaded without submitting to outrageous port fees. The Angelinos are suffering. There are a lot of supply ships that turn around and go up to San Francisco to unload. I need to put a stop to Hastings and his thugs. The Angelinos went down there a month ago in revolt. Hastings and his thugs killed several in the fighting that ensued, and that is when mayor Ryan Anderson imposed the no weapons ordinance. He and Hastings take the lion's share of the port fees and pay the longshoremen and stevedores a pittance to keep them in cheap booze and whores. I'm asking for your help. I can recruit, and I can promote, but I can't promote to or above my rank. I can make you lieutenants, but that is as far as my authority allows."

Eli slid a mail pouch he was carrying from the commanding officer of Fort Leavenworth across the desk to the captain. Hancock opened the pouch. The pouch carried the usual manifests delineating the contents of the shipment, but there was also an envelope addressed to the Captain. He pulled a knife from a sheath in his boot and slit the envelope open. He read the letter out loud after he skimmed through it and smiled. "It looks like I can now promote up to the level of captain," he said with a broad grin on his face. My wife is going to be pleased with a long-awaited pay increase. What say you guys, can I count on some help to take down Anderson and Hastings?"

Eli spoke up for everyone, "Myself, I don't want to be in the Army, but I will help you take control of San Pedro. Jacques here was thinking about the Army; you might get him to join. Roland is married, and I don't think he is looking for army life for his new bride. I will talk to the men and pitch your offer to them. I am sure some of them will join, and a good deal of the rest will stay with you as Army Supply Service teamsters.

Others want to settle and farm. There is a lot of open lands out there in the valley; I am sure some of them will stay here, and some will go north."

Major Hancock looked seriously at Jacques. "Son, I know you are only seventeen, your grandmother told me. I can't make you an officer because of your age, but you deserve to be a captain. I know you are a natural leader, and I can choose to let the charade of your falsified documents continue if you choose to join. Don't answer until you have had a chance to think about it and discuss it with your family. This nation is going to war with itself; it is not a decision to be made lightly to join an army on the brink of war. For now, I want the contents of wagons 34 & 53 brought around to the storeroom behind my wife's kitchen. There is a steel door on the back; I will have it opened for you. You can pull those wagons around close to the door; the crates are going to be heavy. Bring a squad of your most trusted men to unload them."

Roland asked, "Before we get on with the work, when will our grandmother return?"

A broad smile lit up Major Hancock's face. "She and my wife were driving me nuts. Your uncle took them out several days ago to sail around the island. They should be back by tonight. Your uncle Connor has a schooner full of Irish whiskey. He pulled into San Pedro but refused to pay the port fees. He anchors off the beach at Santa Monica. I expect they will be back in the house on the hill by dark. You could wait for them at the house. Your grandmother rented it for a handsome monthly figure. There are maids, carriage drivers, an excellent cook, and hot water plus smoke-free air blowing in off the ocean. The view is spectacular, and you'll be the envy of the entire city."

Eli got the Germans organized to unload the two wagons and had a layout drawing from Major Hancock as to how he wanted the other wagons organized. The mule teams were led out to a grassy field and pranced around happily, free for the first time to roam since they left Missouri. The crates were heavy as promised, especially two that outweighed all the rest. When the men finished, Major Hancock held Eli back and closed and bolted the outside door. He pried off the lid to one of the heavier crates and pulled back the oilskin packing. The crate was full of ten-dollar gold pieces and bundles of paper currency. "I bet you didn't know you were carrying a fortune. This money is the future of the California Brigade. Soldiers receive ten dollars a month, and now I can contract with the local farmers to feed us. Also, there is going to be a real Fort Moore. It won't be huge because there are no foreign threats out here. There are a lot of Southerners in the area, though, and when the South secedes, there is going to be trouble for a while. Frémont is up north with a garrison of soldiers and will have his hands full up there. Fort Moore will be the only US Army presence west of Fort Fillmore at La Mesilla or the small garrison at Yuma, and both of those are a long way away.

Eli and the Major went back through the house, and Eli called all the men to assemble in front of the makeshift headquarters. He felt some pangs of regret as he started to speak to the men. They had been through a lot together, and the regret was to see them break up and go their separate ways when he finished with his speech. "Men, we have been through hell together, and it's going to be hard to say goodbye here at the end of the line. But there is something I want to ask you to help me get done before we go our separate ways. San Pedro Harbor is in the hands of thugs and crooks. I have told Major Hancock here that I would help him take control of the harbor again, but I couldn't do that without your help. I am asking you to stay together for a few more days so we can go down there and oust the mayor and his crooked sheriff. There are longshoremen down there that help the sheriff hold power in the town. It's going to take some serious muscle to kick their asses out of there."

"Major Hancock is going to make an offer for you to join the Army and stay here as a garrison. Also, those of you who don't want to join the Army will be offered to remain in the Army

Supply Corps. The rest of you are free at this moment to do as, and go as, you please. But I am asking you for your help. My family and I are with the Major. If you are with me in this last adventure, step forward, and the Major will swear you into a posse. Then we will make some plans." To a man, other than Señor Francisco, every man stepped forward, including Juan Pedro.

Major Hancock stepped forward and swore in mass the entire wagon train into the military police department of Los Angeles. Then he turned to Eli and pinned the star of police chief on his shirt collar. Eli released the men so they could prepare dinner and bed down for the night. Mr. Sue stepped forward and spoke up for the first time, "I'm going down to the harbor. No one will notice a Chinaman in a port city on the Pacific Coast. I will look it over and be back by morning. It will be good to see what we are up against."

Eli grasped Mr. Sue hard around the shoulders with his left arm and shook his hand, "Be careful, my friend, we need you. I don't want you shanghaied, and if you aren't back by morning, I'm going to take that town apart by force and find you." Mr. Sue laughed and drew his staff out of the back of his chuck wagon. He waved a parting goodbye and walked south to find the road to the port. Eli gathered up his siblings and his sister-in-law and drove them up the hill to the house, a warm bath, a hot meal, and a good night's sleep. Suzette rode behind the wagon on Patches, Juan Pedro, at her side on the big black stallion. Señor Francisco followed along as if not sure what to do with himself and his grandson now that the long journey was over. Suzette and Juan handed over their mounts to the stable hands waiting to greet them. They looked up at the house and marveled at the size of it and its elegant trappings. Suzette and Lia couldn't wait to be clean and well-fed. They walked up the stairs and weren't surprised that the house ran like a hotel. The manager, Mr. Lloyd Jones, introduced his staff, and when Eli started to introduce his party, Jones stopped him and said, "We know all your names except for these Spaniards."

Eli introduced Señor Francisco and Juan Pedro then he asked, "Do you have room for six more men? I have some German friends down at the post that I would like to bring up here." The manager answered that he did if the men bunked up two to a room. He sent one of the Chinese house boys down to get Hans and his men. Suzette and Lia retrieved their things from the wagon and went upstairs to the promise of luxury. The men settled down in a large parlor that served as a bar and drank several more rounds of Irish whiskey they drew directly from a cask, as they started planning for the confrontation down at San Pedro. By the time the women came back down clean and smelling like lilacs, the men were on the verge of total drunkenness. The Germans were in the parlor, and all but Hans were also drunk. Hans was healed up but still had some pain and didn't want to add a hangover to his problems.

Suzette said, "You better get serious and sober up some. There is a telescope on the landing outside our rooms, and I saw a grey schooner coming into shore before I came down. It won't be long; we'll be seeing our grandmother." The lady who ran the kitchen was Mrs. Cheryl Jones; she brought in coffee and warm apple pie. A younger girl, a spitting image of her mother, brought in sandwiches and cookies. Everyone ate and laughed a bit about not being sober when they met up with Denise. As they thought more about Denise, a foreboding of the unexpected dampened the spirit of the impromptu *End of the Line Party*. It wasn't long after they finished eating that they heard a carriage plodding its way up the hill on the cobblestone lane. Everyone rose as one and went to the front porch to watch the carriage come around the last turn of the switchbacks and pull up to the columned entrance of the house. The carriage was nothing more than a stagecoach dressed in finer clothes.

The driver got down and opened the door of the coach and put down a stool. He helped the first person down; it was Lily with Ben behind her. Suzette smiled and whooped for joy and ran down the steps and threw her arms around Lily, almost crying with the happiness for the unexpected reunion. Denise stepped down from the coach, stunned by the swarthy appearance of her grandchildren. Suzette left Lily's embrace and turned to her grandmother with open arms. Denise took Suzette in her arms, and after a long hug and several kisses said with tears in her eyes, "Thank God, you're safe." The boys came down the steps and joined in a group hug. Lia hung back, unsure if the matriarch of the family was going to accept her.

Roland sensed her tension and turned Denise out of the group and said, "I would like you to meet my wife, Lia." Lia met Denise's eyes then demurred, eyes downcast with a reverent curtsy.

Denise ascended the stairs, took Lia's hands, and said, "Welcome to the family." Then she took Lia in her arms and turned to Roland and said, "I wanted to be mad, but I can't conjure up the spirit for it. You have all done incredibly well." At that point, she started sobbing uncontrollably. Irwin and Connor had stepped down from the coach and after shaking hands with the boys, walked up and held Denise. Lily went up the stairs, and Suzette noticed the large knife she still carried in a scabbard on her back. Like the Lefaucheux on her hip, the Bowie Knife was Lily's signature weapon of choice. Suzette couldn't wait to talk to the older woman. She knew Lily was a seer and a healer, well versed in West African herbal medicines.

Lily took Lia's hands and said in perfect Spanish," Hola, mi nombre es Lily. Me encanta tu cabello." Then she turned to Roland and asked in a quiet voice, "Did you know she is pregnant?"

Roland was stunned, and then a look of fantastic joy swept the surprise from his face, and he shouted, "Hey everybody, Lily says Lia is pregnant." Then, seeing his wife deeply troubled, he realized that Lia didn't know Lily was capable of knowing that. He took her aside to explain.

Mrs. Hancock was the last out of the coach, and she walked up to Lia and said, "I can help explain." She took Lia aside and explained Lily's gift in a long dialog in Spanish that only Suzette and the Spaniards understood. Suzette hugged her sister-in-law and assured her again that it wasn't the work of the devil and that Lily was a famous clairvoyant.

Mrs. Jones called everyone into the dining room. A large feast was laid out with fresh fish from the ocean with crab and a variety of meats including fresh fowl, beef, and pork. The centerpiece was a full roasted lamb surrounded by mint jelly. Major Hancock had arrived and sat next to his wife. Roland helped seat Lia, holding her long flowing hair up, then laid a loop around her neck and let the rest stream down her back. It still reached the floor but not by much. Lia sat on one side of Denise and Suzette on the other. Suzette took her grandmother's hand and said, "I'm sorry I caused you so much worry."

The look in her eyes and the sincerity in her voice brought tears to Denise's eyes again. "I was angry for quite a while; I'll admit that. But then I was just worried and scared. I read all the newspapers glamorizing your exploits on your journey west. Did you kill all those people, or was that journalistic exaggeration? Your exploits sold a lot of papers?"

"I did kill them; they weren't people you would want to know. They were savages, outlaws, and renegades. We didn't have a choice; it was a matter of survival. We were better equipped, tougher, and smarter. We did what had to, and nothing more." Suzette thought about the Apache she shot in the back on the San Pedro River and wondered if all of what she said was completely true. The front door was opened wide with sunlight and fall air filling the foyer. Suddenly a shadow dulled the bright sunlight, and an ear-piercing scream split the air. Felipe hovered in the foyer, then saw the group around the dining room table off to the right. He flew into the dining room and landed on Denise's shoulder. She let out a scream, and Felipe screamed back. He spread his wings as she stood to shake him off but then sat back down heavily, there was no getting rid of the bird, and there was nowhere to run. Felipe screamed again, this time, "Apache, Apache!" The only word he knew for danger. Juan Pedro stood up and took the bird off Denise's shoulder. That is when it started.

First, there was a rumble like an approaching freight train. Then the floor started to vibrate, and finally, it shook. The chandelier above the table swayed back and forth, and Mrs. Jones ran through the hall to the front door shouting, "Earthquake, everyone out." Felipe had no trouble; he took wing and followed Mrs. Jones and the kitchen staff out the door. Everyone else was having trouble standing and walking straight. Suzette and Lia each grabbed Denise by her arms and were nearly dragging her toward the front door. Irwin came up behind her and scooped Denise up in his arms, knowing his wife was too terrified to move on her own. Juan Pedro steadied Suzette and walked her out the door. Roland did the same for Lia. They were all safe standing in the drive in front of the house. It was easier to sit down on the lawn in the middle of the carriage circle. Irwin just knelt on the grass with Denise still in his arms. Eli looked around to account for everyone. Jacques was not with them.

There was a resounding crack from the house, and dust swirled in the air as the colonnade of the portico started dancing, separated from the house. Jacques walked out of the front door with a roasted goose under one arm and a platter of Dungeness crab under the other. He cleared the steps and was halfway across the drive when the porch collapsed behind him. The cast iron gargoyle that guarded the entrance to the elegant home broke free of the roof, and clanking like a dull bell rolled to a stop at Jacque's feet. He grinned, "Picnic, anyone?"

The ground shook for another two minutes and then quieted down. There was much shouting and scurrying around in the town down below. Several fires broke out, no doubt from overturned stoves or cracked hearths and toppled chimneys. Suzette grabbed a drumstick and started down the hill. "I have to get to my medical bag," was all she said and let out her ear-piercing whistle. Patches came bounding around the house. Suzette caught a handful of mane as Patches slid to a stop and swung up on her back and galloped down the road riding bareback. Juan Pedro was starting to go around the house when the big stallion came around in a fast trot. Juan leaped upon his back, not quite as graceful as Suzette with one arm still in its cast, but managed to stay on the big stud's back as he nudged him into a long loping stride and followed Suzette down the hill.

The houses in the town were nothing more than shanties and faired a lot better than the front porch of the mansion. Other than the fires, there wasn't much apparent damage. Suzette retrieved her medical bag from Mr. Sue's chuckwagon and headed for the town square. There were no injuries among the teamsters and swampers and Hans, and the rest of the Germans arrived at a run. There were injuries in the town but nothing serious. Suzette treated burns and one trampled foot and set two broken arms and one leg. She was busy setting the leg when she looked up and saw Denise watching her. Denise wasn't seeing a granddaughter. She was seeing a trail hardened young woman going about the business of making people well. Hans and his men circled her, Henry rifles at the ready. One young mother was desperate to have Suzette treat her boy of three. He had been hit in the head by a falling lintel trying to leave their house.   He had a prodigious bump on his head, but his eyes were clear and responsive, and the boy was calm, but the young mother was frantic. Hans had to hold her back while Suzette treated the more serious cases first.

There was a doctor who serviced the Los Angeles area. He strode into the circle of Hans' men and almost yelled with a voice of authority, "What do you think you are doing?" He was enraged and taken aback to have a young woman treating his potential patents. It was obvious he wasn't ready for women doctors in his world, especially one who was still a teenager. "You need to stop," he yelled again. Suzette walked over to him and drew her Lefaucheux and pressed the barrel up under his chin. She didn't have to say anything. The doctor backed away and withdrew more concerned to find patients that could pay rather than taking care of the poor who suffered on his doorstep.

Hans tipped his hat and said, "Have a nice day, Doc."

Denise looked on in wonder. When Suzette finished looking over the little boy with the bump on his head, she walked up and hugged her granddaughter, not knowing what to say. Irwin reached over and gave Suzette an affectionate rub and pat on the shoulder. Denise said, "You have learned a lot since you left Missouri. I can't tell you how proud of you we are."

Suzette smiled and closed her medical bag. Eli pulled up with his wagon, and everyone from the house walked back to the wagon train. There were aftershocks but nothing like the first earthquake. No one wanted to sleep in the great house on the top of the hill. They were comfortable laying out their bedrolls and getting ready for the night ahead. Suzette gave her grandmother her comfortable bed up in the wagon, and Connor had Irwin bed down with the men. Suzette sat up till well after two in the morning talking to Lily and Ben. She wanted to hear all about Africa and South America, and everywhere they had been since they left Missouri some years ago. She was most interested in the voodoo medicine that Lily had documented in her travels. The three of them finally fell asleep sitting by the fire. Sunrise would soon find them slouched against the logs around the fire pit. Suzette had fallen asleep, holding Lily's hand. She was still holding it when Felipe crowed like a rooster to signal the dawn.

Suzette and Lia stirred to the rooster crow and the smell of Mr. Sue's coffee. "Mr. Sue is back from the port," she muttered as she rolled over to get up, still stiff from falling asleep on the ground. Mr. Sue handed her and Lily a cup of coffee as they walked up to his chuck wagon.

"We need to assemble everyone and talk about the port," he said as he was turning bacon in his large frying pan. Suzette went off to wake her brothers. She was still stiff and regretting that the big house on the hill had suffered damaged in the earthquake. She was looking forward to enjoying the luxury of a roof over her head again, but let it pass. There would be plenty of time to live civilized once again when she got to San Francisco. Her brothers were still sound asleep under Eli's wagon. The camp was stirring awake. However, some of the men stayed up all night, waiting for another earthquake. Mr. Sue had their breakfast ready. He told Eli to assemble the men after breakfast, and he would report on what was going on down at the port.

They were just about done eating when a large black man with several helpers pulled into the camp. It was Moses from the ferry operation on the Colorado River. He walked to Eli and said, "Good morning, boss. I've followed you over here to buy another rope for the ferry. I know I can find that down at the port, but a lot of people over in the valley told me not to go down there, so I came to look you up. What's happening at the port, anyways?"

Eli invited him and his men to sit down and finish off the breakfast vitals and let him know that Mr. Sue would bring everyone up on events down at the port as soon as Major Hancock arrived. Moses and his men had already eaten, but being a big man, he had no trouble cleaning up the rest of the leftovers. Major Hancock and Uncle Connor arrived before the newcomers were finished eating. Mr. Sue was invited to report, and he stepped into the middle of the group and waited for everyone to quiet down before he spoke.

"The situation down at the port is not good. The longshoremen treat the Chinese no better than slaves, and there are beatings and killings to keep them in line. They treat the Mexicans no better. The mayor and the sheriff have fifty or more longshoremen armed with bats to enforce the no gun policy. The longshoremen have taken over one of the hotel buildings that has a balcony, and they have fortified it with sandbags and have armed guards on the roof with rifles at all times. The hotel is the tallest building in town and is smack dab in the middle of Main Street with a commanding view of everything from the north edge of town down to the docks at the port. The hotel is a fortress, and I assume that they have rifles and shotguns for all of the longshoremen. There is a Navy frigate in the port named *The Heart of the South*. There is a small contingent of marines on the frigate, but they stay out of town. The US Navy is not ready to shell the town and take it by force. They may be waiting for more troops to arrive, but for the time being, they are just laying-to, waiting to see what happens."

Major Hancock spoke up, "Do any of you men want to take up my offer of enlistment in the army?" More than thirty of Eli's teamsters and swampers raised their hands. They were ready to be sworn in. The rest were either going to stay in the valley to farm or travel further north to the San Joaquin or Sacramento Valleys to do the same. A couple of the Germans were going to head north until they found the timber industry either in Northern California or Oregon. To a man, whether they were in the Army or not, they were going down to the port with the Callahans.

Connor was the next to speak. "If you give me a day to sail down there and get in position, I can take care of the hotel as long as it is visible from the port." Mr. Sue assured him he could see the port clearly from the front porch of the hotel, but Major Hancock asked Connor how he intended to do that with just a schooner.

"The *Blessed by the Wind* is far more than just a schooner," Connor replied. "It has two rifled six-inch guns amidships that have an accurate range of more than three miles. If the hotel is a problem, I can take it down in a matter of seconds." As if to add credence to his statement, the earth offered up a mild aftershock to emphasize his point. Everyone looked around at each other, hardly believing the ominous warning shuttered by the earth. Eli and his siblings knew the exploits of the *Blessed,* and all nodded their agreement that the hotel would not be a problem.   Major Hancock commented that if he fired on the port, the frigate is going to treat the schooner like any pirate ship on the high seas. Connor laughed, "It will be a cold day in hell when I can't outsail a frigate. I've already fought one some years ago in the Caribbean, and while I don't want to kill a US Navy ship, I will do it if they force me into a battle for survival."

Major Hancock asked, "What will you do if they come after you?"

"Sail away to China," was Connor's comfortable reply delivered with a shrug of his shoulders.

Major Hancock ended the meeting with, "We'll be at the gates of the town by 4:00 PM tomorrow if that is enough time for you to sail down there and get into position. For now, it is time for a swearing-in ceremony and to put some men in uniform."

Conner had one more thing to say. "When you come down to the port, I will be flying a green flag from my mainmast. If the flag isn't up, hold off. I will raise it as soon as possible. If the frigate doesn't come out to give chase, I will anchor up here off the beach to take Denise and Irwin to San Francisco. I'll take anybody else that wants to hop a ride."

Suzette was the first to speak. "I won't leave my horse. I will be riding up." She looked over to see her grandmother's worried look. She was hoping that Denise wasn't going to argue that she would go with her on the boat. She didn't want to defy her grandmother again, but she was going with the men to the port, and when she left Los Angeles, she was going to San Francisco on Patches.

SAN PEDRO

I t was a glorious Southern California morning, and everyone was sound asleep when a cannon blast and a bad rendition of *Revile* welcomed the camp to a new day; the first day of army life for more than half the teamsters and swampers. The soldiers were split off from the wagon train in a camp a hundred yards or so, but a cannon blast before dawn jolts the unconscious core of even the weariest dreamer into the reality of another day. The revile that welcomed the new enlistees to their first day of army life also woke Los Angeles. The citizens were aware that morning that Fort Moore was no more a forgotten, nearly abandoned outpost. Mr. Sue was up before dawn as usual and had hot coffee, pancakes, and bacon already cooking on his stove as the sleepy Callahans rolled out of their beds. Suzette, Roland, and Lia, along with Irwin and Denise, chose to risk sleeping in the house on the hill. *Lucky devils,* Eli thought as he drank in his first sip of coffee and flexed his sore shoulders from sleeping on the ground.

Major Hancock was over forming up his soldiers in ranks and told them they would be marching down to San Pedro, and they would be learning the ins and outs of close-order drill after breakfast. The Major came over to find Eli and asked him to provide enough wagons to transport tents, provisions, and arms down to San Pedro to set up a temporary camp for his troops. Eli agreed to take care of it but reminded Major Hancock that he was just a police chief now and not a wagon master. The major would have to appoint a wagon master for his newly formed supply train. Eli recommended a man who he thought would be up to the task.

After mess, Major Hancock issued arms and ammunition from the storeroom. The Major formed up and inspected his troops. Shirttails were tucked in, tunics were buttoned, and one-by-one, the soldiers straightened the lines of the ranks. The troops organized into four squads, one consolidated infantry platoon. A man named Flanigan stepped forward; he had been in the Army in Maryland. Major Hancock promoted him to Platoon Sergeant and handed him the stripes of a Staff Sergeant. Since Flanigan knew all the men, Major Hancock let the new sergeant pick his squad leaders. Four new soldiers beamed with pride as Sergeant Flanigan handed his new squad leaders their corporal stripes. The chain of command took shape. The US Army didn't return to Fort Moore; it simply appeared from the trail hardened men of Eli's wagon train.

Eli and Jacques organized the wagons that would move the troops and supplies to San Pedro, and the soldiers broke camp, loaded their tents and bedrolls on the wagons, and formed up to start the march south. Eli and Jacques went up to the big house for breakfast with the rest of the family. Word had gotten out that the troops were marching down to the port, and the Angelinos were mulling around. It was obvious that a good number of them would be following the troops down to watch the action and take retribution against the mayor and the sheriff's thugs who took part in killing their friends the month before. Major Hancock was going to have a situation on his hands and was briefing his troops that there would be martial law in San Pedro after they arrested the mayor and sheriff. He wasn't going to leave matters in the hands of angry citizens, and he made that clear to the citizen militia, forming up behind his soldiers.

The Callahans were saddling up their mounts, and Irwin and Denise had the carriage hooked up and readied to go. Suzette was on the balcony with the telescope and saw their uncle raise his sails and turn the grey schooner south for the short trip down the coast. Connor wouldn't take anyone from the house with him in case the frigate in the harbor gave chase, forcing him to flee for China. There was a light breeze blowing in off the ocean, the *Blessed by the Wind* would have no trouble arriving at the port long before Major Hancock's column reached the north boundary of the port city. That is where Hastings had posted the **NO WEAPONS BEYOND THIS POINT** sign. There were going to be a lot of guns south of the sign later in the day, but they wouldn't be under the command of Hastings. It would be the first offensive battle the new Army platoon would fight, and Major Hancock would control when, where, and how it would happen. Eli remembered the offensive move they made on the renegades back in Kansas. He knew the men would perform well, but San Pedro was no open prairie, this could turn into an ugly street fight with Major Hancock starting in an exposed position on the north end of Main Street. Today would be a different kind of day. He hoped his uncle's big guns would provide the intimidation needed to make the thugs turn and run. Still, the town would not be secure until every last one of the mayor's outlaws embraced the new order of military command in San Pedro.

As usual, Denise wanted Suzette to hang back and not be in the middle of the fight. Suzette calmly told her, "I am always at the beginning, the middle, and at the end of the fight with my medical bag. There is no way my brothers are going down there without me."

Denise tried to get Lia to hold back but got the same resistance. "I will be with my husband," Lia informed her. And with that, the Callahans and Juan Pedro mounted up and rode down the switchbacks to join Major Hancock at the front of his column. Irwin and Denise followed in the carriage, and Señor Francisco pulled in behind them with his wagon. Felipe was already up in the air circling, looking for Apaches. Denise thought she should buy a publishing house in San Francisco; this was going to be one hell of a story.

Denise was startled as they were waiting for Major Hancock to give the order *Forward March* when a reporter jumped into the carriage. He introduced himself as Edward Sigler and asked if he could ride along. "I go where the Callahans go. I came in on the Butterfield Stage, and I am glad I got here before they went down to San Pedro."

Denise asked, "You're the reporter who has been glamorizing my grandchildren, aren't you?'

"Yes, madam. Only reporting the facts, though, their's is a story that makes its own glamor. And you are the famous Denise Higgins, right?"

"Yes, I am, but I am not sure the Callahan saga should go on and on. I don't want them being *western heroes* to interfere with them having normal lives. The fame you have created has already followed them everywhere and will continue as long as you keep exploiting them for the sake of newspaper sales. Trust me; I know how this works. You are going to make them targets. Every wanna-be gun-happy kid will be looking to make his mark by taking one of them down. You are just setting them up for more danger. I would rather, you, quit. What would that take to make you quit?"

"I'll never quit. Reporting and writing is my life, and if I don't write their story, someone else will. I can assure you that I have not glamorized the facts. I don't need to. They make their news sensational, and your granddaughter is emerging as a symbol for women's rights. Trust me on this. She is changing how women think of themselves, and she is going to be in the news for a long time to come." He opened his satchel and handed Denise a manuscript, the rough draft of a book. The title was *Westward Ho Perils*.

Denise paged through the manuscript and then asked, "Is this complete?"

"It will be after today. I wasn't expecting anything to happen after the journey's end here in Los Angeles. It's obvious there is going to be more to write about."

"What if I offer to buy the book? I, just now, decided to buy or start a newspaper in San Francisco. You could be my first employee, but I would require that you do not report on today's events until then without my review and approval. I'll offer you two hundred dollars right now if you agree, and you can join us for the rest of the trip up to San Francisco. We are going by schooner, I think."

"Mrs. Higgins, you and I have just become best friends." Irwin rolled his eyes, thinking, *here we go again*. The carriage lurched forward as Denise and Edward Sigler was reaching across shaking hands. Irwin took his heavy money belt off and took out ten Double Eagles and paid Sigler with the gold. A different day indeed was underway.

Major Hancock was on foot with his men; his horse trailed behind the first supply wagon. Sergeant Flanigan called out, "Left, left, left right left," as he started marching down the road to the port. Slowly the men caught on and matched him step for step. Paul Hayman ran up to the major and asked him if he could teach the soldiers a marching song. Paul wasn't in a uniform, but the major agreed, and Paul led the men through *The Girl I Left Behind*, stanza by stanza. Within two miles, the men had the song down pat, and it lightened the march as the men moved forward as a polished army unit in a close order drill. The cool air of the ocean breeze made the morning march tolerable, and most of the men were enjoying it.

Halfway to San Pedro, Major Hancock stopped the column and had them break out their rations for lunch. He used the time off the road to brief his men on how they would react if and when the shooting broke out. He was hoping, along with the rest of the soldiers, that San Pedro would not turn into a live fire situation, but he would have them prepared for the worst if that were how it would unfold. He would be on his horse with the Callahans at the front of the column. The men would break into two units and take the town building by building, working their way down both sides of Main Street.

After mess, the men formed up again, and Mr. Sue fell in on the side of the column with Paul Hayman and used his staff like a drum major keeping time – up and down – as Paul taught the men another stanza of *The Girl I Left Behind;* a British tune that saw sailors and soldiers off to war. Their voices boomed for a good distance, and more people came to line the road and watch the soldiers marching to San Pedro. A good many of them fell in behind the militia, curious to know what was happening, or some followed along to enjoy the parade. The soldiers sang:

It was clumsy and discordant at first but was sung well after the fourth or fifth attempt.

The day passed, but the column still reached San Pedro early. Major Hancock had his army issue spyglass out and could see the schooner in the harbor; as of yet, there was no green flag flying from its mainmast. Major Hancock had the men make camp east of the road; he wanted it made clear that the Army was going to be in town for some time to come. He wasn't surprised when Sheriff Hastings rode out to greet him. The sheriff wasn't the most impressive lawman the west had to offer. He slithered out of his saddle in front of the Major's command tent and staggered a bit as a soldier held the flap up for him to enter. He was shabbily dressed, unshaven, and smelled of heavily of rotgut whiskey. A rusty Colt Navy 0.44 caliber revolver hung at his hip. Hastings wasn't just a shabby sheriff; he was far less than a gunman.

"Whatdaya think yer doin, Hancock? Someun could be burnin Los Angeles down while you be down here on a campin trip. Yer soldiers are welcome down in the saloons and brothels, but they have to leave their guns here." Hastings must have felt like he was on a roll yelling at the Major, and he slurred on, "Who're the two lookers out there? If they are the camp whores, I could offer you five hundred apiece for um. Whatdaya say, Hancock?"

Major Hancock stood up, "I say get out of here now before you fall on your ass or I knock you on it. We are coming into town, and we aren't leaving our guns behind. You threaten those two women, and this could be your last day on earth. Now get out of here and sober up." The Major nodded at his two guards, and they grabbed Hastings by both arms and escorted him out. Hastings was still trying to yell at the Major, but between the alcohol and the anger, he couldn't put a coherent sentence together. The soldiers got him up on his horse and then slapped the horse on the rump, and Hastings was riding back into town like a child holding onto the pommel with both hands. Hastings fell off the horse as he turned into Main Street. The camp roared with laughter and cheered Hastings on as he pulled himself up out of the dust and gave the full-arm obscene salute with a bleeding right forearm before stomping off down Main Street.

"So much for the element of surprise," said Eli, but a surprise was out of the question with a full Army platoon parked on your doorstep. No matter what they did, Hastings and his thugs would be ready for them. Jacques was watching the schooner with his spyglass. He could see the crew was shifting whiskey barrels to the starboard side of the boat to make the *Blessed* list in that direction, raising the port gun to bear on the balcony of the Longshoremen's Hotel. Shortly after three, the green flag rose on the mainmast. Anchored bow and stern, the schooner was a dead steady gun platform with hardly a wave in the harbor to spoil the lay of the gun.

Major Hancock gave the signal for his troops to form up. The Callahans, along with Juan mounted up, and the six of them rode over in front of the column and then walked the horses to the north boundary of San Pedro, where Hasting's sign barred armed men from town. Major Hancock threw a rope around the sign and pulled it out of the ground, backing his horse up with the rope around the pommel. He could see Hastings two blocks further south forming up his thugs and sending them to secluded positions up and down Main Street. Hastings, with a longshoreman on either side armed with bats, was waiting for the soldiers to make their move. Hancock and the Callahans got off their mounts and started walking down toward the sheriff. Mr. Sue and Hans held the horses. The troops moved along behind them, scanning the alleys and rooftops of each block of the town as they advanced.

Suzette looked up at a two-story building on the west side of the street that was a saloon and a brothel by the looks of the women in the windows and on the balcony of the second story. She saw a beautiful Asian girl in a sheer light blue dress. She thought she would return in a while when they had the town settled down and see if she could buy the dress. There had to be another one there for Lia; red would be her choice of color to contrast with her black hair and caramel-colored skin. *How silly,* she thought to herself, *here I am on the brink of a serious gunfight thinking about shopping.*

They walked up to Hastings, and Major Hancock threw the sign down at his feet. "Hastings, you are under arrest for failing in your oath to uphold the constitution of the United States."

"Yer talkin bullshit Major. No guns allowed is the law in San Pedro."

"Stand down, Hastings, and hand over your sidearm. We're going down to arrest the Mayor, and you are coming with us." Major Hancock raised his right arm, and the entire platoon raised their rifles aiming at twenty or so men on the balcony of the Longshoremen's Hotel. The men on the balcony raised rifles and shotguns and trained them on the troops.

All was dead still, and the tension in the air was palpable. The citizens of San Pedro were watching from their windows. They expected the Army to arrest Hastings and Mayor Anderson, but suddenly the thought of bloodshed in the streets brought an overwhelming feeling of dread. Not all the townspeople had that reaction, however. Many of them armed themselves ready to join the fight with guns they had hidden after Mayor Anderson and Sheriff Hastings made them illegal. It seems like Anderson's no gun ordinance had little effect on disarming anyone but the most naïve of the people.

Hasting showed the first signs of fear as guns started to appear in the windows and doors up and down Main Street.

But he held his ground knowing even his drunken state that Major Hancock would be loath to fire upon citizens of the United States. But as in all confrontations, there is always the possibility of a wild card -- the unexpected. Felipe, who was content sitting on Juan Pedro's shoulder, eyeing a bird of his species tethered on a stand on the second story of a Chinese market several doors down the street suddenly took flight. He rose up about twenty feet in the air and flew right at Hastings. His aim was deadly as he let fly a long stream of white parrot poop that hit Hastings right in the chest. Hastings swore an oath and drew his revolver and fired three shots at Felipe. A wing shot is hard enough with a shotgun when you are sober, but miserably impossible while drunk with a sidearm and an eye full of parrot poop, however, the shots sealed his fate.

The whine of an artillery round screamed in from the harbor and hit the side of the Longshoremen's Hotel right below the balcony. The shell blew up as designed about ten feet inside the wall, and longshoremen rained down on the street as the balcony collapsed. Hastings turned with the pistol still raised, and Suzette, with her signature move, drew and shot the gun out of Hastings' hand. While the gun was flying through the air, she splintered the bats the thugs were carrying with two quick shots. She then pressed the Lefaucheux up under Hastings' chin and pushed him back down the street. "Let's go see your friend, the mayor." When Hastings didn't move fast enough, she pressed harder, and after a couple of steps, Suzette stood on his toe, and he tumbled over backward. "Get up asshole," and she kicked him in the bottom of his right foot.

The soldiers deployed down alleys on both sides of the street. There was some shooting from behind the Longshoremen's Hotel, but after that brief skirmish, the troops moved down the street, building by building without sustaining any casualties. One thug tried to run into a clothing store, but a blast from both barrels of a 12-gauge shotgun blew him back out the door. Suzette put her 9mm in Hastings' back and said, "Walk if you want to live another day." Hastings had seen the thug fall lifeless on his back on the boardwalk in front of the clothing store, and he knew he had lost control of the port city. The street was full of bleeding and moaning longshoremen from the balcony. Several of them that must have been right above the exploding shell lay riddled with shrapnel, as lifeless as the man on the boardwalk.

There was more shooting from the side streets as they walked down through town. A man rose up on the balcony of the Palace Hotel with a rifle, and Lia shot him before he could swing around and take aim. The standoff collapsed completely, and many thugs were running down the street towards the harbor. No doubt, they would be shipping out soon. Felipe was up on the bird perch over the Chinese market with the other macaw, and from his dancing around and bobbing his head, it was apparent that he had finally found one of his kind and a female at that. Suzette kept Hastings moving toward City Hall as more and more citizens joined their march.

When they got down to City Hall, Major Hancock tried the heavy doors and found them bolted. Juan Pedro rode up on his stallion, and they looped a rope through the handles. The big horse pulled the doors out of the wall, and they fell with a resounding thud on the boardwalk. Suzette walked Hastings in and stood him in front of the mayor's desk. Anderson's eyes were the size of saucers even though he had two armed guards at his sides. He reached to open a drawer on his right, and Suzette shot the little derby off his head. "I have one round left and a dozen soldiers at my back. Which one of you wants to be the first to die today?" Anderson stood up and raised his hands, palms outward in the universal sign of supplication. The armed men dropped their guns and fled through the back door of the office.

Major Hancock strode into the office and told Anderson, "You're all done here, Ryan, now open your safe."

Anderson shook his head *no,* and the major shot the brass ship's clock off the wall next to Anderson's head. Then he pointed his 0.44 right at Anderson's head and calmly said, "One." Anderson was on his knees in front of the safe working the combination before Hancock could say two. His hands were shaking, and he failed to get the combination right on the first and second try. Roland and Lia had walked into the office, and Roland pushed Anderson aside and demanded the combination. Anderson shook his head *no* again, and Roland punched him hard in the solar plexus. Anderson wheezed out a breath and fell to his knees. He reached over to his desk and pulled out the writing shelf and turned it over.   The combination was a series of numbers painted on the bottom of the shelf. Roland opened the safe on the first try. The safe was full of bundled bills and stacks of gold coins, mostly US Double Eagles, but some of every country on earth that minted gold coins.

"That's my money," Anderson pleaded, still clutching his stomach with tears in his eyes.

Major Hancock was unsympathetic. "Taken at the expense of every citizen in this valley!   It looks to me there is enough there to build several schools and at least one hospital here and another up in Los Angeles. Take heart Anderson; we may even put your name on a couple of new buildings."

Hans and two soldiers escorted Anderson and Hastings out into the street. There was a large crowd of townspeople now along with the Angelinos that came down to witness the demise of the mayor and his sheriff. The crowd demanded that Major Hancock charge the two crooks with the murder of their friends and neighbors. Some Chinese families were there demanding that their daughter's release from the brothel. Sergeant Flanigan and several soldiers escorted the Chinese down to the brothels, and the families went about collecting up their girls. The Mexicans were no way as docile as the Chinese. They were demanding that the Major lynch the two crooks on the spot. The soldiers formed a circle around the two detainees to protect them from the angry crowd. San Pedro had a one-room jail behind the mayor's office, and the soldiers took their prisoners over to it and locked them up. Major Hancock had his men loading the heavy safe onto a wagon. It took more than a dozen men to lift it in, and the mules groaned as they pulled it out of town.

No one gave a thought to the *Blessed* as the action wound down in town. When Eli finally looked down Main Street into the harbor, the grey schooner was gone. The *Heart of the South* was making sail to give chase, but the winds were not favorable for turning the big frigate in the narrow estuary. The Callahans wondered when they would see their uncle again, but also rued the loss of a whole ship full of Irish whiskey. Hopefully, the big frigate would give up on trying to pursue the *Blessed*. The lithe schooner could sail almost directly into the wind. The big frigate couldn't come close to matching the seaworthiness of the smaller craft. No doubt, the captain of the frigate was thinking he didn't want to catch the schooner after seeing what it could do with its concealed gun.

Reports were coming in from the soldiers, not a single casualty, not even a wound. The longshoremen that were close to the shell that exploded under the balcony were dead before they hit the street. The local San Pedro doctor treated the rest of the injured longshoremen. There was little for Suzette and Lia to do.

Suzette and Lia asked Mr. Sue to go with them, and they went to the brothels on the north end of Main Street. Suzette wanted to buy the blue dress and also find one for Lia. When they approached the first brothel, Felipe was cuddling up to the female macaw over the grocery store, continuing his courtship. The Madam had two girls waiting for their families out on the boardwalk. Suzette asked Mr. Sue to inquire about the blue dress, and the Madam directed them to a seamstress' shop on the street west of Main Street. Denise joined up with them, and they marveled at the beautiful dresses in the windows of the shop. The seamstress was an elderly Chinese woman who took an immediate shine to Mr. Sue. She sat the three women down in a viewing area and had a servant bring them tea and rice cakes while an endless stream of young Asian girls modeled the dresses. Denise was impressed to see a fashion show with wares every bit as good as New York had to offer. They each bought an evening gown. Suzette got her blue dress, sheer silk brocade with a slit skirt that would show her thigh clear up to her underwear. Lia bought a deep maroon one with a plunging neckline and a white stole that could be used for modesty or flipped aside in an alluring gesture. Denise settled for a more matronly gown of a simple cut with peach color and white lace trim. The three women tried on the dresses, and dressmakers made minor alterations on the spot.

Mr. Sue had summoned the carriage while the women were shopping and loaded their purchases as the girls walked to a cobbler down the street. Denise said she was going down to the Palace Hotel to see if they would rent out their ballroom for a dance. The girls didn't feel like a dance, but Denise argued, "After all, what's the use of buying beautiful gowns if you don't have a place to show off your wares?" Mr. Sue went with Denise, worried that there might still be some of Hastings thugs out and about the neighborhood. He knew Suzette and Lia could take care of themselves.

And the girls did just that. Each bought several pairs of fancy shoes to match their gowns and a new pair of boots for the trip up the coast to San Francisco. Mr. Sue's concerns were justified as two rough-looking men stepped out of an alley as Suzette and Lia walked the side street back to the Palace Hotel. The thugs thought better of any violence though with two determined-looking hard women walking down the street with Henry rifles perched on their shoulders. The two men hustled off toward the port, thinking like the rest of Hastings' men, that it was a good time to leave town. Ships were already offloading cargo down in the port, and they would need sailors to set sail and leave on the first tide.

Irwin went down to the Palace Hotel. It wasn't much, but he arranged for rooms for himself and Denise and the Callahans. There was a dining room that could double for a ballroom. However, there was a large veranda connected to the ballroom with two sets of double French doors. It would do for a party and almost fulfill Denise's idea of what would serve as a dance floor. There were musicians to hire, which was a surprise (and maybe of questionable skill), but they were what the town had to offer, and they would have to make the best of them. Irwin and Eli went down to another hotel called The Rocky Shores and rented rooms for Hans and his men. The entire hotel was in bad need of cleaning after the previous occupants, but the hotel owner and his staff were busy cleaning up the rooms. More than fifty men, soldiers, teamsters, and citizens were clearing what was left of the balcony off the front of the Longshoremen's Hotel, while more soldiers patrolled the streets on the lookout for any continued trouble.

The day passed with a beautiful sunset. The entire town was readying for a grand celebration. Hundreds of people from Los Angeles had remained, and numerous cook fires were emitting aromas that promised a feast of grand proportions. The local orchestra was set up on the veranda of the Palace Hotel, but there were also mariachi bands in the streets, and the townsfolk were already in raucous celebration to mark the end of an era that wasn't by any means the happiest of times for San Pedro. All seemed to be ready. The men gathered in the bar next to the dining room; the women were upstairs in their rooms for hot baths, primping, and donning their new clothes. Roland and Irwin were getting impatient for their wives to make their grand entrance when they heard a line of heavily Irish accented brogue asking for whiskey at the bar. Connor and his two mates had made their way in from the coast to join the party.

Irwin was the first to welcome them. "I thought you would be halfway to China by now."

"It would be quite the contrary for me to sneak off without saying goodbye. Besides, the frigate wasn't even able to turn and leave the estuary. Even if it did, my cabin boy could outsail them even in the worst of conditions. *The Blessed* is at anchor off the first beach we came to after we rounded the point. So, when does this shindig start anyway?"

Just then, the three women started down the stairs. A hush fell over the small lobby, and the men walked out of the bar to greet the ladies. Each one of the ladies was beautiful in her own right, but together they were breathtaking. Denise had the girls wait at the bottom of the stairs as if she was back in the mansion in New York, making a grand entrance to a house full of admiring guests. Irwin and Señor Francisco were at the back of the bar with their four *boys,* happy citizens, and soldiers packed the front of the bar. Slowly a hush fell over the bar as more and more of the drinkers noticed the women standing out in the lobby.

The orchestra took the quiet as a cue to start the dance and did their best to play the only Viennese waltz they knew, Jean-Paul-Égide Martini's *Plaisir d'amou*r. Irwin made his way through the crowd and claimed his wife for the first dance. Denise was still stunning for a more mature woman; she carried herself well, and someone watching from afar could easily mistake her for a woman in her thirties. Denise remembered back to the night when her daughter Anna brought the young Professor Callahan to the Mercier mansion in New York City to the Christmas party she and her husband hosted every year for his clients and their friends. Looking at Suzette, she could only think that Aaden and Anna would arrive any minute to claim her granddaughter.

Roland nudged Juan Pedro and then walked forward and took his wife's hand, kissed her lightly, and led her to the dance floor. Lia wore the red and maroon gown well and had the white knit stole over her shoulders for modesty. Her long hair swung out behind her as Roland waltzed her around the dance floor. The men from the bar started to line the walls of the dining room, and a crowd was forming up on the veranda to watch the gala.

Suzette felt like a wallflower for a moment but then realized that Juan Pedro didn't know how to dance. Señor Francisco pushed his nieto forward. Señor Francisco, Juan Pedro, his abuelo, and Irwin were the only men decked out regally for the dance. Juan Pedro had the local doctor remove the cast from his arm, and he was easily the most handsome man there dressed in a black suit of a Spanish cut with a light blue ruffled shirt and black boots. The blue ruffled shirt matched the blue of Suzette's gown perfectly, and the large turquoise cabochon was a perfect match to the gems in the squash blossom necklace Suzette wore above her ample cleavage. She had the bracelet on her wrist, the earrings hanging at the side of her face, and the barrette fastened in a reverse pull-through-braid ponytail. While all that was stunning, it paled to her tall, slender body tucked into the blue silk brocade gown with the slit skirt showing an immodest amount of thigh when she walked. The white skin of her leg contrasted strongly with her deeply tanned face and arms. The rugged girl from the trail was still there but nicely masked by the rest of the ensemble.

Her Uncle Conner walked up to Juan Pedro and said, "If you don't take her to the dance floor, I will." Embarrassed, Juan Pedro stepped forward and took Suzette's hand, thankful that his tight trousers kept his raging hormones reasonably hidden. Juan Pedro extended his arms to hold Suzette at a respectful distance, mimicking Irwin and Roland as they waltzed around the dance floor. Suzette smiled up at the handsome young Spaniard and pulled him into a close embrace with her arm reaching up, tightly wrapped around his neck. Suddenly, Juan Pedro found his feet and knew how to dance the waltz with graceful sweeping steps all the time, staring down into Suzette's blue eyes. Everyone watched the beautiful couple, and Suzette returned Juan Pedro's intense gaze as the music played on and on.

When the music ended, Suzette stood up on her toes and pulled herself up to give Juan Pedro a short but passionate kiss. Lia could only approve as she watched her young sister-in-law finally expressing her feelings and staking her claim on the handsome young man. Lia looked over at Señor Francisco, who glanced back at her with a wide smile on his face. Lia returned the smile signaling her approval, which in her culture confirmed a betrothal and the blessing of her family's acceptance that Juan Pedro and Suzette were now locked in a committed relationship that could only end in marriage. Señor Francisco's smile grew even wider, and Uncle Connor raised his glass of whiskey in silent approval. Denise couldn't help but smile with joy; she knew full well that Suzette had made a lifetime binding decision, and it would be useless to oppose the will of her strong-minded granddaughter.

Susan Hancock walked into the hotel with her husband's dress blues over her arm and led him upstairs to change him into the proper attire for the dance. No one noticed the reporter Sigler sitting at the bar, furiously penning a report on the day's events. Men were lining up and jousting with each other for their turn to dance with the three gorgeous women. Conner took Juan Pedro into the bar and stood the young man a stiff drink as he explained that if they were in Ireland, Juan Pedro and Suzette would already be married. Juan Pedro nodded his understanding and reaffirmed his commitment to follow and protect Suzette from this day forward.

The dance went on and on. Susan Hancock led her Army Major down the stairs and joined in the fun. Few other men dared to ask her to dance, especially the soldiers who knew they had to show respect for their commanding officer's wife. Señor Francisco had commandeered one of the mariachi bands from the street and led them onto the veranda and called for silence. He announced that he and Juan Pedro would demonstrate Flamenco dancing. He handed his nieto a pair of castanets and pushed him to the middle of the floor. The mariachis opened up with a famous Spanish Flamenco tune, and Juan Pedro struck the classic pose of the Flamenco dancer and then demonstrated that he did indeed know how to dance. Some young women from the street looked on in envy as he reached over to Suzette and pulled her out onto the dance floor with him. His boots were a blur as he beat out the fast rhythm with his feet. Suzette could only stand there enthralled by the dashing young Spaniard and clap her hands to the music. Senor Francisco, however, pulled Lia out of the crowd and while not as fast as his grandson danced with Lia in a sensuous tango as the Flamenco music slowed. When Juan Pedro led into an *Escobilla* to further demonstrate that he was an aficionado of the Flamenco, he ended with sweeping Suzette into his arms and dipping her until her braid touched the floor and held that pose until the music ended. The clapping and cheering brought the house down, and Juan Pedro led Suzette out onto the veranda to cool down in the fresh evening air. The dancing continued well after midnight, and slowly the townsfolk and the soldiers retired for the night along with the well liquored up, male component of the Callahan family; save for Roland who stayed with Lia.

Juan Pedro and Suzette were one of the few couples left on the veranda. He had his back to the wall and was kissing Suzette passionately. His hand slid down to cup her breast, and this time, Suzette did not push him away. She was pulling back from the long passionate kiss and opened her eyes in time to see Hastings rising behind the wall with a bat. She jerked Juan to the side just in time to turn a killing blow to the head to a lesser crippling blow that broke the clavicle in his right shoulder and drove him to his knees. Hastings and two of his thugs jumped the wall and attacked Suzette. One came at her from behind and Hastings from her front, but she had time to arm herself with the barrette and drove the spike under Hastings's chin, piercing his brain stem, killing him instantly. He was still staring at her with the blank stare of the dead when she whirled and drove the spike into the rear attacker's heart. Juan Pedro was in a lot of pain, but when he struggled up off the ground, the third attacker fled. When he reached the exit at the front of the veranda, Roland dropped the assailant with a crushing right hook to his jaw. The crack of his jawbone was louder than the crack his head made when it hit the stone floor of the veranda.

Major Hancock came running out of the bar, and when he saw Hastings dead, he leaped the wall and took two soldiers with him to check on the jail. His guard lay dead with his throat cut. He was a young man from Philadelphia whose dream of a life in California ended with the slash of a longshoreman's knife. The door to the jail was broken through, and the mayor was gone. Hancock gave the order, "Assemble the men and hunt down the mayor and whoever is with him." It didn't take long; the mayor and three of his longshoremen were trying to cross the mudflats east of town. They were easily captured and brought back bound and gagged. Major Hancock was not in a forgiving mood and had more than his fill on Anderson and his men. He asked, "Which one of you killed my man at the jail?" When none of them would answer, he gave the command, "Hang all of them from the portico in front of the mayor's office. This business is going to end if I must hang every last one of them."

The mayor started to sob and plead for his life, "I was locked up inside the jail. I couldn't possibly have killed him." The men were busy pointing at one another, trying to shift the blame to one individual who hopefully would bear the consequences for the rest of them. Major Hancock pulled Anderson aside and then nodded at the soldiers to carry out his order and then turned his back coldly and walked back into the hotel. His word was final. A squad of soldiers led the guilty down the street, and Sgt. Flannigan strung the three men up as per his orders. Anderson was left standing in the middle of an angry crowd of townsfolk; the rest of his life now measured in only minutes.

Suzette and Lia were tending to Juan Pedro. Suzette had asked a young man from the hotel kitchen to find her a short piece of board a little longer than Juan's shoulders were wide.

He returned in a few minutes with a board he had taken from an outhouse door with the quarter moon and a few stars cut out of the center. Lia raised Juan by his head and left shoulder, and Suzette slid the board under his back. Suzette had a long soft cotton rope, and after pushing the clavicle back into place, she started to tie Juan's shoulders down to the board. Juan moaned in pain the whole time, but Lia had given him a stiff drink of Irish whiskey from the bar. By the time Suzette finished several loops around both shoulders and finished the trussing up with tying Juan's right arm to his torso, his moans had subsided to quiet gasps. Suzette had the soldiers carry Juan up to his room and then sat with her back to the wall and closed her eyes. Lia sat next to her, and Denise walked over and sat on her other side. Both women put an arm around Suzette. All of them were thinking, *would the violence ever end?* Suzette finally turned angry, her plans for the rest of the night ruined.

It would be a week before Juan Pedro's shoulder would knit together well enough to travel. Suzette wasn't leaving the Los Angeles basin without him. Denise was pleased; the family reunion would last a little longer even though tainted by the night's events. The two dead men had been removed from the veranda before Suzette was finished tending to the broken shoulder, but the small pools of blood they left behind still glistened as it congealed and dried in the lantern light. Irwin returned with Eli and Roland, and gently they pulled the three women up and took them upstairs to their rooms. Denise held Suzette for a long time in the hall in front of Suzette's room and before letting her go whispered in her ear, "Don't worry, granddaughter. Your time will come, and I will make all this happen for you again when you are ready."

Suzette sat in the darkness of her room a long-time sobbing. She was only fourteen years old, but there had been so much danger and so much death that she couldn't help but think, *will the luck of the Irish hold out?* Suzette was sure there would be more trouble to come. Would there ever be a return to the ideal life they lived in Independence? Would it ever be safe to live again without danger? A million thoughts ran through her mind as she lay back and finally fell asleep wondering, *when will the luck of the Irish come my way?*

She awoke several hours later to nature's call, and even though she had a chamber pot in her room, she quietly went down the hall to the bathroom. On her way back, she listened at Juan Pedro's door to laudanum's quiet snore and then slipped inside and lay down on the bed beside him. She raised his good arm and slid it around her as she nestled up to his side and held his hand to her breast. It may not have been proper, but she finally fell into the deepest sleep she had since leaving Independence. She dreamed, and in the dream, she came to know that the safety she sought would have to be of her own making.

EPILOGUE

On the eve of dark times approaching over the issues of state's rights and slavery, the young nation was poised on the brink of civil war as our young pioneers reached the Pacific Coast. None of the news arriving in Los Angeles via the Pony Express and the Overland Stage sounded good. All of it hung in the air like dark thunderheads on the horizon, and if the Republican candidate, Abraham Lincoln, won the election, radical voices in the South were determined to succeed and fight what they believed would be a short, victorious civil war to defend their way of life. Sentiments in the North also ran high on the side of the war, driven by some who believed in the freedom from slavery and others who coveted with greed, the profits that war would bring. Only the rational on both sides knew that it would only be the young, awash in patriotism or an overzealous sense of duty, were to be ones destined to die for the selfish causes of others. Both sides fervently believed that the war would be a short skirmish; victory would come easy, despite the lessons history offered. More rational and experienced minds knew that no civil war ended with anything other than total devastation, with young men eager to fight, dying until the bitter end of the conflict.

The young Callahan men could easily escape military duty hiding behind their wealth. But that was not how the Callahan men thought or felt. They were poised to go their separate ways after the long trek over the Santa Fe Trail, and the crossing of the Sonora and Mojave deserts. Eli, the oldest of the boys and head of the Callahan enterprises since his father's untimely death, planned on going back to Yuma with Moses, the co-owner, and operator of the Yuma Ferry Crossing. Jacques opted to sign on as a civilian scout in Major Hancock's growing company of soldiers. Roland and Lia planned to accompany Suzette up through the coastal range of California to San Francisco, where she hoped to enter medical school. From there, Roland and Lia were headed to the Mother Lode country to find John Gould, the engineer who built the railroad from the Missouri River to their complex south of Independence.

Others in their entourage were less certain of a direction. Hans and his men were going to stay in the Los Angeles basin and farm. Mr. Sue was going to accompany Suzette to San Francisco, wanting to see her safely to her destination. Paul Hayman was over his fixation on Suzette but also wanted to see the Mother Lode country, knowing that his music would make him welcome wherever he went. Juan Pedro, despite his broken shoulder, would travel with Roland and Lia, still waiting to take Suzette for his lover. His grandfather found his love-struck grandson amusing and was looking forward to traveling north. He had family in the San Francisco area and was determined to find them.

Denise, ever the businesswoman, was on her way to San Francisco to buy a newspaper. Determined to take control of the fame her grandchildren gained from their exploits on the Santa Fe Trail, she knew owning a paper was the easiest way to control the news. Irwin, ever the good husband, was amused as usual but steadfast in his support for his wife. The 1860s were ushering in an era of great conflict and change. Denise was destined to be in the middle of the issues. Slavery, women's rights, the impending war; the list went on and on. Still young at heart, she was anxious to re-establish her influence with a newspaper sympathetic to her causes.

The next decade was at hand, and would indeed be a challenge for not only the young Callahans but for everyone in the tightly wound, war poised nation.